THE LOTT[

Jonathan Tulloch lives in North Yorkshire with his wife and son. He is the author of two previous novels, *The Season Ticket*, which won the Betty Trask Prize and was filmed under the title *Purely Belter*, and *The Bonny Lad*. His work has been translated into five languages.

The Lottery

JONATHAN TULLOCH

JONATHAN CAPE
LONDON

Published by Jonathan Cape 2003

2 4 6 8 10 9 7 5 3 1

First published in Great Britain in 2003 by Jonathan Cape
Random House, 20 Vauxhall Bridge Road, London SW1V 2SA

Random House Australia (Pty) Limited
20 Alfred Street, Milsons Point, Sydney,
New South Wales 2061, Australia

Random House New Zealand Limited
18 Poland Road, Glenfield,
Auckland 10, New Zealand

Random House South Africa (Pty) Limited
Endulini, 5A Jubilee Road, Parktown 2193, South Africa

The Random House Group Limited Reg. No. 954009
www.randomhouse.co.uk

A CIP catalogue record for this book
is available from the British Library

ISBN 0–224–06168–2

Typeset by Deltatype Ltd, Birkenhead, Merseyside
Printed and bound in Great Britain by
Mackays of Chatham PLC

To Mum and Dad

The Quayside for sailors
The Castlegarth for tailors
North shore for Keelers
The Gateshead hills for lovers . . .

Chapter One

The shoppers had departed, the malls were empty. All day long the bright bleep of cash tills, the hum of human voices and the stampede of countless feet had filled the Gateshead Metro Centre, but now silence had fallen. A deep evening stillness hung over the largest retail and leisure complex in Europe. Endless precincts of chrome and glass were disturbed only by the tread of an occasional security guard, and, calling forlornly to one another from the depths of this vast labyrinth, the growled night songs of distant vacuum cleaners.

The fans and air conditioners had been turned off an hour before and the heat was rapidly growing crueller as each brick and block of the sprawling building radiated a whole day's sunshine, and the slowly declining August rays struck fully against the huge panes of the centre's west-facing skylights.

At the furthest reach of the Red Quadrant's upper level, in trading hours the most bustling corner of the Metro Centre, a solitary figure was buffing the floor. Despite the fierce heat, she was working quickly. Moving rapidly down the mall of deserted shops, she swung the cleaning machine in graceful arcs over the tiles. Every five yards or so, she took out a plastic bottle from a pouch at the front of her ultramarine cleaning dress to spray a precise parabola over the tiles in front of her. The squeak of her pink trainers caused by this pivoting movement continually echoed down the abandoned mall.

The cleaner's unruly mass of auburn hair, half controlled by a ponytail, was threaded with grey. And although her face, glowing with sweat, was lined with advancing middle age, she held herself with the power of a young woman. The rolled-up sleeves of her cleaning dress revealed muscles rippling as they absorbed the vibration of the softly humming machine. The top three buttons were unfastened, revealing the deep shadow of a formidable cleavage. The crucifix she wore never rested on its chain, but forever rose and fell, flipping over itself to the rhythm of her work.

The woman worked her way to one of the countless little squares of the Metro Centre. The soft humming of the buffer fell silent as she switched it off and strode purposefully to the fountain. Effervescent in opening hours, the water was now flat as a backwater. Three large metal statues of cows stood in it, watched over by a buxom, life-sized female cowherder who stood on the side of the fountain overlooking them as though from a riverbank: one hand on her hip, the other reaching with a rough tenderness to the nearest of her drinking animals. As the cleaner stood there, staring intently at the water, her posture mirrored the cowherder almost exactly.

She brought out a coin from the pouch of her cleaning dress and flicked it up. The ten-pence piece rose high into the thick sunbeams slanting down from a skylight. Then it plunged, hitting the water with a crisp gulp that resonated in the silence of the square. Greedily, the cleaner watched its silver flashing like the scales of a little fish before coming to rest on a bed of innumerable small coins. Lifting a thick strand of damp hair from her gleaming brow, she closed her eyes. As though in a fervent prayer, her generous lips mumbled while a hand strayed up to the crucifix, clasping the tortured Christ.

As she stood motionless, eyes screwed shut, a man slipped out of the green door of the nearby toilet. Chuckling to himself, he stalked her. He wore the child's pyjamas of a security guard; the Keystone Kop polygon hat. 'Nivver mind, sleeping beauty,' he called when he could contain himself no longer. 'I will awake ye with a kiss.'

'Aye,' the woman shot back without opening her eyes, her voice a rich alto gravelled by a lifetime of cigarettes, 'and I'll put ye to sleep with a black eye.'

With a mock flourish, the security guard whipped off his hat. His hair was crushed against his skull with perspiration. 'Ha'way, man Audrey, ye kna what ye dee to us. Especially in this heat.'

'I kna what I will dee if yus divven't piss off. Haddaway back to Top Cat, Officer Dribble.'

With a laugh the security guard came over to stand beside the cleaner and gazed at the fountain with her. 'Aye,' he mused, taking out a coin from his polyester trousers which stuck to the skin of his thighs, 'it's that time of the week again.' He exhaled wearily. 'Shocking how quick the weeks fly by.' He flicked his ten-pence piece with all his strength, but it rose only a fraction of Audrey's effortless toss. 'I wish . . . I wish . . .' he intoned, and as he closed his eyes a deep need crinkled his face to a shrivelled walnut.

Audrey opened her eyes, scrutinised the bed of the fountain one last time, and then went back to her buffing machine.

'What would yus dee?' the security guard asked, turning with sudden seriousness. 'If yus won, what would yus dee?'

Audrey stopped for a moment, and smiled gently. 'A holiday. Take all the bairns to Disneyland.'

'Me?' the security guard pondered. 'A world cruise. I've always wanted to eat a banana straight from a tree. I don't know why. I just have.' He laughed, breaking the rather solemn, wistful moment. 'We could gan together, pet.'

The buffing machine hummed back into life. 'I'm spoken for,' Audrey returned, and as she smiled widely, she revealed a gap between her two strong-looking front teeth.

The security guard shook his head. 'Aye, that's what I nivver could work oot. Why did yus choose that Ronny lad instead of me?'

'Where d'yus want wor to start, bonny lad?' Audrey looked

3

the security guard up and down suggestively, then threw her head back and roared with a deep, resonating laugh.

The security guard stared at Audrey with undisguised admiration. He put his hat back on. 'So where we all gannin' the neet then?' he asked. 'This heat's bloody cruel. I'm gannin' off me trolley for a nice pint of ice-cold lager. I think we should gan to Shenanigans . . .'

'I'm not gannin' anywhere, tonight,' Audrey interrupted.

The security guard gaped at her. 'Eh? Did I hear Audrey McPhee say that she's not coming for a drink and the lottery draw on a Saturday night after work?'

'Ye deaf as well as stupid?'

'But yus're wor good-luck charm, man lass . . . The syndicate'll nivver win the lottery withoot ye. Six-million jackpot tonight an' all. That's a canny lot of bottles of Diamond White, man Audrey. Ha'way, yus've nivver missed a Saturday for as lang as I've known ye.'

'Aye, and we've nivver won a sausage.' Audrey shook her head. 'Wait and see. The neet I'm not there we'll only gan and win it.'

Perplexed, the security guard gazed at Audrey as she finished buffing the little square, his eyes only lifting from her body to watch the sprayed parabolas describe themselves before settling on the tiles. 'Oh aye,' he suddenly called, 'I forgot to tell yus. Peak's looking for yus. And he's not a happy bunny.'

Audrey's powerful shoulders shrugged. 'If that tosser comes anywhere near me, I'll bloody smash him.'

The security guard chuckled. 'She would an' all. Makes nee difference to her that he's her supervisor.' Only when she had disappeared from view did he shake himself as though from a trance, and go on his way, his slow footsore tread suddenly dwarfed by the endless immensity of the Metro Centre malls: modern starve-crow on the demesnes of Commerce.

Audrey carried on working, moving down the mall like a

4

mower wielding her scythe along the meadow banks. The distant, plaintive baying of a vacuum cleaner steadily grew louder. It was coming from the lower level, which lay in a well twelve feet or so below the upper level, underneath solid green metal railings. A human voice suddenly materialised over the wail of the Hoover. 'Areet, Audrey.'

'Areet, Kaz pet,' Audrey shouted down to the English Teddy Bear Company shop below.

'Feeling lucky, Aud?'

'I always feel lucky.'

'All six balls?'

'I hope it's the lottery yus're talking aboot and not men. I've got enough on me plate with my Ronny.'

'Is he big?'

'Put it this way, pet, there's not much else that can shut my gob up.'

Choking laughter blared up from the Teddy Bear shop. 'Shenanigans or the Thai Gardens then, Audrey?' gasped Kaz.

'Neewhere for me.'

A sweatily confused face loomed out of the entrance of the Teddy Bear shop and peered up to the upper level: 'You're having wor on, aren't ye? It's Saturday neet, man Aud. Saturday neet wouldn't be Saturday neet withoot wor Audrey.'

Audrey continued to buff. 'Aye, well, yus'll have to dee withoot wor this once.'

'What's gannin' on, like?'

'Do I have to tell every bugger me business?'

Kaz watched Audrey for a while longer, a smile on her face. 'Oh aye,' she shouted. 'It nearly slipped me mind. Peak's wanting to speak to ye.'

'Eh?' cried Audrey without turning to look down.

'Mr Peak's after yus!'

In a movement of graceful agility, Audrey hoisted her

5

buttocks on to the green railings. Waggling them contemptuously, she thundered forth a fart loud enough to be heard
above the droning Hoover and humming buffing machine.
Clapping her hands together, Kaz dissolved into cackling
laughter.

Audrey worked on. It was growing hotter all the while, and
she shook her head occasionally to clear the sweat from her
eyes. Reaching a retail outlet named the Gadget Shop, she
turned her buffer off. 'Shop,' she called loudly as she crossed
the threshold.

'Just one moment, madam,' a voice replied through the
open storeroom door. 'Ee, but I'm at the end of me tether
with this bloody heat.'

'Aye, it's like a friggin' sauna,' replied Audrey. She looked
about. The shop, which was so vibrant in the day, was
strangely lifeless at this hour. The winged pigs, which flew
round and round in business hours, hung inertly from the
ceiling; the perpetually somersaulting dog was motionless; and
the perennially drilling soldier lay listlessly on the counter,
heedless of the invasion he was supposed to safeguard against.
The psychedelic water lamps were monochrome. The blow-
up chair appeared to be deflating.

'And was madam looking for summink sexy?' the voice
enquired from the back room.

Audrey grinned. 'Madam's always looking for summink
sexy.'

'Hey, man Aud,' the voice from the back giggled, 'come
and look at some of this stuff. It'll make yer eyes water.'

At that moment a packet was thrown from the storeroom.
Audrey caught it. It was a pair of novelty chocolate-flavoured
knickers. She threw them back. 'Ronny's on a diet, man
Cheryl.'

'Divven't be such a meanie, man Audrey,' Cheryl returned,
throwing the packet at Audrey once more.

Again Audrey caught it skilfully. 'Aye,' she mused. 'Mebbes

6

he does deserve a treat. Even Weight Watchers let you have the odd snack. As lang as yus take yer time and divven't bolt it doon.'

Both women burst into laughter, Audrey's deep-throated bray reverberating down the mall. Cheryl came out from the storeroom. She was a slight, mouse-like figure, wearing the same lapis lazuli cleaning uniform. Audrey flung the packet of chocolate knickers at her with such good-humoured force that the slighter woman staggered under the impact. 'Peak's been in here looking for ye, man Audrey,' Cheryl warned when they had both sobered.

Audrey looked levelly at the other. 'How lang have ye known me, Cheryl?'

'All wor lives,' shrugged Cheryl.

'And when d'ye think I started giving a flying frigg aboot that beanpole?'

Cheryl opened the packet of chocolate knickers. 'I think he's got the hots for ye, mind. I tell ye what, give him these. Ye might as well use them.'

'I wouldn't touch him if his arse was studded with diamonds.'

'What am I gonnae dee with them then?' Cheryl grinned. 'They're melting.'

'Put them on yourself and I'll gan and give Peak a shout. Tell him it's his lucky day.'

'Ee, just 'cos I'm single again doesn't mean I divven't have me standards.'

'Aye,' grinned Audrey. 'Like that fella what used to work at the tip. Kenny Rogers, he calls himself, doesn't he?'

'Ye've made mistakes an' all, man Aud. Remember him with the toupee that came off when ye were . . .'

The women choked with hilarity. 'That's all in the past,' said Audrey when she had recovered enough to speak coherently. 'I'm with Ronny noo.'

7

Cheryl nodded. 'It really is serious this time, isn't it, Aud? Getting on for two years yous've been wed now, isn't it?'

'Aye, getting on for two years.'

'I'm so pleased for you, y'kna, lass.' Cheryl's smile was gentle. 'That yus've found the right one.'

Audrey's face shone and, despite her age, the look of a girl sparkled in her eyes. 'I'd given up even looking.'

Reaching out, Cheryl brushed her hand against Audrey's sleeve. 'Luck of ye,' she whispered in a soft chant, 'for such luck be, make that luck, rub off on me.'

'Ye'll find someone,' murmured Audrey.

Cheryl's eyes widened hungrily. 'Will ye dee the cards for us again?'

Audrey sighed. 'Cheryl man, I've done them loads of times.'

'Aye, but nee man's turned up yet.'

'Have patience, man.'

'Any more patience and I'll forget what you do with one.' The smaller woman hugged herself. 'I need a tall, dark stranger to take me away from it all. Doesn't have to be handsome. Just as lang as he's got a heed on his shoulders. Either that or a win on the lottery.' Cheryl nodded decisively. 'Ha'way then, Audrey, are we gonnae win the lottery tonight or what?'

Audrey pouted her lips in thought. There was a light sprinkling of freckles on her nose, and as the nose wrinkled, they were absorbed like seeds. 'Well,' she pronounced with a new seriousness, 'a black cat crossed me path on the way to the bus stop. And one of the bairns foond a feather in her shoe this morning.'

'Is that good or bad?' demanded Cheryl.

'Good, if it's a swallow or a turtle dove.'

'And which one was it?'

'To be honest with yus, I think it was one of Ronny's bloody parrot's.' Again, laughter gushed out in one of the quiet corners of the Gateshead Metro Centre, irrepressible as a spring of water. Then Audrey clapped her hands resoundingly.

'Why aye. Course we're gonnae bloody win it tonight.' She had walked to the entrance of the shop when she stopped abruptly. Reaching down into her deep cleavage she brought out an envelope. 'Here's the tickets, but.'

'Eh?' asked Cheryl, coming over and taking the envelope suspiciously.

'The syndicate tickets for tonight,' Audrey explained. 'I cannet make it the neet.'

'Oh aye,' chuckled Cheryl.

Audrey shook her head adamantly. 'No. Straight up. I'm not coming.'

'What yus on aboot? It's the Saturday-neet draw . . .'

But Audrey had already left the shop. Cheryl followed her, waving the envelope. 'What's gannin' on?'

'And I'm not joking aboot Peak,' Audrey called as she took up the handles of her buffer. 'If he comes sniffing aboot here again, tell him to keep his distance. I cannet be deein' with him the day. It's the bloody heat. I'll dee summink silly. I kna I will.'

'Sod Peak. What I want to kna is why cannet yus make it toneet?'

'Special occasion.' Audrey winked mysteriously. 'I've got summink important to dee.'

'Summink more important than winning the friggin' lottery?'

The buffer hummed back into life. 'Aye. Summink even more important than that.'

'Bloody hell. Must be a proper big do.' Cheryl watched her friend for a little while as she worked on down the mall. 'Tell wor all aboot it tomorrow then,' she called. 'I'll pop roond to yours after Mass.' Audrey raised a hand and waved. Then shaking her head and hugging herself, Cheryl lifted a hand in reply and whispered yearningly to herself: 'Luck of ye, for such luck be, let that luck rub off on me.'

It was even hotter in the Pegasus travel agency and as

Audrey walked over to the wall of holiday brochures, she gasped. There was a rasp of polish from under one of the large desks. 'Where today, Aud?' a voice enquired.

'Disneyland again,' replied Audrey, selecting a brochure with a picture of Mickey Mouse on it.

'Ee, yus'd think you were in bloody Florida with this heat. I'm that parched. So is it Shenanigans or the Thai . . .'

'Neewhere for me,' Audrey interrupted the woman under the desk.

'Eh?'

'I'm not comin' tonight.'

The voice was outraged. 'What yus on aboot, not comin' oot?'

'What is it with yous lot? Ye'd think I'd bloody gone and robbed a bank. I'm just not comin' oot for a drink tonight, that's all.'

'But you're the syndicate manager.'

'Cannet yus dee withoot wor for once in yer lives? And before ye tell us, I kna.'

There was another hiss of polish and the rubbing of a duster. 'Kna what?'

'That Peak's wanting us.'

'He's stotting mad.'

'I divven't care if he's walking on his hands and spitting fire.'

'He's coming after yus, mind.'

'Let him come.'

A mug of coffee and a huge slice of cake had been left on the counter of Pam's Pantry. When Audrey reached this coffee shop, which stood on the mall itself, she popped the coffee straight into the microwave. Taking a can of lemonade from the large fridge, she pulled the ring, and drained it in one single, mighty draught. She sat at the single table which had not been stacked with chairs and shuddering with pleasure, kicked off her pink trainers.

The cake disappeared in three bolts of her powerful jaw.

Then she took out a cigarette purse. Inside was a litter of cigarette stubs and a single unsmoked Superking. Her work-reddened fingers hovered over the entire cigarette for a moment, and then selected three of the larger stubs. She smoked luxuriously, full lips almost touching over the filter, the smoke thinning lovingly to skeins of blue through the gap in her teeth. Absorbed in the pleasures of her coffee and cigarette, she flipped slowly through the Disneyland brochure. Without looking away from the glossy pages, she brought out a small Argos catalogue pen from the pouch of her cleaner's dress, and, unfolding a little paper serviette, began to write. Her concentration deepened and what had looked at first to be only a doodling on the serviette took more significant shape: row after row of numbers, each series in a column of six.

Audrey was so profoundly caught up in Disneyland and her series of numbers that she did not notice the thin, remarkably tall man staring at her from the mall. He had been there for a whole minute, standing as motionless as the heron that used to fish in the Metro Centre pool before IKEA was built. Despite the rising heat he wore his regulation grey caretaker's coat buttoned to the neck. Not a hair on his head was damp; not a single bead of sweat hung on his pallid brow. At last he moved, stalking her noiselessly. 'Before ye start,' said Audrey, who had still not looked up from the brochure, 'think better of it, and just walk away.'

The man's face twitched with irritation. The tip of his tongue flickered through bloodless lips. 'A mug of coffee and a cigarette,' he said drily, 'and a can of Granny Bryden's Traditional Lemonade.'

'Divven't say I didn't warn ye,' Audrey replied softly. Eyes narrowing intently, she had begun scoring out some of the lines of numbers on the serviette, while enlarging others.

'Yes, Granny Bryden's Traditional Lemonade, and, if I'm not mistaken, what looks suspiciously like the crumbs of a large piece of cake.'

'Shh,' snapped Audrey irritably. Her intense concentration tightened her features painfully. All the rows of numbers had been scored out, except for two. Then at last, having made the sign of the cross while fingering her crucifix, Audrey scored out a set of numbers, leaving one alone on the page. 'That's it,' she said to herself, almost breathless with triumph. 'That's it for certain.'

'Yes, that is it for certain,' the man said curtly. 'I'm sick of telling you. Under the new codes of working practice, cleaners are no longer entitled to a break, yet you insist . . .'

Audrey looked up for the first time. 'You still here, are ye?'

Mr Peak writhed with annoyance as he came to stand right over her. 'I'm going to have to tell Mr Hargreaves. This is Metro Centre time that you're stealing.'

Nonchalantly, Audrey extinguished the last of her butts. 'I'm not in the mood.'

'Not in the mood,' scoffed Mr Peak with aggressive sarcasm. 'Audrey McPhee's not in the mood.' He jabbed a finger at the plate and mug. 'I can see you're in the mood for stealing coffee and cake.'

'Pam puts it oot special for wor,' she replied wearily. 'It's got nowt to dee with ye, lad.' Mr Peak had begun to speak, but Audrey overrode him. 'I've been working in this place since it opened and not once have I left me mall anything other than spotless. The day I do, then ye can come and take wor to your precious Mr Hargreaves.'

'Up you get,' shouted Mr Peak, his face twitching with annoyance again. 'This constitutes a verbal warning. I'm asking you to accompany me to Mr Hargreaves . . .'

In a movement of stunning agility, Audrey leapt to her feet. The mug danced on the table. 'Run alang noo, little lad.' Her voice was low as a growl.

'How dare you address your superior like that, Audrey McPhee?' Mr Peak exploded. 'It's insubordination. Mr Hargreaves will . . .'

'It's Audrey Slater,' Audrey replied quietly. 'I've been married for two years to my Ronny now. I'm Audrey Slater. Audrey McPhee's gone noo. Now get oot my sight.' Audrey went to take her crockery back to the counter, but Mr Peak stepped into her path. Finding her way blocked, a smile glimmered on her mouth. It disappeared as she strode at Mr Peak. The force of her body check sent the tall man reeling. 'How dare you?' she gasped.

Knocked back against a table, he fell to the ground. A stack of chairs thundered down on top of his flailing arms.

After this clatter, the stillness of the evening shopping centre seemed even deeper. Audrey crouched down low over the flinching man so that her breasts were pushed close to his face. 'No, Mr Peak,' she said quietly. 'I divven't want yus to touch wor like that. Get off, please get off.'

'But . . .' stumbled Mr Peak, floundering.

'HELP!' Audrey's mighty roar echoed deafeningly down the cavernous mall. 'HELP! Ye touched me tits!' As she straightened up, her voice grew quieter again.'Ye bumped me boobs. And I can get five girls what saw yus dee it.' She pulled the bewildered man to his feet. 'See me? I get on with anyone. But ye? Ye get reet up me crack.'

Breathing heavily, Mr Peak slunk away. Shaking with rage, he had shambled ten yards down the mall when he stopped. 'You think you're the bloody Queen of Sheba,' he hissed, 'the way you swan about the place. A real Queen Bee, that's what you think you are. Well, I've got news for you. You're nothing but trash. Trash from the Teams. Slater? Slater? Call yourself Slater? You'll always be a McPhee. You'll never be anything but a Tinker McPhee. You'll never be anything but a scum McPhee from the Teams!'

'Well, that just suits me fine,' smiled Audrey benevolently as she took her plate and mug back to the counter of Pam's Pantry. ''Cos scum always rises to the top. And that's where I like to be. In more ways than one. Not that ye'd kna aboot that, ye bloody parcel o' wet fish.'

Now Audrey worked with a real purpose, her strong arms sweeping the buffer ever more rapidly over the tiles until the sweat poured off her in rivulets, and her face gleamed with a sheen.

She finished ten minutes early, and entering the empty sluice room, deposited her buffing machine. Stepping out of her cleaning dress, she padded on bare feet through an arch to the little chamber containing a toilet and two sinks. She plugged the sink with a few paper hand towels, and filled it to the brim with cold water. With a ripple of her shoulders, she freed her hair from its ponytail, and then, slowly, luxuriously, immersed her whole head. For a long, long time she remained under the water, her floating hair fanning out like the fronds of a drowning Ophelia. In a great cascade of droplets, at last she surfaced, her lips parted languorously, her breathing still even despite the length of time she had spent under the water. With a deep sensuous shiver, she squeezed the cool water from her hair, twisted it into a coil and like a mermaid threw it over her shoulder.

From all the innumerable nooks and crannies of that vast consumer cathedral, cleaners were now bearing down on the sluice room. A clanking procession was parading down the empty malls: the pygmy hippos of the ever hungry vacuum cleaners, the llama-necked feather dusters, the clattering elephant-feet mop buckets. And the weary, sweat-shining women.

In the sluice room the silence of the out-of-hours shopping complex was detonated in an explosion of voices. As she was stepping into a pair of cut-off denim shorts, Audrey heard them back through the arch.

'Ee, I'm friggin' knackt oot, me.'

'This bloody heat's enough to finish anyone off.'

'At least ye divven't have to dee the bogs. Smelt like someone had died in there.'

'What aboot me? Some dirty bastard pulled their strides doon and left a big log o' shite for wor in the Antiques Village.'

'Mebbes it was a dog.'

'Some dog. It'd have to be the size of a friggin' shire horse.'

Audrey smiled at the chaos of laughter. The lively conversation continued.

'Where's Audrey then?'

'Did Peak find her?'

'He was looking for her.'

'He's always looking for her. Fancies her, doesn't he?'

'She'll be at Shenanigans already, man. A bottle of ice-cold Diamond White in her hands.'

'We're not gannin' to Shenanigans, are we?'

'Aye, let's gan to the Thai Gardens instead. The music's that bloody loud at Shenanigans, ye cannet even hear the draw.'

'The Thai Gardens is for pensioners, man.'

'Just 'cos you fancy the new barman at Shenanigans.'

'Course I dee. Divven't ye, like? He's proper lush, him.'

On the T-shirt which Audrey was pulling on was written in large letters: THE WORLD'S GREATEST NANA. Back in the locker room the women were stepping out of their cleaning dresses, and the thick scent of body sprays rose in a cloud. In their bird-like babble, the thread of the conversation continued.

'Audrey'll decide where to gan.'

'Aye, she'll say.'

'Audrey's not coming,' Cheryl announced.

'Eh?'

'I said Audrey's not coming.'

'Divven't talk daft.'

'Well, that's what she said.'

'Oh aye, I can just see it noo. Audrey McPhee missing her lottery drink on a Saturday night.'

'Where is she then, with Peak?'

'Has he collared her at last?'

'He's been after her long enough.'

'And mebbes this time he's got her.'

A loud snort sounded from the sinks area. 'Divven't make me laugh. I could chew Peak up and spit him oot in the time it takes to fart.' Cheers greeted Audrey's appearance. She grinned widely at the women who were all in various states of undress, and running at the nearest one, swept her up in a bear hug. Amid laughter and hooting, she lifted the woman higher and higher until she was practically on her shoulders. Then gently she set her down.

'So where we gannin' then, Aud?' asked the woman she had lifted. 'Some say Shenanigans, some say the Thai Gardens.'

'Gan where yus like,' Audrey replied. 'I'm not coming.' There was a chorus of disbelief. 'Bloody hell,' Audrey said. 'D'yus need wor to tuck yus in at night an' all?'

'Peak does,' laughed Cheryl. The rest of the women screamed with hilarity. 'Especially in hot weather,' Cheryl continued. 'Ye see, I telt him that ye divven't wear nee underwear as soon as the temperature gets into the seventies. Should have seen his face. He just couldn't wait to show ye what *he* wears under that grey coat of his.' As the others shrieked uproariously, Cheryl touched Audrey softly on the arm and whispered: 'Come and see what I've got.'

Audrey followed her friend back through the arch. Four women were already refreshing themselves at the two sinks, throwing up water over their greedily gaping faces. Cheryl took Audrey into the toilet cubicle, and then slid the bolt across. She opened the shoulder bag she was carrying, and brought out a box. It was cold to Audrey's touch. 'Chicken tikka masala,' whispered Cheryl with a wink. 'Straight from the chiller.'

'Where did ye get that from?'

'Look,' said Cheryl quickly. 'If yus divven't fancy curry then have this.' She delved into the bag and brought out another cold box. It was a family-sized shepherd's pie. 'That should gan somewhere near to feeding yer five thoosand.'

Audrey's face flickered with suspicion. 'Did ye twoc it, man Cheryl?'

'Ask nee questions and ye will be telt nee lies.'

'It is twocked, isn't it?'

'Put it this way, I haven't been looking nee gift horses in the mooth.'

For a few seconds Audrey looked at the box on which a cooked shepherd's pie steamed invitingly in a dish. Then she slid the bolt free and thrust the door open.

'It's good food.' Cheryl restrained her friend. 'Money's tight, lass. Dee yersel' a favour.'

Audrey looked the other woman adamantly in the eye. 'Things have got a hell of a lot tighter than this in the past, and I nivver broke the law then. I divven't intend to start noo.'

'It's not stealing,' Cheryl snorted with exasperation. 'I've nivver understood your religion. Ye've shagged like a badger all yer life. Each bairn with a different father. Yet ye cannet take summink nee one else will miss. Ye've two grandbairns living permanent with ye, and the rest popping in for virtually every meal, and I kna for a fact yer fuckin' piggy bank went under the hammer lang since.'

'Me religion's got nowt to dee with it. It's just me.'

'Every other bugger does it.'

'Aye, well, I'm not every other bugger.'

Cheryl stared at her friend.

Although Audrey's tone grew quieter, there was a steel in her words. 'I want to be able to look mesel' in the eye when I'm sat at me wardrobe table tonight. Tonight and every other night. I want to be able look mesel' square in the eye before I gan to bed.' She grew vehement. 'Withoot me self-respect? I'd rather drown in the Team gut.'

As Audrey walked past the sinks, one of the women waiting

to cool herself said: 'What's all this aboot ye not comin' for a lottery drink?'

Audrey shrugged. 'There's nowt about it, I'm just not coming.'

'And divven't ask her what she's deein' instead,' put in Cheryl, coming up behind her. 'She's keeping shtum. But if ye ask me, she's copping off with the new barman at Shenanigans.'

The women at the sinks burst into laughter. 'Yer new toy boy, is he, Aud?'

'Or are yus gannin' on a private date with Peak? I heard he thinks yus're lush. A proper Raquel Welch.'

'Ha'way, man Audrey, tell us who yus're seein'.'

Audrey marched through to the lockers. The women there were staring smilingly at her too.

'Aye, spill the beans.'

Audrey took her shoulder bag out of her locker, closed the door and looked at the throng of faces.

'Ha'way,' urged Cheryl. 'What's the big secret?'

For a moment Audrey seemed to be on the verge of making some great revelation, but in the end she simply shook her head. 'That's for me to kna, and for ye to find oot.' And with that she left the sluice room.

The silence in the shopping centre was complete now. As Audrey walked along, one by one the electric lights were turned off so that the tattered beams of the rapidly westering sun slanting through the skylights formed a strange twilight. At intervals of about a hundred yards security railings had been pulled across the malls, and the tiny pass key that Audrey used whispered in the locks like a vole passing through grass at dusk.

A peculiar sound stirred the stillness. It grew louder with each of the small squares that Audrey passed through until at last she reached a larger plaza, a space where two quadrants met. It was from here that the noise was coming. Birds were settling to roost in the copse of real trees which had been planted on the plaza more than a decade earlier when the shopping centre first opened. The forlorn flock of the Metro Centre were arranging themselves for the night. House sparrows mainly, but also chaffinches and greenfinches that had found their way into the vast caverns of the retail and leisure complex, but never managed to find their way out. They lived on dropped crisps and sandwich crumbs, and gazed endlessly at the little tent of blue beyond the skylights. Every so often the cleaners would come across a casualty lying beneath the tantalising ceiling windows: a bundle of fluffed feathers and twisted neck.

Audrey stood for a moment by the bizarre copse. On a nearby branch sat a bird different from any other she had ever seen. The colourful plumage of yellow, red and white was like that of a harlequin clown. It was a goldfinch which had strayed this way down one of the thistle roads of Gateshead: the network of disused colliery railway lines on which flourish thistles and other weeds savoured by the small creatures. 'Hello, my bonny,' she whispered, whistling tunefully. 'Hello. You've brought me luck. Haven't you, my bonny? You brought me luck.'

Slipping through the last of the security railings, Audrey came to the still bustling quarter of pubs, fast-food restaurants and the multiplex cinema. Passing the bright lights of Shenanigans and the Thai Gardens, which stood side by side, she stepped on the escalator. As it took her down to the lower level, she fell into deep thought. One hand clasped her crucifix, whose chain could be seen below the neck of her World's Greatest Nana T-shirt; while the other, having reached into the shoulder bag, caressed the serviette on which had been written the series of numbers. Audrey's lips appeared to murmur as though in prayer. She did not notice Mr Peak moving to the top level on the escalator beside her. He saw her, however, and immediately began to scramble against the flow of his escalator, reaching the bottom just as she did.

At the sight of him, Audrey sighed wearily. 'Audrey McPhee,' he called sharply, following her as she strode to the little newsagent's kiosk. 'I am asking you to accompany me to Mr Hargreaves's office, with which request, in accordance with your contract, you must comply.' Audrey's answer was a rich bellow of laughter. 'I have the authority to dock your wages!' he barked.

Audrey stopped. Without turning, she gazed at the doors to the bus station which lay beyond the kiosk. She was standing beside a thicket of ferns and plants growing from large earthenware pots. On feeling a poke on her back, she breathed in deeply as though to call on reserves of patience.

When she turned she found that a Dictaphone had been thrust into her face. 'Will you comply with the contractual request?' Mr Peak demanded.

Audrey looked at the red light shining on the little machine. She pursed her lips. In an instant, it had been done. Seizing one of the largest ferns, a ripple of her biceps had been followed by a tearing of roots. Then, soil and all, the plant rested on the supervisor's head. 'That's . . . that's . . .' stammered Peak, utterly aghast but determined to keep the Dictaphone recording, 'that's Metro Centre property you have wantonly destroyed . . . Mr Hargreaves will have to be . . .'

Audrey snatched the Dictaphone. 'Message for Mr Hargreaves,' she pronounced slowly into the little microphone. 'Even I cannet keep me tiles as clean as Peak licks your arse.' The pealing decibels of Audrey's laughter distorted the smooth recording on the tape.

The woman in the kiosk applauded Audrey as she came over. 'He had it comin'. That bloody fuss arse.' But Audrey was not listening. She had brought out the serviette and was gazing at the numbers. 'Not oot for a drink tonight?' the assistant continued. She spoke through a jawful of bubble gum, which occasionally ballooned from her mouth.

Audrey made the sign of the cross, kissed her crucifix and

exhaled momentously. 'I've got it,' she intoned. 'I've got it for definite this time.'

The woman looked at Audrey round a constantly inflating-deflating bladder of bubble gum. 'What is it this week, Aud? All the days before the bairns' birthdays or summink last week, wasn't it?'

'Would have come up an' all, but wor Terri-Leigh went and put an umbrella up in the flat.'

The assistant nodded, chewing the gum that had just collapsed against her face. 'They do say that brings bad luck.'

'Still,' said Audrey, 'it's a roll-over jackpot this week. So it was probably for the best anyway.' Her eyes narrowed as she nodded solemnly. 'Took wor ages to work it oot. A proper puzzle. But this is it. I feel it in me waters.' She grinned broadly as she held up the serviette. 'A number from the year me and Ronny first met . . . how many years we've been wed . . . the month we first held hands . . . the day oot o' 365 that we first kissed . . . and the day we first ye-kna-whatted.'

'What aboot your sixth ball?'

'How lang it lasted.'

'In seconds or minutes?'

'That'd be giving it away.' Audrey's laughter hurled itself from the kiosk, but almost instantly she grew serious. 'Just as well I am gonnae win tonight, 'cos otherwise it'll be me for the jobcentre come Monday morning.' She opened her purse and searched among a thick wad of lottery tickets for a pound coin. 'Still, putting up with that one was more than flesh and blood could stand.'

'How much do ye spend on the lottery, Aud?' the assistant asked at the sight of the wad of tickets.

'Too much,' Audrey replied sharply. Then she mellowed. 'Doesn't matter now though, does it? I mean, tonight's the night.'

The assistant took the pound coin. 'They all say that, mind, Audrey.'

'Aye. They might say it, but I kna it.'

'Is it true what they say aboot ye, like, Audrey?'

'What do they say, like?'

'That ye've got the second sight.'

Audrey stared at the whirring of the lottery machine. 'All I kna is that I've got a proper feeling aboot tonight.'

The assistant took out the ticket from machine. 'Ee, I didn't kna it was that late. Yus're just in time. Yours will be the last ticket.' She scrutinised Audrey. 'Mebbes it's a sign.'

'Aye.'

The assistant continued to stare at Audrey for a few more moments then reached behind her and took down a plastic jar from the shelf. 'Sweets for the bairns?'

'Ee, na. I've nee money left.' Audrey closed her purse.

'Pay us next time.' As she filled a large bag to overflowing, the assistant leant forward confidentially. 'Ye still got them two grandbairns stopping at yours?' Audrey nodded. 'Well, get yersel' to Gatesheed market then. Y'kna the stall nearest the café? Just over from where your Ronny's pet shop used to be? Tell Mohammed that I sent yus.' The assistant winked as, with difficulty, she spun the crammed bag closed. 'We're seeing each other. Me and Mohammed. He gets some canny back-to-schools. For the bairns. Genuine labels an' that. From Turkey.'

Reaching out for the bag of sweets, Audrey laid her hand on the other woman's. 'Ta, pet.'

'Ee,' the woman in the kiosk called after her. 'Ye and fuss arse crossed on the escalators. You'll end up getting wed then.'

'Aye, but I had me fingers crossed and I sneezed in your direction. And y'kna what that means!'

Pushing through the heavy doors, Audrey came to the little covered bus station. She walked down the dingy pavement to her stop, where she stood waiting among the cigarette ends and litter which piled like dirty summer snowdrifts in concrete corners. It was quiet. Buses came in, dusty and hot from the day outside the Metro Centre, their diesels wafting a stifling, polluted pollen. Audrey blinked the grit away and ran a hand over her face. There weren't many passengers: teenagers mostly, coming in for the cinema. Boy and girl. Holding hands ostentatiously. Audrey smiled at the sight.

At last her bus came. The word Teams on the destination blind was barely visible beneath a thick coating of summer dust. 'Hard day at the office, pet?' the driver asked.

'Put it this way,' Audrey replied, boarding, 'I'm nee nearer Florida than I was this morning.'

As she walked down the aisle, a sudden weariness came over her. She staggered, half falling into her seat, clashing her arm against the metal bar. All at once her face was old.

She was the only passenger as the bus pulled out of the station into the delicate light of the lengthening twilight. It skirted the precincts of brick, glass and concrete that make up the Gateshead Metro Centre, that sprawling biosphere raised on the low lying marshlands of the River Tyne. Overcome by her exhaustion, Audrey closed her eyes.

She did not see the familiar landscape through which she passed. The rough, exhaust-bitten verges; the stark ranks of rose bushes mulched with polythene bags, polystyrene burger boxes and McDonald's paper cups; the row upon row of parked cars, so many even at this hour.

Neither did she see, as the bus began to move beyond the immediate site of the immense complex, the reed-fringed dykes which once served to drain this lowland for the pasturage of cows similar to those drinking at the Lord Mayor's fountain. Neither did she see, on the rough ground of the overspill car parks used in the Christmas rush, the colonies of orchids lying out of view of the passing traffic, their flowers frayed with the lateness of the season.

And Audrey Slater certainly did not see the shy otter which was raising a family in its shopping trolley and driftwood holt on the river bank beyond the lethal razor-wire fence.

Rubbing her eyes, she opened her mouth wide and yawned

until her jaw could be heard cracking. 'Frigg me sideways,' she whispered to herself. 'I'm oot for the coont.'

2

In Gateshead the land lifts from the river valleys of the Great Coaly Tyne and its tributaries, the Team and the Derwent, into broad-backed hills. Eventually these hills rise into the lonely moorland of the Durham dales, an empty place where red grouse hide from the wind in the heather, and the golden plover give company to the ghosts of lead miners. In the Gateshead portions of this escarpment is a gentler landscape of tall hedgerows, former pit villages vertebrating the spine of the land, and plunging wooded dells, locally called burns or denes.

On top of one of these rural Gateshead hills, on a big house standing rather aloof from the single street of its adjoining village, a figure was sitting astride the apex of a high roof. He was a large man, stripped contentedly to the waist, eyes closed in pleasure at the rays of the sun. It was getting towards evening and the heat of the August day was mellowing. His body was tanned to a deep brown. A small trowel and bucket of cement rested on the ridge of the tiles before him. His legs rode the flanks of the roof as though he were astride a vast horse or riding a flying goose out of the pages of a children's fairy tale.

He was almost totally bald, except for the long ponytail that swung down between his shoulders. Occasionally he reached up to touch this ponytail, as though for comfort or to adjust his balance. He had been sitting like this for a long time; motionless, eyes shut appreciatively, smiling, and all the while softly humming. The tune he hummed was just detectable on the warm air: 'The Bare Necessities'. Every now and again he lifted a hand, and paw-like, wafted away a small but persistent flotilla of gnats.

The peaceful evening was shredded abruptly by a harsh, jackdaw-like voice cawing up from down below. 'Ha'way, Ronny, ye fat lazy bastard! Are we gannin' doon the Wheatsheaf or are ye spending the rest of yer friggin' life dreaming up there?'

Ronny did not open his eyes.

The voice grew querulous. 'You must be finished by now, man. It was only supposed to be a half-hour job, tops.' From below there was the clumsy clang of a boot stepping into a bucket, a stumble and a corvine tangle of swearing. A few moments later the arms of the ladder leaning against the side of the house began to bounce. The heavy breathing of an awkwardly ascending man grew gradually closer. With a small, meditative sigh, Ronny began to hum 'The Bare Necessities' again.

A bucket appeared first, full of rubble and straw; then, peering quizzically through the stalks of straw, a sharp beak-like nose, attached to a rapacious-looking face. 'One Squirrel Kit,' the man said, rattling the bucket fondly and then plonking it on the ledge which passed all the way round the house.

'Areet, Al,' Ronny greeted him, his eyes still shut.

'Jesus, it's hot,' replied Al testily.

'Nice cool breeze up here, but.'

One of Al's eyes was blue, while the other was an opaque white. Both seemed to glint with a cunning intelligence as his head, constantly swivelling, roved acquisitively. 'For frigg sake, man Ronny,' he snapped. 'Put some clothes on. It's like watching a sausage spitting under the grill.'

Al's body breasted into view. It was huge. As he peered up the slant of slates to where Ronny sat, his head craned at countless angles, taking in every detail. Then, just like a foraging jackdaw sighting food, his nose pecked slightly as it zeroed in on the chimney stack. 'Were ye just not gonnae

25

mention it or what?' he demanded in an aggrieved tone. 'Ye kna very well that I can get Surrey prices.'

Ronny opened his mild brown eyes, which were still heavy with daydreams. 'What ye on aboot?'

In his frustration and excitement Al gabbled: 'That . . . that . . .'

Blinking, Ronny followed the pointing finger. 'Oh, that.'

The chimney stack was towering, its brickwork weathered by a century of soot. 'I couldn't see it proper from doon below,' said Al, both eyes shining excitedly. 'It's a friggin' bobby-dazzler. Get it dismantled tonight. If ye're gonnae be up here then ye might as well get some proper work done. I'll gan and borrow the concrete mixer from Trevor. I was wanting a pint of lager pronto, but I'm willing to suffer a bit langer for that chimney.' A cold joy glinted in both blue and white eyes. 'Ronny, auld mate, we're looking at three hundred quid straight profit.'

Ronny shook his head. 'Ye kna the rule,' he said evenly. 'Nee cowboy jobs on auld dears.'

'This one's nee auld dear.' Al grinned. 'She's loaded. Ye saw them antiques in her sitting room. Anyway, this isn't nee cowboy job. In fact, it's deein' her a favour. She gets a new friggin' chimney, and we get Surrey prices for the old one. So ha'way, doon ye come and get the sledgehammer . . .'

'Na.'

Al was outraged. 'What ye on aboot?'

Rubbing his eyes, Ronny tried to wring the dreaminess from them. He yawned. 'What we agreed, nee cowboy jobs on . . .'

'Nee cooboy jobs?'

'That's right, man Al. Nee cooboy jobs.'

'What ye talking aboot? We're the bloody Billy the Kid and Wild Bill Hickock of Gatesheed. We divven't dee anything but cooboy jobs. Anyway, it was ye what strung oot that hour job last month over a whole week and that punter was hardly a

26

spring chicken. In fact, he was more of a grave dodger than this one.'

'That was different. He *was* loaded.'

Al's tone rose with righteous indignation. 'And it was ye what bloody kept that lead we got from that church of Audrey's. Not to mention what ye did last week in Whickham. Them women were ready to tar and feather ye.'

Ronny lifted a hand to touch his ponytail. 'I'm not saying I'm a bloody holy Joe or owt, I'm just not conning this auld dear. Stuck-up bastards in Whickham with sports cars and snotty noses, aye; auld dears struggling on a pension, na.'

Al's huge body writhed with irritation. 'So ye're just gonnae let three hundred quid gan west? I mean, why divven't ye gan the whole hog and change yer name to Mother friggin' Teresa?' Al's good eye narrowed calculatingly as he studied Ronny, whilst the opaque one gaped glassily. 'When did ye win the lottery, like? I mean, ye must be pretty flush to hoy away three hundred quid straight profit. Think aboot it. What's she gonnae lose? Nothing. In fact that chimney looks none too safe. So we're actually providing a service . . .'

'No,' said Ronny, and like a contented bear held his face up to the waning rays of the summer's dusk.

Big Al sighed mournfully. 'Nee wonder we're as poor as friggin' church mice with ye on the job. It's always the same whenever we . . .'

But Ronny was not listening, he was gazing out over the land below. 'Look,' he said.

'Eh?' replied Al, his jackdaw features fixed on the chimney.

'Just look.' Ronny pointed at the view from the roof. 'I've been looking at it all afternoon.' There was wonder in his voice. 'It's Gatesheed.'

'Thank frigg for that,' Al laughed grimly. 'And here's me thinking it was bloody Tenerife.'

'But look, Al. Ye've got to look.'

Reluctantly Al looked out over the panoramic view. Three former pit villages could be seen from where they were. The old colliery workings surrounding these settlements had long since begun the short return to the native heath which once lined so many of the slopes of England, and a blaze of gorse bloom, countless shades of rusty seed heads and gaunt birch trees filled the wide-ranging sight. Here and there among the summer's growth could be made out the bones of some machinery of the Industrial Revolution, its iron slowly returning to the earth from which it had been ripped. 'I divven't see anything,' said Al flatly. 'Just a load o' bloody waste groond. There's not nee pit wheels here now nor nowt.'

Set free to graze on what has become common land once more, skewbald ponies filled the landscape, searching for the delicacies of vetch and clover. The grass stood heavy and high, and some children playing close by to the lone house on which the pair of roofers worked, set the ripe seed heads dancing. Ronny chuckled. 'Look at them bairns. In and oot of the grass all day.' Broom pods were popping in the sun. 'Listen,' said Ronny. 'Just look and listen.'

'Oh aye,' laughed Al, turning away from the view. 'A few scragg ends o' wasteland, and scraps of auld machinery. Very beautiful. Have ye been drinking from the Tyne again?'

'It is beautiful,' mused Ronny. 'I've nivver realised just how beautiful it is.'

'Pass us the wacky baccy if there's some gannin' roond. What's beautiful is that three hundred quid's worth of Victorian bloody chimney.'

Ronny gazed north through a patchwork of field and copse back to the built-up part of the borough. Distant tower blocks rose on this horizon, just the top three or four storeys visible in the folds of the land: monoliths of a strange, long since broken neolithic circle. And then he saw the forest. He narrowed his eyes contemplatively. The trees were mostly larch and oak, and their canopies at this time of the year held a deep, seemingly boundless sea green. There were a number of meadows within the trees, buildings and what looked like some ruins. And, right in the middle of it all, at least half a mile long, a grass avenue leading to a huge statue on top of a pillar. 'Hello?' Al's voice was a sarcastic, sing-song. 'Earth calling Mork. Is yer heed up yer arse again, Mork?' Al shunted the bucket of rubble and straw he had brought up the first few slates of the roof. 'Get busy with the squirrel kit, ye lazy bastard. And remember to make sure she can see a few bits o' straw from doon below.'

But Ronny was still lost in the view. 'What is it?' he mused, gazing at the avenue in the trees. 'What is it?'

'I said there ye gan!' Al shouted.

The loudness of the voice jolted Ronny, and he looked down at his companion. Al was holding out the bucket. Ronny sighed. 'Al man. Nee cowboy jobs, full stop. Squirrel or chimney. It's the same thing. I mean, would ye like someone taking in your auld mam?'

'Chance would be a fine thing,' retorted Al. 'Last time someone tried to get one awer on her, she kicked down his ladder. Broke both his legs. He was lucky she didn't maim him for life like she did me father.' He mused on the memory, and then looked back up at the chimney. 'Look, joking apart, we're in business together, and if ye won't let wor dee the chimney or a squirrel job, then what's the point? We might as well just gan and sign on.'

'Ye cannet sign on when you're already on invalidity benefit,' Ronny pointed out. 'Ye tried that already.'

For a few moments Al seemed utterly disorientated. His eyes darted between the chimney and the bucket of rubble and straw, his sharp nose pecking hungrily at them. Then he sighed loudly, a look of infinite regret on his face. 'Come on then, let's get doon the Wheatsheaf for a pint. That's the least ye owe us.' The mention of alcohol boosted Big Al's spirits instantly. 'Ha'way, it's a Saturday night; let's have a real piss-up. Get proper mortal. Being in this heat all day, I'm that thirsty I could drink the Tyne mesel'.'

'I cannet.' Ronny's voice was quiet.

'Eh?'

'Not tonight, I cannet. I cannet gan doon the Wheatsheaf.'

'Why not?'

'I just cannet.'

'But it's ages since we had a decent night oot.'

'Well, I cannet make it tonight.'

There was a long pause. Al scratched his great belly wedged against the stonework of the house. 'There seems to be a lot of neets that ye cannet make just noo.' He gazed seriously at Ronny, and then winked cajolingly. 'Ha'way. The old firm doon the Wheatsheaf until hoying-oot time. Shooting the breeze, ogling the lasses, puking wor guts oot at half eleven. Mebbes gannin' to a nightclub on the Quayside. The boat mebbes. Just like the auld days.' He studied his friend's shaking head, then grinned mirthlessly. 'Oh, I get it. I kna what this is all aboot. Well. I'll tell ye summink for nowt, bonny lad; ye want to get yer snout oot from between your Audrey's tits for once before the wind changes direction and ye find yersel' stuck there.' Al shook his head rapidly, his flaccidly held cheeks rattling greedily. 'Not that she hasn't got a canny pair. I mean, I wouldn't say na to stringing a pearl necklace roond them beauties mesel', but seriously, man Ronny, ye're in danger of turning into a joke.' Al's body bobbed and lifted slightly as though he was flapping wings in his irritation. 'Ye used to be a proper good laugh, but she's turned ye into a reet boring artichoke. And I'm not just saying this 'cos she cannet stand the sight of me. It's ye I'm worried aboot. The next thing I kna yus'll be wearing a Celtic top and carrying rosary beads aboot. And that's another thing I cannet work oot. What's with the religion? She's had more pricks than a dartboard so . . .'

'She's with me now,' said Ronny evenly. 'We're happy.'

Al shook his head long-sufferingly. 'You want to pull yourself together, son. Before it's too late. It's pathetic to see. She got ye by the balls —'

'What's that?' Ronny interrupted.

'Eh?'

Ronny was pointing over the fields to where the avenue cut a way through the larch and oak forest. 'What's that? All day it's been on me mind.' He smiled thoughtfully. 'I thought I knew Gatesheed, but I divven't. I mean, what's that place . . . ?'

Al spumed with exasperation. In a flurry of incomprehensible crow-like oaths, he snatched the squirrel kit, dipped from view and began his descent. The ladder bounced dangerously.

Left alone again, Ronny pursed his lips contentedly, and staring out over the avenue, hummed 'The Bare Necessities'. After a little while, a dart of suspicion disturbed his ursine peacefulness. A moment later, a second dart hit him. 'Al?' he called down. There was no reply. Very carefully, on his hands and arse, he started to edge down the slant of slates to the ladder. 'Al?' He could just see the top of an extremely dirty white vanette. The door of the vanette could be heard opening and then closing. 'AL!' Ronny bellowed.

'What now?' came the peevish response.

'Where ye gannin'?'

'There's nee reason why I should deprive mesel' of a nice pint, just 'cos ye've signed the pledge. Divven't worry, I'll be back in half an hour.'

'Wait there!' Ronny cried. 'I kna ye. Once ye've got in that Wheatsheaf I won't see hide nor hair o' ye.'

'Aye, well, we cannet all be henpecked hubbies. Some o' wor have got better things to be deein'.'

'I'll be doon in a minute. Just wait there.' There was no reply. An unwonted urgency edged Ronny's tone. 'I said wait there!'

'Ha'way then. Yus're wasting valuable drinking time.'

'I cannet be late mesel'. I've got stuff on tonight.'

'What have ye got on that's more important than a pint with your mates doon the Wheatsheaf?' Al asked. He paused. 'Areet, I'll gan with ye to the Catholic Club if that's what ye want. I'll take ye hyem, ye can square it up with Audrey and then we'll . . .'

Ronny's voice was firm. 'I cannet gan oot tonight. I've summink on.'

'Fine,' came the icy return. 'Then me and Kenny and the rest of the lads'll just have to get mortal on wor own. Leave ye to perform yer fucking cloak-and-dagger act to yer heart's content.'

It was as he was easing himself on to the ladder that Ronny realised he had left the cement and trowel on the ridge of the roof. He swore. For a moment he seemed tempted to leave it there, but then began the precipitous climb to retrieve it. 'I'm just gannin' back to get the trowel an' that,' he shouted. 'Divven't drive off.'

'I'm not yer bloody chauffeur. If ye cannet be bothered to come for a single pint then . . .' Al sighed. 'Get yersel' doon then, I'll just gan and tell her aboot the squirrels.'

'There aren't any,' returned Ronny.

Al's tone was withering. 'That's the whole point, Dumbo.'

The trip back up to the apex was fraught. The slates were smooth and the soles of Ronny's heavy labourer's boots had been worn to a shine. When a lifted slate nail tore into flesh exposed by his pair of Bermuda shorts, he almost lost his grip. By the time he had finally made it to the bottom of the ladder there was no sign of Big Al.

The vanette was still there. Having folded the ladder into itself and secured it on the rickety roof rack with a red rag tied to the end, Ronny opened the back doors, chuckling at the message someone's finger had traced in the grimy glass: *I wish my wife was this dirty*. He placed the cement bucket and trowel among the rest of the debris, a clutter of half-bags of cement, sand, aggregates, blunt saws, rusty hammers, an ancient sledge-hammer, and shovels whose blades were engrained with splashes of concrete and whose shafts were painted in a yellow that only partly covered up the National Coal Board initials.

The donkey jacket that Ronny put on over his naked torso also bore the ghostly legend of the NCB, its stitching remaining after the logo had been ripped off during the grievous time of pit redundancies.

Looking cautiously over his shoulder, Ronny took out a small object from one of the donkey jacket pockets. As he held it in the palm of his hand, staring at it surreptitiously, a deep joy grew in his eyes. It was a jewellery box. He opened it. Inside was a pair of pendants and a ring. A tinny rendition of the theme from *Love Story* played out. His joy deepened. Then he heard voices and he quickly replaced it in the pocket. The tune stopped.

'Aye, it's a tell-tale sign,' Al was explaining to someone in his customer voice. Ronny smiled at the well-known sound. 'It's the straw that's the real give-away. And as ye can see, unfortunately we found that all right. It means they're nesting there. Me main worry is that they've got into your roofing felt.' Ronny had just closed the back doors of the vanette and hurriedly tied them with a piece of orange twine when Al came into view. An old lady was listening to his professional jeremiad with a kind of bewildered horror while looking warily at the bucket of rubble and straw he was carrying. Al took a handful of chipped concrete from the bucket and let it sift through his fingers. 'I mean, look at the damage they've done to your stonework already. And that just the skinny end of the wedge. Ye've got red squirrels here. Thems is like the skinheeds of the animal kingdom. I've heard tales of them gannin' reet through. There ye are sitting on the netty peacefully minding yer own business, and the next moment a geet pair of squirrelly eyes is peeking in at ye.'

'It's areet, pet,' said Ronny, butting in. 'I've sorted the squirrels for ye.'

'Aye,' said Al, flashing his workmate a warning look before adding sanctimoniously to the old lady, 'but to make sure we'll have to check your roofing felt.'

'Na, it's areet,' continued Ronny, dodging the daggers thrown by Al. 'Them squirrels is well and truly finished with. At nee extra cost.'

The old lady seemed even more worried. 'I hope you did it humanely. They're an endangered species.'

'I gave them a month's quit rent,' winked Ronny. 'And shook each one by the paw as he waved ta-ta.'

A huge dark cloud rose from the exhaust of the vanette as it vibrated into life. 'Ha'way, then,' said Al as they pulled away from the house, 'yus'll have to direct us.'

'Eh?' Ronny returned.

'Well, I divven't kna the way to Millionaires' Row mesel', but ye obviously dee.' Al lowered his forehead until it touched the hub of the plastic steering wheel and then groaned. 'Ye must be off yer fuckin' trolley, Ronny. It's two days' work that, a squirrel job. Mebbes even a week. Of deein' nowt.'

They drove in silence through the fields and dells of Gateshead. And as the road took them through the forest that Ronny had gazed at with such interest, they still hadn't talked. 'What is that place?' Ronny mused.

'Snap oot of it!' Al suddenly shouted. 'Get yer head oot o' the cloods for a change. It's just some friggin' auld pile of ruins or summink. It means nowt. Nowt. D'ye hear me? Nowt. Whereas that money yus've just thrown away is real. Real pints. Real bloody food.' He shook his head bitterly. 'Yus would nivver have done that in the past. Ye've changed, man. And not for the better. For a start ye used to be the best laugh in Gatesheed. And noo? Noo, ye're aboot as funny as a lung fish.'

On the dashboard stood a little plastic navvy who, activated by the shuddering momentum of the clapped-out vehicle, raised and lowered his trousers in a crouching posture of contempt. They were driving past the old Derwentheugh coke works, now converted to a country park, when Al suddenly bumped the van up on to the verge and jolted to a halt. He

34

yanked the driver's mirror towards his passenger. 'What d'ye see?' he demanded as the plastic navvy grew still, his buttocks glaring in mid-moony. Ronny gazed up at his reflection. 'I'll tell ye what ye see. Ye see a stetson the size o' one of Kenny Rogers. And d'ye kna why? Because yus're the same as me. We're a couple o' cooboys. That's what we are, that's what we'll always be. The mines have closed, wor little business ventures all disappeared into puffs of fart. And what's left? Cooboy building. How else we gonnae make ends meet with a pair of dodgy ladders, knocked-off coal board clobber and a crappy vanette?' Al's voice had risen to a crescendo of anger, and as he glared at his friend, reproach glinted in both of his eyes. He shook his head and looked forlornly out of the window at the traffic. 'Mebbes it's time,' he began. 'Mebbes this is just the push I need.' Unseen to Al as he continued, Ronny parroted his words as though he knew them by heart: 'Time for me to dee a Lone Ranger, and strike oot on me tod. I'm a faithful soul, and mebbes that's me problem. I stand by a mate through thick and thin, but when that mate begins to take the bread oot me mooth and the pint oot me hand then . . .' Glancing up into the mirror, Al happened to catch Ronny mimicking him. With a face of deep hurt, he stared at him reproachfully.

'Ye divven't have it too bad,' said Ronny reasonably. 'I mean, I dee all the ladder work and since we're mainly roofers that's . . .'

'Oh, I see. I get the picture. It's back to this, is it? D'ye think I asked to be a cripple?'

'Ye're not crippled,' returned Ronny quietly.

'So what's this then?' Al jabbed at his opaque eye. 'Drop a bit of emulsion in it yesterday, did I? I'm wall-eyed, man. I'm bloody wall-eyed!'

'Ye can still see.'

'Then what aboot me legs? One's shorter than the other.'

'So ye say, but neebody can see it. And the doctors have nivver . . .'

'So who's been walking on the buggers for fifty-odd years? Me or some jumped-up quack?' Al shook his head self-pityingly. In the few moments of silence a heavy lorry trundled by, shaking the vanette so the dashboard and navvy fell on to their knees, sending down a shower of old McDonald's wrappers and fries packets. The navvy leered up at Ronny, who rammed the dashboard back into place. 'Anyway,' Al continued, 'I dee the books, divven't I? I'd like to see ye grapple with all them facts and figures. Ye can hardly write yer name. Not that I'm complaining. I mean, I'm the one with the education, and with that comes responsibility.'

'One O level,' smirked Ronny.

'One more than what you've got, Ronny boy.'

'In cookery.'

'Woodwork, if ye divven't mind.'

Al glared at Ronny, who tugged lightly at his ponytail. 'Let's not fall oot, man Al. I'm too happy to fall oot with anyone today.'

Al brought a fist down on the hub of his steering wheel, and the indicator light started ticking. He punched it again, and the light fell silent. 'Are you gonnae tell me what the frigg's gannin' on, Ronny, or do ye usually leave yer best mate in the dark?' Al paused for an instant before muttering darkly, 'Ye nivver used to.'

'There's nowt gannin' on, man Al.'

'So why cannet ye gan oot tonight? It's Saturday night, for God's sake. Ye used to love gannin' on the pull.'

'We nivver pulled once.'

'We did.'

'Aye,' shot back Ronny, 'once. When it was grab-a-granny night on the boat.'

'So? Ye divven't look at the mantelpiece when ye're stoking the fire. And what aboot them lasses we took up to Kielder

36

that time? When I switched the headlights off, mine could have been a Page Three girl.'

Ronny did not answer. He could not contain a dreamy smile as his hand slid into his pocket to feel the jewellery box. 'Anyway, me days of trying to pull are over.'

'Oh, please yersel' then.' Al glowered at his friend. 'Ye can say what ye like, that friggin' chimney would have brought in three hundred quid pure profit.'

The engine vibrated into life and the vanette jolted along the verge for a while before bumping back on to the road. They skirted the old coke works once painted by J.M.W. Turner, saplings now flaming green where once the artist mixed a palette of fiery ambers.

At the traffic lights which separate the rural from the urban portions of the Metropolitan Borough of Gateshead, a red light stopped them. Reaching into his pocket, Al threw down an object on to the dashboard. It was a packet of pork scratchings. 'Not that ye deserve them, like.'

Ronny picked them up and studied the packet. 'Say if I was on desert island and I could only have one food. It'd be these.' He licked his lips. 'Either that or lemon-flavoured scampi fries.'

'Bloody hell. Dee us a favour and just eat the buggers.'

Ronny reached up to feel his ponytail. Then he shook his head. 'I cannet.'

'Well, that's a first,' snorted Al.

'The thing is, I divven't want to spoil me supper.'

'Spoil yer supper?' Al's nose pecked at Ronny's belly interrogatively. 'There's room for the friggin' fatted calf in there and then enough for fish and chips twice.'

'I'm starving,' Ronny admitted. Gazing yearningly at the pork scratchings, he thrust the packet decisively away. 'I cannet. Not toneet.'

Al grew serious. 'For the last time of asking, Ronny man, are ye gonnae tell us what's gannin' on?'

'There's nowt gannin' on.'

37

Big Al's wall-eye scrutinised his friend. Then he shrugged. 'Save them for later then.' And taking the packet of pork scratchings, he made to shove them into the pocket of Ronny's donkey jacket, but something blocked his way. 'What the hell's that?'

'Nowt.' Ronny's reply was rather too quick.

Al's jackdaw swoop penetrated Ronny's paw-like fend. An object was inveigled from the donkey jacket pocket. It was the jewellery box. With the beak of his nose hovering over it, Al placed it on the nub of the steering wheel, sharp elbows jabbing Ronny back. The red light turned to green and the vanette chugged on. Al drove through the scrap heaps and pony fields of Swalwell with his nose over the object and his elbows fanned like the protective wings of a scavenger at a find of carrion.

When Al clicked the box open, the thin, rather tinny version of the theme from *Love Story* played out. Al spluttered into laughter. 'Give it back,' cried Ronny, trying to reach beyond the elbows. The laughter grew guttural as Al lifted up the pendants. They were the two halves of a single disc hung on separate chains. Ronny sat back. A smile replaced the anxiety on his face as he tugged appreciatively on his ponytail. 'I just love her,' he said simply. 'For the life of me, I just love her.' The mirth continued to pour out from Ronny's companion. But he was heedless. 'Geet classy that,' Ronny smiled serenely. 'The way it plays a tune. It's —'

'— aboot as classy as diarrhoea,' Al managed to gasp through his hilarity. A braying of horns brought him sufficiently to his senses to pull the vanette back into his own lane. 'Where d'ye find it?' he spluttered again when he had the vehicle back into control. 'Sellotaped to the back of *Daft Prick Monthly*?'

'Ha bloody ha,' said Ronny as he made a fresh grab.

Al shook his head. His good eye narrowed while the opaque one gazed at Ronny in the driver's mirror. 'So that's what it's all been aboot. Now I see. Now I get the picture.' Al pursed his lips in deep thought. 'It's worse than I thought. It's –'

'Bandits, ten o'clock,' Ronny suddenly cut in.

'Christ on a bike!' Al hissed at the police car parked in a lay-by ahead, scanning the oncoming traffic. He looked at the tax disc holder. It was empty. Desperately, he opened the glove compartment and began to root around among the fast-food wrappings. 'Where the hell's the false tax disc?'

'I threw it away,' replied Ronny.

'Eh?'

'Even that one had got oot of date.'

The vanette bounced like a fairground ride as Al threw the wheel recklessly, and, juddering over some open ground, disappeared down a narrow lane of potholes and dust. The lane thrust them between towering piles of scrap cars. A great claw-grab hovered above them like a monstrous kestrel. 'Is he following wor?' Al demanded nervously.

'I divven't think so,' replied Ronny, turning.

'Just to be on the safe side . . .' said Al and peeped his horn. The man in the cabin of the crane controlling the claw-grab dropped the heavy metal instrument behind the rapidly departing vanette, sealing the way it had come.

'Cheers, Malc,' shouted Ronny through his opened window. 'We owe ye one.'

The man in the cabin waved. The word Wheatsheaf could just be made out from his gabbled shout.

The vanette drove on. 'I've loved her for more than thirty-five year,' Ronny announced. 'Just her. Nee other lass. And to find oot that she's felt the same way. I cannet explain what that feels like. I just cannet say what she means to us . . .'

'Jesus, man,' Al interrupted. 'Have ye farted?'

Ronny nodded. 'Sorry.'

'Wind yer bloody window doon then.'

Beyond the scrap heaps, the road narrowed and deteriorated even further as Al and Ronny threaded a delicate way through allotments. 'I think there's a way through here somewhere,' Al said, his head craning in all directions through the glass.

'Aye,' nodded Ronny. 'We came this way last time there was a copper there.'

When they were certain that the police car was not following them, Al's knuckles, which had whitened on the wheel, ran pink again. 'Right,' he said. 'That's it. Me and ye are gonnae have to have a good talk. Ye've always been a dreamer, but since ye got yer hands on them tits, ye've become a liability. Point one. What the frigg happened to that tax disc? I dee everything else that's dodgy. Y'kna it's your job to keep the false discs in date. Point two. I want to get to the bottom of what's going on or this partnership is gonnae have to hang up its friggin' spurs.'

'I'm sorry,' Ronny mumbled. 'Aboot the tax disc. I forgot. I just cannet seem to think of anything else these days.' He murmured quietly to himself, then turned to Al with the zeal of one sharing a revelation. 'Y'kna what Audrey looked like when she woke up this morning?'

'Have ye farted again?' Al demanded. Ronny shook his head. 'Well, I wish ye would, 'cos I'd rather suffer one o' your minging methanes than listen to ye gannin' on aboot Audrey Bloody McPhee.'

'It's Slater,' Ronny said, almost dazed by the fact. 'She's my wife.'

With the dry heat of August, the dust rose in huge plumes behind them as they continued on the hidden byways. Hens scratching for worms on the patchy surface were sent scurrying. A pig was left coughing in their wake. Mild-eyed goats stared at them.

Al throttled the vehicle over the stone bridge which has crossed the River Derwent since 1778, and trotted it over a piece of scrub. As it mounted a sharp embankment, the dull glissando of the half-bags of cement, sand and aggregates could be heard as they slid down the back of the vanette. 'Did ye at least remember to tie the back doors?' the driver demanded. 'Or did ye forget that an' all?'

'Course I didn't,' replied Ronny.

The bags were followed by the rest of the gear, the shovels drumming against the back doors like a catch of large fish on the deck of a boat.

They had joined the course of an old tree-lined railway line that used to link the steel badlands of Consett to the River Tyne. Their way was smooth for a while now, running over levelled ash, and Al slowed to a walking pace. 'How much then?' he suddenly demanded in a serious voice.

'Eh?'

'For that bloody piece of jewellery.'

Ronny took the jewellery box, and lifted out the double pendant, staring at it as though hypnotised by the gently swinging silver discs. ' "I love ye more today than yesterday," ' he intoned. ' "But less than tomorrow." ' He beamed widely. 'That's what it says on the engraving. On all of it, like. On my half it just says: "I love yesterday than", on hers it says: "you more —" '

'Areet, areet, any more and I'll bloody puke all awer ye.'

The abstracted air deepened in Ronny. 'The way it's one pendant cut into two. That says it all.'

'It says yus've got aboot as much sense as ye've got hair on the top of yer heed.'

'It's a lovely pendant.'

'Sod the pendant,' snapped Al. 'That's one ninety from Gatesheed market. I'm not talking aboot the pendant. What else is in there?' With bewildering speed, Al plucked a ring from the jewellery box, and brought it right underneath his nostrils which flared acquisitively as he seemed to sniff the ruby. There was an audible crack as he bit the gold. Then, with a sorrowful shake of his head, he handed it back to his passenger. 'That cost ye more than ye've got by at least two hundred quid or my name's not Big Al Greener.'

A haunted look seized Ronny's features, and in a gesture of panic he threw up a hand to grab his ponytail. But as quickly as it had come, his terror departed, replaced by a blissful smile. 'I'm in love.'

'Ye're a friggin' moon calf,' Al sighed, and sucked his teeth. 'I love . . .'

'Is that your stomach growling or is there gonnae be a earthquake? Ha'way, get them bloody pork scratchings doon ye before ye deafen wor. Ye'd think ye hadn't eaten all day.'

'I haven't,' Ronny replied solemnly.

Al was incredulous. 'Yus're joking.'

'First time I've ever done that.' He prodded his stomach thoughtfully.

'Nee pork scratchings? Fasting all day? I suppose in a minute yus're gonnae gan and kneel to Mecca.'

'I've told ye. I've summink special on tonight.'

Al scrutinised Ronny. 'Ye must be mad. Why didn't ye come to me? I've got a mate what's big in the jewellery trade. He'd have seen you straight. He'd have . . .' Al broke off and blew through his lips. 'Where d'ye get the money from, bonny lad?' Staring through the open half of his window, Ronny did not reply. Big Al's face grew gentle for one instant. 'You've borrowed again, haven't you?' Al wound down his own window and spat through it. The crunch of the wheels slowly running over the cinder track filled the silence between the two men. 'I cannet believe it. Ye've only gone and borrowed from the loan shark again.' A stone leapt from the wheels and bulleted into the undergrowth. 'What the frigg are ye deein' gannin' to the loan shark again?'

Ronny's reply was quiet. 'I needed money.'

'Money? He needed money. We all need bloody money. I need money.'

'What for?' Ronny tried to smile. 'Pints doon the Wheat-sheaf?'

'No,' said Al. 'Like bloody road tax for this thing.' He struck the nub of the steering wheel. 'How much langer d'yus think it'll be able to stand up to this kind of treatment, up hill and doon dale? Besides,' Al sighed wistfully, 'I'm sick of hiding away, using the back roads, even slinking aboot off road just 'cos we divven't have tax.'

'Or insurance,' added Ronny. 'Or MOT. Or seat belts.'

'Areet, areet,' Al snapped. 'I get the picture. I'm sick of the worry. It's a jail sentence for me if I get caught again. That's what the bloody magistrate said last time. Just for once I want to be able to ride the bloody range openly, withoot me friggin' sphincter throbbin' like a fuckin' grapefruit every time I see a boy in blue.'

In time, the railway cutting debouched them on to an open piece of rough ground. Bordered on one side by the River Tyne and on the other by a tall razor-wire fence, it was a disused siding. Beyond the razor wire, the brick and glass of the Metro Centre could be glimpsed between thickets of birch and alder. Ronny gazed at the retail and leisure centre. 'She'll be in there noo. As we speak. I wonder what she's deein'? Now. At this moment.'

'Probably on the netty, wiping her arse.'

'Ye haven't got a romantic bone in your body ye, have ye, Al?'

There was a pause broken by Al. 'Where did you get the money from? Please tell us I'm wrang. Please tell us that not all your brain cells have migrated to yer friggin' balls. Please tell us yus haven't borrowed from Johno again.' The vanette rumbled to a halt. 'How much?' Ronny did not reply. Al tried to start the engine again, but it was dead. The usual corvine tangle of oaths filled the air. Then he shook his head. 'What's the occasion this time? I mean, it cannet be her birthday again.'

As Ronny got out and began to push the vehicle over the old siding, a troubled look ghosted him. 'Two hundred quid,' he admitted at last. Al closed his eyes as though riding a blow.

Ronny's voice, breathless with exertion, was full of reason-ableness. 'Just two hundred quid. Why, that's nowt. It'll be paid off by Christmas.'

'Two hundred quid,' repeated Al to himself, then thrust his face out of the window at Ronny. 'It was only a hundred quid last time and ye nearly ended up getting yer arms broken.'

At last they came to the hole in the razor wire. Ronny was red-faced and breathless. 'Ye'll have to get oot and push an' all, Al man. Before I have a heart attack.'

Al got out and without a word put his shoulder to the back of the vanette, smudging the graffiti on the grime so the words, '*I wish my wife was this dirty*', now seemed to say, '*I miss my life this dirty*'. With a mighty heave the two men shunted a way through the twisted brambles and longer grass which grew by the wire fence. Al's face was set as stone. 'I'll be deein' me back in next,' he reflected grimly. 'Then what? I suppose I'll just have to starve to death while ye skirmish to yer heart's content in the battles of Venus.'

They came to a chalk track wide enough for the vehicle. 'Speak to us, man Al,' begged Ronny as Al got back into the vanette. But Al did not reply. Ronny watched the vanette coast noiselessly down the slope and disappear in a puff of dust round a corner.

The scent of water was on the air, and as Ronny followed the vanette, he breathed in deeply. The river was close by, its tide on the turn, and in among the salt and slight rotting odour of the sea which high tide carries many miles inland, Ronny could detect the freshness of the Tynedale hills in the river air. He stopped to inhale. It was cooler and damper. Tall river plants grew. And when Ronny rounded the corner, the River Tyne could be seen close by: a great, coaly-black flow. Silent so close-up. And muscular.

He found himself on what once must have been a substantial wharf built for a vast trade of many men. Across the river gleamed the new offices of the recently developed business park. Joggers ran up and down the immaculately revamped riverside area. On this side not a soul was to be seen on the abandoned site. Alder trees grew out of fissures in the old dock. The vanette was parked up right at the edge of the wharf, and Al was trying to drag a large piece of canvas over the dirty white vehicle. 'What ye deein'?' Ronny asked.

'Putting the vanette to bed for the weekend, man,' Al snapped.

'But I've got to get hyem,' Ronny returned. 'I've the bairns' tea to get and then I've got summink on, y'kna I have, summink special . . .'

'So ye keep on saying. But I'm not risking a spell in the friggin' jug just for your "summink specials". Ye can walk hyem from here.' Ronny stared at his friend, his tongue probing the gum. 'Think aboot me for a change,' Al burst. 'I've got to walk all the way to the friggin' Wheatsheaf. Now give us a hand covering this.'

Mechanically, Ronny took a corner of the canvas, and the two men lifted it over the illegal vehicle in a well-practised action. When this was done, Al disappeared over the edge of the wharf. Footsteps could be heard descending a flight of rickety wooden steps. Ronny sauntered to the edge of the wharf and looked down. Al was standing on a dilapidated houseboat. The tide still held it, and the ancient vessel bobbed at its frayed mooring, but already the mud of its ebb berth was beginning to show.

The foredeck of the long, barge-like craft was littered with plant pots in which wilted dead ferns. Al lifted each melancholy pot in turn until at last he had located the key. 'Why divven't ye learn and just put it under the same one each time?' Ronny called down with a smile.

Al glanced up with a chilly look. 'And why divven't ye learn? They nearly broke yer arms last time.'

'Oh, I'll have it paid back in a fortnight.'

'Aye, if ye'd let wor get that chimney stack. Why did ye dee it, man?'

Ronny shrugged. 'I love her.'

Al hawked deeply and sent a glob of phlegm out on to the whispering slide of the Tyne. On the dockside of the boat, in the quickly appearing mud, the wooden ribs of the old keel boats were beginning to show, those long thin coal carriers from past centuries. Al stared up at Ronny. 'There is one way oot, bonny lad,' he said, a new hope in his voice.

'Eh?'

'Let's get doon to brass tacks. Ye've borrowed two hundred quid from Johno. There's only one way to get that kind of money in one gan.' Al paused significantly. 'Ye kna what I'm on aboot, divven't ye?'

Ronny sighed. 'Not that again.'

'Aye, that again.'

'Ye're always bringing this up, man.'

'Only because ye are always acting the prick.'

Ronny's voice rose. 'I cannet believe ye bringing this up again.'

'And I cannet believe yus've borrowed from the loan shark again!' Al shouted back.

'How many times do I have to tell ye?' Ronny cried, his voice echoing against the plush new offices on the Newcastle bank so that the joggers there stared across the river to the rickety houseboat which stood moored to the crumbling, abandoned Gateshead wharf. 'I'm not friggin' well deein' it!'

'So what the friggin' hell are ye gonnae dee?'

Just then the houseboat ground on the mud, and Al was tossed across the foredeck. In a movement of heavy, arm-flapping ungainliness, which made the whole vessel shudder, he just managed to hop back on to the wooden steps. Having gained his balance, he stared up at Ronny. 'Ha'way then, what ye gonnae dee, Ronny lad? Wait for them to break yer legs and hoy ye in the Tyne?' Al threw a hand dramatically over his shoulder to encompass the water flowing behind him. 'These are loan sharks we're talking aboot, man. Loan sharks. D'ye understand? Or are ye so blinded by a pair o' tits that ye cannet see the shit for the fan?'

'I'll pay it back.'

The wood of the stairs creaked under Al's rapid ascent. 'How?'

'Like I did last time.'

'Like ye did last time.' Al's tone was bitter as he reached the defunct wharf. 'Na. There's only one way.' Slowly, he approached Ronny. 'Hello,' Al began, holding his nose and mimicking a call centre customer adviser. 'Have you recently had an accident which was not your fault? And if so, have you suffered financial loss as a result of your injuries? Good, then Claims Direct can help you.'

'For the last time of telling,' Ronny burst out, 'I'm not deein' nee Claims Direct.' Shaking his head, he began to trudge away.

'Ha'way,' Al called cajolingly, 'I'll be yer independent witness. It'll only hurt a bit. Then we'll be in clover. Some of them get six grand. Imagine what we could dee with that.'

Ronny half turned. 'Well, why divven't ye dee it then?'

'I've already done it twice. Three times would be taking the piss. Besides, ye haven't got a criminal record.'

'I have.'

'That was nowt, Ronny; ye didn't even dee time.'

Ronny continued on his way with Al in pursuit, running a few steps and then jumping up with arms spread in gesticulation. 'We could dee it noo,' Al chuntered urgently. 'Ye kna that bit of pavement ootside the Londis shop near yours in the Teams? It's raised. Ye trip awer that and it's pay-oot time. Naughty, naughty Gatesheed Cooncil, give wor five grand. A broken nose? Attendant breathing difficulties? That puts it up to ten grand.' But Ronny did not answer. Al still followed him, stopping only when they reached the hulk ruins of the old riverside flour mill. 'There's nee other way, man,' he called after him. 'Yus're in shit deeper than the Tyne's tide. What else ye gonnae dee? Win the friggin' lottery?'

Wrapping the folds of the donkey jacket closer round himself, Ronny continued. By the time he reached the huge wooden lattice of the Dunston coal staithes where the River Team guts its way into the Tyne, Big Al's shouts had grown indistinct. With each step, his anxiety fell away, until he was smiling. He brought out the jewellery box. Blissful stupefaction came over him. Lifting his arms out wide so that they encompassed the old mill, the staithes and the confluence of the two Gateshead rivers, he shrugged. 'The bare necessities of life,' he mumbled joyfully, 'will come to you. Will come to you. The bare necessities of life will come to ye.'

3

Running parallel to the River Tyne, the bus rattled through Gateshead. Each stop was thronged with people dressed in their Saturday-night best, all waiting for the Quayside or Bigg Market service where the pubs and nightclubs are. Only Audrey rode the bus to the Teams.

Her dusty single-decker passed under the shadow of the massive Dunston Tower, tallest tower block in the north-east of England and shaped like a rocket seconds from launch. Then it crossed the wide expanse of derelict land which rings the Teams estate, isolating it from the rest of the borough. At last it came to the Teams itself.

The outer ring of houses had been demolished: piles of red bricks heaped where homes had been; and in some places just flat green grass where not even foundations remained. On the recently emptied housing, green metal hoardings covered windows and doors, GAS OFF had been painted prominently on the red bricks like the sign for some avenging angel.

Finally coming to the still living streets, the bus's horn blared out. A group of shorn-haired children straddled the road. 'Get oot the bloody way!' the driver yelled. Toothy smiles and scowls answered him on faces ranging from about thirteen years of age down to no more than two. Half of them flicked the Vs, half of them waved, before they all hurriedly disappeared into a single house.

The bus drove on. The hot day was nearly passed. White plastic chairs stood gathered in gregarious little conclaves on the pavements, largely empty now except for a few groups of people lingering in the sunset, their flesh, revealed by shorts and swimming costume tops, lobster red. Children's toys lay scattered in the grime of kerbs. Cairns of Viborg lager cans had been raised by the roadside. And here and there paddling pools still retained one or two bathers from the laughing and screaming multitude of a few hours earlier. A game of cricket held up the bus. And a few yards later, a football did the same, bouncing out from the gathering twilight to cross the bus route and then bouncing back into the dusk on the other side. Radios sang from where they lay hidden in the overgrown grass of gardens like a chorus of evening grasshoppers.

The red-bricked estate lay under an unaccustomed dust: a fine pollen which rises only in the hottest weather from the craters of countless disused clay pits on which the Teams is built. Having passed the Teams Surgery, the bus then skirted the mouth of a cul-de-sac at the bottom of which stood the St Mary Magdalene Church: a large, strange building. Slowing, the single-decker turned the sharp left that brought it right to the heart of the contracting community.

The shops of the beaten-up parade, placed under a wide concrete awning, were all shuttered and closed, except for one. The bus stopped outside this last remaining shop. It was the Londis supermarket. 'Ha'way, sleepyhead,' the driver called as his doors gasped open. 'Yus're hyem.'

'Eh?' replied Audrey groggily.

'Ye fell asleep, man lass.' The driver laughed. 'I divven't kna; burning the candles at both ends again.'

'I'll blow your bloody candle oot in a minute,' retorted Audrey with a weary half-smile.

'Any time.' The driver grinned suggestively.

Audrey hauled herself up, frowning slightly at how heavy her limbs felt. 'Well, I reckon that would only take wor aboot five seconds,' she said, disembarking. 'Mind ye, if I really wanted to make mesel' puke, it'd be easier just to gan and drink a tin o' sago.'

'Areet, Audrey,' a voice called through the open door of the Londis. 'Hot enough for you?'

Audrey peered into the supermarket, and spotting the woman in the sari sitting behind the counter, she waved. 'Any more of this and I'll be gannin' topless, Mrs Singh.'

Mrs Singh tittered, her hair lifted slightly by the breath of a fan. 'Everyone all right at home?'

'Touch wood. You and yours?'

'Very well, thank you.'

Audrey came over to the door. 'Aboot tomorrow morning,' she began, peering into the shop. 'I kna I usually start at half five on a Sunday, but could I –'

Mrs Singh smiled. 'Come in at eleven tomorrow. After your ten o'clock Mass. I've got that lazy husband of mine to help with the papers tomorrow.'

'Thanks. I really appreciate it.'

'I just hope you have a good time. I know it's a special night tonight.'

'It is,' responded Audrey simply.

'Ronny's a good man. You won't find better.'

'I kna,' whispered Audrey. 'It's taken me all me life to realise that, but now I kna.'

Audrey ducked out of the shop. Behind her, the bus was turning. The forlorn parade of shops was its destination; its journey an endless toing and froing between the growing

Metro Centre and the shrinking Teams; its terminus nothing more than this tongue of tarmac, just wide enough to turn on. The driver peeped his horn, and Audrey lifted a hand in parting.

On the other side of the narrow road, parallel to the parade of shuttered shops, ran a thick metal safety barrier. Twenty feet below the barrier boiled the A1. This dual carriageway skewered the very heart of the Teams, the dull roar of its ceaseless traffic hanging heavily above the estate like the drone of monstrous insects.

Audrey walked down the parade and came to the Blarney stones: four immense rocks placed over the road to block joyriders. Pushing through the narrow gap between two of them, she crossed the playground. Scorched by a recent fire, the roundabout was no more than a blackened disc, and the climbing frame a row of charred stumps. The metal of the slide had been buckled to a lethal blade. Hypodermic needles and syringes lurked like snakes in the litter.

After the Blarney stones, Audrey came to the burrow. A concrete tunnel of about thirty dank yards. It was dark. As usual the lights had been broken, and the only illumination was the opened jaw of rapidly declining daylight yawning at either mouth. In the cavern of the burrow, the soft tread of Audrey's pink trainers was amplified into an echoing squeak. The virtually silent scuff-scuff that the walking motion teased from the fraying edges of her denim shorts grew as audible as breathing. Halfway down the cavern, at its darkest point, a broken pipe wept inconsolably down the slickened wall, smoothing the sides of the darkness to a sickly sheen.

'Here she is,' a voice greeted Audrey brightly as she emerged at the other end of the tunnel.

'She's early,' a second voice called.

'Aye, well,' shrugged Audrey, 'I thought I'd better hurry if I'm gonnae catch me flight to Monte Carlo.'

'Is there room in yer suitcase for a little one?' a third voice asked.

Audrey had come out on to a courtyard completely enclosed by flats. She looked up. It was from these flats that the voices had issued. Three women peered down, each on different sides of the square, each on a different floor. The parapets of the walkways on which they stood rose to about chest height, and the points of six elbows could be seen resting on the rough concrete like inquisitive noses. 'Is my Ronny back yet, Bren?' Audrey asked the woman on the lowest floor, her words echoing slightly as all human voices did in the square.

'Not yet, Aud,' Brenda replied. She looked up to the woman next in height to her, calling across the courtyard: 'Ye haven't seen Audrey's Ronny, have ye, San?'

'Na.' Sandra shook her head, and then looked across the courtyard to the woman above her in height. 'Ye seen him, Jen?'

'Na,' replied Jennifer. 'But our lass saw Big Al. Walking. Ye wouldn't see that in a month of Sundays. Must have been pulled for the tax disc again.'

In the middle of the courtyard grew a sorrowful-looking willow. It had not branched wide as was its nature, but tall and spindly in its groping after light. Under the stricken willow, old men, incongruously attired in shorts and T-shirts, sat on a wooden bench and white plastic chairs, playing cards. The courtyard was now in heavy shadow, but the warmth of the day remained. As Audrey passed beneath the tree, the hands of cards were thrown down on to the makeshift table of a tea chest in a storm of laughter. The oldest fingers of them all were reaching for the nest of twenty-pence pieces. 'I divven't kna,' Audrey bantered. 'I thought ye would have known by now. George always ends up fleecing ye.'

'Like taking candy from a babby,' the toothless George grinned.

'What's new then, Aud?' Jennifer called down.

'Ye tell me,' Audrey replied. 'I've only just got off the bus.'

Jennifer paused only for an instant. 'Her at Number 8 on your side has kicked him oot again.'

'Aboot time,' replied Audrey.

'And the pollis came for that young lad at Number 23 on my side,' added Sandra.

'He made a run for it awer the auld rope works,' Brenda continued. 'They had to fish him oot the Team.'

A group of pre-teenage girls that had been bending over something in the far corner of the square scattered at Audrey's approach. 'I saw ye, Toni-Lee lass!' Audrey's sudden shout reverberated round the courtyard. 'Get yersel' in, now.'

With a stab of her strong wrists, Audrey opened the heavy doors and entered her side of the flats. She crossed the breezeblock foyer, chilly even on the hottest days of the year, and went over to the lift. She pressed the button, but it did not illuminate. 'Bloody hell.' With a sigh, she began to mount the stairs. At the third floor, she stopped abruptly. Wrinkling her nose, she smelt the air, and, stooping a little, also sniffed the stairs. Distaste flickered over her features. Her voice became a snarl. 'He's been bloody pissing again.'

When she emerged on to the walkway of the top floor, she paused to enjoy the sun on her face. Her flat had the sunniest aspect of all of them. Her walkway, higher than the others by an entire floor, was a vantage point. As she stood there now, she was raised above everything else like a queen on her balcony. 'Hey, lasses,' she called down to the three women who were all looking up at her. 'That bloody bastard from the third floor's been pissing on the stairs again. Give us a shout when he comes in.'

'Nee problem,' came the three responses.

Audrey breathed in deeply. This high, the evening air felt fresh to her lungs. Bringing out her cigarette purse, she clicked it open, selected a cigarette end and lit up. Inhaling deeply, she leant against the parapet, elbows pointing out: now all four sides of the flats were tenanted by watching women.

From the platform of her fifth storey, Gateshead lay spread out before her like an unrolled map. Windmill Hill rose to the east, its cherry trees drab in the late summer, the sails of their branches dusty. And to the west, the River Team flickered through the wasteland of old rope works and brick kilns to its confluence with the tranquil Tyne. Across the Tyne to the north, on the Newcastle bank of the river, the tower blocks of Benwell and Cruddas Park were already in shadow. Coming back over the water, and screwing her eyes, Audrey just managed to catch the distant glint of the last of the sun's rays firing the chrome and glass of the Metro Centre. 'Penny for them, Aud,' called Brenda from the lowest level below.

Audrey smiled. 'I was just thinking, I'm getting too bloody auld for this game.'

'Ye cannet think that way tonight,' laughed Sandra. 'Special neet for ye and Ronny, isn't it?'

'Oh, aye,' Audrey smirked. 'Just the three of wor tonight.'

'Three?' called Jennifer. 'Ye gannin' in for threesomes now?'

'Why aye.' Audrey's face was deadpan. 'Me, Ronny and wor little fairy godmother, Princess Viagra.'

Leaving a storm of laughter behind her, Audrey moved along to the end of the walkway. The last door was Flat 12A. She reached into her World's Greatest Nana T-shirt, and drew the key from between her breasts. 'Hello!' she called as she opened the door and stepped inside.

It was an open-plan flat with the kitchenette separated from the living room only by a flimsy breakfast bar. One wall was entirely covered in gold-framed photo portraits of children, each one showing a lesser or a greater resemblance to Audrey. A huge sofa and two giant armchairs, none of which were from the same suite, swallowed half the space. 'Hello, Nana,' a voice replied, hidden in the depths of the sofa.

Audrey smiled widely and, having deposited her shoulder bag on the breakfast bar, went over to where a few strands of blonde hair could be seen falling over the back of the sofa. 'Ye areet, Terri–Leigh pet?'

'Yes thanks, Nana. Ye?'

'Champion, hinny. Champion.' With a single kick of her leg, Audrey mounted the sofa and slid down so that she sat beside her granddaughter. 'And divven't ask wor to dee that when I've changed into me skintight leather skirt.'

The girl sitting there laughed. She was about ten years of age with long hair and a pair of glasses held together on the nose by a piece of Elastoplast. Like a puppy, she snuggled in under the arm Audrey extended round her. 'Ee, another book,' Audrey said. 'Are ye enjoying it?' Terri–Leigh nodded. 'What's this one aboot, pet?'

Terri–Leigh thrust a copy of a Harry Potter novel under her grandmother's nose. 'Wizards and that. It's mint.'

Audrey looked with admiration at the girl. 'Ye're a real brainbox, ye. Sometimes I can barely tell the difference between one book and another. But ye, ye could read a hundred and each one would be special.' Audrey pulled Terri–Leigh towards her and planted a kiss on her forehead.

The pieces of upholstery, gathered round a wonky coffee table, were grouped as though facing a television. But there was no television, just a television-sized patch on the wallpaper which was darker than the rest. Audrey closed her eyes. 'Ee, it's fatal to sit doon. I'll nivver get up.'

'And it's yer special night tonight.'

'Aye, it is, pet.'

'Have ye had a hard day, Nana?'

'Nowt that I couldn't cope with twice over, Terri lass.' Audrey kept her eyes closed and a corner of her mouth gaped slightly with exhaustion. 'I can see why ye like to read,' she said, luxuriating her body into a more comfortable position on the sofa. 'It's so peaceful.'

'Nana,' whispered the girl, 'if yus're tired, shall I read to ye?'

'Aye,' said Audrey smiling through a wide yawn. 'That'd be grand.'

Moving deftly from under the arm that held her, Terri-Leigh flitted through to one of the rooms that gave off from the main room of the flat. She came back with another book. 'What bit were we up to?' Terri-Leigh flicked through the pages of a slim volume as she reinserted herself under her grandmother's arm. 'Oh aye, the bit where the donkey gets ill.'

For some time the child read, filling the silent flat with the words of Paul Gallico's fable, *The Small Miracle*. With her eyes still closed, Audrey listened as though transported into another world. A hand gently caressing the blonde hair of the reader, who read fluently, was her only movement. Five, ten minutes passed. 'Ee.' Audrey tried to stir herself, but yawned. 'I cannet sit here all night. Where's your Auntie Leeanne, Terri pet?'

'She's not here.'

Audrey opened her eyes abruptly. 'Eh?'

'She had to gan to work. They started early today.'

'Who's been looking after ye and Toni then?' Terri-Leigh did not reply. Audrey hauled herself to her feet. 'And has Toni been oot since Auntie Leeanne left?' Reluctantly, Terri-Leigh nodded. 'Reet,' said Audrey, clapping her hands together. 'I'll skin that madam, she knas not to gan oot when neeone's in the flat.' Audrey stalked across the room to the kitchenette. A large pile of towels was piled on top of the fridge. She selected a green one, and then strode back to the front door. 'TONI-LEE!' Audrey's voice echoed deafeningly down in the courtyard. The green towel flopped down over the parapet like a flag as Audrey secured the specially added loops of elastic over the screws put into the concrete. 'I've put yer towel oot, Toni lass,' thundered Audrey. 'Divven't make wor have to come doon.'

As Audrey stood there scanning the square, voices raised in a domestic argument were gushing out from one of the open doors on the lower levels. 'And what the fuck d'yus think ye look like, dressed like that?' a man demanded passionately. 'Ye cannet gan to the Wheatsheaf in a bikini top.'

'I'll gan the fuck where I want, dressed like how the fuck like I want,' a woman countered.

'Hey,' Audrey yelled. 'There's bairns what live here y'kna.'

The voices immediately fell silent. The three women had left their sentry positions, but a moment later Jennifer appeared through the open door of her flat. 'Your Toni's on her way,' she called over to Audrey. 'I've just seen her through me back window.'

'Who's she with?' Audrey asked.

'Briony Chapman,' Jennifer replied. 'And the two pixie lasses.'

'Ta, Jen,' said Audrey.

Below, there was a blur of movement across the courtyard, and a flurry of sprinting footsteps. Audrey only had time to stroll to the end of the walkway before a breathless child threw herself up the stairs, nearly bumping into her.

Toni-Lee was so similar to Terri-Leigh that they might have been twin sisters rather than cousins. Toni wore the same glasses, hers being patched up at the arm; she also had the same blonde hair, although she wore her hair cut short. 'I had to rescue a wolf, Nana,' Toni-Lee burst out before her grandmother had a chance to begin.

Audrey was dumbfounded. 'Eh?'

'It was trapped in a one of them knocked-doon hooses,' Toni-Lee continued, 'under a geet pile of bricks. Ye could hear it whining for miles off. I couldn't leave it. Not after what Father Dan said aboot St Francis.'

'Ee,' said Audrey shaking her head in disbelief. 'Where d'ye get it from?'

'I swear doon it was so a wolf, Nana,' the girl gabbled. 'Mebbes he was looking for Gubbio. Got lost in Gatesheed.'

'He'd have to have caught the wrang plane on his way to a funny forest if he was.' Audrey bit back her laughter, and adopted a stern face. 'Ye kna yus're not allowed oot when there's nee adult in.'

'But . . .'

'Get in that flat noo.'

Toni-Lee ran past her frowning grandmother and disappeared into the flat. Left alone, Audrey roared with laughter. She was still chuckling when Jennifer cried over the courtyard to her. 'Hey, Audrey, the pisser's there.'

Audrey lowered herself over the parapet until, with hair flaming out wildly, she was looking directly into the walkway below. 'Now listen to me, ye, and listen well,' she growled at the bewildered, thin man with a purple drinker's face. His key was already in the door. 'If ye divven't stop pissing doon that stairwell, I'll come doon noo and tie a knot in it so tightly that yus'll end up pissing oot o' yer arse.'

She flipped herself up, bowed to the applause from the three sentinels and then disappeared back into her flat.

Toni-Lee was in the kitchenette area holding the packet of fish fingers she had just got out of the fridge. 'I thought I'd give ye a hand with the tea,' she said dutifully. 'What with ye and Granda Ronny having a special night tonight.'

Tipping a wink to Terri who was kneeling up on the sofa watching proceedings, Audrey folded her arms. 'I haven't finished with ye yet, madam.'

Toni-Lee dipped from sight and brought out a gigantic bottle of tomato sauce from a cupboard. Then she went to a drawer and brought out the cutlery. 'Ye'll have a lovely time tonight, Nana,' she declared, a look of busy innocence on her face. 'And I'll even hoover for ye.'

Audrey winked at Terri again, who smiled. 'Ye've crossed them knives, lass. Means there's gonnae be a argument.'

Toni hurriedly rearranged the offending cutlery. 'Ye gan and get changed, Nana. Granda Ronny'll be back soon.'

Audrey could restrain herself no longer. 'Come here and give us a love, ye daft kipper!' Toni-Lee flew over to her grandmother, and buried herself in the embrace. 'And ye,' Audrey added to Terri-Leigh, who came over with her book, and also disappeared in the all-encompassing love of their grandmother like a bookmark slid into a favourite passage. 'God love yus, the pair o' yus,' Audrey whispered fervently. 'Me best bairns. Me very best grandbairns. Me very own lasses. Me very own cwins.'

'I'll still dee the tea,' said Toni.

'And I still mean what I said,' continued Audrey. 'I cannet have ye oot when there's neeone in. And if I catch ye deein' it again then there'll be hell to pay. There's anything gannin' on these days. It's not like when me and Granda Ronny was bairns. It's dangerous noo. So promise wor, will ye? Promise not to dee it again?' The embrace grew so ardent that the two girls were lifted off their feet.

'I promise, Nana,' said Toni-Lee. 'Cross me heart, hope to die . . .'

'Until ye see an elephant fly,' Audrey finished, and hoisting the girls under her arms, she spun them round and round until they were screaming with delight. Still laughing, she set them on their feet. 'Now gan and get the telly and get oot from under me feet for ten minutes while I get yer teas on the gan.'

Toni-Lee ducked back into the kitchenette and opened one of the low-standing cupboards. From this cupboard she wheeled out a television and a video. 'Cannet we just leave it oot all day, Nana?' she asked.

'Aye. If ye'll pay the fine when they catch wor withoot a licence.' Audrey opened the fridge. On seeing how empty it was, she sighed. She took out the packet of oven chips. 'And another thing,' she called. 'I've telt ye not to play with Briony Chapman.'

'Why not, Nana?'

'Nivver ye mind.'

'What aboot the pixies?' Toni asked as she wheeled the TV and video to the darker patch of wallpaper overlooked by the higgledy-piggledy three-piece suite. The sound of applause from a game show soon filled the flat. 'Can I play with them, Nana? The pixie lasses?'

A wave of compassion froze Audrey for a few moments so that she stood there with her arm reaching into a cupboard and her fingers clasped round a tin of beans. 'Aye, ye can play with them. There's nee badness in them bairns. But what'll come of them God only knas.'

Audrey had lit the gas oven and laid the fish fingers under the grill when there was a knock at the door. Toni dashed over and opened it. Two little girls stood there. Toni-Lee ushered them in. They were small, frail beyond the reckoning, though their faces were old and knowing. Large-chinned and pointy-nosed, they had the coarsely delicate pixie-like features of those born from a womb abused by alcohol. 'Can the pixies come in, Nana?' Toni asked.

'Course they can.' The compassion which had seared her features minutes earlier burnt across Audrey again. 'Are ye areet, lasses?' The pixies nodded with a barely perceptible movement of their heads. 'Have ye had your teas?' Almost equally as imperceptibly, the two sisters shook their heads.

'Their mam's strung oot again,' Toni said.

'Does she need an ambulance?' Audrey asked quickly.

Toni shook her head. 'It's not heroin this time.'

The cutlery in the drawer clattered as Audrey yanked it open and rifled out two more sets of knives and forks. The eldest pixie girl looked up at Audrey. Everything else about her was small, only her eyes were large: the staring, disproportionately big eyes of a baby.

Audrey emptied the bag of oven chips on to the baking tray. Then she took down a second tin of beans, and opened the two cans of tuna she found in the cupboard. There was also a can of tomatoes. 'It's just gonnae be a Nana special tonight, girls, areet?'

'Belter,' Toni and Terri called back.

'Ye haven't seen Ronny, have ye, lasses?' Audrey asked.

The pixies shook their heads. Toni came into the kitchenette. 'Gan and get ready now, Nana. Granda Ronny'll be back soon. I'll look after the tea.'

'Ye can drop the act now, man,' said her grandmother.

'There is nee act, Nana. I just want ye to have a good time. Ye've been looking forward to it for ages.' Audrey smiled. 'I'll give ye a shout when the lottery draw's on,' Toni added.

Audrey nodded. 'Uncle Bill's babysitting tonight. He's as soft as sausage so I want yus in bed by half nine. Areet?'

'Did ye really see a wolf?' Terri-Leigh asked her cousin when Audrey had gone through the door in the middle of the wall on which the portrait gallery hung.

'Course I did,' Toni replied from the kitchenette. Her face widened with invention. 'Huge eyes, and geet big jaws. Mind ye, he didn't half wag his tail when we pulled him oot.'

In her bedroom, Audrey sat heavily on the foot of her bed. The springs rippled. The double bed took up most of the room. For the rest there was a window, covered in net curtains, a rickety wardrobe and a truly substantial dressing table into the mirror of which Audrey now peered. A huge, disconcertingly realistic crucifix hung on the wall above the bedhead.

There were three panels of mirror on the dressing table, and Audrey gazed into the central one. 'Ha'way,' she upbraided the weary face staring back at her. 'I cannet sit here all day. Ronny'll be back any second. What the frigg's the matter with ye, lass? Ye've had harder days than this.' With both hands, she tugged at her thick hair, and after another few moments of stupefaction, abruptly rose, scattering the pile of pink, heart-shaped cushions heaped behind her on the duvet.

From the wardrobe she selected two articles of clothing, and laid them on the bed: an imitation leather miniskirt, and an imitation leather jacket. The black PVC of both garments was silvered here and there by zip chains. The neck of the jacket had a little ruff of fake leopardskin.

Stepping out of her shorts, she lifted off her World's Greatest Nana T-shirt. Her underwear dropped to the carpet. For a while she stayed in the same position, stooping a little in her nakedness as though under a heavy burden, her face downcast, her hands lowered. Until, with a mighty stretch, she cast off her load of weariness and straightened.

Adjusting one of the outer panels on the dressing table, she was able to view herself from knee to head. Taking her breasts in her hands, she lifted them until they stood high like a young woman's. Then she tilted her body so that the thick rope of a varicose vein and the worst sagging of her buttocks were hidden from the reflection. With a sharp intake of breath, she sucked in the mound of her stomach. 'Mirror, mirror on the wall . . . who is the . . . who is the . . . who the frigg is the . . .'

Audrey held herself like this for a few moments more, then, with a gush of breath, released herself. Her booming laughter filled the room as the great ageing bounty of her body shook, her hair cascading over her breasts. On one of her bouncing buttocks a tattoo showed, its design faded by the years. Capering like a girl, Audrey jiggled her sagging body joyfully. 'Well,' she said to the crucifix, 'it's nowt ye've nivver seen before.'

Sitting at the dressing table, wrapped now in a yellow towelling robe, she took up her hairbrush. It was silver-backed, and of a piece with the craftsmanship of the dressing table. There was a knock at the door. 'Come in,' she called. In the mirror, Audrey could see Terri-Leigh standing there. She turned and, winking at the child, nodded.

As her granddaughter ran the stiff bristles of the brush through it, Audrey's thick hair crackled. 'Ye're gannin' grey, Nana,' the little girl said. 'Yus're gannin' proper grey.'

Audrey smiled a little wistfully. 'I couldn't be your Nana, but, withoot a few grey hairs.'

Rhythmically, gently, the brush passed through the hair, teasing straight the grey as well as the auburn. 'Shall I sing, Nana?'

'Aye,' smiled Audrey.

In nothing more than a whisper the grandmother and her granddaughter sang in time to the brushing. It was a song about a man who, many years ago, had lived on the Tyne, no more than a stone's throw away from the high rise.

> Bobby Shaftoe's gone to Sea
> Silver buckles on his knee
> He'll come back and marry me
> Bonny Bobby Shaftoe.

Terri-Leigh was nearly finished when the sound of a man's voice could be heard from the main room. 'At last,' said Audrey. 'Gan and tell Granda Ronny to hurry up.'

Terri-Leigh laid the brush down and, having swapped a final smile with her grandmother in one of the side panels of the mirror, left the bedroom. Audrey had changed into her leathers when the child knocked again. 'It wasn't Granda Ronny,' the girl said. 'It was Uncle Bill.'

New juvenile voices could be heard through the open door. 'First time he's been early to babysit in his life,' Audrey mused.

'He's gone,' Terri-Leigh replied solemnly. 'Said he couldn't stop. Summink's cropped up.'

Audrey came into the living room to see two more bodies on the sofa: a pair of shorn-haired boys, both in old Newcastle United shirts. 'Areet, Brosnan,' she called to the oldest of the two boys, who was about eight.

'Areet, Nana,' he replied.

'Areet, Keegan,' Audrey called to the five-year-old beside him.

'Areet, Nana,'

'Come and give us a love then, boys.'

The two lads got up and disappeared in the embrace of their grandmother.

'Where's yer sister?' Audrey demanded, releasing them at last.

There was a sudden crash from the kitchen area where Toni stood poring over the grill pan. In a burst of energy that sent the gilt-framed photo portraits dancing on the wall, Audrey sprinted over to the kitchenette. At first she could find nothing, and her face puckered with agitated puzzlement. Then the cymbal clash of a pan lid alerted her to one of the low cupboards. Reaching down, she plucked out a baby girl, a one-year-old with a dirty face and a filthy red ribbon tied in her baby-fine hair. 'Hello, me little sweetheart,' Audrey cooed, rubbing noses with the baby. 'Hello, me bonny little princess.'

The bonny little princess gurgled with delight.

Audrey started to swing her. 'And who's her nana's little pride and joy?' Swung higher and higher, the baby cooed delightedly, until in her excitement she deposited a small but heartfelt offering of puke on the little leopard-fur ruff of Audrey's jacket.

'Cara's puked up on ye, Nana,' Brosnan called from the sofa.

'And we haven't had wor tea yet,' put in his brother, Keegan.

'I've turned the fish fingers,' said Toni, 'but the pan's starting to bubble.'

'Turn the heat reet doon,' Audrey said.

Keeping her shoulder lifted so that the delta of posit spread no further, Audrey carried her most recent granddaughter through to her bedroom. 'That's a fine trick to pull,' she laughed. The back-up imitation-leather jacket Audrey took from the wardrobe had no zips and no little embellishment of fake leopard fur. It was worn smooth, and criss-crossed with little rips. 'There.' Audrey winked at Cara as she glimpsed herself in the mirror. 'Cinderella can still gan to the ball.'

Cooing at the contentedly bouncing, beaming baby wedged between her legs, Audrey sat on the edge of the bed and began hurriedly to apply a deep red lipstick. Among the shrapnel of cheap cosmetics on the dresser top stood a single framed picture. It showed Ronny and Audrey on their wedding day standing outside the St Mary Magdalene Church. Kissing a piece of toilet paper, she gazed smilingly at the photo. The bright imprint of her puckered lips was stamped on the paper. Still gazing at the photograph, she reached out for her mascara.

She had done only one eye when she stopped abruptly. 'D'ye kna summink, pet?' she asked the infant who beamed back. 'I haven't been to the netty since just after dinner. And if I divven't gan soon, I'll piss mesel.'

Plucking up the laughing baby, Audrey carried her back to the living room. 'Take yer cousin,' she said to Terri-Leigh who was sitting reading on the sofa, seemingly oblivious to the loud babble of the television set.

'The lottery draw's on soon, Nana,' Brosnan warned her.

'Oh aye.' Audrey plucked her shoulder bag from the breakfast bar and ran to the bathroom. A contented sigh eased from her as the urine gushed. Trembling with relief, she opened her bag. Her hand encountered something cold. She drew out the family-sized shepherd's pie. 'Bloody hell, man Cheryl,' she gasped, as, with a firm shake of her head, she thrust the food back in her bag.

In the bag her hand encountered something soft and feathery. It was the crumpled serviette on which she had written the lottery numbers. Audrey peered at the row of six digits. There was no paper in the toilet, so having torn off the numbers carefully, she dried herself with the serviette, and tossed it into the bowl before flushing it away.

The smell of burning food greeted Audrey as she emerged

from the bathroom. Toni-Lee was sitting on the sofa, bouncing Cara on her knee. Nobody was in the kitchenette. Audrey ran over, reaching the cooker just as a pan boiled over.

Having scraped the charred edges from the fish fingers, and stirred the pan, she began to ladle the food on to four plates. There was only enough for three. 'Terri, pet,' she whispered. The little girl came dutifully over. 'Pop doon to Mrs Singh and get summink for ye and the boys, will ye, hinny? And when yus're doon there get some milk and bread an' all.'

'How much should I get?' Terri asked.

'Get three hours' worth. I'm not working a full morning tomorrow.'

'Should I take Mrs Armstrong, Nana?'

Audrey nodded. She looked over to where Toni-Lee was bouncing Cara higher and higher. 'She's already puked once, man Toni.'

'Nana,' said Terri-Leigh quietly, 'it takes ages for Mrs Armstrong to gan up and doon the stairs.'

'She thinks the world o' ye, pet.'

'And she has to keep stopping to get her breath.'

'She's been poorly, love.'

A look of sorrowful wonder came over Terri's face. 'Is she dying, Nana?'

Audrey looked at her granddaughter for a few moments. 'Put it this way, pet. The good Lord's not lang off wanting her with Him. She was a bonny lass in her prime, mind.' She kissed Terri on the top of the head before she ran to the door. 'Ha'way, yous,' she called to the others. 'Yer teas are ready.'

Just as the children were gathering round the breakfast bar on which stood only three plates, the door to the flat opened, and a teenage girl entered. 'Hello, Mam,' she said. 'Me and Corky haven't had wor tea.'

The defunct Teams Hemp and Wire Rope Works provided the rope that pulled Cleopatra's Needle from Egypt to London. It also manufactured the submarine cable which runs under distant fathoms from Suez to Karachi. Some of the foundations of the grand old workshops still show, a few scattered piles of bricks remain, but it is stunted birch trees, scrub grass and thickets of willowherb which flourish now on its derelict space. Across this wide-open area, Ronny was hurrying home.

Every now and again he burst into song and, grinning widely, kicked his arms and legs out. In rhythmic imitation of *The Jungle Book* cartoon character Balloo the bear, he shimmied over the wasteland.

He boogied into one of the willowherb thickets, and boogied out again, his shoulders covered in the white wisps of their seeds. Jiggling on his way, he wiped the froth from his donkey jacket, but the tenacious seeds clung to him. Most of the flowers were dying for the year, but the clumps of meadow cranesbill still bloomed, tickling his legs as he minced past them. The dance took him up on to a little bank on which grew a drift of harebells, and despite his haste, he stopped to admire the colony of the summer's most beautiful flowers.

The bank was once a wooden industrial bobbin around which the thick rope had been wound. Over the years the wind had knitted it a skin from the loose sand of brick and cement, the grains of dust and leaf mould, which it continually carried over the wasteland. Shallow, and prone to drying, this soil was the perfect bank for the needs of harebells. His face transfixed, Ronny hunkered down and reached out to caress the delicate cup of a harebell. A dust of pollen lightly coated the work calluses of his forefinger.

Ronny looked up abruptly. Something above had caught his attention. The house martins were gathering high above Gateshead, filling its sky with their twittering. He watched them for a time, a great glow of happiness on his face, and then he hurried on, crossing the River Team on the concrete platform which serves as a bridge.

Having passed through the hole in the perimeter wire fence, Ronny then walked down the avenue behind the Spartan Redheugh engineering plant. The dog roses of high summer were long gone. Entering the Teams, he scurried over the rubble of recently demolished houses.

'Areet, Ronny,' somebody greeted him when he reached the parade of shops. 'How's it gannin'?'

'Canny,' Ronny beamed. 'Canny, Kenny. What time is it, like?'

'Getting on for lottery time.' Kenny wore a ten–gallon hat and chewed an unlit cheroot. 'So what's the joke tonight then?'

'I'm on a special diet, me.' Ronny cupped his stomach in both hands. 'A seafood diet. I see food and I eat it.'

'Get a move on, Ronny,' a voice called from the Londis shop over Kenny's laughter. 'She's waiting. And didn't I tell you that Tendulkar would certainly score a century today?'

'Just ye wait and see, Mrs Singh,' Ronny laughed. 'Hussain and Butcher will rip yer opening bowlers to pieces in the morning.'

'Is that your second joke of the evening?'

Ronny walked hurriedly on, the traffic from the A1 groaning from the other side of the safety barrier. At the Blarney stones roadblock he met a man with an arm in a sling. 'Let's have tonight's then, Ronny lad,' he said.

'Doctor, Doctor,' Ronny began as he pushed his way with difficulty through the roadblock, 'I'm geet stressed. Why's that? Well, I cannet make me mind up whether I'm a teepee or a wigwam. Relax, yus're just two tents.' Entering the burrow, Ronny could hear the man's laughter.

Ten yards into the concrete cavern, Ronny threw his head back and yodelled: 'Ronny's hye-e-e-e-m.' He chuckled to hear his voice echoing. 'Are ye ready for the neet of yer life-e-e-ey?'

'Areet, mate.'

Startled by the closeness of the quiet voice, Ronny stopped. Through squinting eyes he made out the shape of a body standing halfway down the tunnel beside the wet wall beneath the broken pipe. It was not a large body. Nothing more than a child. But the voice was deep. 'Areet,' Ronny returned uncertainly.

The next moment a bright light was dazzling his eyes, and Ronny threw up his hands in protection. As quickly as the blade of light had stabbed him, it was withdrawn. 'There's nee mistaking ye, baldy-lang hair,' the deep voice grunted.

'Who are ye, like?' Ronny asked anxiously.

As his eyes grew used to the darkness, Ronny could see that the figure's head was short-cropped, and large for the body on which it rested. The outline of the face was disturbingly babyish. 'Look oot for a fat, baldy-lang hair. That's what they said, and that's what ye are. I'm looking for someone else an' all. D'ye kna some cunt with a cowboy hat what calls hissel' Kenny Rogers?'

'Aye,' croaked Ronny as though his throat had run dry.

The youth rasped with cruel laughter. 'Are yous lot on day release from the funny farm or what?'

'What's it to ye, like?' Ronny asked, bristling.

'Ye divven't ask me questions, ye fat fucker,' snarled the youth. Ronny tried to walk on, but found his way blocked. 'Ronny Slater,' the small figure mused. 'Fat fucker Ronny Slater.' In the gloom, the whites of Ronny's eyes darted about as he tried to see more clearly the features of the one blocking his way. 'It's time for yer repayments, Ronny boy.'

Ronny gasped softly with recognition. 'Aren't ye Jimmy Walsh from Lobley Hill?'

The reply was menacing. 'For the last time, ye divven't ask

nee questions. Ha'way, fat cunt. Ye've borrowed money. Two hundred pound. It's time to start paying it back.'

'I borrowed from Johno,' Ronny protested.

Jimmy spat contemptuously, adding his slime to the slickening wall. 'Johno's finished roond here. Macca's taken over.'

Ronny froze. For a few seconds he could not move. Then he backed off a single, cautious step before breaking into a sprint. His massive bulk tore out of the tunnel, shuddering as he raced across the charred playground. On finding himself at the safety barrier above the dual carriageway, in an ungainly and painful scramble he hauled himself on to it. He threw a glance over his shoulder: Jimmy was approaching, jogging almost nonchalantly through the wrecked playground, a small, lethal baby-faced figure in a blue tracksuit. Below, the cars whirled along the dual carriageway. Lowering himself as far as he could, Ronny dangled above the A1 for a few seconds and then dropped.

There was a sharp stab of pain as he hit the ground. Crying out, he crumpled into a heap, arms huddled protectively round himself like an oversized foetus. Through a web of fingers he saw that he had managed to land on the small ledge just to one side of the thundering traffic. If he had rolled another foot or so with the impact of his fall, the car bumpers would have closed over him. 'What the fuck are ye deein' doon there, baldy-lang hair?' Ronny looked up to see a baby face leering down at him from the safety barrier. 'Divven't be a prick,' the taunting voice added. 'Ye cannet hide from Macca.'

As soon as Ronny stood, he felt the weakness of his left ankle. He could only shamble across the dual carriageway, heedless as a mouse to the roaring metal of the vehicles which tore by inches from him. Somehow he managed to make it to the middle. Then his momentum deserted him. Perched on the central reservation, he gazed numbly at the torrent of traffic roaring by on either side of him. Back the way he had come, he could see Jimmy sprinting up the parade of shops, heading for the road bridge.

Rousing himself, Ronny stood swaying on the central reservation like a great bewildered bear. Then he plunged from it. He did not see the faces of the drivers gaping at him, nor hear the blaring of the horns, but walked as though in a trance.

Cruel laughter greeted him as he finally hauled himself on to the crash barrier at the other side and flopped helplessly over it. He lay on the pavement looking puzzledly at his injured leg. A grunt escaped his lips as a hand yanked him roughly to his feet. 'If ye ever dee that again, I'll make sure ye nivver walk another step. D'yus understand?' Ronny nodded. Jimmy took a small black book from his pocket. 'Now. Ye owe wor money.'

Ronny blinked helplessly. 'But I only borrowed it a fortnight back.'

'Just give us a tenner, baldy-lang hair. I've got that nut job in a cowboy hat to see yet.' Jimmy held his hand out.

'I haven't got owt this week, I swear doon, I —'

'Turn them pockets oot.'

'I —'

The blow knocked Ronny sideways. He quickly turned out one of the pockets of the donkey jacket. A hail of small screws and bent nails pattered to the ground. 'And the next one.' Ronny hesitated, but only for a second.

Jimmy grabbed the jewellery box. The theme from *Love Story* played out forlornly, almost lost in the thrum of the speeding traffic. With skilful fingers Jimmy had discarded the halved pendants, the box, and pocketed the ring. 'That'll dee for this week. But next week I'll be wanting money.'

'I paid awer two hundred quid for that!' The pitch of Ronny's voice rose wretchedly. 'That's what I borrowed for in the first place.'

'Time is money, fat knack, and that's what you've cost me today.' Jimmy took a step towards Ronny so that his breath

71

scoured the older man's face. 'Next time you play the prick with Jimmy Walsh, I'll winkle your eyes oot.'

After Jimmy had gone, the empty ring box continued to play until Ronny stooped to pick it up and close it. He pulled gingerly at his ponytail, and as his hand came down over his shoulder, it brushed against the willowherb seeds. Some of them fell and landed in the thin spit of grit between paving stones. Blinking, Ronny gazed at where the seed lay.

5

Audrey's hair flared like flames as she flicked it from out of her eyes. Rifling through a drawer, she brought out an elastic band and tied up the unruly tresses into a ponytail. The heat from the oven was rising as the pizza Terri-Leigh had brought back from the Londis shop began to cook. 'Are ye sure ye divven't mind, Audrey pet?' said the old woman who stood at the breakfast bar which was littered with emptied plates.

'Not at all, Mrs Armstrong,' replied Audrey, smiling. 'I've a full fridge.'

Mrs Armstrong's eyes, set in a flaky, puffy, unhealthy face, shone with gratitude. 'I was just wondering what I could find for me tea when the little poppet knocked. She's a darling, your Terri.'

'She is,' Audrey nodded.

'Just like her nana.' Mrs Armstrong scrutinised Audrey. 'Yer mam would be proud of ye, Aud. She was a fierce lady, auld Ma McPhee. But one of the best.'

'Me mam thought the world o' ye, Mrs Armstrong, and so do we.' Audrey looked over to the television set to where the children sat. 'Get oot that armchair now, Brosnan McPhee, and let Mrs Armstrong sit doon.'

Audrey squatted to open the oven door. The heat blasted

over her as she stared calculatingly at the pizza. 'Hands up who hasn't had their tea yet?' she called.

'Just me and Mrs Armstrong,' Terri-Leigh returned.

'And Theresa and her new boyfriend,' put in Toni-Lee.

'Oh aye.' Audrey straightened. 'What do they call him again? I'm dying to meet him. I thought they were in the flat. Where are they?'

'I think he's a bit shy,' Brosnan said. 'He's just oot on the walkway, but he's flapped to come in. Mebbes ye should put a towel oot for him. So he sees it's time to come in. What colour's he gonnae have?'

'There's only pink left,' Audrey smirked, looking at the pile of towels on the fridge.

'The lottery draw's on in a moment, Nana,' Keegan said.

Audrey was washing up when the door opened. 'At last. Where've ye been, man Ronny.'

But it wasn't Ronny.

'Ee, hello, Mam,' said the woman coming into the flat.

She had the same wild hair as her mother, a similar vigour of body, and also a loud, wholehearted laugh, but all on a lesser scale. 'Areet, Leeanne pet,' Audrey called. 'Am I glad to see ye.'

'I'm sorry aboot before, Mam. They rang us from work.'

Audrey nodded. 'Couldn't be helped, pet.'

As Leeanne came into the flat, she was followed by four children in descending order of size. The teenaged Linzi, who grinned with her whole face, Skye, two years younger but a whole decade more serious, Elliot, who wore a Celtic football strip and came in doing kick-ups with a worn plastic football, and a little girl of about three. They all gathered in the kitchenette and stared solemnly at the oven. 'Yer big night tonight, Mam,' Leeanne winked.

'Aye,' Audrey replied. 'It's just that . . .' Audrey hesitated unaccustomedly.

73

'There's neeone to babysit wor, Auntie Leeanne,' Terri-Leigh called over.

'The lottery draw's coming on,' Brosnan added.

'Ee, course I'd dee it,' said Leeanne, 'but I've got to gan back to work. I'm just on me break. They've let wor oot to gan and get the bairns. Paul's been called on a job, ye see. In fact, Mam, I was wondering if ye could take mine.'

'Have they had their teas?' Audrey asked, a blink the only sign of her weariness.

Leeanne shook her head, and her four children took a step closer to the oven. At that moment Toni-Leigh came up urgently to the breakfast bar. 'The lottery draw'll be on soon, Nana. D'ye want wor to check the tickets?'

'Aye,' Audrey said. 'I haven't had a chance to turn round yet. Give us me purse.' Toni brought out the purse from the shoulder bag. Audrey took out the wad of tickets, then singled one out. The most recently purchased. 'Keep yer eye on that little winner,' she winked.

Leeanne looked at her mother. 'Got a feeling aboot it, like?'

Audrey smiled awkwardly. 'Aye, ah have.' The two women stared at each other for a while. Then Audrey laughed. 'D'ye see wor Theresa oot there?'

'Aye. She was under the tree snogging with some lad.'

'That's Corky,' said Linzi with a grin. 'He's proper lush.'

'We're still waiting to see him,' Audrey said. 'Anyway, Leeanne lass, get yersel' off to work. And tell Theresa to bring this lad of hers up.'

'Aye, I'd better gan. Ye'll be areet? Just give them that for their tea.' Leeanne pointed at the shepherd's pie that could be seen poking out of Audrey's shoulder bag. Then she turned to her children. 'Reet, ye lot, sit doon in front of the telly and Nana'll make ye a nice shepherd's pie.' The children went over and squeezed themselves on to the sofa. 'Hello, Mrs Armstrong,' Leeanne called. 'And for the last bloody time of telling, divven't play football in the flat, man Elliot.' And with that she was gone.

For a long time Audrey stared at the cover of the shepherd's pie. She jumped when she heard the whispered voice. 'What ye gonnae dee?'

Audrey looked up in confusion to see Terri-Leigh gazing at her. 'What d'ye mean, pet?'

'Aboot tonight I mean. How can Granda Ronny give ye the best night of yer life when ye're stuck in here with us?'

For a few seconds, Audrey did not reply. Then she winked at her granddaughter. 'We'll just have to have it here. Why not? If we cannet gan to the Catholic Club, we'll bring it here. That young lad of Theresa's, he's supposed to be a DJ, isn't he? Ye'll see. We'll have the best night o' wor lives and we'll be stopping reet here.'

'Nana, did y'kna ye only made up one eye?'

The pizza steamed as it was cradled from the oven. Taking the newly washed plates from the draining board, Audrey set them on the breakfast bar. 'What are ye deein'?' Brosnan demanded angrily of Elliot who, ball under arm, had pushed his way into the queue.

'Divven't talk to yer cousin like that, man,' growled his grandmother.

'But it's not his turn.'

'Nivver mind that.' Audrey turned from the aggrieved face to the prematurely triumphant one. 'And as for ye, Elliot, gan and sit doon and wait. And divven't play football in the flat.'

'Nana,' Keegan shouted from beside a birdcage covered in a tartan cloth, 'can I get Slim Jim oot noo?'

'Ye kna the rule,' Audrey replied sharply. 'Ye divven't gan near him until Granda Ronny's back. The last thing I want is bloody Slim Jim roond me neck!'

'Where is Granda Ronny? He's usually back by noo.'

'He'll be here any minute. And if I have to tell ye once more aboot that football, Elliot . . .'

Audrey closed her eyes and breathed in for a few moments, resting her weight against the breakfast bar. A resounding clunk roused her. She opened her eyes to see that the shepherd's pie had been put in the oven. Linzi was smiling widely. 'I've put it in for ye, Nana,' she said.

Before Audrey had time to react there was a huge roar from the sofa. She looked over. All the children were crammed into a single armchair, holding their noses. Baby Cara, toddling unsteadily, was beaming at them. 'Nana,' Brosnan shouted, 'Cara's filled her nappy!'

Cara fought her grandmother tooth and nail. Linzi spread out sheet upon sheet of the *Gateshead Herald* as the toddler kicked and rolled her way across the carpet. Skye hovered with more sheets of newspaper and the warm water bowl. At last Audrey got a grip. There was a rasp as the nappy fasteners were pulled. She had just began to lift the heavy, fragrant nappy when a spherical object sailed over her head with a flurry of flapping wings, followed by a crash. 'Slim Jim's oot,' Keegan cried ecstatically.

'Elliot knocked the cage doon with his ball,' announced Brosnan with his mouth full. 'After ye telt him not to.'

'Ee, what a lively parrot,' Mrs Armstrong remarked, staring at the squawking bird.

Audrey's attention captured by the bird, Cara managed to roll free. 'Nana,' whispered Linzi. 'Ye've got shite all awer yer skirt.'

'And yer jacket,' added Skye.

'The lottery draw's on now,' announced Toni.

'Where's me tea? Where's me tea?' demanded the African grey parrot from its perch on the tapestry picture of *The Angelus*: a portrait of a man and woman of the earth praying at sunset as they paused from their labours.

The door to the flat opened. Skye and Linzi giggled. 'Nana, look,' they whispered. 'Theresa's brought in her new lad.'

Pinioning the struggling toddler, Audrey looked up. The new boyfriend was dressed in a capacious smock-like top. On his head was a hat with a brim so pendulous that it shrouded his features. The seat of his trousers hung down to his knees. Adopting the pose of an American rapper, his thin arms gave a flurry of gestures. Theresa looked on in admiration, then explained, bursting with pride, 'Corky says hello.'

Corky nodded at Audrey. 'Areet, Mrs Audrey?'

When the baby had been cleaned, and Audrey had changed out of her imitation leathers and back into her shorts and World's Greatest Nana T-shirt, she grabbed her cigarette purse and strode to the front door.

'The lottery draw . . .' said Toni.

'Listen, the lot of yus,' Audrey announced. 'I just want yus all to leave wor alone for five minutes.'

'But what aboot the lottery draw, Nana?' all the grandchildren asked.

'Even that will have to wait.'

The air was beginning to cool as Audrey leant against the parapet. Night had fallen over Gateshead and countless lights twinkled. The radios had been turned off, and a stillness hummed at the edges of the noise of the A1 and the babbling argument from the feuding couple below.

She inhaled. The breeze held the scent of water. The Team and the Tyne were at low tide, and their currents, running fresh, brought the clean tang and playfulness of sources springing in the heart of wide-ranging northern hills, right into the guts of the inner city. Trembling pleasurably, Audrey clicked open the cigarette purse, and selected the last of her Superkings.

In a trance of relaxation, she watched the smoke from her cigarette drift over to the spindly branches of the willow. She had only smoked half of it when one of the sentinels called over. 'Your Ronny's on his way.'

'At last.' Audrey had just finished her cigarette, docking it close to the filter and placing it back in her cigarette purse for later, when she heard the well-known footsteps on the stairs. 'Happy anniversary, love!' she called down the stairwell. Her own words echoed but there was no reply from Ronny. She listened. His steps sounded more laborious than usual, as though he were dragging them up the concrete stairs. He was a long time reaching their walkway.

'Hello, pet,' Ronny said as he stepped into his wife's view.

'Where've ye been, man Ronny?' Immediately she saw that he was limping. 'What is it, pet? Did ye hurt yersel'?' She came to him tenderly, but as she reached out, he grimaced as though with a jolt of pain.

He waved her away. 'It's nowt, man. Just a sprain.'

'What's happened?' Her concern deepened. 'It was the ladder, wasn't it? Ye'll end up breaking yer back one of these days.' Her voice grew sharp. 'That bloody Al Greener, I keep on telling him ye need proper ladders and scaffolding. But he –'

'It wasn't any ladder.' Ronny's voice was full of an unwonted agony. 'It wasn't any ladder,' he repeated, more quietly. Then, in a whisper fretted with deep misery: 'It wasn't nee ladder.'

The two of them stood there staring at one another. 'Happy anniversary,' Ronny breathed. 'It was supposed to the best night of yer life but . . .' Ronny trailed off again.

Audrey's face puckered with puzzlement. 'Theresa's here. If it's only a sprain we can still gan oot. Come on, let's get ready. Meet her new boyfriend an' all. Corky they call him. Strange lad. But seems nice enough. Ha'way, Ronny, let's gan and paint the toon –'

'Audrey, we're in trouble.' Ronny's words were toneless.

'Yer leg, is it that bad?'

He smiled bitterly, his face a travesty of its usual uncomplicated serenity. 'I wish it was just the leg, hinny. In fact, I'd rather lose me leg than this.'

'What the hell are ye gannin' on aboot, man Ronny?'

Sighing, Ronny leant over the parapet. 'It's not as if me life's insured or owt, so there's nee point jumping.'

Audrey stared at him bewilderedly.

Ronny turned to Audrey. 'Macca's back.'

Audrey gasped softly. There was a long pause. They looked at each other with dread. 'It had to happen,' said Audrey at last. 'Anyway, he still doesn't kna that . . .'

'That it was us what called the pollis on him that time?'

'Shh!' Audrey hissed. When she spoke again it was in a whisper. 'As far as we're concerned that nivver happened, reet? We nivver phoned the pollis or the fire brigade. None of that had owt to dee with us. Reet?'

'Won't he put two and two together?' Ronny clutched at his ponytail. 'I mean, he knas we were there at the scene when his bedsit was burning doon. For frigg's sake, man Audrey, I was in all the papers when I rescued auld Joe O'Brien —'

Audrey cut in urgently. 'We'll cross that bridge when we come to it. We cannet live in fear for the rest of wor lives.' She exhaled and, despite her words, fear clearly clouded her face. With an immense shrug of her shoulders, she tried to throw it off. But the monkey clung to her back. 'The best thing to dee is not to worry. I mean, we both knew he'd be back. He only did six months for possession.' She nodded decisively. 'We'll keep oot of his way, that's what we'll dee. We'll dee nowt to draw attention to worselves, we'll . . .'

Ronny dropped his head, and buried it in his hands. 'It's too late. It's too late. Audrey man, I've done a really stupid thing, I've —'

But before he could finish speaking, the door to the flat was opened. 'Nana,' said Toni-Lee in a small voice.

'Audrey man,' agonised Ronny, 'I meant well, but I've done a really stupid thing.'

'Nana,' Toni-Lee repeated.

'Just a moment, pet,' said Audrey distractedly. She was

barely able to keep the panic from her own voice. 'Me and Granda Ronny have got to –'

The little girl was holding out a lottery ticket. 'Nana, Granda Ronny. I'm not sure, but I think we've won the lottery.'

Chapter Two

I

In the small hours of the morning when even the most committed Geordie reveller has crashed to rest, but before the rising of the early-morning cleaners, two absurdly elongated limousines were driving down the A1. One was white, the other shocking pink; both turned off at the Teams junction. From the pink stretch limo issued a ceaseless singing of many raucous voices, while two people sat facing each other over the roof of the white one: their backsides hoisted up on the rim of opened windows, their legs dangling inside the car, a heavy bottle standing between them as though on a table. This strange convoy proceeded to crawl through the silent streets of the deserted estate.

Having refilled their glasses from the jeroboam of champagne, Ronny toasted Audrey. 'Mebbes this'll dee the trick.'

'Let's give it a gan,' she replied.

They both gulped down their champagne and then yawned hugely. Audrey still had not changed out of her denim shorts and World's Greatest Nana T-shirt. Ronny wore a pair of Bermuda shorts and the old donkey jacket. He shook his head. 'It's nee good. It still hasn't sunk in.'

'Me neither.'

Just then the white limo came to a halt, and the driver's outside window whirred down. A face peered up at the couple above, its features haggard with exhaustion under the peaked chauffeur's cap. 'Can I go home now please?'

'We're just starting to enjoy worselves, man,' Audrey replied.

'But we've been on the go all night,' returned the ashen chauffeur.

'It's booked until tomorrow dinner time,' burst out Ronny proudly. 'Courtesy o' *News of the World.*'

The driver scratched a cheek. 'Have you really won or are yus just taking the piss?'

'Get back in yer box, ye miserable bastard,' Audrey shot back.

With a sigh, the driver disappeared, and once more, at nothing more than walking pace, the long vehicle paraded through the empty streets. 'Na,' said Ronny after a while, shaking his head. 'It just won't sink in.'

'We'd better have some more bubbly,' Audrey recommended.

Ronny lifted the jeroboam. 'It's not all it's cracked up to be, champers, is it? I mean, it's pleasant enough. But there's nowt amazing aboot it.'

'Ye just haven't drunk enough yet, man Ronny.'

They filled their glasses again.

'I think I've drank mesel' sober.' Ronny closed his eyes and drank down the sparkling drink. He shook his head with a vehemence that betrayed his inebriation. 'I still cannet believe it.' Ceremoniously, Audrey emptied her glass. 'Well?' Ronny asked.

For a while, Audrey seemed to be deep in serene thought, then suddenly she lifted herself right on top of the roof and yelled at the top of her lungs: 'THREE BLOODY MILLION POONDS!' Disturbed by the explosion on the soft air of the night, cats plunged down the alleys, their wailing reverberating.

'Shh,' said Ronny, drunkenly holding a finger to his lips. 'Divven't wake the bairns.'

Audrey slumped back into a sitting position. 'Oh aye,' she returned in a stage whisper. 'I forgot.'

They drove on. 'One minute ye're working on a roof,' Ronny mused, 'the next . . .' He trailed off with an uncomprehending, Gallic shrug, which, overbalancing him, nearly sent him dropping to the road below. Swaying after his balance, his speech grew suddenly slurred. 'Blows yer bloody brains oot, man.' He pondered this, increasingly philosophical. 'I mean, one minute I'm sitting on a roof, and the next I'm in a friggin' stretch limo. It's –'

The driver's outside window whirred down again. 'Are you sure them bairns haven't been sick again?' the driver asked blearily.

'Where did they find ye?' Audrey demanded. 'Driving a hearse? Why cannet ye be like yer mate? He's really enjoying himself.' Audrey pointed to the pink limo which was some yards distant. The driver of the pink vehicle was tooting his horn in time with the drunken choir packed in his vehicle.

'He's not the one who'll have to clean up me upholstery,' the driver pointed out.

With a graceful feint of her body, Audrey slipped inside the stretch limousine. Sleeping children lay scattered all over the many yards of plush, luxury upholstery. Their gentle, untroubled breathing rose and fell peacefully. Most of the tribe was there, including the two pixies who slept as soundly as the rest. Audrey smiled. In the well of an empty jacuzzi lay a deep litter of pop cans, crisp packets and pizza boxes. All three television screens showed silent snow blizzards. Deftly, Audrey moved through the sleeping bodies. Despite the alcohol she had consumed, her movements were perfectly poised. As though overcome with a sudden insurmountable tenderness, she went round each one, planting a fervent kiss on cheek or forehead.

Terri-Leigh stirred on feeling the lips, and, still sleeping, enquired: 'Have we really won?'

Her grandmother nodded with the solemnity of one greatly moved. 'We've really won.'

With the same graceful agility, Audrey lifted herself back on to the roof where Ronny was deep in metaphysical pondering. '. . . Whichever way I look at, I just cannet take it in. I mean one roof, withoot scaffolding, withoot even a safe ladder, will not gan into a stretch limo. Nee matter how many times ye divide it, multiply it or subtract.' His tone grew gabbled, panicky. 'Audrey, summink's not reet. There must be some mistake. We've got it wrang. It cannet be us. It —'

Kneeling up on to the roof, Audrey silenced him with her lips. Clamping her mouth on his, she breathed: 'We've won, lad.' A long, passionate kiss followed. When they broke from each other, a single, piercing squeal escaped Ronny's lips. Immediately he rammed a fist in his mouth.

'Shh,' he scolded himself, adding, as though it were a tongue twister: 'Canny bit bairns is sleeping . . .'

For a third time the driver's window whirred down. 'I'm begging you. Please let me go to my bed. There's no one else up to see you.'

'I'll tell ye summink,' said Audrey. 'The first thing I'm gonnae buy is a big fat smile for ye, 'cos ye obviously cannet afford one for yersel'.'

Meandering through the Teams, the white limousine eventually drove down the parade of shops. The square flats beyond appeared ghostly in the orange light of the urban small hours. They drew up alongside the pink limo. 'Areet, Mam,' a drunken head greeted Audrey from the pink limo.

'Areet, Bill,' Audrey replied.

One by one the windows of the other vehicle wound down, and the song burst out from its confines on to the still, pre-dawn air. 'Areet, Mam.'

'Areet, Leeanne.'

'Areet, Mam.'

'Areet, Theresa.'

'Areet, Mrs Audrey.'

'Areet, Corky.'

'Areet, Audrey.'

'Areet, Cheryl.'

'Areet, Audrey!' many voices cried.

'What's gannin' on here, like?' Audrey demanded. 'Someone won the lottery or what?'

There was an explosion of cheering, and a chromatic, ever more deafening version of 'Who Wants to be a Millionaire?' broke out. 'I dee! I dee!' they yelled joyously.

'We're just gannin' back doon the Bigg Market, Mam,' Bill drawled, his eyes bloodshot. 'Buzz the latecomers. Then we'll gan and buzz thems comin' oot the casino.' Bill whooped like a drunken cowboy. 'I love seeing their faces when they see wor in the limo.'

'We might catch Peaky oot on the razzle an' all,' cackled Cheryl.

'I dee! I dee!' the chorus rang out.

Audrey's voice dropped to a whisper. 'Yous gan. I divven't want to wake up the bairns again. They've only just gone over.'

The pink stretch limousine had just disappeared below them on the dual carriageway when Ronny and Audrey heard a plaintive goose-like honking. The honking grew louder. A moment later the dirty vanette could be seen mounting the slip road and waddling into the Teams. 'Bloody hell,' said Audrey, 'I thought we'd shooken him off, miles back. How does he always know where we are?'

'Instinct,' Ronny shrugged. 'Ye cannet shift big Al.'

'Not withoot a bloody geet bucket o' stewed prunes anyway.'

There was a tut of disapproval from the driver. He looked up. 'That's no way to talk aboot your brother.'

'Me brother?' Audrey demanded.

'Aye. Him with the wall-eye.'

'He's not me brother.'

'He said he was.'

'Eh?'

'When he tried to borrow a tenner off us.'

'More fool ye. Now go.'

'Where to now?'

'Anywhere he isn't.'

The white limousine turned in the bus circle and was coming back down the parade when the vanette drew up. Al hopped out heavily. 'Hold up,' he called. 'I'll get in with yous.' He was halfway to the limo when it pulled away sharply. 'Hey,' he shouted, left in the middle of the road. 'What's gannin' on?'

'They've gone doon the casino,' Ronny called apologetically.

Al continued to stare after them, then he raced back to the vanette, his face that of a jackdaw in pursuit of the seagull which has just snatched the biggest piece of bacon rind from the bird table.

'I think yus'd better get inside now,' the chauffeur said as the limo began to run down to the dual carriageway. Having grabbed the heavy jeroboam, Ronny wriggled himself obediently inside, wincing slightly as he sprawled on his sprained ankle. 'And ye, Mrs Wild One,' the driver said to Audrey. The car rolled nearer and nearer to the dual carriageway. 'Please!' Urgency heightened the pitch of his voice. But Audrey was not listening. Holding her arms out wide she lifted herself higher and higher. Supported only by the strength of her calves, she was practically standing out of the elongated limousine. With her arms stretched out massively, she threw her head back and roared with laughter: a wild, chaotic Angel of the North made flesh. A heavy-goods lorry thundered by, but Audrey just laughed louder. 'Bloody hell,' whimpered the chauffeur. 'Bloody, bloody hell.'

But before she could either fall or fly, Audrey was back inside. 'Na,' she said quietly to Ronny. 'I still cannet take it in.'

Ronny gazed at her, utterly sobered. 'Ye could have . . . fallen.'

Audrey smiled. 'Not tonight, pet. Tonight we can dee owt, ye and me. Tonight's magical.' The electric window sealing the driver's compartment from the rest of the limo opened. 'He's like a bloody jack-in-the-box, him,' Audrey chuckled.

'Now that ye haven't quite managed to kill yourself,' the driver said tartly, 'where we going? Me shift ended three hours back.'

'Anywhere,' shrugged Audrey, lying beside Ronny across the last available piece of upholstery. 'Just Gateshead.'

'But we've already been everywhere in Gateshead.'

'Well, go there again then, Eeyore.'

Audrey and Ronny continued to lie across the lavish upholstery. 'Aye, it's hard to take in,' mused Audrey. She lifted a hand and flexed the fingers. 'That's been in buckets of bleach since I was nowt but a bairn.'

Ronny stretched his own hand out. 'And that's either dug coal or climbed ladders.'

They fell into silence, contemplating their hands, their fingers entwined until it was difficult to see which one belonged to the other. Suddenly Ronny sat bolt upright. His face was shining with inspiration. 'Go to that place.'

'Eh?' the driver replied.

'Oot the back. Rowlands Gill way. It's in the woods. Ruins an' that. A long avenue.'

'Do you mean the Derwentside Estate?'

'Is that what yus call it?' Ronny demanded, his whole body animated.

'Just up from the old coke works?'

'That's it.' Ronny continued to sit up as though transfixed.

'It's a National Trust property,' the chauffeur said doubtfully.

87

'Take us there,' Ronny cried eagerly. 'Take us to the statue.'

The driver shrugged helplessly. The stretch limousine whispered its way through the sleeping streets of the Metropolitan Borough of Gateshead, purring through the Whickham Thorns towards the scrap heaps of Swalwell with the hulk of the Metro Centre sprawling below them. At the traffic lights they passed into the rural quarters of the borough where Ronny had been working the day before.

When they were in the middle of the forest Ronny had seen from the roof, the driver suddenly slipped down a concealed, tree-fringed private road. It was potholed and narrow, and despite the expensive vehicle, they bounced on their plush seats. Away from the city lights the full power of the moon could be felt, its light shimmering on the traceries of oak and larch branch tangles like gossamer on spiders' webs. Every now and again there were glimpses of ruined walls and skeleton buildings. And, still driving slowly, as they penetrated yet further into the estate, high wrought-iron gates concealed flashes of stone-built residential houses with expensive cars on their drives.

There was a soft rasp as the wheels of the stretch limousine pulled on to the ash of the car park. 'Well, that's it,' said the driver, collapsing over his wheel. 'I divven't care what you do, I'm gannin' to sleep.'

Within moments, the driver's breathing was as audible as the children's. Eagerly, Ronny got out of the limousine. 'Ha'way,' he whispered. 'I want to show ye summink.'

Under the shine of the moon, they stumbled by the wooden hut of the National Trust tea rooms, and then, hand in hand, skirted a high wall. 'Where we gannin'?' Audrey asked as Ronny led her through an open door in the wall. He was hobbling badly from his fall, but his face was glowing. 'What is this place, Ronny man?'

It was a walled garden, and Victorian glasshouses ran

endlessly under a wall on which apple trees were trained. Vegetable plots and flowers filled the heart of three acres while mazes lost themselves among trestled beans and vines. The path was sown with camomile so that as the couple walked along their footsteps disturbed the herb, filling the air with a delightful, ghostly fragrance. Finding an opening at the far side, they passed out of the walled garden. The door slammed behind them and they found themselves rolling down a grassy bank.

The laughter started when they were still rolling, and by the time they had reached the bottom, they were almost helpless with hilarity. They tried to stifle it, but it kept on bubbling out. It was not loud, not even Audrey's voice was raised much above a whisper. It was the silent, tremoring, almost hysterical seizure of pure ecstasy that robs the body of everything but a silent shaking. 'Has it sunk in yet?' Ronny asked when at last they were sober enough to talk.

'No,' replied Audrey simply.

Their cry of joy rang out in the night.

A long grass avenue running between towering oaks stretched out before them. Audrey kicked off her pink trainers and gasped with pleasure on feeling the grass on the soles of her feet. She hurled the pink trainers into darkness. 'They always pinched me feet, them.'

Ronny did the same. His heavy labouring boots vanished into the shadows beyond the moonlight. 'I feel as though I've nivver had them off.'

'Where are we?' Audrey asked. Ronny hobbled forward. 'Ye'll feel the pain o' that tomorrow, mind, pet.'

But Ronny simply smiled. Down the avenue a quarter of a mile to the left, a large building was just detectable in the moonlight. To the right, at a similar distance, a huge pillar rose. Ronny set off for the column.

'Where we gannin'?' Audrey asked.

'I'm not sure.'

'I bet this place is haunted,' she said softly.

Ronny laughed, but when he looked at his wife, she was serious.

Barefoot, hand in hand they walked, two intruders from the twenty-first century in a Noble Pleasure Garden of the eighteenth. On the avenue was a lily pond, and they paused when they reached it. Audrey took out a cigarette purse. The purse was crammed to capacity with Superkings, although the charred, hard, brittle flakes from earlier dog ends still encrusted the lining. The column was close now and they stared at it over the lily pond. 'What the hell is this place?' Audrey whispered. 'I feel as though we've come through the back of a friggin' wardrobe.' The pillar was silver in the moonlight, the figure at its top now discernible: a woman holding the scales of justice. 'I mean, is this place here all the time or just when ye've won the lottery?' The smoke from Audrey's cigarette drifted over the lily pond like incense.

When they were twenty yards or so from the foot of the pillar, they stopped again. Audrey laid her hand on her husband's arm. 'Why've ye brought wor here, pet?'

Ronny's gaze came down from the female figure at the top of the pillar. He tugged gently at his ponytail. 'We've won the National Lottery.'

'Yes,' replied Audrey solemnly. 'We have.'

A long silence was broken at last by Ronny. 'Before we won. Before I foond oot we'd become millionaires, I sat on that roof and looked at this. And summink struck me. Summink, like, knocked us between the eyes.' Ronny exhaled. An animal cried from somewhere in the forest, some small creature whose life had been snatched in an instant by a fox. 'Ye work all yer life, but what can ye ever kna? That's what I was thinking. I'm Gatesheed through and through but I've nivver even heard of this spot.' Audrey nodded gently, and waited. 'We'll be a lang time in wor grave, pet,' Ronny began again after a long pause. 'And yet we hardly know the half of it. Ye kna me. I'm nee depressive. I'm a happy-go-lucky frigger. But today, on that roof, I knew I was bound to die. I kna we all are, but today I realised there was nee hiding from it. I knew that there'd come a time for me to . . . stop. And what a shame. That's what I thought. What a shame to have to leave so much unknown.' Ronny shook his head, pausing only for a moment in his unaccustomed fluency. 'What a shame to die with so much love in me heart left to give. What a crying shame to die withoot even knowing what it was that I could see from that roof. What a shame to gan away when all of this was lying undiscovered.' Ronny trailed off. 'I'm not explaining mesel' very well. But I felt it. On that roof. Summink too deep for words. Ye must work all yer life, and meanwhile ye miss the hidden things. Ye miss the . . . delights. Aye . . .' He broke off to gesture at the column. 'If ye're not careful, ye miss the delights. And that's what life's all aboot. The delights.' He smiled broadly. 'So that's why I brought wor here.'

Gently, Audrey kissed him on the cheek. 'Ye can see everything there is to see now. All the delights there are.' Their arms entwined round each other. Ronny kissed one of his wife's chapped hands, the one holding the cigarette. 'Look at me poor dishwater hands,' she said quietly. 'Ruined. A cleaner since I turned fourteen.'

Ronny's voice choked with emotion. 'There'll be nee more cleaning for ye, hinny lass. We've won the friggin' National Lottery.' Their embrace grew tighter. 'I think it's beginning to sink in, Audrey.'

'Aye,' she replied.

There was a short pause. Ronny's voice was still thick with emotion. 'Can I have another blow job, love?'

'Oh, I think we can dee better than that.' Audrey's own voice grew husky as she pulled him down on to the soft grass, freshened by a hint of dew. 'Let us just finish me fag first.'

The pillar rose above them. And around them the silent

night pressed tightly. Until, all at once, a bird began to sing: the first of the new day.

2

Light began to kindle itself in the east, and slowly the fire took, until dawn came to the souls of the Metropolitan Borough of Gateshead and beyond.

The sun rose on the concrete walkways of the Teams' high-rises, deserted at this time save for the odd woman heading wearily for work. The sun rose further upstream of the River Tyne, that umbilical cord of the world's Industrial Revolution, lighting up both the dilapidated houseboat beneath the crumbling wharf and the gleaming Metro Centre. And the sun also rose on the Pleasure Gardens of the Derwentside Estate, picking out two figures who lay gently slumbering near the foot of the vast column of liberty.

They had been asleep for only about an hour when Audrey stirred, her cheeks twitching as the first rays of the sun caressed them. The beams reached her eyes and she blinked once, twice, and then woke up. She lay still for a while, her hand raised slightly to block the slanting sun. Then she looked at the one slumbering beside her and smiled.

Stretching massively, she climbed to her feet. Suddenly she leapt. Then she leapt up again. Time and time again she leapt with a silent euphoria that lifted her higher and higher like a spawning salmon at the breast of a weir. As abruptly as she had started, she stopped leaping, and with a huge yawn of contentment, wandered peacefully over to the column. She sat with her back against it, and thoughtfully smoked a cigarette.

Ronny woke a little later. He sat up quickly, casting about like one lost, tugging disorientatedly at his ponytail. 'It's true,' Audrey said softly. Gingerly, she lifted a hand to her head.

92

'That bloody champers kicks a punch, but. I mean, did we drink it or just heed-butt the bottle?'

Ronny collapsed with a pleasurable groan. 'This is the worst I've felt since me stag do.' He smiled. 'And the best.' But worry clouded his features. 'Audrey man, are ye sure we've won? I mean, there cannet be nee mistake?'

'Ronny man, have ye ever known me to be wrang aboot anything?'

Ronny inhaled deeply and then, having exhaled like a giant whale, began to chuckle. 'The lottery. The friggin' lottery.' The chuckling continued, neither building to a guffaw nor declining to a titter: a steady stream of joviality. Smoking contentedly, Audrey continued to smile at him.

'Someone's coming,' she said at last.

Ronny followed his wife's pointing finger. A figure was walking down the avenue towards them. Behind the figure, who walked with a rather staccato gait, half a mile away from the base of the column, the building shape of the night before was revealed as an ornate chapel. The pillars of its Grecian colonnade still lay in shadow, but its dome sparkled in the rays of the sunrise. 'Whoever it is,' said Ronny, staring at the approaching figure, 'he's a big lad. A gamekeeper mebbes. Come to turf wor off.' Worry edged his voice. 'Mebbes we're trespassing, pet. Mebbes he's come to prosecute wor.'

Audrey had stood to her full height. 'We've won the lottery. We could buy this place.' With the sun in their eyes, shining directly down the avenue, it was difficult to see who the approaching man was until he was directly upon them. 'What the hell are ye deein' here?' Audrey demanded when he came into their ken.

'Message for Ronny and Audrey,' announced Al, ignoring the barb in his friend's wife's voice. 'Yus've won three million poond.' He smiled ingratiatingly. 'Divven't worry, I've looked in on the bairns. They're still asleep.'

With a long stride, Audrey began to step up the avenue.

Al stared at Ronny for a while. 'Well, bonny lad. Ye've hit the big time.' They followed Audrey, but she was too fast for them, and she pulled further and further ahead. 'She doesn't seem too happy aboot it,' Al pointed out.

Ronny shrugged. 'Hasn't sunk in yet.'

'And what's the matter with ye, hop-along Cassidy?'

'I sprained me ankle yesterday. It's nowt.'

A light mist hovered on the avenue, and ahead of them Audrey seemed to be wading through water. 'Well, well, well,' chuckled Big Al.

'Aye,' replied Ronny. 'Hard to believe, isn't it?'

'Understatement of the friggin' year.' Al cupped his hands together and then declaimed loudly: 'In yesterday's corner we have a clapped-oot auld cowboy builder without a penny to his name what's nivver been further than Hartlepool in his life. In today's corner we have a millionaire with the world at his feet.' He laughed silently. 'Sprained ankle or nee sprained ankle, ye're still walking on air.' He stopped abruptly and, deeply moved, squeezed Ronny's arm while hissing something so vehement as to be inarticulate.

Ronny shook his head. 'At first, when I'd just woke up there, I forgot. Just for a second. All I knew was that me heed was throbbing fit to burst.' Ronny exhaled dazedly. 'I still cannet take it in. Does yer heed in good and proper when ye stop to think.'

An arm was laid over Ronny's shoulders. 'Bound to happen. A touch of the heebie-jeebies. It's the scale of it. Some of them what win cannot even make a cup of tea for the best part of a fortnight. I was talking to the adviser last night. Y'kna. The lottery winner's adviser. I rang her up.' Ronny looked questioningly at the other man. 'Well, someone's got to take charge,' Al returned. 'So divven't worry, marra, I'm here to pilot yus through it all. And first things first. A trip to Carl's Pie Cart. We need a fry-up.' Al nodded. 'We need to come up for

94

air. Get wor bearing. Get some sustenance. This winning countless millions is hungry work.'

At the chapel, they mounted the bank and saw both limousines in the car park. And the vanette. Ronny hung back. 'Ha'way, man,' said Al. 'What's the matter?'

'We came through a geet big garden. Weird it was. Like summink from that bairns' telly programme. But bigger. *The Secret Garden* or summink. Where is it? We walked through it.'

'Aye, yus'll be having trouble distinguishing between fantasy and reality. The adviser mentioned it.'

'It was real.'

'Course it was, course it was. And the fairies took yer boots?' Al propelled Ronny on. The pink limousine was disgorging its passengers: a group of drunken, singing, shouting people staggering blinkingly into the dawn light. The children were running about the car park. A ball was being kicked perilously close to the windows of the National Trust tea rooms. Barefoot, Audrey could be seen bending over a rolling Cara to discard a heavy nappy. 'Reet,' said Al, speaking quietly but urgently. 'What are ye gonnae dee now, Ronny boy?'

Ronny lifted his arms out wide with a shambling smile. 'I divven't kna. Buy a Rolls-Royce or a Ferrari, I suppose. Take the bairns to Disneyland . . .'

'Not that now. I mean *now* now. As in the next hour.'

'I suppose Audrey'll be gannin' to Mass as usual.'

Al tutted darkly. 'What aboot ye?'

'Well, I've always gone to the allotment on a Sunday morning.'

Al seized on this. 'And that's exactly where'll ye gan this morning. In a situation like this. It's routine what matters.' He glowered over at Audrey. 'Make nee mistake, bonny lad. She'll try and get ye in there God-bothering this morning. Special occasion, she'll say. But if ye dee that, all will be lost.'

'What the hell are yus gannin' on aboot, man Al?' Ronny chuckled.

Al drew his friend closer. 'Now I kna ye love her and all that, and I'm all for that. I must admit I felt a pang when I foond yus at the bottom of that statue. Canny spot for a bit of ootdoors shagging that. Put us in mind the time I had Audrey's mate Cheryl.'

'Ye shagged Cheryl?'

'In Washingwell Woods. She's small but she gans like a piston.' Al nodded. 'She was canny.' He paused for a moment and then continued. 'Anyway, we've got to keep ye oot that church at all costs. We'll gan to the allotments as we always dee.'

'Ye nivver gan to the allotments.'

'Aye, well, it's a special occasion today. What time's the photo shoot?'

'Noon.'

'Reet. Ha'way then.' Al moved Ronny forward towards the vanette.

'What's gannin' on?' Ronny asked.

Al stopped, and looked at his friend significantly. 'I'm saving you, that's what's gannin' on. That church is nee place for us. We're modern men, ye and me. Free thinkers, man. Darwinisms, aren't we? I mean, we divven't believe in summink just 'cos we're telt to.' Al shook his head superciliously. 'Na. Modern people like ye and me only believe what we can prove. Y'kna, what we can see with wor own eyes. The big bang what went off three billion years back. Sea slugs growing legs, coming on to the land and turning into men and women. Millions and millions of genes all gannin' radgie to pass themselves on. That's us. None of that other nonsense. We only accept what's common sense. And, see, ye winning the lottery? It just proves it. Darwin an' that. Genes. The whole kit and caboodle. It just proves that everything's just a geet fuckin' lottery.'

'D'ye think so?' Ronny asked with sudden hunger in his

eyes. 'I'm not so sure any more. Winning the lottery . . . well, there's got to be a reason.'

From the car park area there was a storm of laughter. Audrey, holding the giggling, nappyless Cara, was dancing uninhibitedly with her. Al shuddered slightly. 'Anyway,' he added, 'the beer tastes like piss doon the Catholic Club.'

3

The strange cavalcade of two stretch limos and a dirty white vanette bounced down the private road of the Derwentside Estate through the crystal air of early morning. At the traffic light which divides the rural from the urban quarters of the borough, the convoy divided. The pink limousine headed for the Teams.

St Mary Magdalene Church, and the cul-de-sac at the bottom of which it stood, was still slumbering. There was an abandoned feel about the church building. It was like a large boat which, having been brought into dry dock and upended hull-upwards, had been forgotten. Its grey concrete façade was pebble-dashed as though with barnacles, and faultlined with fissures that widened a little more every year.

Once, twice and then three times the pink stretch limo drove slowly past the mouth of the quiet cul-de-sac, the inebriated voices unceasingly throbbing their tuneless song from within. On the fourth time, the luxury car pulled up.

From the bedroom window of the house nearest to the church, a man was watching. As he yawned, he scratched his light beard. Then, as he saw Audrey climb out of the car, he swore softly. She strode down the cul-de-sac, and a few moments later, the bearded man felt his house shaking beneath his feet. He yanked open the window and glared down at Audrey, who, having just let fly another knuckle volley against

97

his front door, was squinting up at him. 'Get lost,' he said irritably.

'But I've got summink to tell ye,' Audrey burst out excitedly. 'Ye'll nivver guess.'

'No, and I don't want to.'

'But Father Dan, man, I've –'

Having slammed the window, the priest had gone from view. He appeared at the front door a little later, in a dressing gown. 'What the hell are you bothering me at this ungodly time of the day for, woman?'

Audrey smirked. 'Just wait until yus've heard what I've got to say.'

'Audrey, I haven't even had me cup of tea and a fag yet.'

She thrust three packets of Senior Service at him. 'Smoke yersel' silly, hinny.'

He disappeared inside, but the door was left open. Behind her the slurred singing rose and fell. 'Just take them roond the block again,' she called to the driver. The house was sparsely furnished. *The Angelus* by Millet hung above a gas fire, as it hung in Audrey and Ronny's flat. 'I've got news that'll blow yer heed off, man!' With a wince, Audrey threw a hand up to her brow. 'It's already blown my mind away. I've got the hangover from hell.'

Muttering came from the kitchen where the priest held the kettle in his hand. Audrey watched him as he shook the appliance vigorously. 'The bloody thing's broken,' he snarled, giving the kettle a particularly savage shake. When he plugged it in, the little red light came on. 'Thank the Lord for that. I've mended it.'

'Father, ye've got to listen to wor,' Audrey demanded. 'I cannet believe ye divven't know already. We've been ringing you all night.'

'So it was you. I switched the phone off. Thought it was just a pack of drunks.'

'It was.' Audrey's laugh filled the council house. 'Listen . . .'

'Audrey, I'm not listening to a word until I've a fag in one hand and a mug of Assam tea in the other.'

Audrey watched Dan open the fridge, recoiling savagely as he held up a milk bottle to his nose. 'The fridge is on the blink again,' he moaned. 'Why doesn't anything work in this place? I'll just have to have it black.' Going over to a cupboard he opened it. 'Bloody hell. Now the sugar's gone walkabout.'

Audrey stepped forward. She placed a Senior Service in his mouth. She lit it. 'Just go and sit down, man. I'll get yer tea.'

The priest retired into the other room, slumping into an armchair. Without removing the cigarette from his mouth, he smoked with his legs dangling over an arm rest. Gradually his late-middle-aged features seemed to grow mollified. 'How much did you win then?' he called nonchalantly at last. Audrey came from the kitchen carrying a mug of thick, tarry tea in one hand, and a pint glass of black coffee in the other. She stared at him. 'Well, I presume you had a win on the bingo last night.'

A single scream rang out. The priest looked in puzzlement at Audrey, who, despite the scalding heat of the coffee, was drinking it swiftly down. A little spoon clanked against the glass as she gulped. A horn beeped on the cul-de-sac, and Dan looked out of the window to see the stretch limo reappear. 'Although you must have spent a good deal of your winnings on hiring that.' Outside, the driver could be seen remonstrating with Cheryl who was squatting to urinate against the wheel. 'God, it's that mad woman,' he added. Then he looked back at Audrey. 'So how much did you win then?'

Audrey finished the pint pot of black coffee and smacked her lips loudly. 'It isn't nee bingo.' She wiped her mouth. 'Ye're not gonnae believe us what it is.'

'So what's the point in telling me then?'

'The mad woman's coming over,' Audrey said with a throaty chuckle.

Cheryl was staggering down the cul-de-sac towards them pulling up her skirt. After ten yards she fell, and lay there in a giggling heap. The priest groaned. 'What's going on, Audrey?' he demanded sharply.

'Father man,' replied Audrey, 'we've won the lottery.'

Without looking away from Cheryl who was trying to rise, Dan said quietly: 'You've what?'

'We've won the National Lottery.' Audrey ducked back into the kitchen. There was a chink of glass and she came back with a bottle of whisky and two large tumblers. 'Hair of the dog what bit wor.' Audrey toasted the priest and then tossed back her whisky.

'What are we talking about here, Audrey?' Dan continued, still staring through the window at the helpless Cheryl. 'Four balls?'

Audrey's voice was hoarse. 'Na.'

'Five Balls?'

'Na.'

'Five balls and the bonus?'

'Na.'

'My God.'

Audrey's voice was a whisper. 'We've won awer three million pounds.'

The priest downed his whisky then accepted the second dram Audrey had already poured into her own glass. 'My God, I can't believe it.'

'Neither can we, man Father.'

'And after all these years of me telling you not to waste your money on those bloody tickets.' He laughed with Audrey. 'Glad to see you listening to your priest when he tells you that gambling's stupid when you've got twenty mouths to feed.'

'Well, God obviously knas better than ye.'

Dan shook his head. 'So that's what the limousine's all about. At first I thought it was Johno playing gangsters.' He suddenly glared at Audrey in alarm. 'You haven't gone and bought it, have you?'

'We don't get wor money until Monday,' Audrey chuckled.

'Thank goodness for that.'

'But we'll be getting a whole fleet of the buggers just as soon as the bank's open.' Audrey mulled over a mouthful of whisky. 'Divven't worry, man. I wasn't born yesterday. I've brought up a tribe o' bairns and grandbairns in the Teams. I'll kna how to spend me money, and I'll kna how to keep a hold of it.'

'Three million pounds, you say?'

'More than.'

'And you've checked it over? There's no mistake? You really have won?'

'We've talked to the advisers already.' Another high-pitched scream reverberated around the room. 'It keeps on coming over me,' she explained, 'but it won't sink in.' Yawning widely, she pointed through the window to where Cheryl was back on her feet. Audrey chuckled. 'She's got the hots for ye, and she's pissed mortal.'

'Audrey, I don't know what to say. It's the best news I've heard for a long, long time. I'm so pleased for you.'

Audrey grew suddenly serious. 'Offer this morning's Mass up for wor. To say a thank-ye.' She grasped the crucifix that lay outside the neck of her T-shirt, and closed her eyes. 'I cannet make sense of it yet. All I can dee at the minute is say thank you. Thank you, God. Thank you. Thank you.' There was a rattle of fingernails on glass. They looked to see Cheryl at the window. Pushed against the glass, her nose was distorted to a pig's snout. 'Hello, Reverend! I've come to see ye. I need a bit o' spiritual advice. I've got summink to confess to yus. Ha'way, gorgeous, let wor in.'

Audrey grinned at the priest. 'I hope your lock's been put back on yer door.'

4

'Are ye sure this is a good idea?' Ronny asked as the white
limo pulled effortlessly up Dunston bank. He yawned. "Cos to
be honest with yus, Al, I'd just as soon gan doon the allotment
and crash oot. Me heed's gannin' twenty to the dozen.' He lay
right back over the plush upholstery, stretching while scratching his stomach like a cartoon bear. 'I haven't told the lads
doon the allotments yet.' The thought struck him forcibly. 'Joe
and Ginga divven't even kna.'

'I've told ye,' replied Al, determination in his white and
blue eyes. 'This is gonnae be the best laugh we've had since we
took them lasses up Kielder forest.' The gradient of the hill
sharpened. 'Have ye tied the back doors?' Al grinned, then he
shook his head wonderingly. 'One minute yus're tying the
back doors of a crummy vanette to stop a half-bag of bloody
cement falling oot, the next, yus're in a stretch limo.'

Ronny nodded. 'Every noo and again I forget. Just for a
nanosecond, like. And then, bam! It clocks yus reet between
the eyes. Three million poonds. I mean, three million poonds.'
Ronny made an effort to rise, but couldn't. 'Ha'way, Al, let's
gan to the allotments.'

'Look,' said Al solemnly. 'It's for ye we're deein' it, man. It
wasn't me what them wifies chased doon the road in
Whickham.' Al pondered. 'They've tret wor like shite for
years, people like them, and I just want to see their faces when
they see us in this.'

At the top of the bank they turned right along the Whickham
Highway. Whickham holds itself aloof from the rest of
Gateshead. Although it lies on the Durham side of the Tyne,
officially it is part of Northumbrian Newcastle. A place of stone
houses with a village church and a well-kept park, it is tree-
lined with wide verges. Here the beleaguered professional classes
of the borough congregate. At last Ronny managed to haul
himself back into a sitting position. 'I'm not sure aboot this.'

'There!' Al suddenly called. He drummed against the

driver's window which opened wearily. 'Turn left here,' he commanded. He turned significantly to Ronny. 'Elm Road, remember it, bonny lad?'

'How could I forget?' Ronny replied simply. 'I asked them if they wanted their ridging tiles renewed and they nearly knackt me wedding tackle.'

'Aye, and it's payback time, Ronny boy.'

The car drove down the residential road, Al's roving eyes scanning the numbers. 'Stop!' he ordered the driver. 'That's the one.' Ronny nodded. 'Reet then, driver,' Al continued, 'gan oot and knock them up. Gan on, he'll pay ye fifty quid. Gis a pen and I'll write yus oot an IOU.'

The driver's eyes were lifeless with exhaustion. 'And you'll pay for any damage?'

Al dismissed the cavil contemptuously. 'He's a fuckin' millionaire this lad, y'kna,' 'He could buy a whole bloody fleet o' these Ladas.'

The driver got out of the car and reluctantly approached the large front door of 19 Elm Road. He pressed the bell. There was no reply. The chauffeur looked back helplessly to the limo. 'Just keep on pressing that bell,' Al told him. 'It'll be even better if ye have to get the buggers oot o' bed.' Al prodded Ronny and pointed at the downstairs window of the house. 'Look at that, bloody Indian sign. Really gets my goat, that.'

Ronny peered at the square sticker on the pane of glass. It was a Neighbourhood Watch Area sticker.

A woman in pyjamas eventually answered the door.

'That's her areet,' Ronny nodded as he and Al stared through the black tinted glass.

Al clapped his hands. 'Ha'way then.' Pushing a button, the window wound down. Gingerly, the chauffeur retired to the car, leaving the woman on the doorstep staring bemusedly at Al. 'Excuse me, madam,' Al began in his best touting voice, 'but are ye the hoose owner?'

'Yes,' the woman replied, baffled.

'Me and me partner here just happened to be passing in wor stretch limo when we noticed that yer ridging tiles are in a bad way.'

Ronny thrust his head out of the window beside Al's. 'They're purely shocking,' he said.

'It's eight o'clock on a Sunday morning,' the woman said incredulously. A cat appeared; it stared haughtily at Al and Ronny.

Al heaved a professionally gloomy sigh. 'Well, if ye divven't get it sorted oot, it'll only end up . . . falling doon.'

'Falling down?' the woman demanded irritably. 'What on earth are you talking about?'

'Crash!' cried Al. 'On yer heed. And poor little kitty cat, crushed to a hamster.'

The cat mewed aggressively. 'Don't I recognise you?' The woman strode down the little garden path towards the stretch limo. 'Weren't you those cowboys?'

'Hold fire,' whispered Al to Ronny. 'Hold fire, hold fire . . .' Ronny gazed anxiously at the woman who had hurled her gate open and was now only yards from their vehicle. 'Fire!' Al suddenly shouted.

The woman stopped dead in mid-stride. Her mouth fell open. Her eyes narrowed in disgust. A naked arse had been thrust out of the window. She gasped as a second pair of buttocks appeared beside it to wails of laughter. 'Give us a kiss, pet,' one of the two just managed to say.

'Aye,' the other one added. 'A peck on the cheek.'

The limousine began to pull away, and as quickly as the backsides had appeared they were retracted. Big Al and Ronny appeared in their stead. 'Look at us,' Al called, struggling to pull his trousers back on.

'Look at us,' Ronny echoed, helpless with laughter.

'Aye, it's us. Yer friendly, helpful neighbourhood cooboy

builders.' The woman continued to stare, open-mouthed. 'In a stretch limo,' Al added.

'A stretch limo,' Ronny gasped.

The elongated car drove on, Al and Ronny's voices shredding the Sunday-morning calm. Al grew louder, his tone more intense. 'We're in a stretch limo. Can ye see? We're in a stretch friggin' limo.'

'Calm doon, man,' Ronny coaxed, tugging his ponytail anxiously.

Al's face was tightening with passion. 'We're in a stretch limo!' he shouted, his body rising out of the window.

'Nee need to gan mental, man Al.'

But Al was not listening. 'It's us what's in the stretch limo. Not ye. Us. Us. Us!'

Ronny tried to haul his friend back inside. Faces had appeared in windows and at opened doors. Newspaper boys were staring. Al's passion grew belligerent. 'What the frigg are yous geeking at?'

At last Ronny managed to get him back in the car. Al stared at him, his chest rising and falling agitatedly. He seemed dazed by his own ardour. 'I've dreamt of this moment,' he said softly, a curious gentleness on his jackdaw face, 'Ronny boy, for years I've dreamt of this moment.'

Lulled by this seeming calm, Ronny loosened his grip. In an instant Al had wriggled through the open window. He landed heavily on the road. His white eye glinting crazedly as he sat there, Al held his arms out wide as wings. Cords roped his neck as he began to yell to the population of Whickham in general. 'Ye think we're summink yer shoe trod on, divven't yus? Trash from the Teams. But look at wor noo, gan on, look at wor, we're in a stretch limo!'

Ronny hammered at the driver's window. 'Stop!' he shouted. The limo stopped, and Ronny bundled himself out. 'Ha'way,' he begged Al, running over to him.

Like a bull near heifers, Al shrugged Ronny off. 'What have

we ever done to ye?' he screamed. 'All we ever wanted was to scratch worselves a living. And yous? Ye tret wor like scum. Yous slammed yer doors in wor face, yous pushed wor from yer doorsteps, yous shooed wor from yer bairns —'

'Al, man.' Ronny tugged at him, looking about anxiously. The limousine was pulling away, while, watched by a crowd of peeping faces, the woman was striding towards them with a large boyfriend in tow. 'Stop!' Ronny shouted helplessly at the chauffeur.

'No way,' the driver yelled back. 'Lottery win or no lottery win, I'm not going to have my limo damaged.' He wagged his chin at Al who was sitting dazedly in the middle of the road. 'Ye're a friggin' psycho.'

'Al,' Ronny begged. 'Get up!' He heaved at Al but his friend was a dead weight. Ronny glanced at the large boyfriend who was now only fifty yards away. His shoulders were perpendicular with bodybuilding. 'Al man . . .'

'Fat knackers!' the boyfriend suddenly yelled at the top of his voice. 'Wait until I get my hands on you. Scum fat knackers!'

'Al man,' screamed Ronny. 'Brick shithouse bandit at twelve o'clock!'

Ronny's unaccustomed agitation jolted Al from his trance. 'Friggin' hell,' he whispered as he saw the bodybuilder. He jumped up. He and Ronny began to sprint. In a desperate pelt of waddling bodies and elbows, they hurled themselves over the road, vaulted the fence that skirted open countryside and half screed, half rolled down a bank of brambles and nettles.

'The next time I see your ugly mugs round here,' the boyfriend yelled from the other side of the fence. 'I'll . . .'

But Al and Ronny did not wait to hear the threat. Hobbling like a crab, mincing in bare feet, Ronny crashed through the undergrowth, followed by a blindly blundering Big Al.

Without stopping, they scrambled over a stile and, following a grass lane, plunged into the depths of Washingwell Woods.

They only stopped when they could go no further. Having long since left the path, they flopped down on a grassy bank, chests heaving like bellows, lungs screaming for breath.

It was a fine, late summer's morning and little birds sang from every tree. Though early, the sun shone brightly, its light the dapple of a thousand pointillisms in the canopy above them. A roe deer peeping from the brake, watched them with a timid fascination. 'I went a bit mad back there, didn't I?' Al said at last.

'A bit,' Ronny replied, looking ruefully at the soles of his feet which were white with nettle stings, and kneading his ankle tenderly.

Al reflected. 'It's with winning the lottery. Knocks ye off kilter. Sends yus a bit bonkers.'

'It's gonnae take a bit of getting used to,' Ronny said.

'I'm areet noo, mind.'

'Why aye.'

'Nee need to tell anyone aboot it, eh?'

'Na.'

There was another long pause.

'What ye gonnae dee?' Al asked finally.

Ronny got up from the soft grass of the bank, whose green was tinged with the pink of red campion. 'Gan and get a pair of shoes on.' He picked up a long stick which lay in the grass. 'And then gan doon the allotments. I've got to tell Joe and Ginga.'

'Na. What are ye gonnae dee big time?' Al chuckled. 'I mean, yus're hardly gonnae gan up nee roofs nee more.'

Ronny sank back on to the grass and rubbed his feet. There was a silence as both men looked about the woodland. 'It's a canny spot this,' Ronny said at last. He seemed to come to a decision. 'I'm gonnae see more places like this. That's for one thing. As for the rest . . .' He shrugged.

'I've been here before, me,' Al announced.

'Have ye?'

A contemplative look had come over Al. 'It was somewhere roond here that I shagged that Cheryl.' He sighed. 'Back in 1971.' He got up abruptly. 'Aye, somewhere here. Got nettle stings all awer me arse. That'll friggin' teach wor to let a woman gan on top.' Mounting the little bank, Al crashed into some bracken, breasting through the fronds.

They pressed on for a while. 'Did ye see their faces?' Al suddenly hooted with hilarity. 'When we –'

'Aye,' Ronny roared back. 'I thought she was gonnae pass oot when she saw yer . . .'

Still laughing, they mounted the steep sides of a bank and, following an old pitman path, emerged from Washingwell Woods into a large bowl of land whose steep sides concealed it from prying eyes. Two thousand years before, the Romans had built a fort here. Its shape still lingered on the land. 'This was it,' Al announced. He went over to where a thicket of gorse and broom grew in the rough pasturage. 'Just here. I can still remember it an' all. Every detail.' A smile twinkled in his white eye. 'The thing aboot Cheryl is, she doesn't just drop her knickers for anyone. At least then she didn't. It was special. But such a lang time agan.' He lifted his eyebrows. And confused by his sudden emotion, he spat. 'Life's short, bonny lad. Short as a shag with a girl ye fancy.' When he began to speak again, his tone was wistful, slow as the changes of sunlight over the ancient fort. 'Ye might want it to last. But it cannet. That's the nature of the beast. And the more ye enjoy it, the quicker ye feel it rushing to its end. And if ye try and hold back? The whole friggin' thing just pushes ye on.' Puzzled by his own thought processes, he broke off. 'What the frigg am I on aboot?'

A loud snoring mixed with the sound of a passing bumblebee. Ronny was asleep on a soft bed of grass. Al looked at him for a while, and then gazed over the field. He sat down, and continued to stare as though gazing on things long gone: a great fat man sitting in a local lovers' bower, motionless with a memory. If jackdaws had a concept of a morally dubious Buddha, this is how they might have sculpted him.

Ronny came round at last, woken by his own snoring. Al was still sitting there. 'Ye've won the lottery,' he greeted him.

Ronny gaped disorientatedly. 'I've just had a dream. At least I think it was a dream.'

'I'm surprised it was quiet enough for that,' smiled Al. 'Ye were snoring like a pig.'

'I dreamt that I was shagging Audrey.'

Al rolled his eyes. 'Surprise, surprise.'

'The thing is, we were young. She had nee wrinkles, and I had nee belly.' He reached for his ponytail. 'I had a full heed o' hair an' all.' His eyes narrowed ruefully. 'I could have had her back in 1962.' Al looked at him questioningly. 'Audrey man,' Ronny explained. 'Like ye shagged Cheryl. I could have had Audrey. But I didn't have the bottle. We could have been married all this time. Shared a life. Had kids.' A sudden panic seized Ronny. 'I've wasted me fuckin' life. I could have had her forty year back. What's the point in winning the lottery when . . .'

There was a loud clap. Al had slapped his friend. Stunned into silence, Ronny gazed at him. 'Ye were getting hysterical, man,' said Al simply. 'Divven't fall into that trap. The what-ifs. That's a mug's game. Anyway, what are ye whining aboot? Ye've got her noo. Ye've got the rest of yer life left.'

'But I might die soon.' Al shook his head, and with a sheepish smile Ronny's panic drained away quickly. 'Aye,' Ronny mused. 'This winning the friggin' lottery business, knocks ye reet off kilter.'

'Divven't worry, bonny lad,' said Al soothingly. 'That's what I'm here for.' He stood up. 'I'll see yus're areet.'

Ronny smiled like a child. 'Ha'way, Al. Let's gan to the allotments. Joe and Ginga, they're like family, y'kna. I want them to hear aboot it from me.' Ronny rubbed his hands together. 'They'll be that pleased. I cannet wait to see their faces.'

'Come on then, bonny lad,' nodded Al. 'We're finished here now.'

Ronny hobbled on his way, leaning heavily against his staff like a pilgrim. As Al was leaving the hollow, he secretively plucked at the exquisite golden bloom of the gorse. "Shit-cakes," he hissed as a large thorn pronged him. But he carefully placed the golden flowers in a pocket.

5

'Where is everyone?' Standing at the altar, Father Dan examined the sparse congregation of St Mary Magdalene's ten o'clock Mass. He marched irritably down the aisle of the huge church. 'Any more for any more?' he shouted through the open church door. 'I see Steve hasn't even bothered to turn up,' he added as he came back up the aisle. 'I don't suppose there's anyone else that can play the organ?'

There were a few coughs. 'Ee,' Cheryl said getting up suddenly from the pew under which she had been noisily slumbering. 'Hasn't he got lovely eyes?'

'I'm going to make this short,' the priest announced. 'I know everyone wants to talk about one thing and one thing only, and we'd much rather be sitting in the club with a cup of coffee than clanking about in this great warehouse.'

The Mass lasted twenty minutes, and the congregation streamed out as quickly as possible. By the time Dan had reached the back door where he usually greeted everyone at the end, only Audrey was waiting. 'Where've they all gone?' he asked.

'I think they've gone to the club,' she replied evasively.

'But it's not open yet, and I've got the key.'

'The thing is, man Dan, one or two of yer parishioners, like, have done a bit breaking and entering in their time.'

The club was a large hut leaning in the corner of the churchyard under tall poplar trees. As Audrey and Dan walked towards it, a man wearing a ten-gallon hat with an unlit cheroot in his mouth bustled past them. 'Are ye gonnae turn the beer on, Father?' he asked.

'And what's it to you, Kenny Rogers?' the priest retorted irritably. 'I didn't see you at Mass.'

Without replying, Kenny hurried to the club. He opened the door and disappeared within.

When Father Dan Boyd opened the door to the St Mary Magdalene's Catholic Social Club a fug of freshly poured ale and thick cigarette smoke engulfed him. Gabbing voices thrummed the air. 'What the . . . ?' the priest cried. The place was packed. The church choir was serving drinks behind the bar. The pair of octogenarians in charge of the offertory were dancing arm in arm. The entire corpus of Eucharistic ministers were elbowing their way through the crowd to the bar. When Audrey walked in, there was a drum roll and a band began to play. Everyone sang: 'For She's a Jolly Good Fellow.'

The band was on the stage, a flimsy affair with strips of silver paper hanging along the back wall, and a spinning disco globe suspended from the ceiling by a length of washing line. The keyboard player of the band was waving. 'Hello, Father,' he called.

'Where were you for Mass?' Dan returned acidly.

The rest of the band waved. A motley crew of bass guitar, guitar, accordion and drums. On the large drum was written, in faded print: THE GEORDIE SHAMROCKS.

'Will someone just tell me what's going on?' the priest suddenly yelled.

'Bill said Audrey's paying,' one of his wayward parishioners said.

'We've decided to make it a Lourdes Benefit night,' another one explained sheepishly.

'But it's half-past nine in the morning,' Dan pointed out.

'And d'ye think Our Lord waited until teatime to get oot the tomb?' Audrey asked, coming up behind him with a smile. 'He was oot as soon as he saw his mam and Mary Magdalene coming doon the lane.'

'Yes,' returned the priest, 'but he didn't go on to have a monumental piss-up.'

'Course he did,' laughed Audrey. She looked through the crowd of heads to where Bill had just lifted Cara on to the bar. 'And divven't ye be giving them bairns nee more shandy, Bill man!' she suddenly cried.

The band began to play another number: 'If Ye're Irish, Ha'way into the Parlour.'

Everyone was pressing round Audrey, pushing and pulling, congratulating her as they tugged at her as though for a relic from a saint. 'Geet oot me face,' she suddenly snarled. 'I've got the hangover from hell and yus are just getting on me bloody tits.'

People melted from Audrey and the priest as she led him to a quiet corner by the safety exit where the empty beer bottles were stacked in crates. For a while nothing was said as they looked about the club. Damp streaks discoloured the walls on which hung paper from the Festival of Britain epoch. Framed pictures of Newcastle United, Celtic and the Pope hung behind the bar. On the bar itself was a range of gallon whisky bottles filled, to lesser and greater degrees, with coins. 'This is the first time I've had a moment to mesel' since we won,' Audrey mused. She touched her World's Greatest Nana T-shirt and then twiddled the frayed ends of her cut-off shorts. 'I'm still wearing these.' She lifted her feet and wriggled her toes. 'At least I've lost them bloody trainers.' Raising two hands to her head, she yanked powerfully at her thick, dishevelled hair. 'I still cannet take it in.'

'Where's Ronny?'

'He always gans to the allotment on Sundays. He'll be telling auld Joe O'Brien and Ginga the good news.'

'Ginga's the one who salvages things, isn't he?'

'Owt that other folk divven't want. Just like a Womble.'

'He's a good man. Your Ronny.' Father Dan looked closely at Audrey. 'You're not going to . . .'

'Start shagging someone else behind his back?' Audrey shook her head. 'I only used to sleep aboot 'cos I was looking for the right one. I divven't need to now I've foond him. Some folk divven't kna what I see in Ronny. They ask us. They say, "What d'ye get from him that I cannet give ye?"' She hugged herself. 'I nivver bother to answer. He just fits us. That's all. We're like pieces in a jigsaw puzzle.' She pursed her lips. 'He'd come to Mass if I asked him to. But I divven't. I want him just to be himself.'

The priest nodded. 'God's just as likely to be in the allotment as anywhere.'

She smiled wistfully. 'We should have got married forty year back, but we were both too shy. Can ye imagine that? Audrey McPhee being shy? If I was sixteen now, I'd have him in that bed and up that aisle before he could turn roond.'

'There's a time for everything under the sun,' Father Dan mused.

'Eh?'

'Nothing. Enjoy your dancing, Audrey McPhee.'

Cheering greeted a new arrival. It was a man carrying a child on his shoulders for whom he had to stoop drastically to get under the door jamb. 'Wor Paddy,' grinned Audrey. 'I was wondering when he'd get wind of it.'

'The clans are gathering.'

Paddy set his little girl on the floor and went over to Bill at the bar where a pint was held aloft for him like an Olympic torch. A few moments later the child had reached Audrey. With a great shout of delight from both little girl and grandmother, Audrey hoisted her granddaughter on to her knee. 'This is me lottery win,' said Audrey, hugging the Down's syndrome girl, Bernadette, close to her. 'Me real jackpot.' She kissed Bernadette with an almost painful fervour. 'I divven't seen enough of her, but. Do I, Bernie? Not since her daddy went to live so far away.'

'Where is Paddy these days?' Dan asked.

'South Shields.'

The band finished their song. 'Ha'way,' someone shouted, 'get Audrey up.'

The call was taken up. 'Aye. Give us a song, man Audrey.'

'There'll be a riot if ye divven't,' Dan laughed.

Audrey rubbed noses with Bernadette. 'What d'ye say, bonny lass? A proper McPhee duet or what?' Bernadette nodded solemnly and Audrey threw her head back, shouting, 'Make way for the McPhee singing hinnies!' With Bernadette on her hip, she made her way through the crowd. The Geordie Shamrocks offered their hands to pull her up but, spurning them, Audrey leapt effortlessly on to the stage. She waved aside the microphone they offered. Standing on the stage, she scanned the audience for a few seconds, and then said: 'We've just won awer three million poond.' Cheers broke out and the old place was filled with a great roar. 'And we're gonnae enjoy worselves. Aren't we, Bernie pet?' Bernadette nodded and the crowd burst into fresh delirium. They were silenced instantly by a single look from the matriarch in bare feet. 'He's . . .' Audrey held the opening word of her song lingeringly, tantalising the members of the band and the packed club. Then, with a wink, and still holding the three-year-old on her hip, dressed in her crumpled World's Greatest Nana T-shirt and cut-off denim shorts, with a cigarette wedged between forefinger and middle finger, Audrey began to sing:

He's a broken-hearted pitman
Head awer heels in love,
With a big lass from Gatesheed,
And he calls her his dove . . .

The entire Teams gathering breathed in mightily in preparation for the chorus, and then all burst into song. And as they sang Audrey and Bernadette stood above them, the object of everyone's attention. Her voice, a powerful, rich alto, caused the picture of the Pope behind the bar to wobble against its nail.

She's a big lass, she's a bonny lass
And she likes her beer.
And her name is Cushie Butterfield,
And I wish she was here!

6

The lane down to the allotments ran into an open countryside of high hedgerows and small meadows. It was an old cart track and the long generations of wooden wheels had cut a deep way into the earth so that tall banks rose on either side. Hawthorn trees grew on top of the banks, forming a leafy roof over the sunken way. 'See me,' said Ronny, his fingers flitting playfully at his ponytail as he hurried down. 'I love it doon here. The cares of the world drop from yer shoulders with every step.'

'What cares? Ye've won awer three million poond.'

'Oh aye, I was forgetting.'

Their laughter roared out so that in the fields beyond the hawthorns a hare drowsing under a wizened oak tree stopped to listen.

The allotments were a shanty town of corrugated iron and salvaged wood. Ronny's plot lay at the heart of it all and as they passed by the other holdings they heard the sounds of husbandry: the rasp of spade in earth, the dull cloching of a hoe, the tinkerings of cockerels, and the hissing of geese whose beady eyes could be seen bridling at the passers-by through knot hole and metal slit.

Despite his hobble, Ronny continued to walk quickly.

His allotment was no different from the others, fenced with the same corrugated iron and commercial property hoardings that periodically mushroom fruitlessly in Gateshead's countless brown-field sites. The opening was a front door from one of the first streets to be demolished in the Teams at the time of Margaret Thatcher's first harrowing of the Northern marches. Ronny banged twice on it, and the padlock fell into his waiting hands. Following him into the plot, Al looked about with an unimpressed air. A path took them between vegetable paths to a wooden shack. Some of the produce had already been harvested and the good earth of Gateshead gleamed blackly between flowering rows of potatoes and wigwams of scarlet runner beans.

Ronny broke into a sprint, his limping bare feet teasing puffs of dust from the beaten-earth path. He mounted the creaking wooden steps in one bound and landed on the little veranda. His hobbling clog-dancing routine sent the whole wooden structure wobbling. For a while it seemed that the place was going to collapse. Then with a final jump, he stopped abruptly. 'Three million pounds,' he whispered to a little gnome sitting on the edge of the veranda with a tiny fishing rod.

'More than,' Al corrected him.

Ronny nodded proudly, then stared at the substantial, higgledy-piggledy hut. 'I made that meself. Auld floorboards mostly. D'ye kna what was Russell Street? Ginga borrowed Terry's horse and cart when they pulled it down.' Ronny pointed at the ornamental turning of his corner poles. 'Banisters,' he said.

'Canny, canny. Still, yus'll be glad to get shot of it.'

'Eh?' Ronny asked absent-mindedly, still peering up at the shack with the fond eye of a craftsman.

'Well, noo yus've won the lottery, ye won't want this. I mean, when all's said and done, it's pretty crap.'

Ronny continued to gaze at the shack. 'Get shot of it? I hadn't thought aboot gettin' shot of it.'

Al shrugged. 'It's hardly the sort of thing ye can boast aboot doon the country club.'

But Ronny had disappeared inside.

The hut was a darkened world of secret shelves and improvised tools. Everything required by the tiller of the earth was there. And more. A veritable museum of old biscuit and tobacco tins containing screws and bits for every conceivable piece of joinery. 'I got most of this when the pit closed down,' Ronny said, rattling a tin of drill bits. 'Thought it might come in handy. It hasn't yet. Still, there's time.' Light flooded the interior when Ronny took down the wooden casement from the window and black dust could be seen riding the sunbeams. 'Look at that. There's been nee coal dug here for years, but it's still in the air.'

'Get it knocked doon,' said Al, slumping into an armchair. He kicked the stove, fashioned from an oil drum, and it clanked. He kicked the wooden water barrel and it clunked. 'Places like this? It's for auld gadgies with nowt. And ye'll have to get rid o' that friggin' donkey jacket.'

'But it's comfortable.' Ronny felt along the shelf, in his eagerness knocking a few tins and jars over. 'He's up here somewhere,' he said. 'Aye, here he is.' Al looked up to see his friend beaming widely and holding a ventriloquist's dummy. It was a dachshund dog. 'Hello, Denny!' Ronny said to the dummy. 'How's it gannin'?' Pressing his lips tightly, Ronny attempted to ventriloquise an answer, but it was an inaudible growl. 'How many doggy biscuits could ye buy for three million, Denny me auld doggie?'

'Not that thing again,' said Al with a dismissive wave of his hand. 'I thought ye'd given that up years back.'

Ronny gazed fondly at the puppet. 'I've nivver given up being a comedian.' He turned to Al eagerly. 'D'ye think I could make it as a comedian?'

Al's head shook vehemently. Then he checked himself. 'Ordinarily no, but then ye've won the lottery, haven't ye? Ye can dee owt.'

'D'ye hear that, Denny?' Ronny cried. 'D'ye hear that, me auld doggy-do?' The hut reverberated with the dog's howls of delight, mixed with a cacophony of other canine noises. 'Doon, boy, doon,' Ronny laughed, but the panting and barking continued as he made the puppet jump up enthusiastically. Then he set the dog on his friend, pretending it was copulating against his leg. Wearily, Al cuffed the puppet away. Ronny stopped at last, eyes shining and face beaming.

Al yawned. 'Reet then, ha'way let's gan.'

'Gan?'

'Why aye,' said Al. 'Ye said ye wanted to come doon here, so we did. Now let's gan.'

Ronny put the puppet down. 'We've only been here half a minute.'

'Lang enough, if ye ask me. We've got things to dee. We're busy men noo, y'kna, Ronny.'

'But I haven't told Joe and Ginga.'

Al sighed indulgently. 'Areet then, get them told. Then let's vamoose.'

'No. No. I always spend the whole morning here.'

'Deein' what?'

Ronny shrugged. 'Pottering aboot. For a start, I usually light the stove and make a cup of tea.'

'Living dangerously for a millionaire that, isn't it, bonny lad?'

'Joe and Ginga come awer for a cuppa.'

'The excitement's killing wor.'

Ronny plucked a fork from a corner. 'I kna. We'll dig up some spuds.'

Al flinched as Ronny marched excitedly past him and bounced down the steps brandishing the fork. 'I've got a bad back, remember,' Al called. Standing on the veranda, he watched Ronny striding to the potato patch. 'Morning after yus've won the lottery and what're ye deein'? Grubbing up spuds.' He watched Ronny carefully testing the earth around a potato plant. Then he came down the steps himself. 'Look, I'll tell ye what. Ye stay here, and I'll buzz off for a bit. There's a few things I need to dee.'

Ronny looked up from the soil. 'Hold on a second, ye'll see me bringing up potatoes in a moment.'

'I'll just be five minutes.' Al opened the old Teams front door through which three generations had gone out and come home, never to return now. 'See you in a bit,' he called as he closed it behind him.

When he had grubbed up his first potatoes Ronny hunkered down to stare closely at them. They lay in the earth like a clutch of eggs, creamy against the black soil. The green of the tops, so vibrant only a minute or so before, already seemed to be wilting. A wondering expression came over Ronny's face as though this was the first time that he had witnessed the fructification of the earth. He gazed and gazed in fascination, only looking away when he heard a sharp cough. He looked up to see an old man standing on his path. Leaning heavily on a walking stick, the old man was frowning. 'Ye areet, Joe?' Ronny greeted him with a broad beam across his face.

'Aye, but you're not,' the old man replied. 'What the hell are ye deein' staring at them potatoes like that? And what was all that caterwauling a few minutes back?'

Ronny tugged gently at his ponytail, leaving a dirty smear on his head. He chuckled. 'The thing is, Joe. Summink's happened.'

The old man's hands were as gnarled as the hawthorn brake

above the allotment path. He wore an old pair of black boots, and peered irritably at Ronny through rheumy eyes as he headed up the path to the shack. 'Gan and make the tea.'

'I've got summink to tell ye, man Joe.' Ronny ran past him and pulled the armchair on to the veranda. The old man's face flashed with pleasure as he eased his bones into the armchair. 'Ye'll nivver believe wor, Joe,' said Ronny as he brought out a small deckchair and a little wooden stool. 'It's so –'

'Well, in that case divven't bother telling wor.'

The sound of a goat bleating reached them from another allotment. 'Ginga an' all,' Ronny whispered to himself. 'I'll tell them together.'

'Stop wittering and get the tea on,' Joe said.

Ronny looked at the hut. 'I haven't lit the stove yet.'

Joe shook his head. 'If there was a way of making tea withoot the trouble of boiling water, ye'd have come up with it by now. But there isn't, so get the water on.'

'Mebbes we can have summink different this morning. Have a change.'

'Like what?'

'I divven't kna. Champagne or summink.'

'I can see yus're in one of them moods today, lad. Ye stink an' all. That donkey jacket mings to high heaven.' As Ronny lit the stove, Joe O'Brien gazed critically around the allotment. 'Ye haven't sown yer mustard crop yet, have ye? Ye want to get it done, lad. Every day's a loss. Have ye still got them seeds what I gave ye last year?'

'Aye, somewhere,' returned Ronny distractedly as he watched the flames begin to lick round the kindling. 'But just wait until ye hear what I've got to tell ye.'

'Somewhere,' the old man repeated to himself as he shook his head. 'I'd love to see this precious somewhere of yours. Half of everything yus have ever owned is there. And half of mine. If only I could find this somewhere, I'll be the richest man in Gatesheed.' A strangulated shout of joy emanated from the hut. 'Somewhere?' continued the old man, shaking his head. 'It's the same place as nowhere. There's no such place, Ronny lad.'

'There is,' Ronny replied with gusto, 'and I think I've foond it.'

'The King of Somewhere, ye. Anyone would think –' Joe broke off as yet more laughter gushed from the shack. 'What is it with ye this morning, Ronny lad?'

'Summink massive's happened.' Ronny had come out on to the veranda.

Joe stared at him. 'Yer compensation? Is that it?'

'Eh?'

'Y'kna, for when you knackt yer back?'

Ronny spread his arms out wide and smiled expansively. 'For the life of me I divven't kna what yus're gannin' on aboot.'

'From when ye went into that fire, man,' Joe said crossly. 'Pulled me oot. Ye did yer back in. Lost the pet shop 'cos of it. I've nivver been one to sponge on the state, but ye're entitled –'

'Shh!'

Joe was puzzled at the terrified vehemence of Ronny's reaction. Fear showed where a moment before joy had been bubbling. 'What the hell's the matter with ye, Ronny?'

'It's not that, man Joe,' Ronny replied quickly. 'It's got nowt to dee with that.' He glanced about rapidly as though to find eavesdroppers at the corrugated-iron fence. 'Anyway, Joe marra, I thought I'd telt ye not to mention that to anyone.'

'Eh?'

'Do ye not remember?' Ronny's voice dropped to a whisper. 'There was bad people involved.' His voice dropped even further. 'Y'kna, Macca. And if they ever foond oot it was me and Audrey what called the pollis an' that . . .'

'Oh aye,' mumbled Joe. 'I forgot. I . . .' An apology hovered in the air before being replaced with a growl. 'Well, it was your fault. The way yus've been gannin' on all morning. And it makes us angry the way ye gan up that ladder and fetch and carry for Al Greener five-bellies, while all the time yus're entitled to –'

Ronny sighed and sat on the little wooden stool. 'Joe, as far as I'm concerned that fire nivver happened. And if ever he foond oot it was us –' Ronny broke off. And then grinned. 'Bloody hell, this changes everything. What happened last night. Bloody hell.'

'What the hell are yus gannin' on aboot noo?'

But Ronny had dissolved into laughter. He was still laughing as he went back into the hut. Plunging his head into the water butt, he drank deeply, his laughter bubbling the water. Drops cascaded from him as he lifted himself free and, like a dog, shook himself dry. He looked over to see Joe standing in the door, blocking the light. 'If ye were badly,' the old man said doggedly, 'y'kna, ill. Yus'd tell wor, wouldn't ye? Ye'd tell me and Ginga.'

Touched, Ronny nodded. 'It's not so much being badly, man Joe, but more of a career change.'

'Eh?'

In one quick movement, Ronny had scooped up the ventriloquist's dummy. 'Gottle o' geer,' he growled. 'Gottle o' geer.'

'Not that again,' the old man moaned. 'I thought that was bloody lang gone.'

'Divven't listen to him, bonny lad,' said Ronny to the dachshund.

With a snort the old man went back outside. Whining like a dog, Ronny crept out, and coming up behind the armchair, made the dummy cry in the old man's face. 'Ye've hurt his feelings, man Joe. Say sorry.' The old man grabbed the dummy. It sailed into a patch of mint.

When the billycan boiled on the stove, Ronny made the tea. He brought three mugs out on an old Double Diamond tray and placed it on an upended tea chest serving as a table. Ronny sat thoughtfully on the stool. At the foot of the wooden veranda steps a little group of sparrows were playing in the dust. Their chirping rose and fell, but they scattered at Ronny's sudden burst of laughter, taking cover in a sorry-looking fruit bush. They stayed there, continuing to bicker in greater safety, returning only after a long silence between the two human beings sitting above them.

'Joe?' said Ronny at last.

'What?'

'What would yus dee if you were rich?'

The old man, watching the sparrows as they dust-bathed, screwed up his face. 'Rich?'

'Aye. Say ye came into a fortune or summink.'

'How would I come into a fortune?'

'If ye won the Grand National or summink.'

'I divven't gamble.'

'It doesn't matter how ye got it.'

'But it's pointless. I'll nivver have money.'

'Just say ye did!' Ronny's ringing voice caused the sparrows to flee their dust-bathing once more. 'What would ye dee if suddenly ye had so much money that ye didn't kna what to dee with it? What would ye dee if ye had so much money that ye wouldn't be able to carry it, let alone coont it? Even if it was in twenty-poond notes, and ye had a friggin' geet wheelbarrow. What would ye dee . . . ?' He broke off. 'Oh, where's Ginga got himself to? I cannet keep this to mesel' any longer. I've got to get it off me chest . . .'

At that moment the door to the allotment opened and a goat came in. 'At last,' cried Ronny. A long rope was attached to the goat, and it took a few moments before the entrance of the man holding it. Ronny jumped eagerly to his feet. 'Ye'll nivver believe what's happened, man Ginga.'

Ginga was old, though not as gnarled as Joe O'Brien. A thick mane of ginger hair covered both his head and his face.

Shrewd yet benign eyes glinted fox-like through a rufous tangle of lash and brow.

'Hurry up,' Ronny called.

'He won't have his hearing aid on, man,' Joe said testily.

Ginga dropped to his knees to slowly haul in the goat. The goat was headstrong and intent on a patch of strawberries, but at last Ginga had an arm round it. Ronny brought an enamel mug over to him, and in a minute or so, the goat had been milked. Ginga tethered it to the knob of a banister on the steps, and then, having completed his tasks, smiled at Ronny and Joe.

'Ronny's got summink to tell wor,' Joe said as Ginga sat in the small deckchair.

'Eh?' replied Ginga.

'A big announcement,' Joe said.

'Eh?'

'A big announcement,' Joe repeated loudly.

Ginga shook his head. 'Hold on, marra. I'll just turn me hearing aid on.' A rapt look of attention seized his faculties as he grappled with the hearing aid. 'I nivver kna how to work this. That's better,' he said when he had finally managed to switch it on.

'Ginga . . .' Ronny began excitedly.

But the russety old man had turned to Joe. 'Ye kna that gadgie what works at the frozen-chip factory?' Joe nodded. 'He'll give ye a regular bag of offcuts for a couple of vegetable boxes now and again.'

'Tell him I'm interested.' Joe's brow wrinkled with thought. 'Is it your turn for the poultry pen?'

'Ronny's,' Ginga replied.

'We'll get it pegged oot this morning.'

Ronny suddenly stood. 'Three million pounds!' he declared. 'Awer three million pounds,' he repeated more quietly. 'Awer three bloody million pounds,' he finished in a whisper.

The others looked at each other and then looked at Ronny. 'What ye on aboot?' Joe demanded.

'We've won the lottery,' Ronny shouted.

'Pull the other one,' said Joe sarcastically. 'It's got bells on it.'

'Straight up! I swear on anything ye like. I swear on me and Audrey. We've only gone and won the bloody lottery!' The ensuing silence was filled by the chirping of the sparrows who had just flown back to the fruit bush. 'We've won –'

'We heard what ye said,' Joe snapped.

Another strange silence followed. Still standing, Ronny stared down at his two friends but, baffled and disorientated, they were staring expressionlessly at each other. 'Are ye sure, Ronny lad?' Ginga asked at last.

'Talked to the adviser. Audrey double-checked.' A butterfly flew in from over the makeshift fence. It meandered over the vegetable plots, jaunting at last over the sparrows' dust bath, settling in it for a few moments. 'So what d'yus think then?' Ronny pressed when the silence had become oppressive to him. 'Me and Audrey, we've just become the richest couple in Gateshead.'

'Who's getting your plot?' Joe's voice was terse.

'Eh?'

'Well, ye won't be wanting it no longer.'

Shaken by the unexpected hostility of this outburst, Ronny tugged bewilderedly at his ponytail. 'But I'm not gannin' anywhere.'

'Divven't talk daft,' Joe continued bitterly. 'Yus've won the National Lottery, what'll ye want with an allotment now?'

Ronny sat down heavily. Joe spat rancorously. 'Ginga man,' Ronny appealed, 'can I get some sense oot o' ye?'

Ginga looked away uneasily. 'Congratulations, lad. Aye. Well done, an' that.'

'Is that the best ye can dee?' Ronny replied, staggered. 'Think aboot what I've just telt yus. I mean, it's not aboot a bag of bloody oven chips or moving a poultry pen aboot. It's the friggin' National Lottery.'

Joe sneered as he slurped his tea. The goat bleated at the end of its tether. Ginga shifted positions awkwardly. 'The thing is, Ronny lad,' Ginga began, 'we've nivver really seen much money. We barter an' get by. Why, ye used to yoursel'. I suppose we just cannet take in what's happened.'

The butterfly meandered back over the dust, and one of the sparrows, having come back to the earth patch, watched it for a while, and then flew up after it. 'I thought yus'd be happy,' said Ronny through narrowing eyes.

'Happy?' His face twisted bitterly, Joe looked Ronny in the eye for the first time.

'Aye,' replied Ronny, throwing his arms wide. 'Happy.'

After two attempts, the sparrow managed to stab the butterfly with its blunt beak. 'Happy?' Joe echoed incredulously. 'Are you off yer rocker? I wouldn't wish it on me own worst enemy.'

Injured, the butterfly fell to the ground. The sparrow lost interest for a moment. But seeing the desperate wing fluttering in the dust, instinct impelled it to finish the maimed creature off.

7

'Right!' said the man with the huge camera dangling round his neck. 'I want you all on the bridge.' The boards of the Gateshead Millennium Footbridge drummed with the step of countless feet. 'Family only!' the man screamed.

'It *is* the family,' an onlooker said from the crowd watching on the quayside. 'And they're not even all there.'

Occasionally a raucous song still rose and fell from the crowd and family, but it quickly died. Exhaustion hung heavily over them all. Beneath the bridge ran Coaly Tyne, sluggish with the high tide. Leaning against the parapet, the family stared down at its water.

The cameraman stared at them in dismay. 'Bit miserable, aren't they? I thought they'd just won the lottery.'

'They've been up all night,' someone answered from the quayside. 'Ye should have heard them at two in the morning.'

'Well, maybe this will put them back in the mood.' The photographer scurried over to the large four-wheel drive parked between the two stretch limos, perched precariously near the edge of the Gateshead quay. He brought back with him a jeroboam of champagne.

'I'll take that for them,' said a figure materialising out of the crowd. 'I'm practically one of the family anyway.' Having snatched the champagne, Al took it on to the bridge.

Twitching like a shrew, the tabloid photographer looked about. Ten feet below, the water streamed, its current a sleek sheet. Looking up from the water, he stared at the bridge which played itself over the river like a metal harp. On the Newcastle side stood the new restaurants and brasseries of the revamped legal district, and the magnificent white structure of the old Co-operative Society now converted to a luxury hotel. His gaze travelled back to the Gateshead side to the Baltic flour mill, in the process of becoming a massive art gallery. 'We'll have that in the background,' he decided, adding in a loud voice: 'Now which one of you is Audrey?'

The pop of the champagne cork rang out. A cheer rose. 'That one's Audrey,' Al told him, having delivered the champagne and elbowed his way through the crowd to the photographer. 'The canny totty with the big bazookas.'

The photographer smiled. 'Quite an eyeful for an old bird. No wonder they hired the limos. She done glamour work?' Al shrugged. The photographer's features crinkled thoughtfully. 'I don't know about what she's wearing.' He stared at the World's Greatest Nana T-shirt through squinting eyes.

'Audrey love,' he called. 'This is just a thought, but I don't suppose you'd go topless?'

The wailing laughter on the quayside fell silent as Audrey stared over at the photographer. Her voice was quiet. 'What did you say?'

'Just boobs,' said the man, frantically searching through his camera bag for appropriate lenses.

'Aye, get them oot!' someone sounding suspiciously like Big Al shouted.

'Ta for the limos,' said Audrey softly, 'but if ye think that allows ye to get fresh then yus'll regret it.'

The photographer twitched. 'Let's have everyone a bit closer together then. Hutch up, everyone.' The family bunched closer together round Audrey. The photographer dropped his camera from his face. 'Hold on, hold on. Do we have to have you right in the middle, mate?' Ronny looked about. 'Yes, you, the bald one. No disrespect, friend, but our readers like something a bit bouncier with their cornflakes than that big bald egg.'

'He's beginning to annoy me,' Audrey remarked. She looked about. 'Put the champagne down, Bill. You're legless enough already.'

The photographer's eye roved over the family group. 'You,' he cried, pointing at Theresa. 'And . . . you.' He gestured at the young teenager Linzi. 'You stand with yer nana.'

'She's my mam,' said Theresa.

'She's my nana,' said Linzi.

Ronny was still standing beside Audrey. 'Come on, mate,' the tabloid man continued. 'A joke's a joke. No offence, but the ponytail with the bald head. You've got to be having a laugh.' When the group was assembled to his liking, he gazed thoughtfully at it. 'There's still something not quite right,' he muttered. With a flash of inspiration, he rifled through his camera bag and brought out three bikini tops. 'Here, mate,' he said to Al. 'Let the dog see the rabbit.'

'Eh?' Al replied.

'Take these over to the girls.' The photographer called over to those on the bridge. 'Best-quality Gucci wear. Why don't you try them on? You can have them. Just try them on for size.'

No sooner had Al delivered the skimpy tops than Audrey hurled them back. They landed among the crowd on the quayside. There was a scramble like children rushing for the pennies scattered after a wedding. 'Get a move on,' Audrey ordered. 'We haven't got all day, y'kna. We've got the Winners' Adviser coming this afternoon.'

Shadowed by Big Al, the photographer began to shoot. 'So what does it feel like to win over three million pounds?' he called to them. 'That's better. Let's have a few more smiles. You're never going to have to work again. How does that feel? Sweet, sweet. You can tell your boss where to shove it. Tell the jobcentre to . . .' Breaking off and lowering the camera, he spoke to Ronny. 'Look, pal, I thought I'd told you to shuffle off to Buffalo.'

'Reet, that's it,' snarled Audrey. 'That jumped-up little pantry boy . . .'

'It's all right,' said Ronny, moving to the edge of the group.

'It's still not working,' the tabloid man mumbled. Inspiration flashed in his eyes again. 'I tell ye what, Audrey love, can you just give me a quick turn?' Sighing, Audrey turned round. 'A butt-cheek shot,' nodded the photographer. 'Can the ladies all turn round for me, and you, Audrey love, can you lift your shorts up a bit . . . ?'

'No, I couldn't. And me lasses aren't showing nee bum neither. Unless ye want to end up in the water.'

The photographer sighed, then flinched slightly when he felt a large belly pressing interrogatively against him. 'D'ye dee the Page Threes an' all?' Al asked.

'Are you one of these three-belly characters you have on Tyneside?' the cameraman asked curiously.

Al shook his head. 'Five-bellies, lad. Five-bellies.'

'Well, I tell you what then, five-bellies son. I'm going to go and get another bottle and I want you to . . .' The words passed from hearing as he whispered into Big Al's ear while miming the spraying of a bottle of champagne. Big Al croaked with dry laughter.

On the bridge Theresa was yawning. 'Ee, if I divven't get hyem soon, I'll fall asleep on me feet.'

Corky, his features invisible under the floppy brim of his hat, gave a flurry of rap-like hand gestures, finishing off with both hands cradling his head. 'I'm knackt oot an' all, pet.'

'What's he deein'?' Audrey demanded suspiciously as Al began to creep over the bridge towards them. He was crouched low and moved like a lobster.

When Al was within a few feet of the family, he began to shake the bottle. 'Now!' the photographer shouted. Opening the bottle, Al sprayed it all over Audrey's front.

'Wet T-shirts,' said the pressman appreciatively. 'That's more like it.'

Carried away, Al aimed the foam-gun at Cheryl, who tittered coyly.

The photographer was still busy taking pictures when his viewfinder abruptly lost focus. An instant later, he felt himself being grabbed bodily, and hoisted off his feet. The next thing he knew, the water of the River Tyne was rushing to meet him. Audrey stood on the bridge looking down as the wretched man surfaced. 'I told ye yus'd fall in if ye didn't look where you were steppin'.' She turned to the rest of those gathered. 'Didn't I?'

'Aye,' the gathering cheered, in one voice.

8

Unusually for Gateshead, the dog days of August stretched on and on so that it seemed summer would never end. The vegetable crops of the allotments grew thirstier and thirstier, and the grass of the Derwentside Estate Long Walk, from chapel to stone pillar, yellowed under the constant sun. Dogs grew irritable; cats were nowhere to be seen, lying deep in shade.

A week had passed since six balls had altered the destiny of a family from the Teams, and night had long since fallen over the Square Flats, slowly spreading its welcome cool. Still the party raged, as it had done for seven days and nights. Music pulverised the courtyard, while the walkway outside Flat 12A was crammed with people.

The flat itself heaved with bodies. And right in the middle of it all, surrounded by rings of clapping, laughing people, Audrey and Ronny were dancing to the 'Birdy Song'.

Audrey's leopardskin dress clung revealingly to her body. Her chunky bracelets and crucifix, overlaid with masses of heavy gold jewellery, jiggled in time to her dancing knee-length, square-toed boots. Her hair, recently dyed blonde and teased up into a towering beehive, shimmered in a solid, hairsprayed mass. Ronny was sweating profusely in a gleamingly black Roy Orbison suit and tie. The parrot dozed on his shoulder. From time to time somebody threw a bottle of Diamond White at Audrey, who screwed off the top with her teeth and threw it back.

The crowd brayed out the chorus of the 'Birdy Song' as the two lottery winners pecked over each other's shoulders like mating birds before corkscrewing down, elbows flapping like a pair of laying hens.

Toni-Lee lowered her new digital camera. 'I've definitely got them this time,' she announced to the other children sitting on the breakfast bar with her. They gathered round to look at the digitally captured picture. 'Perfect,' nodded Toni-Lee at the image of Corky and Theresa kissing in the kitchenette.

'I've got them on this as well,' Skye pronounced solemnly

131

while indicating the large image display of her Sony digital camcorder.

Oblivious to all of this, Theresa and Corky continued to kiss passionately, bending over the throbbing Sony DHC-MD373TC minidisc mini system complete with DJ microphone and record turntable, which stood on a kitchen surface.

Just over the din of the 'Birdy Song' a mobile phone could be heard ringing. Brosnan reached over the high tower of Argos catalogues, and, rooting through a great pile of cellphones, picked the one with a picture of Buffy the Vampire Slayer. 'Hello,' he said into the mouthpiece.

'It's your gan,' the voice of Elliot told him.

'OK.' Dextrously, Brosnan edged down the breakfast bar between his cousins right to the end where Elliot sat with Olympus Etetrek goggles over his face and the games console in his hands.

'Cheryl's still trying to get off with Father Dan,' Linzi pointed out to Terri-Leigh. But Terri-Leigh did not look up from her de luxe hardback copy of the latest Harry Potter.

'And Uncle Dick's on to his tenth bottle of Budweiser,' said Toni-Lee. She pointed the camera at the little old man who was drinking with Bill and his friends.

'I'll tell ye summink,' Uncle Dick was explaining, his hook nose, wrinkled bald head and constant toothless smile reminiscent of a benign vulture. 'I've had two strokes, but I can still lift me own body weight.'

'He can,' nodded Bill vociferously.

'And d'ye kna why?' Dick asked, licking his gums. Nobody knew why. ''Cos I eat a raw egg for breakfast every day of me life.'

'He does,' Bill continued to nod. 'Ha'way, Uncle Dick, gan and ask Mrs Armstrong to dance again.'

Uncle Dick stared over at the massively overweight Mrs Armstrong who was wedged in an armchair talking to Father

Dan. Uncle Dick nodded seriously. 'I've always liked them big. Some like blondes. Some like brunettes. Me? I divven't care aboot none o' that. I just like them big.'

The 'Birdy Song' began to fade, and breaking off his kiss with the audible pop of a sink plunger, Corky eagerly selected one of his own discs. A loud, bass-thumping dance anthem flared out. 'DJ Corky here,' he shouted into the microphone with Theresa hanging proudly on his arm. 'The hardest core on Tyneside, the softest mix on —'

A hail of shouts rained down on him, and with a long-suffering sigh, he lifted off the dance anthem. A few moments later 'Agadoo!' from the Black Lace *Party* album rang out through the flat. There was a roar of approval.

In this brief lull the crowd had descended on Ronny and Audrey. 'If I was ye, Ronny lad,' somebody was saying, 'I'd just disappear into the big blue yonder . . .'

'I'm telling ye,' someone else advised, 'ye want to put a good half of it away pronto. Get it safe, then whatever happens it's always there . . .'

'No, no, no,' a third person cried. 'Spend every penny today, tomorrow can look after itself.'

The group pressing round Audrey was also full of helpful tips. '. . . All I'm saying, Audrey pet, is that if it had been me what had won I'd sod them all and gan on a world cruise.'

'Aye, with him from Shenanigans.'

'He said he'd gan with ye an' all, if ye take him to Goa.'

As Ronny's eyes glazed over, he felt an arm encircle his shoulder protectively. 'Give him some space, lads,' Al said. 'None of yus have got any idea aboot it. Let's face it, it's hardly benefit fraud we're wanting to kna aboot.' As he guided Ronny away, Big Al whispered: 'Divven't worry aboot what the plebs say. We've got it sussed. Ye and me. We kna one end of a Coutts chequebook from another.' Ronny nodded as he yawned. 'The same banker as the Queen,' continued Al, impressed by his own words. 'Now we've really arrived.'

Ronny yawned even more widely. 'Ye're knackered,' said Al indulgently, continuing to draw Ronny away from the pressing offers of advice. 'Bound to be, it's been Party City here for a week. Your nerves are strained to a pitch.' He thrust a bottle of Newcastle Brown Ale into his friend's hand. 'Here, the answer to all life's questions.'

Ronny lifted the bottle to his lips automatically. But he did not drink. 'I think I've had enough.'

Al studied him closely. 'Aye, good idea. Let's gan and get some air. We need to talk. I've had a few more ideas aboot the future.' As Al led Ronny to the front door, he pointed at the priest who was talking to Audrey. 'He knas when he's on to a good thing. Ye'll have to watch him.'

'Have a drink, man Father,' Audrey was urging Dan.

'No,' the priest replied after a moment's pause. 'I think I've had enough of that for a while. I'm going now.'

'But the party's only just getting gannin'.'

'It's been going for a week, Audrey. Look, I need to talk to you.'

'Areet then.'

'Not here.'

Audrey and Dan elbowed their way to the front door of the flat, reaching it a number of minutes after Ronny and Al had disappeared through it. Then, having pushed down the walkway, they descended a flight of stairs and came out on the walkway below Audrey's.

Leaning against the parapet, they looked out over the courtyard. The music continued to pump out from above. For a while they breathed the cooling night air in silence. 'The party can't go on for ever,' Dan said at last.

Audrey yawned. 'Actually, I'm getting a bit sick of it mesel'. I haven't had time to think. To take any stock of it. I haven't really had time to turn roond.'

'By the way, thanks for the Celtic season ticket. Now all I need is to be able to get up there every week.'

'I'll buy ye a car,' Audrey said impulsively.

'And will you teach me to drive it?' he asked with a wry smile.

'Ronny'll go with ye. As lang as the Toon aren't playing.'

He handed her a cigarette and they both lit up. Dan's smile faded. 'There's no easy way of telling you this, Audrey. There's bad news.'

Audrey peered at him through a cloud of smoke. 'Eh?'

'I've known about it for a week. Kept it from you. Didn't want to ruin the party.'

'Will yus just tell us what ye're on aboot?'

Dan took a deep draw on his cigarette and with the smoke softly exhaled a single word: 'Macca.' He watched Audrey's reaction then added in a whisper: 'Johno's finished round here. Macca's taken over the Teams.'

Audrey continued to smoke silently for a while. 'It had to come.'

'And you're sure he doesn't know?' the priest asked quietly. 'About you-know-what? About the . . .' He leant right over and dropped a single, barely articulated word into Audrey's ear: '. . . Fire.'

'I'm certain.'

'Well, that's a relief anyway.' A pause fell between them. The smoke from their cigarettes drifted over to the frail canopy of the spindly tree. 'It's just as well you've won,' Dan began again, his voice a murmur once more. 'Now you can go away. Get free of all of this. It means you can live your life without any fear.'

Audrey was staring thoughtfully over the courtyard. 'I suppose it does.'

'What are you going to do?'

Audrey nodded at the courtyard. 'It's all I've ever known. I moved in here the day they put the flats up. Nineteen sixty-eight. I was here before man was on the moon.'

'He's a wild animal, Audrey. If ever he did find out, it would be better if you were well away.'

Audrey looked levelly at the priest. Then, without a word, she stooped down to her knee-length boot. In a movement so fast as to blur, she had pulled the zip down and brought out a small object. The priest heard a click and found himself staring at the spitting snake's tongue of a flick knife. 'If anybody tries to hurt me or mine,' she said with a soft menace, 'there's nowt I wouldn't dee. D'ye understand? Nowt.' She growled like a tigress protecting her young. Then, as quickly as it had appeared, the knife was back in her boot. 'I've worked it oot,' she said soberly. 'What would I get? Hard-working nana of bloody umpteen kills gangland psychopath in self-defence.' Audrey shrugged shrewdly. 'Two years? A year? A suspended sentence. Ye'd give wor a character reference, wouldn't ye?'

'You're a one-off,' Dan said, simply.

Audrey smiled, revealing her lucky gap-tooth in all its glory. 'I've lived here all me life. Brought up bairns. Grandbairns. It helps if y'kna how to stand up for you and yours.' She took a long drag on her cigarette. 'As for taking the life of another, man. Well, I've telt God aboot it. He might not like it, but He knas.'

The priest gazed wonderingly at the woman standing at the parapet of the flats with him. 'I think He might understand.'

Just then there was a drum roll of court-shoe heels on the stairs above. Dan turned just in time to find Cheryl flinging herself into his arms. 'Father Dan,' she sighed, 'I've got summink to confess. Will ye hear me confession?'

The priest pushed her off wearily. 'You're beyond hope.'

'I fancy the arse of yus. There, now y'kna. Let's gan away together. Just the two o' wor. Cannet ye see I've got the radgie hots for yus? Ha'way, let's dee a *Thornbirds*.' Dan's shoulders shuddered with laughter as he walked down the stairs. 'Ee, Audrey,' Cheryl whispered in ecstasy as she watched him turn from view. 'Mebbes I should become a convert.'

'Convert from what? Ye divven't believe in owt.'

Cheryl shrugged. 'I've been to the spiritualists a couple o' times, but I'd dee owt for that Father Dan.' The two women looked at each other, and then burst into laughter. Cheryl clinked together the two bottles of Diamond White she was holding. 'I was gonnae give it to Father Dan,' she smiled, 'but ha'way, let's gan and sit somewhere by worselves, and have a quiet drink. I feel as though I haven't seen owt o' ye since ye won.'

When they had mounted the stairs and disappeared back into Flat 12A, a lull seemed to come over the courtyard they had left behind. Those on the walkway outside the party happened to fall silent, and nobody else came and went. All that could be heard was the chum-chum of the *Party* album. The only movement: a stirring of limbs from someone sitting on the bench under the ailing willow. It was Ronny. He stretched his legs and arms, and yawned. 'Reet,' said Al in a brisk, businesslike tone. 'Where had I got to? I think I'd covered most of the pitfalls we have to avoid.'

'Al man, cannet we dee this another time? I'm bushed.'

'Oh, I see. I'm sorry if yer own welfare bores ye.'

'It's not that. It's just that I've had people in me face for a week. All telling us what I should dee. I'm proper shagged oot.'

Al beamed. 'And they're all full of crap. At a time like this, what ye need aroond ye is someone in the know. Someone what's been where ye are gannin'. Someone what's tasted the high life.'

'And where the hell am I gonnae find someone like that roond here?'

'Look nee further.'

Ronny looked about the courtyard puzzledly. 'Eh?'

Al winked. 'Yours truly.'

Just then a figure began to walk across the yard. It was the priest. 'Watch oot,' whispered Al. 'It's the enemy.'

Dan paused and peered at the bench. 'Is that you, Ronny?'

'Aye, Father,' Ronny nodded.

'Enjoying a moment's peace?'

'That's right. I'm fit to drop. Too much partying.'

'Well, I hope you clear your head a little. I'll see you later.'

'Aye, see ye later, Father.'

Dan had walked on a number of yards when Al called to him: 'Ye not gonnae say hello to me then, Father?'

'No,' he replied without stopping.

Al scoffed. 'That's not very Christian o' yus.'

'I'll say hello to you when you return that lead you stripped from the church roof.' And with that he was gone.

Al shook his head and poked Ronny confidentially in the ribs. 'He's on the make areet.' They sat for a while in silence. 'It's time to start thinking aboot the future,' Al began again at last. 'Work oot what ye want to dee. I mean, have ye any idea?'

Ronny exhaled wearily. 'I cannet even think of tomorrow let alone the future.' There was another long pause, during which Ronny began to nod off.

'I've been thinking it over,' Al said, trying to stir his friend. 'And I've decided to take it on. On a proper footing, like. As an adviser. A pukka consultant. I've decided to become your own personal mentor.' Ronny was softly slumbering. 'So I'll take that as agreed then,' said Al, rubbing his hands together. Lower and lower Ronny slumped until he was lying over the bench, forcing Al to perch on the edge. 'There's summink else I've been thinking aboot an' all,' whispered Al to himself after an interval. 'D'ye think that that Cheryl is worth another shag?' Craning his neck round, Al gazed up wistfully at Flat 12A. Still gazing up, he climbed to his feet. He stood there for a long time, utterly motionless, both eyes glinting. 'That's agreed an' all then,' he whispered at last.

Inside the flat, Audrey and Cheryl finally managed to push their way into Audrey's bedroom. An unknown couple was cavorting on the new waterbed. 'I'll give ye ten seconds,' said Audrey, 'and then I'll droon the pair o' yus.' Scrambling for clothes, the couple hurried out of the room. 'What a friggin' cheek,' said Audrey. Then she and Cheryl burst into laughter.

The waterbed left precious little space for anything else in the room. The doors of the wardrobe only opened six inches; the drawers of the dresser two or three. Cheryl sat on the bed as Audrey liberally sprayed an air freshener around the bed. A cloying Pine Fresh fragrance filled the room. Audrey dropped beside her friend, and the bed rippled. 'Bloody hell,' laughed Cheryl, 'ye'd have to be a synchronised swimmer to shag on this.'

'Stop the friggin' world,' Audrey begged, stretching out, 'I want to get off. Honestly, Chez. A week of parties. It's beginning to dee me heed.'

Cheryl lay down beside her. 'I'll have to be gannin' back to work tomorrow.' Yawning, she pursed her lips. 'I divven't kna how Peak's managed this past week. Half the bloody cleaners have been roond here on the razzle.' She smiled. 'What a week.' Cheryl lifted herself up, and propping her head on her hand, studied Audrey closely. A seriousness came over her. 'What ye gonnae dee then, Aud?'

'We're gannin' to Disney World. The whole family. It's all booked.'

'No,' her friend replied softly. 'I mean, what are yus gonnae *dee* dee?' Audrey did not answer. 'Well, ye cannet stop here, can ye?' Again Audrey did not answer. Cheryl prompted her. 'Look at this bed. There's nee room to swing a cat. Ye'll need somewhere bigger. Yus've hardly bought owt yet, but you will, and then where's it gonnae gan? Every hoosebreaker between here and Middlesborough will be camping oot on the walkway.' Cheryl thought for a few moments. 'Ye cannet stay in the Teams.' The two women looked at each other for a little while, then Audrey broke the shared glance. The waterbed rippled as she bounced off it. She lifted up the net curtain and slipping behind it, stared out of the window. 'It's the end of an era,' Cheryl pronounced as she looked over at the gauzy shape of her lifelong friend. 'Audrey McPhee leaving the Teams.' She lifted herself into a sitting position. 'Where ye gonnae gan to?'

'I've told ye,' said Audrey, stretching so that the net curtains billowed round her like a huge veil. 'We're not deciding anything until we've had wor holiday. The adviser said not to make any snap decisions.'

'Sod the adviser. Ye'll have to face facts.'

Audrey sighed. Cheryl wriggled off the waterbed, and joined her behind the curtain. 'Here,' she said, lighting two cigarettes.

Their smoke drifted through the window as they gazed down over Gateshead. The window gave a view of Windmill Hill where once the great five-wanded windmills ground corn, their sails singing in the wind. Closer could be seen the moat of the dual carriageway. Laughter exploded from the teenagers gathered on the playground that they themselves had destroyed. 'Mind ye, I thought she would have been here by now,' said Cheryl at last. She paused weightily before adding: 'Y'kna, Toni-Lee's mam.'

Audrey took a deep draw on her cigarette, her lips clenching fully round the filter. 'Aye, so did I.'

Nothing was said for a while. 'Where is she at the minute, like?' Cheryl asked.

Audrey shrugged lightly. 'Ibiza, I think.' She took another deep draw on her cigarette. 'She'll come when she hears.'

They smoked on. There was a scream from the playground, then a barrage of screeching hoots. Cheryl's voice had grown breathy. 'What aboot Terri's mam; have ye told her?'

'Terri's gonnae tell her herself. We've got a visit coming up next week.'

'But she'll have heard already, won't she? I mean, they get newspapers inside, divven't they? And they have radios.'

Audrey took a third deep pull on her cigarette and leant heavily against the window sill. All at once she seemed utterly spent. Reaching out, Cheryl laid her hand on hers. 'There's not neeone else is there?' Cheryl asked.

'What d'ye mean, man Chez?'

'The fathers of yer bairns. Will they not come roond?'

'Except for Paddy and Leeanne's dad, they divven't kna who they are.' Audrey nodded her head. 'I divven't even kna who they are.'

'And what happens if Paddy and Leeanne's dad shows his face?'

'I'll bloody hoy him back doon the stairs.' Audrey's fingers searched for the crucifix among the clutter of her other necklaces, impatiently tossing them aside until at last the totem rested in the crook of her index finger. 'See, them two years being married to him? They were the worst I've ever known.'

Cheryl rotated her cigarette between thumb and forefinger. 'I remember how he used to slap yus aboot.'

'I wouldn't stick for it now. I was just a lass meself at the time.' Audrey gazed at the crucifix. 'I'll tell ye summink, Chez. If I ever see him again, I'll kick him in the balls. And I won't stop kicking until he can get a job as a choirboy.'

They gazed at the continual, grim procession of traffic, and then at the emptiness of the Windmill Hill which rose in the orange twilight of the urban night like an ancient burial mound, its cherry trees ghostly shapes. 'And there's not neeone else,' Cheryl probed. 'Neeone else what might turn up unexpectedly? Not nee skeleton to fall oot o' the cupboard?'

'No,' Audrey answered immediately, but she grew thought-ful. Deeper and deeper the thought seemed to bury itself.

'What is it, man Aud?'

'Nowt,' snapped Audrey. A sudden need appeared to consume her. She shovelled the cigarette, wedged between wedding and middle finger, into her mouth like a starving person feeding. Sucking powerfully, she shivered with the nicotine rush. 'There's nobody else,' she added more softly, peering furtively at her friend through the cloud of smoke.

'Ha'way, man Audrey, what aren't yus telling me?'

'Eh?'

'I kna ye, and yus're keeping summink from wor.'

Audrey shook her head tersely.

Cheryl studied her a little longer. 'Well. Y'kna ye can rely on wor, Aud,' she whispered simply. 'I'll always be here for ye.'

'Aye. I kna, lass.'

There was chink of glass and Cheryl handed the two bottles of Diamond White to Audrey. 'Three million poond,' she said simply.

'Aye. Three million pound.'

The net curtain billowed a little as Cheryl's arm gestured over the view below them. 'Ye've got enough to buy this whole place.'

Clamping both bottles between her teeth, Audrey twisted the caps off. Cheryl grabbed the foaming bottles. 'In the name of the Father, the Son and the Holy Spirit,' she intoned as she began to pour the seething sweet cider over Audrey's head, 'I baptise ye the Queen of Gatesheed. Wor Lady of the tower blocks. Patron saint of every bugger what's ever bought a lottery ticket with her last poond coin!'

Audrey's full-throated laughter sounded out through the window like the call of a strange nightbird. It shimmered on the soft air for a while, and then dissipated in the fragile foliage of the willow. The sleeper beneath the tree did not wake at the sound of the laughter. Ronny lay in a delicious sleep on the wooden bench. Whatever his dreams held, they brought him no disquiet. His slumbering face, nosing cosily into his ponytail, was fixed in a broad beam.

Time passed, and the party continued to rage, although, with sheer weariness, the revellers were beginning to quieten. The three sentinels had staggered from the revels and now stood at their posts looking down over the courtyard, blinking in stupefaction. Each had a nightcap of a bottle of Babycham on the parapet at their elbows. 'Well,' yawned Jennifer, 'they've had a good time, but it cannet gan on like this for ever.'

'Why not?' Sandra demanded.

'Ye can have too much of a good thing.'

'Can ye?' Sandra asked, genuinely intrigued. 'Can ye have too much of a good thing?'

'Who says it's a good thing?' the third woman, Brenda, interjected.

'What ye talking aboot?' laughed the others. 'All that money? Nivver having to work again? Course it's a good thing.'

'Aye, but ye hear things, divven't ye?' Brenda continued gloomily. 'They're always in the papers them what win. And they're back in them six months, mebbes, a year later. When everything's gone wrong.' She paused for a moment to take a drink from her bottle of Babycham. The other two followed suit. 'Aye,' mused Brenda darkly. 'Summink usually gans arse-up.'

'There's nee way that could happen to wor Audrey,' Jennifer said. 'She's too strong-willed, man.'

Somebody crashed out of the party and leant heavily against the parapet. Puking noises were followed by the slop of liquid on the stones of the courtyard below. The puker remained there for a while, as though dazed by the experience, and by the sudden shedding of toxins; then he wiped his mouth and returned to the party. 'Doesn't look like Bill McPhee is worried aboot winning the lottery,' Jennifer chafed Brenda.

'He was nivver one to hold his drink,' Brenda said disparagingly.

There was admiration in Sandra's voice. 'He's been drinking solid for a week. Twenty pints a day, or so wor lass reckons.'

'It's Audrey and Ronny I'm worried aboot,' returned

Brenda. 'I've just got a feeling. I even heard that she walked under a ladder this morning, when she was coming back from the Londis shop with booze.'

'Nivver,' replied Jen. 'Audrey wouldn't dee a thing like that.'

There was silence, broken at last by Brenda. 'Say what ye like, there'll be trouble.'

Sandra shook her head. 'If there was any trouble brewing then Audrey would see it comin' herself.'

'Aye,' nodded Jen. 'After all, she knew she was gonnae win before the draw. The lass at the kiosk was telling us. Psychic, she reckons.'

Brenda shrugged. 'Mebbes she's lost the sight. Or her luck's changed.'

'Aye, well,' returned Sandra, 'I'd run the risk of a few tears before bedtime for three million pound.'

But Brenda was not listening. Like a drunken Cassandra, she shivered dramatically and then whispered: 'Just ye wait, it won't be many tides of the Tyne before trouble comes. Aye. Trouble. I saw it the moment she walked under that ladder.'

The sentinels continued to stand there, drinking. 'There's one thing for sure,' said Jennifer finally. 'We'll need a fourth.'

'Eh?' the other two asked.

Jennifer pointed at the three sides on which they stood. 'North, west and east,' she pronounced in turn. 'We'll need a new south. Nothing's nee good withoot a south. She's the only one what can see the dual carriageway and the shops proper.'

They stared for a while at the untenanted walkway. Then, as one, finished their drinks and retired within their own four walls.

When Ronny woke, he sat up quickly as though mysteriously refreshed by his couple of hours on the hard wooden bench. He sprang to his feet. 'Aye, that's what we'll dee!' he exclaimed to himself, his voice echoing about the courtyard.

144

The walkways were deserted. Even the queue had disappeared from outside Flat 12A. Only the thump-thump of the music could be heard. He bustled out from under the cover of the ailing tree and, with a whoop, crossed the square. He took the stairs two at a time. 'That's what we'll dee,' he chanted joyfully to himself. 'That's what we'll dee!'

He was halfway up when a sudden breathlessness disabled him. Doubling up on the concrete landing, he staggered against the cold wall. He strained for oxygen, the look of a frightened animal rolling in his eyes, his chest heaving. His breathlessness seemed only to grow worse. A tight pain seized his left side and, bewildered, he clutched his heart.

Then, all at once, it was over, and he could breathe with ease. He sank into a sitting position, gingerly flexing his left arm. Two people thundered down the stairs, and he did not even look up at them. He seemed to be in shock. Still flexing his left arm, he gaped at the cold concrete stairs.

At last he stood up and began to climb the rest of the stairs. He was still dazed when he reached the top floor. The air remained hot, but at this height the gentle, refreshing, river breeze whispered its rumours of the clean, upland interior where Cumbria, Northumbria and Durham meet. At last, with a puzzled shrug of his shoulders, Ronny carried on to the flat.

He found Audrey talking in the middle of a group of people, and marched straight over. 'Audrey,' he began, recovering his original excitement, 'I want to have a word.'

'Ronny, are ye areet?'

He nodded, urging: 'Ha'way.'

She followed him to their bedroom door. 'Ye look canny peaky, pet. Y'kna, as if yus'd seen a ghost.'

'Let's gan away,' Ronny said impulsively.

'We are gannin' away. We're gannin' to Florida a week on Wednesday.' She looked more closely at her husband. 'Honest to God, pet. You look terrible. Have you been sick or summink?'

'I'm fit as a fiddle.' He shook his head, grinning vehemently until Audrey had been persuaded. 'Let's gan away noo. This minute.' Audrey scrutinised him. 'We need to get away from all of this.' He gestured at the determined partygoers. 'We divven't even kna half of these folks.' Audrey looked about at a particularly motley crew who stood singing by the bathroom door. 'It hasn't sunk in yet, and why? Because we haven't had a second to worselves. We need a bit space.'

'But –'

'Nee buts.' Ronny laughed. 'We've won the lottery. The rules divven't apply nee more. We can dee whatever we want.'

'When, where?'

'Now. And leave the rest to me. The world's wor oyster. And talkin' of oysters, I want to see the sea again.'

'The sea?'

Ronny's mild brown eyes flickered dreamily in his pasty face. 'Aye, the sea. The deep blue sea. We'll be able to talk there.'

Audrey mused for a bit longer, then, having looked about the flat, nodded. 'A week's holiday before wor holiday of a lifetime.' She began to grow excited too. 'Tenerife, Goa, the Seychelles?'

'Better than that.' Laughing, Ronny clapped his hands.

'Better?'

Ronny took Audrey round her middle and began to dance with her. 'We're gannin' to Hartlepool!'

'Hartlepool?'

'Aye, to the caravan.'

They packed two black bin liners with bedding and a change of clothes. Terri and Toni were slumbering on the waterbed. They woke them gently and led them, still more than half asleep, through the party. As they moved through the flat, a huge drunken conga had just collapsed, and the four of them slipped through without attracting attention.

146

It was way past midnight as they led the two girls down the stairs, and then down the burrow. When Toni fell back asleep, Audrey swept her up in her arms, carrying the bin liner between her teeth. The vanette, standing just the other side of the Blarney stones roadblock, was dirtier than ever. In the grime of the back window a fresh legend had been scripted: *My other car's going to be a Porsche.* Audrey glowered at the clapped-out vehicle. 'We'll have to get a new car.'

'Ye kna what we agreed. Nee big decisions until we've been to Disney World.'

Audrey sighed dreamily. 'It's a dream come true. Taking the bairns to Disney World.'

The vanette started eventually in a dirty explosion of thick black exhaust smoke. In the back, the girls slept among the half-bags of cement and shovels on a nest of duvets. Audrey scooped away the detritus of McDonald's waste and other fast-food trash from the front. 'It's like a skip in here, man Ronny.'

'Aye, well, we used to get hungry gannin' up and doon them ladders.'

Set off by the motion of the vanette, the navvy began to pull his endless moonies. Audrey dropped an empty paper cup over his leering head. 'I divven't kna why yus bothered with this when ye've got the real thing.' She smiled, but as she gazed at her husband a look of concern grew on her face. 'Are ye sure ye're areet, pet?'

'Course I am, love.'

'Yer colour's all drained away.'

'I'm fine. How could I not be when I'm on me way to Hartlepool with me baby beside wor at the wheel?'

'No, man, I'm being serious.' She paused for a moment. 'Before, in the flat, ye really looked bad. I mean, ye really looked ill. Are ye sure there's nowt the matter?'

For an instant, a look of uneasiness flickered over Ronny's features, then he dismissed it with a grin. 'Just a bad pint. Nowt that a couple of days in auld Hartlepool cannet sort.'

9

Al found Cheryl at last in the queue to Carl's Pie Cart, a fast-food caravan which from time to time parked up outside the beaten-up parade of Teams shops. She was three or four people ahead of him and when she happened to turn, she caught him gazing at her. She looked away. But when she turned back, he was still looking. She snorted haughtily. 'Pie and chips,' she said to Carl when it was her turn at the hatch. 'And mushy peas.'

'There's nee mushy peas left,' sighed Carl, a large, melancholy individual in an apron which might once have been white.

Unabashed, Big Al stared at Cheryl as she administered her salt and vinegar. The ketchup bottle farted as she squeezed it peevishly. 'I'll pay for hers,' he called.

With her nose in the air, and the steam coming off her food, she passed Al, brushing him lightly with the tip of her elbow. Al's opaque eye glinted at the sight of her so close, while his belly rumbled at the smell of the food. His eyes followed her distractedly, while his nose pulled him back to the pie cart. There was a brief tussle within him during which he looked now at Cheryl and now at the chalkboard menu, which simply said: ALL KINDS OF PIES + CHIPS. After a few moments of struggle, Al pulled himself from the queue and lumbered after Cheryl.

He caught up with her in the burrow. 'What the hell do ye want?' she demanded.

'Nowt.' Al tried to appear nonchalant.

'If yus're following me, ye can fuck reet off.'

'I'm just walking,' he said, adding lamely, 'it's a free country, isn't it?' Al followed her across the courtyard. 'Are ye gannin' back to the party or what?'

'What's it got to dee with ye, five-bellies?'

'Where ye gannin' then?'

'Hyem.'

Cheryl entered the foyer door to the east-facing flats and pushed the lift button. It opened, and she went inside. Al had to push back the closing door to get in beside her. The lift began to rise. 'Cheryl,' Al blurted, 'do ye remember that time in Washingwell Woods?'

A mocking hoot reverberated in the lift. Uncharacteristically, Al grinned obsequiously, cringing like a cur when the hoot grew crueller. Only once or twice did he look at her food. His gaze seemed riveted on Cheryl's face as her mouth chewed chips disdainfully. 'And yus're not getting any o' this,' she said, biting into a pie. The gravy dribbled down her chin. Al shivered slightly at the sight.

The lift reached Cheryl's floor, and she got out. 'I've started thinking aboot ye all the time,' he called after her. 'I keep on thinking of when ye and me —' But the door to the lift closed, and he felt the sinking beneath his feet. As the lift descended, he closed his eyes and breathed in tenderly. On the odour of the pie and chips, he could now detect the fragrance of Cheryl's Impulse body spray. He groaned with yearning.

Stumbling across the courtyard, he collapsed on the wooden bench. Reaching very carefully into a pocket, he brought out a tiny, seemingly frail object. It was the gorse bloom he had picked from Washingwell Woods.

With his eyes closed, he was holding the bloom to his nose, dried now and brittle, when he felt someone sitting down beside him. His heart missed a beat. 'Is that ye?' he whispered, almost tenderly.

There was no response for a moment, then suddenly, shockingly, the bloom was knocked from his fingers by a powerful blow. Yelping with annoyance, Al opened his eyes. 'Areet, Al five-bellies,' Jimmy greeted him. The anger evaporated from Al's features, replaced by fear. 'I hear ye've got summink for us,' the baby-faced youth said. Al nodded. He began to root about in a pocket. But his fingers fumbled nervously. At last he managed to find what he was searching for, and presented Jimmy with a wad of notes.

'From Ronny,' Al explained quickly. 'Y'kna him what –' Al broke off abruptly.

'Won the lottery?' Jimmy finished for him.

'He borrowed two hundred quid.'

Jimmy snatched the money. 'But it's five hundred quid with the interest payments.'

'Aye,' said Al. 'There's five hundred quid there.' He looked at Jimmy nervously, and tried to smile ingratiatingly. 'Now, that's him done,' he said. 'He won't be borrowing nowt more.' Al tried to get up but found Jimmy had pressed him back with a hand.

'What's all of this to ye, five-guts?' the youth demanded.

'Nowt.' Al shrugged with an attempt at nonchalance. 'Just passing on a message.'

Jimmy's tone was bloodless. 'Divven't play the prick. He must be a mate o' yours or summink, to have given ye that money just now.'

Al looked wretchedly about the courtyard, then, as though swelling with a sudden reckless, helpless pride which his jackdaw nature could not help but vaunt, said: 'I'm his number two, aren't I.'

Jimmy's laughter creaked round the square. 'Thunderbirds are gan, or what.' Al grinned feebly while desperately casting about the square, searching for a way of escape. Abruptly, Jimmy stopped laughing and moved closer to Al, causing him to inch away deferentially. He moved right along the bench, but at last could go no further. He felt the press of Jimmy's leg against his. Jimmy's breath felt cold on his face as he said: 'I think mebbes ye and me can come to a business arrangement, Mr Number Two.'

'What d'ye mean, Jimmy?'

'Ha'way, man fatty, ye're not gonnae keep the golden goose to yersel', are ye?' Jimmy took one of Al's cheeks between his thumb and forefinger. Playfully, he rattled it. When he withdrew his hand, an angry welt ran across the skin. 'Ye and me are gonnae come to some arrangement.'

'Arrangement?' Al's face twitched.

'Aye. He's won the friggin' lottery, hasn't he? I think he can afford more than five hundred. I think wor Ronny can lay us a whole load o' lovely golden eggs. If he's handled properly. And that's where ye come in, number two, five-bellies.'

10

The traffic on the dual carriageway was light at that hour, and the vanette quickly passed through the Team Valley Trading Estate. It rattled under the embrace of the Angel of the North which, in the corroded dust of the urban night, was as rusty-seeming as the acre of seeding sheep sorrel in which it stood. Beyond the span of its wings twinkled the lonely lights of the Beacon Lough tower blocks.

On its way to the A19, the vanette threaded through the skirts of the Metropolitan Borough, then laboured up the rising hinterland of tussocky grass and tethered skewbald ponies where the winds of Gateshead, Sunderland and Washington mingled. It crossed the high bridge over the River Wear. Far below could be seen the metal skeletons of old steam packets and tugboats embedded in the mud, and revealed at every tide. On the banks of this river, close to the great grey North Sea, lay the shipwright city of Sunderland.

The dirty vanette continued on its ponderous, shaking progress, drilling a way bluntly through the East Durham coalfield, the signposts a litany from the harrowing of the mining industry: Houghton-le-Spring, Seaham, Murton, Eas-ington, Shotton, Trimdon, Horden, Blackhall and Peterlee. Each name a pithead of syllables crouching at shafts of toil, generations deep. 'Wynyard Hall,' mused Audrey, reading out another, newly erected signpost. 'Nivver heard o' that before.'

'Hasn't been built long,' Ronny replied. He looked in his driving mirror and then elbowed Audrey. 'Look at the pair o' them bairns; sleeping like a litter o' puppies.'

The thin tink-plish tink-plish of the indicator light sounded as Ronny pulled out to pass a vehicle even slower than his. It was a small wagon with a cement mixer and stack of shovels in its open hold. 'Yee-ha!' Ronny whooped, waving at the wagon as they inched past it. 'Cowboys oot riding the range. Why, it takes one to kna one.'

'Them days are over,' said Audrey.

'Aye, they are,' replied Ronny as though just realising this for the first time. The indicator light continued to tink-plish; a blow on the hub of the steering wheel from Ronny's fist finally silencing it.

They came to another sign for Wynyard Hall. 'Why does it get two?' Audrey asked.

'Eh?' said Ronny, pulling himself back from a reverie.

'Why does that Wynyard Hall get two signposts?'

'Oh, that.' Ronny tugged lightly at his ponytail. 'Only the most expensive hoosing estate in the whole of the north-east. What's-his-name built it.'

'Who?'

'Ye kna. The same gadgie what did the Metro Centre. Sir John Hall, that's him.'

Audrey peered over the dark fields towards the development. 'Can anybody just live there?'

'Aye, anybody with a few hundred grand up their sleeve.'

Impulsively, Audrey turned to Ronny. 'Can we turn off here and have a quick look?'

'Na. We cannet. It's all cut off, isn't it? Security guards and a road block. To keep the plebs oot.'

'Who stops there then?'

'Anybody who's anybody in the region. Put it this way, man Audrey. Kev Keegan used to.'

'And Tony Blair?'

'Eh?'

'Does Tony Blair live there then?'

Ronny shook his head. 'They haven't come to that yet, thank God. New Labour. Na. He lives in Trimdon Colliery.'

Audrey wrinkled her nose in thought. 'Isn't that where that other Tony lives an' all?'

'What other Tony?'

'Ye kna him. Tony what's-his-name. Used to have a blind dog. And a nose like a bottle.'

'Oh aye. Tony Greft. Na. He lives in Shotton Colliery. That dog of his used to lock its jaw on wood. Once it hung from the beam above the bar in the Collier's Rest for an hour. D'ye remember? Used to sup ale from an old chamber pot.'

For the third time, a signpost for Wynyard Hall came up on the side of the road. 'Let's turn off,' urged Audrey.

'I've told ye, man, it's all sealed up . . .'

'But we can just look at it from the outside.'

'Why, man Audrey?'

Her voice grew compelling. 'Three times I saw the sign. Mebbes it's meant to be.'

'I hope not,' countered Ronny. 'I couldn't bloody stand living there with them nobs.'

'Divven't talk daft, man Ronny.'

'How am I talking daft?'

'Well, we're nobs now, man.' Ronny shifted uncomfortably in his seat. 'Listen, pet,' said Audrey in a reasonable tone, 'we've got to be thinking of moving somewhere.'

Ronny's face rippled with puzzlement. His mouth gaped a little. 'What, leave Gatesheed?'

'I'm not saying that. Not necessarily. But we'll have to shift to some place.' Audrey broke off to look at her husband. He was fidgeting distractedly with his ponytail, his face full of apprehension. 'We've won the lottery, love,' she said softly. 'We cannet stay in them flats for ever.' She paused for a few moments. 'It's gonnae be all change, Ronny pet.'

Suddenly Ronny wriggled his back against the seat as though to scratch an itch. The wriggling became more intense. 'Ha'way, pet,' he pleaded, 'I'm driving.' Audrey leant over and began to scratch him on the small of the back. 'Up a bit,' he begged. 'Across a bit. Now doon a smidgen. Aye, that's it.'

'Ronny man, ye cannet avoid the question for much langer, y'kna. We've got to −'

'Both hands, man Audrey,' he demanded. 'Both hands.'

Sighing, Audrey began to scratch her husband's back with both hands. A look of ecstasy came over him. 'That's it.'

'Ronny, we've got to face the future.'

'Well, pet, we divven't need to decide. Not yet. We've got Disney World to enjoy first. Wor holiday of a lifetime. And Hartlepool.'

'We cannet put it off for ever, mind. We'll have to come to grips.'

The plateau of the East Durham coalfield began to run down to a wide, marshy coastal flat. From one horizon to another, lit up by bright lights and pipe flames, stretched the tortured metal forest of countless petrochemical installations. In the brittle scrub of these endless steel thickets grew colossal cooling towers and smoke-belching chimneys: the dreaming spires of Teesside. Ronny smiled. 'A sight for sore eyes.'

Vast concrete edifices; uncoiling intestines of pipes; huge spherical containers webbed by an ivy of clinging, climbing gantries; plantation after plantation of humming, pendulous pylons; and there, right in the heart of this unimaginable tract of girder, rod and rivet: the Transporter Bridge, the inter-locked beaks of two giant cranes kissing over the sad waters of the gentle, sloe-black Tees. And beyond that, on the south bank, the vast orange dunes of the iron-ore piles in among which the steel works shimmered like an unlovely mirage.

A thick, multicoloured smog hung above the whole place, forming a dense, permanent primeval dusk. Here and there the luminous flames of gas pipes pricked the mist like giant will-o-the-wisps.

The indicator light tink-plished back into life as they turned from the dual carriageway and followed the supine course of a giant metal pipe. The indicator light continued to sound, this time silencing only on the second blow of Ronny's fist. After some slow miles through dereliction, they skirted the shell of an Empire Social Club and passed between two vast cooling towers. Emerging, they found themselves in a wide, empty, flat expanse of rough pasture fretted with dykes. It was as though they had plunged from the dark satanic mills and come out on to the fens of Cambridgeshire.

In the midst of this expanse, a number of miles across and framed entirely by the precincts of a poisonous industry, was a signpost. Standing in a fathom of creek water, its lettering was corroded by salt, the name it bore only just decipherable. 'Hartlepool,' nodded Ronny smilingly. A curlew, standing on the sign, rose at the vanette's approach, and was caught in the headlights. Its eerie call sounded over the fen. 'Hartlepool,' Ronny repeated.

While the lights of Hartlepool were still at some distance, the vanette bumped off the road on to a rudimentary track running between sand dunes. The indicator light was jogged back into life. This time even three blows on the nub of the steering wheel did nothing to silence it, and it continued to sound as they penetrated further into the dunes. At last they reached a place of flattened sand. 'Belter,' said Toni-Lee drowsily, having been shaken awake. 'It's the caravan.'

There were about ten of them drawn up wagon-train fashion against the prevailing sea winds. They were not large caravans, nor were they plush, and most seemed riveted with rust. Many of the tyres had been punctured. There were only two that appeared habitable behind their shrivelled net curtains. On the ground around one of these stood a few garden ornaments which Ronny tripped over as he excitedly carried the bin liners to it. Audrey followed with the sleepy girls.

It was small inside, but cosy. There was no sink or toilet, but a bunk bed, and a plastic-topped table, whose seating pulled out to form a small double bed. 'Good news,' Ronny greeted the others. 'Nee new leaks.' Having fetched water from the tap in the stark toilet block, Ronny assembled a little camping stove and began to boil a kettle. 'I've always loved Hartlepool, me,' Ronny chuntered. 'I used to come here with me mam and dad. It was the only place me dad used to really enjoy himself at. He loved it here, me auld dad. Christ, he had a hard time. Me mam had his life. But whenever he came here he –' Ronny broke off. 'Are ye areet, pet?'

'Course,' Audrey replied. 'I was just clearing me throat.'

Ronny continued to gaze at his wife for a while. 'What is it, love? Ye seem . . . sad or summink.'

'It's nowt. I'm just tired, Ronny.'

By the time the tea was ready, the girls lay fast asleep in the bunks, and Audrey sat slumped over the plastic-topped table. She too slept.

Placing the plastic cups of tea carefully on the table, Ronny slid into the seat opposite Audrey as quietly as he could. Motionless, he studied his wife. All he could see behind the tresses of her pillowing hair was the curve of a cheek and the tip of her nose. Reaching out gently, his work-calloused fingers hovered over her as though to offer a blessing. Then, overcome by the strength of his emotion, he closed his own eyes. His snoring soon filled the caravan.

He woke up to find Audrey staring rigidly through the little window. The blackness of the sea could be made out beyond the pane, strung with the lonesome lights of the container and bulker ships awaiting entrance to Teesport. He did not know how long he had been sleeping, but his plastic tea cup had gone cold. The light from the paraffin lantern caught Audrey's reflection in the window. Ronny's eye narrowed at the look on her face. It was one of lingering brooding. 'Audrey . . .'

Audrey jumped with shock, knocking over the cups. The tea cascaded over the edge of the table, soaking into Ronny's suit. 'Ronny man, ye gave us the shock of me life.'

Ronny looked at her in confusion, a hand worrying the tip of his ponytail. When he had stripped off into a pair of shorts and his donkey jacket, he said with a forced briskness: 'I'll make another cup of tea, shall I?' But Audrey did not seem to notice the fresh tea when he placed the cups on the table, or even Ronny. 'What's the matter, pet?' he asked at last.

Her jaw was clamped tightly, her eyes were distant. Ronny peered at her helplessly. Their shadows, cast by the paraffin lantern, hung motionless on the ceiling of the caravan, twitching occasionally as the flame bobbed in the draught which came in through the open door of the caravan. Ronny gazed up at these shadows as though mesmerised by them. The rise and fall of the sea rinsing the shore could just be heard.

A sudden darting of the shadows jerked him from his absorption. He looked down. Audrey had risen abruptly. 'Audrey pet,' he called softly.

She turned to answer from the door, and a sob tore from her.

Face contorted with bewilderment, Ronny went to her. 'Silly bitch,' she was castigating herself through clenched teeth. 'Silly, silly bitch. Weeping cannet mend nowt.' There was an audible crump of knuckle on bone as she punched herself full in the face, staggering under the strength of the blow.

'Audrey man!'

As she jumped, Audrey's shoulder struck the door surround, causing the whole caravan to shudder on its wheels. Panicking, Ronny hurried to the door. Already she was on the sea defences, climbing recklessly down the concrete blocks and stone boulders down into the darkness of the beach below.

He found her standing in the sea. A wave, still fizzing at her knees, had soaked her dress. 'Hey,' he appealed softly. She did not turn. Stumbling into the water, Ronny staggered at the thrust of a powerful wave. 'I've nivver seen ye cry before, pet,' he whispered when he drew level with her.

'I wasn't crying.' She turned to look at him but in her smile he could still see the sadness.

'What's the matter?' he asked, baffled. She shook her head. 'Audrey, what's the matter?'

'It doesn't matter,' she replied.

'But . . .'

'It doesn't matter.'

For a long time neither of them spoke. Behind them the blocks of the coastal defences towered, to their left and right the beach stretched like a curlew's beak towards the many jetties of Hartlepool. In front of them was the sea.

The tide was ebbing, and all along the foreshore could be seen pricks of light: the lamps by which the sea coalers of Hartlepool work, men who gather the coal brought in on the tides. 'Me cousin Warren'll be doon there somewhere,' said Ronny. 'It'll be good to see him again. That's why we used to come here. Every holiday. Me mam's sister lived here. The two of them were so busy gabbing that it gave me dad chance to breathe.' Ronny broke off. 'What's the matter, love?'

'Come on.' Taking his hand, Audrey began to wade further out in to the sea.

'It's bloody freezing,' he groaned. A wave broke at his middle. 'Reet in the ye-kna-whats.'

With a sudden laugh, Audrey ran at her husband, spraying great fans of water. Retaliating, he soaked her too. They grew more and more boisterous. Playing like children, their voices rang over the sea. They wrestled each other back to the shallows, and fell on soft sand. 'I think it's beginning to sink in,' Audrey whispered.

'Aye,' returned Ronny and then he whooped.

'Nee more scrimping and saving. Nee more twocking from Peter to keep Paul off wor backs.'

'Nee more gannin' up ladders . . .'

'And doon malls . . .'

'Nee more.'

'Nee more.'

'Audrey man, what was the matter before?'

Beyond them the sea heaved massively. At the Tees mouth peninsula a blast furnace winked like some infernal lighthouse. 'I love ye, Ronny Slater.' Audrey's voice was as tender as the breeze coming from the sea on the hot air of August. 'I love ye with all me heart, and every other part o' wor.' Their lips came close. 'I used to think we were so lucky. Having each other. And all the family. But now we've got it all. D'ye hear me, my love? Now we've got everything there is to have.'

As the lottery winners kissed, the lights of the containers and bulkers continued to twinkle beyond the bar. From time to time the blast furnace winked. And, all along the beach, the men with the lamps collected the coal brought to them by the retreating tide. 'Aye,' whispered Ronny when their kiss broke. 'Now we've got everything there is to have.'

Chapter Three

I

After the hot summer, a mild autumn came to the Metropolitan Borough of Gateshead.

Feasting on the seed heads of September, the goldfinches travelled the thistle roads, those disused branch lines and colliery railways that network the old coalfield of County Durham from Hartlepool to the Metro Centre. And as the green growth of summer began to die back, the wastelands of Gateshead revealed more of their origins: the foundations of a workshop under what had been an impenetrable tangle of brambles since May; a little beehive of bricks, small remnant of the kiln apiaries, exposed by the dying back of nettles; and everywhere, four or five to each square mile, shown by the black ash soil emerging from under dying grass, the earthworks of extinct coal pits.

A dirty white vanette was crossing the Tyne Bridge from Gateshead to Newcastle. The driver was a bald man with a long ponytail. He was wearing a pair of Mickey Mouse ears. The woman in the passenger seat wore a skimpy white T-shirt, its large swell emblazoned with the word HOOTERS. Her hair had recently been dyed black and permed. She was examining the deep red gloss on the nails of her manicured hands. A massive golden crucifix lay over the letters OT of her T-shirt. 'I'm telling ye, Ronny pet,' said the woman, 'this is the one for us.' The driver did not reply. The woman lifted up a plush brochure from her lap, and waved it under her husband's nose. On its cover was written: NEW HOMES OF DISTINCTION.

'I'm trying to drive, man Audrey,' Ronny complained.

Suspicion narrowed Audrey's eyes. 'Ye haven't even looked at this, have yus?'

'Course I have.'

'Well, what did ye think of it then?' Ronny shrugged. Audrey turned to the two girls in the back of the vanette. Both of them wore God Bless America T-shirts. 'Me and the cwins think it's ace, divven't we, lasses?'

'Why aye,' said Toni-Lee turning from the grimy back doors through which, with a camcorder, she had been filming their passage over the bridge.

'It's mint,' nodded Terri-Leigh without looking up from her giant, fully illustrated copy of *The Hobbit*.

'Aye,' nodded Audrey solemnly. 'I've got the feeling that this is really gonnae be the one. Wor future home.' She mused on this. 'Y'kna how I thought we were gonnae win the lottery? Well, this is the same feeling.'

Ronny grunted.

'What's the matter with ye?' she demanded. 'Ye've got a face like fat.'

'Nowt's the matter.' Ronny shooed away Toni-Lee's camcorder which was now zooming in to film his face.

Audrey sighed. 'It's because we're gannin' to look at a hoose, isn't it?'

'Course not,' he retorted evasively.

'I'm gettin' sick of this, Ronny. Ye're already working oot a reason for not liking it, aren't ye? And it's been the same ever since we got back from Florida.'

'It's not my fault. When ye've been on as many roofs as I have, ye get bush eyes.'

'Well, ye need a bloody pair of specs then, 'cos there cannet have been something wrong with all of them. We've seen more than twenty since coming back from Florida.'

They drove along the urban clearway to the northern

suburbs of Newcastle. 'Hey,' chuckled Ronny suddenly. 'It was brilliant in Florida, but, wasn't it?'

Audrey smiled at the memory. 'A real holiday of a lifetime.' But tightening her grip on the estate agent's brochure, she shook her head. 'We've been back for a fortnight now, Ronny, and we're nee nearer moving.' For no reason at all the vanette's indicator began to tink-plish. Ronny did not even bother to try and punch it into submission. 'And I swear doon,' Audrey continued, 'if ye divven't gan and get that new car, I'll just gan and hire one.'

'Wait until we've moved,' reasoned Ronny. 'Then we'll get the cars. It's a big decision. A couple of new cars. We divven't want to rush it.'

'Rush it? If we gan any slower we'll be deed by the time we get sorted.'

They turned off the dual carriageway and Ronny accelerated at a speed bump. The indicator light stopped its drone. 'Take all small children by the hand and secure all jewellery,' Ronny boomed in an American accent as they rode another traffic bump. He laughed to himself. 'Them rides were summink, mind, weren't they? In Florida. Them rides were –'

'Ronny man, the rest o' wor love this hoose. We want it. It's time to move.'

They came at last to the Meadowings, a so-called Prestige Development of large mock-Tudor houses squatting on the green belt. 'That's the one,' said Audrey. 'The one with the treble garage.'

'Loads of footballers live here, y'kna,' said Toni, thrusting the camcorder between Audrey and Ronny to film the houses.

Audrey nodded. 'There ye gan. Yus'll be able to gan for a pint with Alan Shearer.'

Three BMWs stood on the drive. The nearest number plate declared: TRISH 5. Ronny began to back up. 'I just cannet believe we're still gannin' aboot in this auld banger of a vanette,' said Audrey in despair. But her despair disappeared into a paroxysm of joy as she got out and stood there gaping at the house.

Ronny grimly tweaked his Mickey Mouse ears and pulled his ponytail. 'Let's see the worst then.'

'It's a fairy tale,' whispered Audrey, tottering to the huge front door as fast as her tight white pedal-pusher trousers and towering high heels would allow. She pulled a wrought-iron bell pull, and the Big Ben chimes could be heard sounding cavernously. 'Classy,' she nodded, impressed.

The owner of TRISH 5 answered the door. 'Yes, can I help you?' she asked suspiciously, her accent recognisably from the Essex marshes despite efforts at geographical camouflage. Her dyed blonde hair showed dark roots.

Audrey beamed. 'Y'areet, hinny?' Trish looked down in puzzlement. Toni-Lee was filming her; Terri had her nose buried in her book. Ronny was striding across the stretch of bowling-green grass which made up the front lawn. Still wearing his Mickey Mouse ears, he was carrying a garden fork. 'What the hell are ye deein', Ronny man?' Audrey shouted. She turned back to Trish. 'It's Mr and Mrs Slater and family. We've come to view the property.'

Trish looked doubtfully at the vanette. 'Oh.'

There was a crisp rasp as the prongs of the fork pierced the lawn. 'It's as I thought,' Ronny called over. 'It's sodden.'

Audrey dashed over and, snatching the fork, hurled it away like a javelin. 'This is Ronny,' Audrey explained, shunting Ronny to the doorstep, 'and if he doesn't stop deein' me heed in, I'm gonnae hoy him in the Tyne.' With an apologetic sigh, Ronny began trudging back to the vanette. 'Where the hell are ye gannin', Ronny Slater?' Audrey shrilled.

Ronny did not turn. 'It's only September and me prongs came back wet. The water table's sky-high. See, the Meadow-ings? It's built on a flood plain.' He turned apologetically to Trish. 'Sorry, pet. But come the turn of the year I divven't

163

fancy being on *Look North* carrying a bairn in each arm through waist-high water.'

Nothing was said for a long time on the return journey. At last Ronny broke the silence. 'Look, pet, let's gan and have another look roond the estate agent's if that's what ye want.'

'What's the point? Ye divven't like anywhere. Anyway, I've got to gan and meet Cheryl and them in the Metro Centre.' Audrey sighed. 'This cannet go on much langer, Ronny man. I mean, anyone would think ye didn't want to leave the Teams.'

Suddenly Ronny threw the wheel. The other vehicles beeped angrily as the vanette lumbered across lanes. The half-bags of cement, shovels and other building equipment which still remained in the back, slid across with the two cousins. 'Careful,' said Audrey sharply. Leaving the stream of traffic heading for the Tyne Bridge, Ronny drove down to the quayside. He bumped up on to the kerb, and hurriedly got out. His face was animated.

He was halfway across the low swing bridge when he clambered up on to the wooden railing, and jumped. 'Bloody hell!' gasped Audrey, running after him.

'Has Granda Ronny gone for a swim?' asked Toni-Lee, following with her camcorder.

They spotted him down on one of the pier-like wooden pontoons on which the swing bridge rests. He was sitting right at the far end, where the cormorants often perch with their wings held out to dry. 'Yous wait here,' Audrey ordered her granddaughters, and, ignoring the DANGER UNSAFE sign, she vaulted the railings.

The decaying wood creaked beneath her feet. Through the many missing planks, she could see the river flowing. Audrey sat down beside Ronny, and with their feet dangling together, the gulls flying just above them and the river breeze caressing their faces, they gazed at the Gateshead bank. The flats and red roofs of the Teams peeped out from a great swathe of greenery. From somewhere came the scream of kittiwakes.

'We always used to come here as bairns,' said Ronny, breaking the silence at last. 'Ye weren't supposed to, but we did. To watch the boats.' He extended a foot. 'Sometimes they got that close. Ye could smell what the crew were gonnae have for their tea.' He laughed, but as his gaze travelled back up the river, he grew solemn. 'It's all changed so much now, Audrey. Gateshead. Like a different place. Y'kna. Somewhere else. Not here. Sometimes I wonder where I am.' For a few moments he seemed lost in bewilderment, then he smiled. He pointed at the view. 'The thing is, but, pet, it's still home. It's still, y'kna, hyem.' He took his wife's hand and jumped up with fresh enthusiasm. 'I've got to show you summink. It's been on me mind since before we went to Florida.'

'Careful on them friggin' planks,' warned Audrey as they picked their way back to where Terri and Toni waited patiently: one reading, one filming proceedings. 'It's been a lang time since ye were a bairn, and even langer since ye weighed four stone two.'

They returned to the Teams, pulling up at one of the recently demolished streets. Having scrambled to the middle of a huge mound of rubble, Ronny sank to his knees and began to dig, lifting the broken bricks and concrete with his bare hands. 'Ronny man,' Audrey demanded, 'what the hell are ye deein'?' Like a man possessed, Ronny ripped at the debris, hurling it aside. With a whoop of triumph, he pulled out a long, thin object. It was a street sign. Giggling excitedly, Ronny held it out to the cousins, who took it and held it between them. 'Y'kna what this means, divven't ye, Aud?' he shouted.

Audrey drew out a Superking from her cigarette purse. She placed it carefully in her mouth and lit it. 'Keir Hardie Avenue,' she said, reading the street sign.

Ronny threw his arms out wide. 'I was born here,' he

yelled. 'And this?' He frantically gestured at the rubble beneath his feet. 'Would ye say this is aboot where number 19 was, Audrey?'

Having kicked off her heels, Audrey was walking towards him. She went a few yards beyond where he stood. 'So this would be number 21,' she said quietly.

'Ha'way over here, lasses,' Ronny called to Terri and Toni. They scampered to him. He was sitting on an old toilet. 'This is where ah was born, man cwins.' He pointed to Audrey. 'And there? That's where yer nana first saw the light of day.' The girls rushed over to their grandmother. 'Why leave what we've always known?' Ronny demanded exuberantly. 'We don't need to move. We can dee it the other way.' He plucked off his Mickey Mouse ears and hurled them up in the air. Then climbed up on to the toilet. 'We were born here,' he cried, his feet dancing precariously round the rim. 'Why shift? Make Mahomet come to the friggin' mountain.'

After this frenzied shouting, the silence of the derelict place seemed ghostly, like that of a battlefield after the fighting has passed on. With one hand Toni-Lee held the sign, with the other she held up the camcorder to her eye, trained on Ronny who had just stepped off the toilet and now stood on the rubble of Keir Hardie Avenue with the pair of Mickey Mouse ears in his hand and the wild look of a prophet in his eye. A moment later, Audrey's laugh rang out. 'Well?' Ronny asked.

Audrey nodded. 'Well, well, well.'

'But d'ye think it's a good idea? We could build exactly what we want. Just here. A swimming pool. Tanning studio. A snooker room. And all here. A mansion. On Keir Hardie Avenue.'

2

On its way from the rubble of Keir Hardie Avenue to the Metro Centre, the dirty white vanette drove under the

Dunston Rocket. Then it pulled past the hulk of the flour mill, and rattled on alongside the Tyne. In the back, placed between the two cousins, lay the Keir Hardie Avenue sign. At last the vanette entered the Green Quadrant car park.

'I divven't believe this,' said Audrey. Al was standing in the only empty parking space. He had with him a bag on wheels stuffed to capacity. 'How the hell did he kna we were coming here? I thought I was the one what was supposed to be psychic.'

'I've telt ye,' said Ronny. 'It's instinct.'

'Aye, well, find another space.'

They found nowhere else to park. And as they drove back to Al, he was still at his spot, beckoning them as he shooed away another vehicle.

'He's not coming with us to meet Cheryl and the other lasses from work,' Audrey said. 'Cheryl said he's been pestering her to death.'

'He fancies her, man,' explained Ronny simply.

'Aye, well, she doesn't want owt to dee with him.' Audrey shivered. 'I mean, look at him. He's always oot for number one. I wouldn't trust him as far as I could throw him. Ha'way, gan roond once more. Someone might have come back to their car.'

The vanette began yet another circuit of the car park. 'Keir Hardie Towers,' mused Ronny. 'It's got a ring to it.'

Audrey smiled. 'Ronny love, I think it's a brainwave.'

'D'yus really think so?'

'Why aye! The more I think aboot it.'

The vanette stopped abruptly. Leaning over, the two kissed, ignoring the camcorder and the beep of the cars stuck behind them.

As soon as the vanette backed into the space, Al opened the door for Audrey. 'Remember, Ronny,' Audrey said, ignoring Al, 'I'll see ye at the Hoose of Fraser restaurant at twelve.' Ronny groaned. 'What's the matter with ye?'

167

'Ye kna ye cannet get a decent bacon stotty there.'

'Aye, well, ye cannet expect wor to gan to Gatesheed market noo that we're millionaires.'

By the time Ronny climbed out of the vanette, Audrey and Toni-Lee had gone. Terri-Leigh stood leaning against the bonnet, reading. 'And how's me millionaire this morning?' Al greeted Ronny.

'Canny as can be.'

Al turned to Terri-Leigh and stared at her. 'What's that cousin of yours always poking a camera in yer face for?'

'She's making a film,' Terri replied.

'What aboot?'

Terri shrugged. 'Everything.'

As the three of them walked through the thronged car park to the Green Quadrant entrance, Ronny stared at the bag on wheels Al was pulling. Al winked. 'Ye wouldn't believe the paperwork involved in being your personal assistant, Ronny lad.' They entered the centre. 'I've been deein' some more research on new motors. Yer mouth'll water fit to fill the Tyne when ye see the size of the engines. Oh aye, I've put me thinking cap on aboot the move an' all.'

'We've had some thoughts aboot that worselves,' Ronny said quietly.

At this hour on a Saturday morning, the Metro Centre was packed. As they negotiated the shoppers Ronny explained excitedly about Keir Hardie Towers. 'Ye're joking, aren't ye?' Al responded as he sat down in the café at Littlewoods.

'Belter idea, isn't it?'

Al shook his head. 'I think you're extracting the Michael, Ronny lad.' He looked over to where Terri-Leigh stood in the queue to the food counter, nose deep in her book. 'Ye'd better make that two chocolate brownies, Terri pet,' he called. 'Two just for me, that is.' Al licked his lips. 'I cannet help but think of what ye were telling wor aboot America. Y'kna, the size o' the portions. Sounds just like my kind of place . . .'

'Al man. I'm not joking. Aboot building a hoose in the Teams.'

'Keir Hardie Towers?' said Al witheringly. 'Why divven't ye just gan the whole hog and move into yer friggin' allotment?' Al broke off to call over to Terri-Leigh again. 'Remember to get them to put an extra sausage on me all-day breakfast, an' all, love.'

'Doesn't have to be called Keir Hardie Towers,' Ronny reasoned. 'We could call it Keir Hardie Hall. Or just Keir Hardie House.'

'Ronny, Ronny, Ronny,' Al overruled him patronisingly. 'Yus're forgetting the golden rule aboot a good gaff. One: near to a good local. Two: next door to a piece of hot totty. Three . . .' Al snorted. 'Three, the Teams is a shitehole.'

'Aye,' nodded Ronny. 'But it's our shitehole.'

The arrival of the food stifled the argument. For five solid minutes the two men ate in silence, knives and forks chattering noisily against the rapidly emerging plate pattern. Ronny's ponytail swayed slightly in time to his shovelling motions, and as Al scooped the bacon, eggs and sausage into his mouth, his opaque eye closed with pleasure. When their cups of tea had been refilled once from the metal pot, Al emitted a connoisseur's belch, then reached into his bag on wheels. He brought out a load of envelopes and placed them on the table. Then he reached down for another load, and laid them out. Again and again he dipped down to bring out envelopes, until eventually, losing patience, he picked up the bag on wheels and tipped out the contents. Looking on in puzzlement, Ronny only just managed to lift away their empty plates before the deluge covered them. Every inch of the table was covered in envelopes. He looked questioningly at Al. 'Paperwork,' Al shrugged.

They were all addressed to Ronny and Audrey. And had all been opened. 'What's gannin' on?' Ronny asked.

Al was leaning back on two legs of his chair, idly picking his teeth with a plastic tea stirrer. 'It began when ye were in Florida. After a few days I arranged with Marco just to drop them off at me hooseboat instead.'

'Marco?'

'Postman.'

Ronny's face screwed in confusion. 'The postman's been dropping wor post off at your hooseboat?'

'Well, technically no. 'Cos technically it's not an address. The hooseboat. With me not paying cooncil tax an' that. And technically it's a treasonable offence, redirecting mail. But Marco doesn't mind. We gan back a canny way together. It saves wor the walk roond to the Square, y'kna. Just when ye were in Florida. I forgot to tell him ye were back.'

Ronny exhaled and tugged at his ponytail. 'Audrey would gan radgie, if she knew.'

'Well, I am yer personal adviser, man. It makes sense. The hooseboat's like me office.' Al lifted up a handful of envelopes and let them drop. 'They're just begging letters.'

'Begging letters?'

'Harmless.'

'You've read them all?'

'I take me new job serious.' Al rifled through the pile, and scattering a number on to the floor, extracted a single envelope. 'There's only the one nasty.'

'Nasty?' Ronny drew out the rather grubby letter from the already opened envelope. Its message was scripted in letters cut from the headlines of a tabloid newspaper. 'You have broken the circle,' read Ronny. 'Beware.' He gazed at Al, mystified. 'What the hell's that all aboot?'

Al plucked the letter from him and crumpled it into a ball. 'Pay nee attention. Occupational hazard. Just some crank.' He gestured at the rest of the correspondence. 'What d'yus want wor to dee with this little lot?'

'Ye say they're mostly begging letters?' Ronny felt his ponytail tentatively.

'Mostly bairns what'll die if ye divven't give them the money for an operation in Cuba or somewhere.' Al plucked a number of letters at random and, with a card sharper's speed, exposed their contents. Most contained a picture of a child along with a handwritten appeal. He read one of them in bored tones. ' "You have been blessed with good fortune. Will you now bless our lives? For without the gift of a special guardian angel, our little Chloe will surely die ..." ' Al dropped the letter. 'Blah–blah–blah.' His hand dived back into the pile, and once again expertly plucked out a few. 'Some of them are from women, mind. Hoying themselves at ye. Their measurements. Their sense of humour an' that. There were even three pairs o' knickers.' He looked at Terri–Leigh who continued to read her book as though oblivious to them. 'I've left them zipped up in the bag.' He cleared his throat. 'I didn't really kna what to dee with them. Then there were men after Audrey. Gigolos, y'kna. One of them was from that new barman in Shenanigans. He's a bloody dark horse, him.'

But Ronny was not listening. He was gazing at the photograph of the child which went with the letter Al had read. She had huge, imploring eyes. He read the accompanying letter. ' "Will you bring the darkness down on our little ray of sunshine? It is your choice. You decide whether our little Chloe lives or dies." ' Ronny shivered.

Al snorted. 'How much do they want? No. Let me guess. A hundred grand.'

Ronny's finger traced down the letter. He shook his head. 'Fifty grand.'

'It's a mug's game, that,' Al said sharply, grabbing the paper. 'Divven't even think aboot giving them owt.'

'Why not?'

'They're just made up. Hoaxes, y'kna.'

Ronny stared at the child's eyes. 'How d'ye kna?'

'Human nature, isn't it? People'll say owt to screw money oot o' yus. I'll tell ye one thing, Ronny boy, since we won this lottery I've had me eyes opened to folks. And it's not a pretty sight. Letters like this? If ye gan doon that path, ye'll be fleeced before ye've time to say baa.'

'But what if it's true?' Ronny gazed at the imploring eyes of Chloe. 'They're right. I mean, it is up to me. I can decide whether —'

Al snatched the photograph from Ronny. 'So shall I get rid of this lot then?'

Ronny stared in confusion at the profusion of correspondence. 'No,' he said quietly. 'We'll keep hold of them for now.'

'So be it. You're the boss. But I'm telling ye. Ye'd be better off putting them begging letters from your mind.' Al pointed at the poison pen letter which had been screwed into a ball. 'At least that one's an honest scam.'

Ronny gazed mistrustfully at the ball of paper. 'Do yus not think that I should gan to the pollis aboot it?'

'Ye've nee idea, have ye? Ye gan from one extreme to the other. Just as well I'm here.' He chuckled. 'Ye always were a bit fey, ye, like.'

'Fey?' asked Ronny. 'What the hell do ye mean by that?'

'Y'kna. A dreamer. Away with the bloody fairies. But divven't worry, it'll all be taken care of. Now, I've been looking at car performances, I think the best thing for ye is —'

'But it might be serious. The poison pen letter. I mean, him what wrote it might be a psycho.'

'Am I your personal adviser, or not?' Al suddenly burst out. ''Cos I advise ye just to ignore it. Besides, the winners' adviser was telling us, it happens all the time. These poison pens. The winners always get them. That's why ye have to move. Change addresses. Ye have to —' Al broke off. He peered at Ronny suspiciously. 'I mean, I am yer personal adviser, aren't I? Proper, like? A kosher job?' Ronny nodded evasively. Al fixed him with his wall-eye. 'We'd better set a salary then. It's been a month since ye won. I divven't want to press ye, but I'm totally broke.'

'The thing is . . .' Ronny breathed in deeply. 'Aboot money. Well, y'kna how me and Audrey are having that meeting . . .'

'What meeting?

'Did I not mention it?'

'No.'

Ronny cleared his throat guiltily. 'It's to sort out the money once and for all. To tell everyone what they're getting. Y'kna, family and friends. It was the winners' adviser's idea. Get everyone together. Dee it all in the open. Above board. So everyone knas what everyone else is getting.'

Al grunted. 'Doesn't everyone already kna I'm yer assistant?'

'Course they dee,' nodded Ronny uneasily, avoiding Al's piercing white jackdaw eye. 'It's just that the winners' adviser said —'

'Oh what the hell does she kna?' Al thundered. 'She's not on the ground here like I am.' He studied Ronny. 'The old team's the best, isn't it? I mean, when them kids from Bensham stole yer medicine ball, who got it back?'

'Ye,' returned Ronny simply.

'Me,' nodded Al.

'That was forty-five years agan, mind,' said Ronny mildly.

'Aye, well, us Keir Hardie lads have to keep together through thick and thin. We —'

'Exactly,' Ronny said. 'Exactly!' he suddenly erupted. 'That's why we should buy that land. Where the auld avenue stood. And build worselves a hoose there —'

'Ye're not still gannin' on aboot that, are ye?' Al shook his head sombrely. 'Forget aboot it. People will just laugh at yus. Now, ha'way, let's get a new car sorted. Are we still sticking with the original plan what I worked oot? A sensible family saloon, and summink —' He broke off to wink at Ronny. 'Summink a bit tasty. A proper fanny magnet.' Al chuckled, but the chuckle died peevishly. 'Are ye listening to me or what?'

173

Ronny's eyes shone with inspiration. 'It's been the dream of a lifetime, only now I can realise it.' He gave a great flourish of his ponytail. 'I've seen the future, Al lad. I've seen what the days ahead hold, and it's looking good. It's looking bloody purely belter.'

'Now listen to me, and listen to me well,' snapped Al. 'Ye've always been full of ideas. And every single one of them has been cuckoo.'

'No they haven't . . .'

'Buying the Team Valley and turning it into a nature reserve? That was stupid.'

'No it wasn't.'

'Crossing the North Sea in a beer barrel?'

'Na. Anyway that was never a serious one, man.'

'It was, man Ronny. Ye even wrote to the Dunston Fed brewery to see if they'd sponsor ye. Then there was the time when ye were gonnae open up a bloody clapped-oot auld closed-doon pit as a cooperative –'

'That would have worked.'

'Reintroducing wolves to Keilder Forest? Bringing steamer ferries back to the Tyne? Translating the *Kama Sutra* into Geordie?'

'That's already been done.'

'Buy a job lot of garden gnomes, paint them in Toon colours, and sell them ootside St James's on a match day?'

'We did that one.'

Al nodded. 'On the day Sunderland came. We'd only got two sold before they smashed up the rest. Bonny lad, the list's endless. In fact, all ye have ever done in life is dream.'

'Exactly,' said Ronny with sudden certainty. 'Exactly. And at last I can start to live me dreams. Me and me childhood sweetheart living at Keir Hardie Towers. And that's not all.'

'God help wor.'

'It's not just the hoose. I'm gonnae be a comedian an' all.'

'A comedian?'

'I've decided. A comedian. And a singer. All me life I've been forced into a box. A pitman. Then the pet shop and all them friggin' hamsters. After that, a bloody cooboy builder. But now? I'm not only gonnae be a stand-up comedian but a singer an' all. I'm gonnae be Gatesheed's answer to Vin Garbutt.'

'Who the hell's Vin Garbutt?'

Ronny thought for a moment. 'Put it this way, he's like a cross between Roy Orbison, Bob Dylan and Eric Morecambe. But better.'

Al snorted. 'Ronny, face facts, yer jokes are aboot as funny as a heart attack. Ye cannet –'

'Yes I can. Yes I can. I can dream to me heart's content. And live me dreams an' all.'

It was as they were packing the paperwork back into the bag on wheels that Al handed Ronny another envelope. 'I nearly forgot.' Ronny took it, and looked questioningly at his personal adviser. Al shrugged. 'From her dad.'

'Whose dad?'

'Audrey's dad.'

Ronny shook his head. 'Cannet be. He's been dead for years.'

'Christ,' sighed Al with a shake of his head. 'I can see I'm gonnae have me work cut oot with ye.' He looked at his friend with a patronising smile, and then shook the bag on wheels. 'In here somewhere are a host o' similar resurrections. Nee wonder your Audrey's a religious freak. If them letters are to be believed then she's had more dads than Christ had apostles . . . and more bairns.'

Ronny gazed at the envelope. 'How the hell could anyone be so cruel?'

Al shrugged. 'It's a common occurrence. I was talking to the winners' adviser aboot it. She said it happens all the time. Long-lost relatives turning up oot o' the blue. From the grave.'

'Bloody hell,' gasped Ronny. 'I'm only glad I got to it first. Audrey'd be creased. She never knew her dad, y'kna.'

'On the other hand. I suppose ye cannet rule it oot.'

'Eh?'

'Well, it might really be from him.'

Ronny's face puckered. 'How the hell might it be him, when he's been deed for decades?'

'Mebbes he isn't deed.' Al stared at the letter. 'This one did seem more real than them others. Y'kna. Had the ring of truth.'

'Are ye joking or what?'

'Winning the lottery often throws up such shocks. Thems is the winners' adviser's words.' Al weighed it up. 'Still, all things considered, I'd put it doon to just another con trick.'

Ronny's mouth twisted. 'He left her when she was two. Three mebbes. He did the dirty. She won't talk aboot it. Won't have him mentioned. Every time there's summink aboot dads on telly, she gets up.' He tugged anxiously at his ponytail. 'Talk aboot a skeleton tumbling oot the cupboard. If it really was him, it'd . . . Christ, I cannet even begin to think what she'd dee.' Ronny began to read the letter. 'He says he's lived in London all his life since leaving here. He's just come back. He knas he doesn't deserve it but he wants to explain. He wants to make his peace.'

Al snatched the letter, and shoved it into the bag on wheels. 'Just another con merchant after some money.'

Ronny gazed at his friend solemnly. 'He says he doesn't want any money, Al.'

For a moment Al seemed to be lost for words. Then he laughed disparagingly. 'He's playing the lang game, man.'

'The lang game?'

'Y'kna, worm his way into her affections and then the money comes of its own accord.' Al clapped his hands together. 'Ha'way, pull yourself together. Divven't take it to heart. Anyway, if ye have to worry then worry aboot yersel'. I mean, there's three or four of your long-lost sons and daughters knocking aboot in this bag on wheels.'

Ronny's jaw dropped. 'Straight up?'

'So divven't tell her nowt. And forget aboot it yersel' an' all. If the deed really are rattling at the window then ye'll find oot soon enough without getting oot of bed to shake them by the hand.'

3

Eyes fixed on the tiles, Audrey walked slowly down the mall. 'I knew it.' Stopping, she grunted with satisfaction. 'She's nee good, that lass what got my job. That stain's been there for three days noo.' Toni zoomed in her camcorder on the stain. Audrey chuckled as she rubbed her hands together. 'Ee, it'll be canny to see the lasses again. Divven't get wor wrang, I divven't miss the work, but I cannet wait to have a bit crack with them.' Audrey shook her head as she looked triumphantly at the offending tiles one more time. 'Na; she's nee idea how to use a buffer, that new lass.'

They walked on, Audrey's eye roving critically over the nooks and crannies which she used to clean. 'Nana?' asked Toni-Lee after a while.

'Yes, pet.'

'When d'ye think me mam's gonnae come?'

Audrey halted instantly. She looked tenderly at her grand-daughter. 'I divven't kna, love,' she whispered, placing her hand gently on the child's cheek. 'Soon. Mebbes soon.'

Hand in hand, they walked on through the well-known precincts of the Metro Centre, coming at last to the fountain in which the metal cows drank. Audrey brought out a new leather purse from her designer shoulder bag, and took out a coin. 'What yus deein', Nana?'

Audrey smiled. 'I've been wishing here since this place

opened. Hard to get oot the habit of it.' She looked at her purse which was full of notes. 'I've more twenty-knicker notes now than I had twenty-pence pieces then.' She held out a coin to her granddaughter.

'But we've already won it, Nana.'

'There's other things to wish for.' Audrey smiled sadly. 'For yer mam. That she comes hyem soon.'

'When she does, will I have to leave ye and Granda Ronny?'

'Toni pet, ye dee exactly what ye want to dee. Ye can stop with us. Or ye can gan with yer mam. It's your choice. Now, ha'way, toss the coin.'

But closing her eyes, her granddaughter shook her head. 'Ye dee it, Nana. Ye've got the luck.'

Audrey nodded, and taking the money, flicked it high. 'We'll have yer mam back before ye can open them eyes,' she whispered as the coin spun. 'Good things come in groups, hinny. We've got the money. And next, we'll get yer mam back.' Hitting the water crisply, the twenty-pence piece flashed to the bottom of the fountain. 'And mebbes this time, Toni, she'll settle doon and make a home for the pair o' yus.'

'I divven't want her back. I nivver want to see her again.'

Audrey gaped at her granddaughter. All at once she seemed to have become an old woman. 'But, Toni pet, how can ye say that about yer own mam?'

Toni-Lee seemed to be fighting against tears. 'She doesn't want me, Nana.' She tugged her grandmother's arm. 'What can I dee if she just doesn't want wor?'

'Well . . .' Audrey faltered. 'Well . . . Just say a little prayer.'

'But what'll I pray for?'

Audrey thought for a long time. 'Happiness, pet. That ye and yer mam will find a bit happiness.' She took her granddaughter in her arms, and held her there securely until the child opened her eyes and smiled. 'Ee,' whispered Audrey, 'look at them coos. They haven't been polished for a fortnight. Me? I tended them like they were flesh and blood.'

There was a soft splash. Audrey was wading towards the sculpture cows as though through the shallows of the Tyne.

'Nana!' called Toni-Lee in horror, then, chuckling, trained the camcorder on her grandmother as, breathing on the metal flanks, she rubbed vigorously with her lifted T-shirt.

Audrey had just finished polishing the cows and was still standing in the fountain admiring her work when she let out a laugh that resounded about the square. The security guard had just emerged from one of the malls. 'I'd like to say ye were a sight for sore eyes,' Audrey yelled good-naturedly over the square, 'but I divven't tell porky-pies.' The security guard took one glance over, saw Audrey and then scurried back the way he had come. 'It's me!' Audrey called after him. 'Awer here, Officer Dribble, at the friggin' wishing well, wishing ye well . . .'

The security guard had gone. Audrey stared after him in puzzlement, but before she had a chance to shout anything else, another voice filled the square. 'What the hell are ye deein' in there?' Cheryl demanded good-humouredly. 'Ye've already won once. Get oot o' it, and give another body a chance.'

Audrey's face lit up. 'Ha'way into the water, Chez. We'll have a swim. Ye divven't need a cossie.' Cheryl was wearing the same pair of leggings that she always wore to work. Her Gateshead Garden Festival T-shirt was torn slightly and faded with a decade of washing. For a moment her eyes rested on Audrey's new pedal pushers and Hooters T-shirt. 'I swear doon,' said Audrey, clambering out of the fountain, 'Officer Dribble's just blanked wor.'

Cheryl shook her head. 'He's just shit-scared. Peaky telt him he's not allowed to chat to anyone. If he sees him deein' it, he's oot on his ear. He's already had one warning.'

Audrey rolled her eyes. 'I'd just tell him where to gan, me.'

'He's got two sets o' child maintenance payments to meet.'

Cheryl glanced furtively down the mall where the security guard had gone. 'He won't have been blanking ye on purpose, man Aud.'

'I was gonnae say,' laughed Audrey. She paddled round the rim of the fountain, leaving wet footprints. 'I worked with him for ten years.' She looked about the square. 'Where's the other lasses then?'

Cheryl looked away evasively. 'Oh, they cannet make it.'

'Eh?'

'The lasses. They cannet make it.'

'None of them?'

Cheryl pretended to examine her hands, studying the coarse, red fingers, puffy with constant dipping in hot water and bleach. 'They've got to get the shopping in an' that.' She glanced at the deep red of Audrey's manicured nails. 'They're all really gutted. They want to meet another day.'

'Cheryl man,' said Audrey, her face set hard, 'what the hell's gannin' on?'

'Nowt, nowt,' Cheryl said quickly, her hands raised in a conciliatory gesture. 'Y'kna how it is, man Audrey. Most of them lasses were like ye. They've got other jobs. There isn't always time.'

Audrey's face remained hard for a while before softening. 'I suppose. Anyway, you're here, hinny.'

Cheryl beamed, and then turned to Audrey's granddaughter whose face was obscured by the camcorder. 'How's the film comin' on, Toni-Lee pet?'

'Cheryl,' Toni-Lee suddenly said, without lowering the viewfinder, 'will ye just look at yer fingers again, like ye did before.'

Cheryl blinked. Then she looked at Audrey. 'Ee, yus've had yer hair done again. Permed and dyed. It looks great.' She reached out to finger the ringlets. 'Ye look like a proper Nell Gwyn.'

'Eh?' Audrey replied, puzzled.

'Y'kna that advert. Have a orange, Charlie. It used to be on the box. Nell Gwyn. She was Prince Charles's girlfriend.'

'Are ye sure?' Audrey asked.

'Before Princess Di.'

Audrey led them down the malls. 'I've always loved it in here,' said Cheryl as they crossed the threshold of House of Fraser, her voice lowering to a whisper as though entering a cathedral. 'The times you and me have come in here. Just window shopping. Fantasising.' She smiled wistfully. 'Totting up the price of wor dreams. And now? Ye can have anything you can see.'

Audrey strode into the lingerie department. Impulsively, she plucked a negligee from a stand and held it out to Cheryl. Cheryl shook her head. Audrey thrust the garment in her hands. 'Audrey man,' Cheryl protested.

'What?'

'What ye deein'?'

'Well, ye want it, divven't ye?'

Cheryl glanced at the camcorder. She sighed. 'Aye, course I dee, but –'

'Even Father Dan wouldn't be able to say na to ye in that.' Audrey walked through the clothes department. Her eyes were lit with a hunger as she scanned the array of clothes. 'Besides,' she called over her shoulder, 'if I divven't get ye summink, I'll feel bad aboot treating meself.'

For about twenty minutes, Audrey pillaged through the clothes, lost in a lust of purchasing. Cheryl browsed more sedately, casting a glance at her friend every time Audrey selected a garment.

At the till Audrey brought out a platinum store card and handed it to the assistant. 'Ee,' Cheryl grinned, 'the last time I saw one of them was just before me ex was arrested.' The assistant glanced at Cheryl. 'Divven't worry, pet,' Cheryl explained, 'House of Fraser wasn't one of his.'

The assistant smiled weakly as she began to sort all the clothes Audrey had bought into bags.

'Is he oot yet?' Audrey asked.

'Got another six months to dee. But divven't bother. I'm not having him back. Father Dan's the only one for me.'

Audrey grinned. 'What aboot Big Al? I hear he's falling head awer heels for ye.'

'Dee us a favour, man Audrey. I'm not that desperate.'

'I divven't kna,' laughed Audrey. 'The pair o' yus could sail away somewhere on that boat o' his.'

'Aye, aboot as far as Jarrow.'

As the women chatted, the sales assistant surreptitiously lowered her hand under the counter. A bell rang out. Almost instantly a woman in a formidable blouse and a face orange with foundation make-up, bustled over. 'What seems to be the trouble?' she demanded self-importantly.

The assistant blushed hesitantly. 'Can you just check something for me please, Mrs Collie.'

'I see.' Mrs Collie eyed Audrey and Cheryl significantly.

'What's the matter with ye?' Audrey demanded.

Mrs Collie tensed. Then grew haughty. 'You're cleaners, aren't you?'

Audrey nodded. 'So?'

'I recognise you both. And you,' she pointed at Audrey, 'are a known troublemaker.' Mrs Collie nodded at the assistant who pressed another bell under the till. Then she demanded: 'And the child's camcorder, where did she get that?'

'What's it got to dee with ye?' Audrey retorted. She turned to the assistant. 'Are ye gonnae run them things through for me or what?'

The assistant began making the semblance of an effort to seem to be cashing the goods, but Mrs Collie stopped her. Her tone became inhumanly official. 'I'm sorry but I would like to verify your entitlement to a platinum store card. Would you accompany me please, ladies, there's one or two things —'

Not listening, Audrey tapped the assistant on the arm. 'Run them through.'

The peaked hat of a security guard could be seen wending its way towards them through the hosiery department. Mrs Collie drew herself to her full height. When he saw Audrey, the security guard blanched. 'Surprise, surprise,' Audrey grinned. 'It's Officer Dribble.'

'Take these three to the security room,' Mrs Collie ordered. The security guard looked blankly at all three. 'Suspected credit card fraud,' Mrs Collie pressed irritably.

'Ye what?' Audrey demanded. 'I'm not putting up with this.' She reached out and grabbed Mrs Collie by the arm.

'Security,' the supervisor shrieked.

'I'm taking ye to the manager,' Audrey explained.

'Security,' the supervisor repeated. But the security guard simply looked on helplessly.

'Aye,' continued Audrey. 'I taking ye to the same manager what personally signed me Privilege Platinum card and membership of the Silver Service loonge.'

'What?' Mrs Collie cried.

Audrey rounded on the security guard. 'Tell her then, Dribble. Tell her who I am.'

'She's Audrey McPhee,' the miserable security guard replied. 'She's a millionaire, man. She won the lottery.'

Mrs Collie's face knotted with confusion and the beginnings of fear. 'I didn't know . . .'

'Aye, well, ye dee noo,' Audrey said, 'ye sour-faced cow.'

'Run them through then, girl,' the supervisor ordered, hastily picking up the goods Audrey had brought to the till.

'Get us the manager before I slap yer face.'

'Oh, there's no need for the manager. Just a misunderstanding,' said Mrs Collie, trying to smile. She inhaled and then swallowed. 'I am so sorry. I didn't realise who you were. I just –'

'Aye, well just make sure it doesn't happen again, lass.'

Audrey squared up to her. 'I'll be watching oot for ye in future, droopy drawers, so behave yersel'. Oh aye, and if I decide to sue yus for defamation o' character, the bairn here's got it all on film.' Mrs Collie stared at the camcorder lense in horror and then bustled away, mortified. Audrey's laugh followed her humiliatingly through to the soft furnishings department. Audrey turned to share her triumph with the security guard. But he had gone.

Audrey pushed the bag with the negligee into Cheryl's hands. 'Ha'way,' she said. 'Dinner time.' Cheryl followed her at a distance of some yards. 'What's the matter with ye?' Audrey called.

'Why divven't we just gan to McDonald's, Aud? Or Pam's Pantry?'

'I want to gan here.' Audrey strode on, but stopped when she saw that Cheryl still lagged behind. 'What's the matter?'

Cheryl sighed. 'Now they won't let me in here no more.'

Audrey led them through the heavy door of the Silver Service lounge. 'Bloody hell,' gasped Cheryl at the sight. 'It's like summink from *The Forsythe Saga*.'

'Posh, eh?' Audrey chuckled.

They walked past a grand piano being played in the corner, and sat down at a table. Entranced, Cheryl gazed at the vase of flowers set in the midst of the heavy cutlery. The other diners stared discreetly at them, but Cheryl was too busy looking at the flowers to notice. 'Nana?' Toni–Lee asked. 'Can I gan and dee some more filming in the shop?'

'Be quick,' said Audrey. 'What d'ye want for yer dinner?'

'Big Mac and fries,' the girl replied.

'Ee, I divven't think they'll dee summink like that here,' Cheryl warned.

'They'll dee owt we ask them for,' replied Audrey.

When Toni–Lee had gone, nothing was said for a little while as Cheryl gazed in awe at the opulence of the surroundings. The light sparkled on the crystal of the wine glasses, the starched linen tablecloths gleamed almost translucently and the tread of the waiter was silent. Cheryl shook her head and pushed the menu away. 'I divven't understand a word of it.'

Audrey read her menu calmly. 'It's just all bloody pretend. Y'kna, code. Ye pick it up canny quick.' She jabbed a lacquered fingernail at the printed card. 'See that, *pommes frites*? It just means chips. And that, *filet mignon*? It's a steak.'

'It's a different world in here,' Cheryl whispered, awestruck. 'Ee, Audrey, ye won't be talking to the rest o' wor soon.'

Audrey shrugged. 'I take people as I find them. And ye, ye are me auldest mate. I'm not gonnae turn me back on ye.' She mused. 'Officer Dribble can piss off, but, if that's his attitude.'

Cheryl sighed. 'The thing is, Audrey . . .' She broke off.

'What is it, Chez?'

'Nowt.' Cheryl shook her head.

'Canny funny nowt.'

'It doesn't matter.'

'Must dee since yus've mentioned it.'

'Honest, Audrey, really, it's nee big deal.'

'Well, just tell wor then.' Audrey's ringing voice caught the attention of the dining room, but the diners quailed from her questioning glare.

Cheryl seemed reluctant to speak, but at length admitted: 'It's just that one or two of them have been saying a few things aboot ye, like.'

'Eh?' Audrey seemed amazed.

'Oh, nowt that matters,' Cheryl assured her. 'Nowt that matters. Just bloody tittle-tattle. But I thought ye had a right to know.'

'Who?' Audrey demanded. 'I'll bloody knock them into the middle of next week.'

'I wish I hadn't said owt now.' Cheryl hurriedly dipped into her Kwik Save carrier bag and took out a cigarette purse. She clicked it open. Inside were three full cigarettes and a litter of dog ends.

'Ee, na . . .' began Audrey.

But Cheryl had already got two cigarettes out. 'No, have one o' mine, man Audrey. Ye're always lashing oot . . .'

'I mean, there's nee smoking in here.'

'Nee smoking?' Cheryl was aghast.

'Aye.' Audrey shrugged. 'It's posh.'

Cheryl glanced at the grand piano, and then put her cigarettes away.

They sat for a while in silence. 'Who's gannin' behind me back at work?' Audrey asked at last.

'Forget aboot it,' said Cheryl. She brightened her tone. 'Tell us aboot the hoose then. The Meadowings. Have ye told Ronny that yus've put an offer in on it already?'

'No, not yet,' returned Audrey evasively.

'Ye'll have to tell him soon.'

'I will.'

'What, on the day ye move in?'

'I'm gonnae dee it before wor meeting.'

'Meeting?'

'Ye kna, man Cheryl, I telt ye aboot it. The winners' adviser telt wor it was a good idea. Get everyone together and tell them what we're giving them. Like the reading of a will, except neebody's died. All above board so neebody can complain later. It's supposed to stop folks falling oot.' Audrey wrinkled her nose so that the light freckle dusting shimmered. 'I was gonnae give the lasses at work summink towards their Saturday neets, but I divven't kna whether I will any more.'

'So ye've worked oot what everyone's gonnae get?'

Audrey nodded. 'We've just got to like finalise it. And then we'll tell everyone. At the same time. Y'kna, at the meeting.'

Surreptitiously, Cheryl stared at her friend, and then, just as Audrey caught her glance, said: 'What aboot the Meadowings then, when are yus moving in?'

'Actually, there's been a change of plan.'

'Eh?'

186

'It was Ronny's idea, but the more I think aboot it, the more I like it.' Audrey nodded. 'We might not be moving after all, man Cheryl.'

'Not moving?'

'We're Teamsers born and bred. So is the bairns. Where would we gan?'

'Stay in the Teams?' faltered Cheryl. 'Stay in that little flat?'

Audrey shook her head grandly. 'We're gonnae buy the land where Keir Hardie stood. Build wor dream home there.'

As Cheryl stared dumbfoundedly at her friend, the waiter came over. 'Areet, Franco,' Audrey smiled.

'Hello, Audrey. How is it going?'

'All the better for seeing ye, bonny lad. This is Cheryl, me best mate.' Cheryl giggled as the Italian waiter bowed.

'Charmed, signora.'

'Cod and chips twice,' said Audrey. 'Done in proper batter, mind.'

Cheryl watched the waiter as he strolled to the kitchens. 'He's not called Franco. And he's not an Italian. He's from Darlington. He gans to Shenanigans.'

'Aye, well, I won't tell if ye divven't,' smirked Audrey.

'I'm gannin' radgie for a cigarette,' said Cheryl, drumming her fingers on the table.

'Me too,' Audrey replied. 'We can always gan to the ladies and have one after wor meal.' Audrey grew thoughtful for a while. 'But ye didn't say.'

'Say what?'

'What ye thought aboot wor staying put in the Teams.'

There was a pause. 'But I thought that one at the Meadowings was your dream home.'

'This one will be a dream home an' all. Built to wor own specifications.'

'Ye're really gonnae stay in the Teams?'

'Aye, mebbes. What d'ye think aboot it?'

Cheryl shook her head. 'Everybody else would give their right arm to move.'

'It's not that bad.'

'The Teams? Course it is, Audrey man. It's the devil's arsehole.'

Audrey stared at her friend, taken aback by her ferocity.

'I'll say one thing aboot it,' Cheryl began again. 'Yus'll give folk a reet sickener.'

'Eh?'

'Think aboot it, man. Neebody else has got a brass farthing. For a start yus'll have to build a friggin' geet security fence the size o' Hadrian's Wall.' Cheryl paused weightily for a few moments. 'They'll be queuing up to rob you. Besides, what aboot . . .' She grimaced. 'Ye kna who.'

Instinctively, Audrey dropped her voice to a whisper. 'Macca?'

'Why aye. The fire an' that.'

Audrey flinched. Her eyes widened in alarm. 'How d'ye kna aboot that?'

'Ye telt wor.'

'Did I?'

Cheryl nodded. A sharpness entered her voice. 'I haven't told neeone, if that's what yus're worried aboot.'

'I'm not saying that. It's just that —' Audrey broke off. 'When did I tell ye?'

Cheryl shrugged. 'When ye were pissed one night.'

'I just cannet remember telling ye.'

In the silence that followed, the piano threw its blossoms of melody over the beautiful place. Wine sang as it was poured. Hushed voices discoursed. 'Just say what ye mean, man.' Cheryl's voice suddenly rose above the harmonious hum of the restaurant. 'Ye think I'd grass on ye or summink?'

'Course I divven't,' countered Audrey defensively. 'It's just that —'

'Ye cannet trust yer auld friends any more. Is that what ye

188

want to say?' Cheryl snarled bitterly as she rose. 'Well, if that's the case then ye kna what ye can dee with yer posh fuckin' fish and chips. Ee, but there's been nee living with ye since ye won the friggin' lottery.'

'Eh?' replied Audrey. Then, losing her cool, she rose too. 'Gan on then, piss off, if that's your attitude.'

'It is.'

'Good!' Audrey's voice had grown to a shout. 'So frigg off oot of it then and gan and talk aboot wor behind me back with Dribble.' Cheryl strode across the restaurant.

'I'll tell ye this for nowt,' Cheryl shrieked. 'They're all cracking on aboot ye. All having a bloody geet slag on ye. How ye think ye're the bloody bee's knees. How there's nee living with ye since ye won. With yer bloody hairdos, and yer bloody Florida.'

With a gasp, Cheryl ducked as a wine glass smashed against the wall just above her head. The wine ran down it like blood. 'I'll let ye off because ye used to be a mate,' Audrey said in a quiet voice that nevertheless could be heard in the kitchens. She pointed at the broken glass lying on the deep shag carpet. 'If ye hadn't been, then that would have been yer heed. Now fuck off oot of it.'

4

There was line dancing at the St Mary Magdalene's Catholic Social Club that night. The dilapidated old Portakabin shook as the line of dancers stamped and bounced in time to the hillbilly riffs of the Geordie Shamrocks. Kenny Rogers was there with his huge ten-gallon hat perched on top of his diminutive frame, and the rest of the dancers had made some attempt to appear Texan: denim jeans, checked shirts and the odd holster of cowboy guns. But Ronny and Audrey had gone the whole hog. In her little skirt, fishnet stockings, cleavage-

189

revealing jacket and cowgirl hat, all made of red suede and trimmed with white tassels, Audrey danced beside Ronny, who was dressed Clint Eastwood style in a poncho with hat and heavy boots complete with spurs. Big Al was the only person not dancing. He sat at his table grimly interrogating a bottle of Newcastle Brown Ale. From time to time, roaring with laughter, Audrey threw her lasso round his middle, and tugged him on to his feet.

A huge cheer greeted the end of the song and the dancers broke drunkenly from their line. Immediately, everyone gathered round Audrey, yapping and barking for her attention. One of them was drunker than the rest. 'Buy us another pint then,' he demanded. Audrey did not reply. 'Gan on,' he ordered, growing indignantly self-righteous. 'If I'd won the lottery, I'd buy every bugger a pint for life.'

Audrey glared at him. All those crowding round her held empty pint glasses or Diamond White bottles in their hands and eager hungry-dog looks in their eyes. She knitted her eyebrows for a few instants, and then turning to the barman, pulled out a wad of notes from between her breasts. There was a huge cheer and the entire gathering surged to the bar. Swinging her lasso, Audrey caught the one who had demanded the drink, and pulled him to the door. He struggled like a netted fish, but was helpless to resist. 'And divven't bother coming back,' she ordered as, thrusting open the club door, she dumped him outside.

He walked away, but after about ten yards he stopped. 'Ye think ye own this place divven't ye, Audrey McPhee? But people are just aboot getting sick o' ye.'

'Are they?' Audrey returned coldly.

'Aye, ye think ye're the bloody Queen o' the North but . . .' Before he could complete his sentence, his legs seemed to fall out from underneath him. Lying on his chest with his chin on the ash of the church car park, he began to vomit.

With a laugh, Audrey returned to the club.

Ronny had just sat down with Al. 'What d'yus think yus look like in that bloody poncho?' Al demanded. 'And you're sweating like a pig. Are ye ill or summink?'

'I'm areet, man Al.'

But Al's face was serious. 'Na, straight up, marra. Ye divven't look too fettled.' Ronny waved away the concern. Al took a drink and his face twisted. 'If I'd known that Audrey had fallen oot with Cheryl, I'd nivver have come here. I divven't trust Catholics.' Al shook his head. His voice became a peevish whine. 'And I wish ye'd tell her to stop bothering us with that bloody lasso.'

Ronny shrugged. 'Y'kna how it is, Al. Ye annoy her.'

'Well, it's not very professional. I mean, I suppose I work with her as much as I work with ye.' Al's opaque eye narrowed calculatingly. 'I could sue her for harassment.' He nodded at Audrey who, in the midst of a throng, was starting on another bottle of Diamond White. 'I must admit, I thought Audrey might have had summink to say aboot it. Me being made yer personal adviser on a permanent basis. I mean, ye have definitely telt her –' Al broke off. 'Are ye listening to me or what?' Al gazed at Ronny. His face was white and gleaming with sweat; his eyes seemed to be faraway. 'Hello, Houston calling.'

'I could start here,' said Ronny dreamily.

'Eh?'

'Here. Do me first one here.'

'Yer first what?'

'Gig. Booking. Y'kna, me new career.' Ronny paused proudly. 'As a singer-comedian.'

'Oh aye, Vin Barbutt.'

'Garbutt. Vin Garbutt. Start here, who knas where it might end?'

'Christ on a bike, I thought yus were just taking the piss with that. Ye a comedian? Let alone a singer. I'm gonnae give it to ye straight, man Ronny. It's for yer own good. Ye cannet sing, ye cannet tell jokes, yus've got as much charisma as a . . .' But Al broke off to peer closely at his friend. 'Are ye sure you're all right? I think ye must be gannin' doon with summink. Ye look proper ill.'

'I'm just a bit hot.' Ronny wiped his brow. His hand came back beaded with sweat, and he looked at the clammy skin in mystification. 'I wish someone would open a door in here, but.'

'It's not that hot, Ronny. Ha'way, man Clint bloody Eastwood. Nee wonder yus're sweating. That poncho's pure wool. Take it off.'

'I cannet,' said Ronny. 'I've nowt on underneath it.'

Suddenly Steve of the Geordie Shamrocks made an announcement. 'I'd like to call on Gatesheed's very own Patsy Cline to give us a number.' There was loud applause, and those around Audrey started cheering. One or two began to push her towards the stage. She turned on them, and they melted back with fawning smiles. 'Ha'way, Aud,' Steve begged, 'dee a Patsy Cline.'

'Na,' called Audrey back, stifling a yawn. 'I've got to gan hyem and check on the bairns.'

'Gan on. Give wor "I Fall to Pieces".'

Audrey sighed, and then smiled. 'Areet, just quickly, mind. Wor Theresa and Corky are babysitting, and it's them I want to check on more than the bairns.'

Amid tumultuous applause, Audrey vaulted on to the stage. She pushed aside the microphone, as, with broad grins, the Geordie Shamrocks started to play the lilting country ballad.

Ronny rose rather unsteadily to his feet. 'I think I'll just gan and get a breath of air,' he explained to Al.

'Are ye sure ye're areet? Here, I'd better come with ye . . .' But Ronny waved him back.

It was cool outside, and the autumn air was laced with dew. Ronny stood by the church for a moment and breathed in deeply. His spurs rattled as he walked out of the cul-de-sac and continued through the estate until he came to the bombsite that had been Keir Hardie Avenue. With an excited whoop he clambered over the rubble.

For a long time he stood there, gazing at his demolished birthplace. A solitary street light cast a jaundiced glow over the rubble of bricks and timber of roof beams. Someone had smashed the toilet, and its pieces lay as forlorn as a swallow's broken egg. Just then, someone whistled from close by. Ronny spun round. The whistling sounded out again, this time from what seemed to be the opposite direction. Ronny swivelled, but he could see no one. The whistling continued. A soft, mocking jingle: the theme tune from *The Good, the Bad and the Ugly*. 'Who is it?' Ronny cried.

'Hello, Ronny boy,' a voice answered so close that Ronny jumped. 'Looking for yer marbles, are ye?'

Ronny gave a sharp intake of breath as he recognised the baby face leering at him. 'Areet, Jimmy.'

'The good, the bad and the friggin' ugly.' The youth laughed raspingly. 'Nee prizes for guessing which one ye are, fat lad.'

'What ye deein' here then, Jimmy?' Ronny asked, trying to force a lightness into his tone.

'Little birdy telt me you were leaving the club. Decided to have wor little chat now.'

Ronny tried to smile. 'Wor little chat?'

'Aye. Wor little chinwag.' Despite the gentle chill of the September air, Ronny felt a trickle of sweat run down into his mouth. Puzzled, he tasted the salt. 'So what d'ye think then?' Jimmy asked, an edge sharpening his tone.

Ronny was confused. 'What aboot?'

'Wor little proposal.'

'What little proposal? Honestly, Jimmy, I divven't kna what yus're talking aboot.'

Jimmy paused for a moment. Then he tutted. 'Dear me, hasn't five-bellies number two been talking to ye?'

193

'No.' Another drop of sweat coursed down Ronny's face.

'I'll have to sort him out then, the naughty loser. He telt me he was gonnae put it to ye.'

'Jimmy man,' said Ronny hesitantly, shaking his head so that the sweat sprinkled from him. 'I've paid ye. If that's what yus're meaning. I mean, he did give ye the money, didn't he?'

'Aye, I got that money.'

Ronny touched his ponytail anxiously. 'I divven't owe ye any more then.'

There was a cruel burst of laughter. 'Oh dear. Since Greener hasn't put ye in the picture, I suppose I'll have to.' Jimmy paused. 'Ten grand should dee it.'

'Ten grand?'

Jimmy smiled. 'What's that to ye? Ye've got millions.'

'But I divven't owe ye owt.' Despite his fear, Ronny's voice rang out over the demolition site. 'We're all square.'

'D'yus want to upset Macca, is that it?' Jimmy's stark words hung between them for a while. 'The thing aboot Macca,' Jimmy continued, his tone lightening again, 'is that he's like the Incredible Hulk. Y'kna. Divven't make him angry. Ye wouldn't like him when he's angry. So ha'way, Clint, keep him happy. Give us the ten grand.' Jimmy's voice became a low snarl. ''Cos if ye divven't, he's liable to break every bone in yer body . . . and that's if he's in a good mood.'

Ronny blinked as though unable to focus on the youth in front of him. A drop of sweat had run into his eye, and even when he had cleared this with a forefinger, his vision remained clouded. 'If I pay ye,' he managed to say at last, 'is that the last I hear o' ye?'

Jimmy nodded. 'Aye. That'll be it. Everything cancelled. A fresh start for yus.' The youth sprang lightly over the rubble of Keir Hardie Avenue. 'Give the money to yer number two. He knas the drill. Ten grand. In twenties.'

It was as he was staring after him that Ronny realised he could not breathe. He struggled for air, but he could manage only wheezing gasps. He sank to his knees, his mild eyes widening like a cow before the abattoir stun gun. Just then the music from the club drifted over to him: somebody opened the door to leave. Silence returned: the club door had closed again. 'Oh God,' whimpered Ronny, his fingers digging into masonry dust. 'What the hell's the matter with me?'

4

It was Audrey who had left the Catholic Club. 'Well, I'm just a coal miner's daughter . . .' she sang to herself as she walked up the cul-de-sac.

Suddenly a presbytery window was flung open. 'Right, that's it, we'll lose our licence for certain now,' Father Dan cried angrily.

'Divven't be such a wet blanket, Father Dan man,' Audrey returned.

'I told you to keep things quiet for a bit. But you –'

'Just 'cos ye divven't like line dancing. If it had been a ceilidh ye wouldn't mind.'

The priest shook his head. 'There's been complaints about the noise. And the fighting in the cul-de-sac afterwards.'

'What's that got to do with me?'

'You're the one who buys the drink,' the priest spluttered angrily. 'Without you, people wouldn't be out partying every night that God sends. If needs be, I'll bar you myself for a week. It's time things got back to normal round here. We can't all be like you. Some of us have to do a day's work. You're just disrupting everyone. I've told you, but you don't seem to listen to anyone any more.'

After Dan had slammed the window, Audrey stood there for a bit longer staring up, and then, shrugging, went on her way.

She was halfway down the burrow to the Square Flats when it happened.

At first all she knew was that she had been knocked down, powerfully, irresistibly, as though by a swinging dead weight. Having hit the ground, she was stunned for a few seconds. Lying there, she became aware of something prying into the crannies of her body, running over her flesh like an army of rats. The security light was broken as usual, and she could see nothing. It was only by the warmth of the breath on her face that she realised her attacker was human. The fingers searching her were as sharp as hypodermic needles. A man was perched on top of her, but the voice that suddenly rasped out was so dry as to barely sound human. 'Give us yer money. Just give us yer fuckin' money.'

In less than a second it had been done. Audrey forced some leverage for her knee, and then rammed it up with all her strength. The man's gasp echoed in the tunnel as the blow to his testicles flung him from her.

She leapt to her feet and stood above him. He lay there in helpless agony. Again and again she raised her sharp-footed cowboy boot to kick him violently in the side. The strength of the blows shunted him across the underpass, until, curled like a foetus, he was piled up against the concrete side. She knelt down to him. 'Who the fuck are ye?' He did not reply. She took out her cigarette lighter. The flame clicked into life and her shadow on the concrete ceiling yawned over the motionless body like a minotaur.

He wore a Donald Duck mask which she ripped from his face. 'Christ,' she gasped on seeing him. 'It's ye.' There was an instant's pause. 'What the fuck are ye deein', man?' His face was yellow and desiccated. Flakes of sallow skin formed unhealthy patterns in the deep shadows of his sunken eye sockets. His eyes glowed like cigarette ends. Audrey shook her head. 'Sean Macarten. I've known ye all yer life, lad.'

Sean Macarten was somewhere in his mid-twenties but

looked aged with the premature senility of a heroin addict. His limbs were wasted to chicken legs. 'I need money, man Audrey,' he said simply. 'You've got some.'

Continuing to stand above her assailant, Audrey sighed. He just had time to look up in appeal before he was knocked unconscious, the tip of her boot shattering a cheekbone. Audrey watched him fall still, made the sign of the cross and then hurried on.

At the mouth of the burrow, she paused and, leaning heavily against the side, stared at the ground in disbelief. She grew shaky for a moment, but then drew herself resolutely to her full height and entered the courtyard.

Mrs Armstrong was standing against the parapet outside Flat 12A. The three sentinels were in position on the other sides of the square. 'Areet?' Audrey called up questioningly.

The response was subdued. 'Areet, pet.'

'Areet, Audrey.'

'Areet, love.'

'Areet, lass.'

Audrey stopped and stared up. 'What's the matter?' She tried a joke. 'Somebody died?'

'Ye better come up here, lass,' said Mrs Armstrong heavily.

'Has summink happened?'

'Aye. Summink's happened.'

Audrey tore across the courtyard. Without even bothering to try the lift button, she sprinted up the stairs. So great was her adrenalin that when she reached the top she was barely out of breath. 'Well?' she asked Mrs Armstrong. Shaking her head Mrs Armstrong walked inside the flat. Audrey strode after her.

As soon as Audrey crossed the threshold, Theresa threw herself into her mother's arms. 'Me and Corky had just popped to the Londis Shop . . .' she sobbed.

'We were only oot for two minutes, Mrs Audrey,' Corky explained.

'And when we got back . . .'

'They were here . . .'

'They've cleared . . .'

'The whole place . . .'

Still holding her youngest daughter, Audrey walked mechanically into the flat. The younger children all sat on the floor with their backs against the wall where the television had been. There was nowhere else for them to sit. The new double suite which had taken up half of the room had gone. So had everything else. The children, subdued and frightened, looked at her silently for a while, and then getting up, surged at her. With a great silent scream, Audrey ran to them with her arms wide and, staggering under the press of their embraces, lifted them. 'Neebody's hurt?' she demanded in a voice compressed with countless layers of emotion. 'Tell me neebody's hurt.'

Breathlessly, she went through each child. Calling their names and then rubbing their faces protectively with her nose.

When the first passion of her love had subsided, Audrey looked at Mrs Armstrong. Mrs Armstrong shook her head, then burst into tears: a wheezing squeeze box playing a lament. 'How could they, Audrey pet?' Mrs Armstrong keened asthmatically. 'After all ye've done for people since ye won that lottery, how could they come in here and do this?'

'Who was it?' Audrey's voice was a low growl.

Mrs Armstrong wrung her hands, and then covered her face with them.

'They came in,' explained Linzi. 'Told us to sit doon. Then they took everything.'

'Everything,' Mrs Armstrong repeated. 'There's not a stick o' stuff left.' Audrey plunged into her and Ronny's bedroom. The waterbed had been slashed, and the carpet was awash. 'It was when the water started dripping through me ceiling that I knew summink was wrang,' Mrs Armstrong said. Everything portable had been taken. The wardrobe door was open. It was empty.

'They just walked in here and took everything,' said Toni-

Lee. 'And when Theresa and Corky come back they told them that if they did owt stupid they'd kill them.'

Corky's hands flourished in rapper sign language. 'They were proper gangstas.'

'Who was it?' Audrey repeated, her eyes dull with hatred.

A voice called out quietly. 'Macca's crowd.' Audrey looked over to where the voice had come from. It was Terri-Leigh still sitting against the wall. 'That's who they were,' the girl explained. 'Macca's crowd.'

'How d'ye kna, pet?' Audrey asked.

'They talked to him on their mobile phones,' the girl added simply. 'I heard them.'

A bewildered look had come over Audrey's face now. The hatred remained, but it was baffled with fear. 'Macca?' she repeated to herself. 'Macca?' Suddenly she threw her arms wide again, and gathered her family to herself. 'It doesn't matter that they've tooken everything,' she cried. 'The main thing's that nee one's hurt. The only thing that matters is that me bairns is all areet. They can have everything else. Just not me bairns. Not me bairns.'

5

Under a slate-grey October sky, the dirty white vanette had been coming and going all morning in the Teams. Now it stood parked at the Blarney stone roadblock, its back doors open to reveal a hold of battered cardboard boxes and black plastic bin liners. A host of children sat close by on the safety barrier above the busy A1. 'Are ye still gonnae come back to the Teams and play?' Brosnan was asking his cousins, Terri and Toni.

'Course we will,' replied Toni from the other side of her camcorder.

'And can we come and play with ye there?' Keegan asked.

'Why aye. There's gonnae be a party, remember.'

'Is it posh where yus're gannin'?' Elliot demanded. 'Or can ye play football?'

Terri-Leigh looked up from her book. 'There's room for a whole football pitch, man.'

'And yus'll tell wor if there's any nice lads?' Linzi asked, bouncing baby Cara on her knee.

Terri and Toni laughed. 'Na,' said Toni. 'If there's any that's proper lush, we'll keep him to worselves.' She dropped the camcorder. 'We'll still see ye every day at school, man. And it's not as if we're gannin' to the other side of the world.'

Just then, the burrow echoed with the sound of heavy breathing. Ronny and Al staggered out. They were carrying five or six bulging bin liners wedged between their bodies. 'Divven't drop owt,' warned Ronny as they reached the van. 'It's valuable gear this.'

'I thought everything valuable got twocked in the burglary?'

'Sentimental value, man,' Ronny explained.

'Ye mean useless tat.'

'I mean things what mean summink to me.'

'Ye mean useless tat.'

'Na. It's what's special.'

'It can't all be special, man Ronny. I mean, we've been loading them boxes and bin liners all day. Couldn't ye just ask the burglars to come back and take what they've left an dee wor all a favour?'

Dancing the bin liners into the van, they dropped the last one on the ground. There was a dull clump. Ronny dived down and gingerly felt inside the bin liner. His anxiety cleared. 'Nowt's broken,' he called.

'What is it, like?' Al asked. Ronny carefully brought out a nest of three pet tanks. They were filled with the fluffy hamster bedding which had cushioned the fall. Big Al flashed angrily. 'Ye've got me sweating like a bloody pig, risking me back, for a few auld glass tanks?'

'Not just any auld glass tanks. It's all I've got left from the pet shop.' Ronny smiled. 'Ironic that. Hamster bedding saved them.' He shook his head. 'I used to hate hamsters. Just wanted to sell the exotic pets, y'kna. That was me vision, like.'

'Aye, and that's why the whole bloody enterprise went arse up.'

Ronny dwelt on the tanks for a little longer, then ceremoniously blew the particles of hamster bedding from his fingers. Wisps of the material fell into a puddle which had gathered from the morning's intermittent rain. Querulously, Al watched Ronny place the black bin liners in the hold of the van. As he closed the back doors and tied the twine, Ronny sighed nostalgically. 'That's me life in there. You see, we made an agreement. Audrey and me. Apart from the new things we've bought since the . . .' Ronny paused delicately. 'Since we got turned awer, we agreed only to bring what was special. To the new place, like. What really had, y'kna, sentimental value.'

'So where's her stuff then?'

Ronny reached into one of the bin liners and brought out a single shoebox, bound with rubber bands.

'Is that all?' Al asked.

'Apart from that dresser we shifted before. And all the framed photos of the bairns.'

Al groaned. 'That dresser was taking the piss. Me arm's still badly, y'kna.' He reached round his back for the sling hanging there, and popped his arm in it. 'Better keep this on, just in case anyone sees. Y'kna, videos me workin'. I'm deein' a Claims Direct on me bad arm.' He turned to the children on the safety barrier. 'Seen anyone suspicious hanging aboot, yous lot?' he asked.

'Just ye,' Brosnan replied.

'Cheeky bastard,' Al laughed.

Ronny was looking at the arm in the sling. 'Are ye sure ye got that falling after ye'd left the club that neet?'

'Why aye,' Al nodded, evasively.

''Cos after Jimmy left me on Keir Hardie Avenue that night, he said he was gonnae to give ye a talking to . . .'

'We've been through all of this,' Al interrupted him. 'It was just a joke. He wasn't being serious. It was Jimmy just taking the piss. He's a cunt and that's how he gets his kicks. Terrifying poor tossers like ye and me.' Both Al's eyes narrowed. 'Ye didn't give him that money, did ye? The ten grand he asked for?'

'Course I didn't.'

'Are ye sure?'

'Why aye.'

''Cos once you start paying him, he'll nivver leave up . . .' But Ronny had already got into the vanette. Al got in behind the wheel. 'If he starts blackmailing ye . . .' he continued.

Ronny's tone was businesslike. 'Ha'way, Al, we'd better get this lot to the new hoose. The meeting'll be starting soon.'

'That bloody meeting,' huffed Al. 'I'm getting sick of hearing aboot it. More cloak and dagger than *Carry on Dick*. It's pathetic. Why haven't ye just told everyone what they're getting? I mean, it's been ages since ye won. Why have you taken so lang?'

'It's what the winners' adviser said was best to dee. Divven't rush into things. She said that me and Audrey had a lot to work oot. With such a big family. The winners' adviser said –'

'Oh aye,' muttered Al, 'and of course Lady Muck knas best. She's probably not a real person anyway. Just a computer or a hologram or summink.'

Ronny looked out the window at the Teams. 'Moving oot o' after all these years. It's the end of an era.'

'I'm only glad yus gave up on friggin' Keir Hardie Towers.' Al threw his thumb over his shoulder, gesturing at the back of the van where the Keir Hardie Avenue street sign could be seen. 'The Teams is finished. Ye want a fresh start. Ye cannot

202

live in the past.' He broke off as though to mull over his own words. 'The Geordie's day is awer. What I mean is that gadgies like me and ye, why, we're dinosaurs. When they closed the pits they might as well just have left wor doon there an' all. Nee wonder they're knocking the place doon. Mind ye, for us two Geordies life is just beginning. We're the exception that proves the rule. The beagles what've escaped from the laboratory.' The smile turned into a frown. 'I divven't kna aboot where yus're moving to, but. It's in the middle o' neewhere. I've advised ye against it, so divven't come moaning to me when all them trees and fields start to dee yer heed in.' Al laughed and looked to share the joke with his friend, but Ronny was thoughtful. 'What's the matter with ye?'

'Mebbes God exists after all.'

'What the hell are ye on aboot now?'

'Well, where's the sense in it all otherwise?'

'Is it sense ye're wanting, bonny lad?'

'Aye.' Ronny nodded his head. 'It is. Since we've won, I've been thinking. I mean, how can it all just be a lottery?'

Al exhaled as he shook his head. 'Ye'll be the first person what ever foond religion because o' money.' Al put the key into the ignition, but before he turned it he suddenly stopped. 'Here's some more food for thought, Reverend bloody Slater.' He dug into his deep pockets and brought out a sheaf of letters. 'More paperwork. Came this morning. And every one a bairn what's gonnae die withoot yer help.'

Ronny sighed profoundly. He tugged disconsolately at his ponytail. 'When we won the lottery, I wasn't expecting anything like this. How the frigg do they kna where we live?'

'There's nee calculating the lengths that greedy people'll gan to.'

'Or desperate ones.' Ronny narrowed his eyes. 'I mean, if there was ever owt the matter with Terri or Toni and I didn't have the money for a operation or drugs . . .'

Al clicked his tongue. 'Ye still thinking of that Chloe, aren't ye?'

'I cannet get her oot me mind.' Ronny closed his eyes. 'I'm the sort o' person what likes to think that everyone's happy. I cannet abide to think o' folks suffering. Especially not bairns.'

'Just consider yersel' lucky to have been lifted oot o' it, bonny lad. As they say, life's nasty, British and short. So we might as well have some fun alang the way.' Al checked himself. 'And talking about fun. Here's another one of them nasties.'

Ronny stared at the envelope being held out to him. It was the same small white envelope, slightly grubby. 'What does it say?' Ronny whispered.

'Same auld shite, really. Aboot the circle being broken an' that. They're asking for money now.' Al picked the letter from the envelope. The same tabloid headline lettering littered the page. '". . . To mend broken circle you must pay. If not, the bad luck of a thousand broken mirrors be on you."' Al held the letter out to Ronny. 'Bit awer the top that like, eh?'

'I just hope they're not some bloody axe-wielding maniac.'

'Na, it'll be some auld gent from a bungalow in Surrey.'

Al turned the key. It took him three attempts to start the engine, and then the whole vehicle shuddered forward, belching out a cloud of thick smoke from its wobbling exhaust. 'For the last time,' said Al solemnly, 'see sense and divven't move to this new place. For a start there's nee local for miles; and then there's aboot as much chance of being able to watch some hot totty sunbathing topless next door as there is of seeing a ghost . . . Na, there's more chance of seeing the ghost.'

Its indicator light tink-plishing, the dirty white vanette drove unsteadily down the parade of shops. Passing the Londis supermarket, Ronny lowered the window to wave goodbye to Mrs Singh. As the vanette slowly mounted the slip road out of the Teams, once again rain began to fall from the slate-grey sky.

The rain grew harder, and the children jumped from the safety barrier. With a great shout they ran towards the burrow. The concrete cavern rang with their voices, as did the courtyard when they emerged. 'What's the matter with them bairns o' yours?' one of the sentinels called over to Audrey, who had just emerged out of the door of Flat 12A.

Audrey looked down at them; they had all settled under the ailing tree to shelter from the rain. She smiled to herself. 'They're high as kites, man. Bairns always is when there's summink new gannin' on.'

'So when yus off then?' the sentinel asked; it was Jennifer.

'Soon,' returned Audrey. 'We're having wor little meeting, and then that's us.' She looked over. 'Did Corky and Paddy carry that chair to yours?'

'Aye, ta pet,' Jennifer replied.

'And we got the fridge,' put in Brenda.

'Ta for the washing machine,' called Sandra.

The branches of the tree, famished with mid-autumn, afforded little shelter. And when the rain grew heavier, the children ran from it, screeching and laughing. 'It's gonnae be quieter roond here, mind,' said Brenda.

'Ye'll still be popping roond, mind, won't ye, Audrey?' Sandra asked.

'Why aye,' Audrey returned.

'Them pixie lasses will miss ye the most, man,' mused Jennifer. 'I divven't kna what they'll dee for a square meal noo.'

The children could be heard screaming down the burrow. 'Nee McPhee in the Teams,' sighed Sandra. 'That's a turn-up.'

'Get inside,' laughed Audrey, 'before yus have me mascara running.'

When the other sentinels had gone, Audrey remained at her parapet listening to the pounding hiss of the rain. She stared at the courtyard, greyed with drumming water, and at the drops creating a puddle in the groove of the walkway parapet, a furrow formed in the concrete by the press of her body over the many years.

In the flat the rain could be heard in a different key: a bass drumming against the roof. It seemed to mesmerise her. When at last she walked across the room, the unfamiliar noise of her tread in the empty flat pulled her up abruptly. She sounded like a stranger in her own home.

The pictures of the children had been taken down from the wall, but they had hung there for so long that the wallpaper still held their shadows like the negatives of photographs. Closing her eyes, Audrey sat on the only chair left in the flat, a stool from the breakfast bar.

She did not hear the man who came into the flat and stood watching her, so when she opened her eyes and saw him, she jumped. 'You look miles away,' Father Dan said.

'I was just wondering. How many times have I sat here listening to the rain, man Father Dan?'

'Well, that's one thing we're not short of round here. Still, I think you're doing the right thing.' The priest shook the rain from his jacket. 'You couldn't have stayed here. Not after the burglary.'

'And that Macarten lad in the burrow. It fair shook me up. If someone who's known you all his life can dee that, then anything might happen. But it was more than just that. We couldn't have stopped here anyway. It was impossible. People treat ye differently. They try not to, mebbes. But they dee.'

'Not to mention my friend and yours.'

'Macca? Aye. It's for the best. Thank God that chapter can come to an end at last.'

The priest brought a briefcase over to where Audrey sat on the stool. 'All the documents are here.'

Audrey took the briefcase. 'I'm nervous as a kitten. I've nivver had to face me family like this before. Y'kna, officially an' that. I think that's why we've put it off for so lang.' She looked at the door. 'They'll be here soon. They've just popped to the Wheatsheaf. To celebrate wor leaving.'

'Did you not feel like celebrating?'

She pursed her lips. 'I'm just having five minutes to mesel'.'

'And is Ronny all right about the move?'

'It's a compromise. Where we're gannin'. He's always loved nature an' that. And he doesn't want to leave the area, ye see, Father.'

'And do you?'

Audrey smiled. 'No. I wouldn't have chosen that hoose. It's an auld rambling place. But Ronny loves it. It had to be south of the Tyne and north of the Wear for him. Besides, he's had a feeling for the place right from before we won the lottery. Y'kna. A feeling.' Audrey laughed. 'Ye kna me, Dan, as lang as me family are happy, then I am.'

She fell into silence, her eye straying up to the dark patches on the wallpaper where the portrait gallery had been. 'Look at them faces,' she began. 'Before ye came in, I was thinking of them. Some of them grown-up with their own bairns noo, but I can remember seeing each one for the first time. Their faces all puckered up and angry with the birth. And none of them weighing nee more than a handful of feathers. Aye, each one resting so light in me arms that I could of carried them for ever and nivver ever got tired nor nothing.'

'The pictures have gone, Audrey,' whispered the priest. 'Ronny and Al have taken them to the new house.'

'Oh aye. So they have.' Audrey stared at the dark patches. 'The thing is, I've looked at them that often that I'll always see them. I just need to close me eyes. And there they are.'

'Sorry I gave you a shock when I came in.'

'I suppose ye could say I was saying me goodbyes.' She lit a cigarette, and held the light out for the priest who took out one of his Senior Services. The smoke from their cigarettes drifted across the emptied room. 'When ye live in the same place for so long,' Audrey began again, 'sometimes ye divven't notice time passing. Ye divven't see the changes. Then comes the day when ye have to shift. And all the goodbyes of the long years have to be said in a single day . . .' She broke off. 'I didn't think it would be this hard to say goodbye, Dan.' Distracted by emotion, she brought out a small object from the pocket of her real leather trousers. 'I foond this when we were packing.' She handed the object over to Dan. It was a keyring with writing on the fob. 'Bill gave it to wor when he became a father for the first time.'

The priest read out the message on the fob: '"A mother holds her child's hand for a few short years, but their heart for ever."'

Audrey nodded. 'See the way we call God wor Father? We've got that wrang. Only a mother could understand the pain and the pricelessness of the whole thing. The joy what gans hand in hand with the agony. The weirdness of it all. All them little moments that cut yus to the quick but are worth everything else put together. The start to the finish. It's a mystery really, isn't it? I mean, why do we feel such love for a little thing what's covered in shite and cries all the time? And why do we keep on loving them when they're big, ugly and stupid? No matter what they dee.' She pointed at where the pictures had hung. 'Ee, but they grow up so quick. One moment they're in your arms, the next they're oot through the door with their own lives to lead. And . . . and . . .'

The priest took out a quarter-litre bottle of whisky, toasted Audrey with it and drank. 'Here's to God, our Mother.'

'I must be gannin' bloody soft in me auld age. Here, give us that bottle before I start proper blubbing.'

Dan watched Audrey drink, the whisky tinking audibly as the air bubble bounced up the neck of the bottle. 'We're going to miss you round here, Aud.'

'Haddaway. It's only just up the road, man. We're still gonnae come to Mass with ye.' Audrey took another draught of the spirit. 'Funny thing is, it wouldn't surprise me if Ronny starts coming to church an' all. He keeps on asking all these questions.'

'Questions?'

'Aboot the meaning o' life an' that. Ye see, it's done his heed in. Actually winning the lottery. He keeps on gannin' on aboot the chances against it. He thinks it, I divven't kna, shows summink aboot the universe.' Audrey handed the bottle back. 'Then we get these begging letters. Full o' bairns what's dying. It really chokes him.' She broke off thoughtfully. 'The other day he asked us whether I thought animals went to heaven. It's as if he's becoming, I divven't kna, more spiritual.'

Father Dan looked at her steadily. 'Do you not realise yet, Audrey?'

'Realise what?'

His Adam's apple bounced as he drank. 'Ronny's one of the most spiritual people I know.'

'Eh?'

'Do you know anyone kinder?' Audrey shook her head. 'Do you know anyone who dreams more?' Audrey shook her head again. 'Do you know anyone who can spend a whole day's hard graft on a roof and at the end of it be full of a view he'd seen countless times before? There's something he's got that keeps him going.'

Audrey smiled. 'His delights.'

'What?'

'He calls it his delights. Y'kna. All the little things that ye might miss in the day-to-day. A tree, a view, an auld friend. That's what he sees. His delights.'

A look of awe came into the priest's eyes. 'He's seen God.'

Nodding, Audrey smiled. She held out a hand. 'I'm shaking like a leaf. I'll be glad when all of this palaver's awer and done with. Once I've telt them what they're getting, we can get on with the rest o' wor lives. It's been playing on me mind.'

'Are they all right about it? The family?'

'Course they are. They keep on asking about it, mind. Wanting to know how much an' that. That's been the hardest bit. Keeping it quiet. I've nivver kept a secret before. And they've kept on chipping away asking. Hinting. Driving us mad really. And all the way through it I've been sorting oot their hooses what I'm buying them.'

'Maybe you should have told them that they were getting property. I mean, they might have been expecting money.'

'They'll be fine.' Audrey nodded emphatically. 'I kna people always say that trouble comes hand in hand with fortune. That them that win the lottery end up fighting with their own family like rats in a sack. But that's not us. We're close. Besides, I read the cards. Everything's set fair.'

The priest's laugh boomed through the empty room. 'Deep down you're just a heathen, aren't you? I mean, you really believe that a pack of playing cards can tell the future, don't you?'

Audrey smiled. 'Me mam used to do it. And hers. It just gets passed on. Comes with the territory.'

'I don't understand that part of you,' Dan said simply.

'I divven't neither.'

'This business of you knowing things. Like that you were going to win the lottery.'

Audrey did not speak for a while. 'The thing is, man Father, what I've learnt awer the years is that it's better not to think too much aboot it. I've frightened mesel' a lot in the past.' She paused to inhale deeply on her cigarette. 'That's why I haven't passed it on to my bairns.' She shook her head adamantly. 'There's things my mam taught me aboot the gift that I haven't passed on. And I won't. It's better to leave it. Easier. They divven't kna. Leeanne and the others. They divven't kna I haven't passed it on. I've taught them the cards and that kind o' little stuff, but the rest? It's better being left.'

'The gift?'

'That's what me mam called it.'

'What is it?'

'I divven't kna. All I kna is that it's all mixed up with me faith. 'Cos you kna me faith? Well, ye'll see it soon. Ye'll see it when me family come through that door. Because that's what my faith is, Father. Me family.'

They smoked thoughtfully for a while. 'There might be a few problems,' Dan began again. 'It's inevitable that money brings them. It would probably be just as well to expect them. Then you can overcome them.'

'I kna me family, man Father. There'll not be any problems. Oh, I kna what they're like areet. A rough lot. But we're solid. Nothing could break us.'

Father Dan walked over to the breakfast bar to bring back an empty beer can as an ashtray. It was a tin of Alloa Sweetheart stout. For twenty-five years it had lain behind the cooker. When he came back to the stool, Audrey had stood up. She had her back to him. All at once her body seemed to have sagged. Her shoulders were rounded, and the hands that he could see hugging herself were those of an old woman. The face that turned to the priest was, despite the expensive make-up and the frame of recently styled hair, faultlined with the weight of years. And as she spoke, her voice too seemed husky, its fabric worn. 'There's been something else on my mind.'

'What?' The priest took the bottle and screwed the cap on after a final slug.

'Something I thought I'd forgotten all these years past. But it's come back to me with a bang.'

'Terri and Toni's mams?'

'No. Not them.' Audrey took a deep pull on her cigarette. 'Terri's mam's coming oot in under a year. She'll be areet. It was that friggin' boyfriend of hers what did it. I think she genuinely thought she was just carrying for that fella of hers. Toni's mam, Donna? She's a different kettle o' fish. She's . . . lost. She's not a bad lass. I mean, look at Toni. That's what her mam was like at that age. But somehow I lost her. I thought she'd have come back by now.' An uncertainty hovered in Audrey's eyes for a while, then resolution sharpened her features. 'We'll sort her out.' As Audrey continued to smoke, her hands trembled noticeably. 'It cuts me up to think of them two bairns growing up withoot a mam. Makes us wonder where I went wrang. What I did to make them lose their way.' Audrey bit her lip. 'For frigg's sake, man Dan, give us a drink.' After a sharp pull of whisky, Audrey stared back at the priest with an imploring look that was foreign to her nature. 'But that isn't what's been on me mind.'

'Audrey, what are you trying to say?'

'It started aboot a week after we won. The night me and Ronny went to Hartlepool. It came over me that night like a slap in the face.'

'What did?'

'This thing what's been bothering us. And it's been growing on my mind since.' There was a long pause broken at last by Audrey herself. 'You see, I keep on thinking he might turn up. That he might read the newspaper and come. That he might still be alive somewhere.'

'Who?'

'I haven't seen him for fifty years, but I keep on thinking . . .'

'I see,' the priest closed his eyes as he inhaled his cigarette again. 'Your father.'

Audrey looked at her friend. 'How do ye kna?'

'How long have I known you for?'

'But I've nivver once mentioned him.'

'You didn't need to.'

With the cigarette wedged between her lips, Audrey clenched her fists tightly. 'How could he have just gone off like that? And me only a bit bairn?' The knuckles reddened and then turned white. 'I've blocked him from me mind for fifty-odd years; and the lottery, it just knocked the barrier clear away. Like a tidal wave. Bam! The dam's doon.' Audrey raised her fists and for an instant rage contorted her face. 'The bastard,' she spluttered. 'The fuckin' bastard. He makes us feel like hitting oot. He makes us feel like murder. He makes us feel . . . he makes us feel . . . like a little lass what's lost in the rain . . . and neebody wants wor . . . and there's nee where safe to gan.' Her shoulders heaving, she grunted as though shrugging off a great load. Then her voice brightened. 'To hell with him. I'll get over it. I get over everything, me.' She suddenly laughed. 'Ye'll have to get in there with Cheryl quick smartish, mind, if ye divven't want to lose her to Big Al.'

The priest grunted with laughter. 'I'm glad that you two made it up.'

'She's worth a hundred of the rest of that back-stabbing crew. In fact, I've changed the money roond a bit. I was gonnae give the lasses from work a bit, to drink with, y'kna. But I'm gonnae give it all to Cheryl instead.'

'Is that wise?'

'What d'ye mean?'

'Won't it create bad feeling?'

'Tough.'

Father Dan extinguished his cigarette in the Sweetheart stout can. 'Is Ronny's family coming?'

'There only is two. His auntie, Queenie they call her. And cousin Warren. He's a sea-coaler in Hartlepool. I divven't kna whether they're gonnae be able to come today. Cousin Warren works the tides.'

The priest and the grandmother had lapsed into silence, so that only the falling rain could be heard, when the door was thrust open and the group from the Wheatsheaf burst in dripping with water. Immediately they fell silent too. Bill walked over to his mother; on his arm was the barmaid. 'This is Karen, Mam,' he said, his whisper slurring under the weight of four pints of lager. 'She's the barmaid at the Wheatsheaf. And me fiancée.'

Karen looked levelly at Audrey, holding out her hand to show the ring. 'We've just got engaged.'

'Well, let's get a move on,' said Leeanne quietly, ignoring Karen disdainfully. 'Paul's got to get back to work. Even if neebody else has to.'

With the others had come a woman nobody else knew, accompanied by three teenage sons. 'This is Michelle, Mam,' added Bill. 'Y'kna, me ex.'

Karen gripped Bill's arm in a passion of possessiveness. 'I divven't kna what the fuck she's deein' here.'

Michelle glared coolly at Karen. 'I've got more right to be here than ye.' She pushed her three sons forward to Audrey. 'Here's three grandbairns ye didn't kna ye had, Ma McPhee.'

Mrs Armstrong's asthma rattled loudly as she took off the plastic rainmate which glistened with drops. Cheryl held her walking stick for her. Paddy and old Uncle Dick, despite the alcohol they had consumed, stood there silently. Corky and Theresa stared at Audrey. Joe and Ginga stood at the back of the group, a hessian sack between them. 'Suppose ye're happy,' Joe murmured to Ronny. 'Now that yus're turning yer back on yer roots.'

Ronny chuckled. 'Glad to see the auld Joe back with us.'

But their banter died on the muted atmosphere. Even Al was quiet as they all stood bunched in the room, waiting in sodden suspense. Just then a loud shouting exploded into the flat as the children ran inside in a body. They too quietened instantly.

They had been waiting for a number of minutes when an odd couple knocked at the door. The man was shy and middle-aged. He bore some resemblance to Ronny, except for the hair: pulling the thick woollen hat off he revealed a flattened quiff of immense proportions, which he proceeded to tease back into rigid life. With him was a woman. Her features were also reminiscent of Ronny but where he was easygoing and open, she was harsh and crabbed. 'Cousin Warren,' Ronny greeted the man. 'How's it gannin'?'

'Champion, Cousin Ronny,' said Warren, smiling.

'And Queenie. How are ye?'

Queenie allowed Ronny to kiss her on the cheek. 'Now then, our lass's lad,' she growled at last. 'Fat as ever, eh?'

'Areet, Joe,' said Warren. 'Areet, Ginga.'

'Areet, Cousin Warren,' the old men replied. Joe turned to Ginga. 'Give him the veg sack.'

'I've got a load o' sea coal for ye doon below,' Warren replied, taking the hessian sack.

'Christ,' Al whispered to Cheryl, having inched up behind her unawares. 'The heady world o' finance or what.'

Dan nudged Audrey. She walked uncertainly over to the breakfast bar, and placed her briefcase on top of it. She beckoned Ronny who came over rather uncomfortably and stood behind the bar with her, fiddling with his ponytail. The briefcase opened with a click that resonated in the pregnant silence. All eyes followed Audrey as she brought out a number of documents. 'Ye kna why we're all here,' she said. 'So I won't waste nee more time.' Toni-Lee's camcorder was trained on her grandmother's face as she began. 'To each of the following we are giving a one-off payment of five thousand poonds. Cheryl . . .' At the mention of her name, Cheryl solemnly lifted her hand, a gesture copied by the rest of the people whenever they heard their name being called. 'Big Al, Mrs Armstrong, Joe and Ginga . . .'

'I divven't want nee charity,' Joe growled.

'I'll have yours then,' Al quipped.

'. . . And Cheryl gets another two and half grand on top of that for being the only mate I can proper trust.' Choosing another piece of paper, Audrey continued, reading from the new sheet. 'For each of me grandbairns, we're setting up a trust fund so that on their eighteenth birthday they each get ten thoosand poonds, and on their twenty-first birthday they will receive a payment towards a hoose to the equivalent value of fifty thoosand poonds.'

The silence deepened as everyone continued to stare intently at the bits of paper on the kitchen surface in front of Audrey. Mouths were tight with calculation. Cracked lips were tentatively licked.

'Auld Uncle Dick and Father Dan will both receive a one-off payment of ten thoosand poonds. And to each of me bairns, and to Ronny's cousin Warren and Auntie Queenie, a hoose on Woodside Gardens.' Audrey breathed in, flushing with satisfaction now that the proceedings were coming to a close. 'We've already bought them. Y'kna, top o' Dunston, near Lobley Hill, they're lovely.' Hurriedly, Audrey added: 'I should just add that Queenie and Warren's hoose, not yet purchased, will be the same value in Hartlepool.'

The silence held for a moment as everyone took in all the information, and then pandemonium broke out. A chaos of countless voices gushed forth peevishly.

'So it's not gonnae be money?' Bill's fiancée Karen demanded.

'Donna and Becks get the same as me and Paul?' Leeanne gasped in disbelief. 'We work every day that God sends, and thems dee nowt but cause trouble, and we get tret the same?'

'And what aboot these three lads?' Michelle demanded. 'Are they getting the same as the others?'

Leeanne rounded on her. 'She's only giving money to her own grandbairns. Not every rag, tag and bobtail that crawls in off the street.'

'They *are* her grandbairns, man. I was married to him, wasn't I? And he kept on coming back when he wanted to get his leg awer.'

'All three o' them are mine?' Bill asked, staggered. 'And they've been brought up in Sunderland an' all.'

'What aboot grandbairns-to-be?' Karen asked, forcibly yanking Bill away from Michelle and placing his hand on her womb. 'Do we get double if it's twins?'

'Does it have to be Woodside Gardens?' asked Paddy. 'I've sort o' settled in South Shields.'

The individual speakers became lost in the general mêlée of dissent. 'I divven't kna why ye're giving anything to Donna and Becks after the way they've behaved.'

'Why give us hooses anyway, what's wrang with money?'

'I'll take oot a friggin' paternity suit if I have to.'

'There's been nee mention of me being tooken as a proper adviser.'

'What the hell is she giving money to that priest for?'

'It's just not fair.'

'It's a proper rip-off.'

'I feel really cheated, me.'

Then a harsh, icy voice cut through the rest. It was Queenie. 'There's awer many of thems,' she intoned. 'We want more. Give us ninety grand, that's only fair. We need a hoose with off-the-road parking for Warren's Land-Rover and wagon.'

After a few moment's silence once again the flood gates opened. 'Who the hell does she think she is?'

'Aye, what's it got to dee with her?'

'What a bloody cheek . . .'

In disbelief, Audrey watched her family fall on each other.

When at last they had all gone, Ronny and Audrey still stood behind the breakfast bar. They did not move for a long time. 'Divven't worry,' said Ronny calmly. 'They'll get over it. Once they get used to it. I mean, look how happy they were in Florida.'

Without answering, Audrey went through to the bedroom. When Ronny joined her, she was standing at the window gazing out over Gateshead. He watched her from the door. 'Divven't worry, man,' he cajoled. 'You'll see. The family, they'll settle down.'

'It's not that.'

'What is it then?' He fell silent for a time, and gazed at his wife who continued to peer at the well-known view. 'Is it the same thing upsetting ye now that was upsetting yus in Hartlepool? I mean, is there summink yus're not telling me?'

'Na.'

'Ye're not . . . seeing someone else, are ye, Aud? Another man?'

'Ronny man,' whispered Audrey hoarsely, 'will ye just leave us alone for a bit.'

Ronny withdrew. Waiting in the main room, he stared at the Sweetheart stout can that stood forlornly on the breakfast bar: the last of their belongings. Then he trailed disconsolately through the rest of the flat, pausing in each room. He was in the bathroom when he heard the hammering. When he came back into the sitting room, it had been strangely darkened. Puzzled, he looked about. Just then Audrey came out of the bedroom. 'What's gannin' on?' she asked.

The hammering continued, a violent banging that seemed to cause the whole place to shake. They could also hear the sound of voices. And then they realised. A green metal hoarding had been placed over the front door. The council was already boarding up their flat. They were being sealed within.

Chapter Four

I

'Ee, Audrey,' gasped Cheryl. 'It's just so beautiful.'

The two women gazed at the lounge of the new house. 'It is, isn't it?' Audrey replied.

Cheryl clapped her hands silently together in rapture. 'It's like summink from *Hello!* magazine.'

The huge room was large enough to have swallowed the entire floor space of Flat 12A. Chintz festooned the lavish furnishings. The luxurious salmon carpet absorbed the foot. 'This interior decorator from Bainbridge's came,' Audrey explained. 'But it was us what chose the colours.' Cheryl stared in speechless adoration at the tied-back curtains which billowed from the massive poles like a pair of pink bridal gowns. 'In fact,' added Audrey, looking about proudly, 'we ended up choosing everything really.'

'It's just so beautiful,' Cheryl managed to gasp at last. 'Like summink from the telly.' She paused and looked at Audrey's freshly peroxided hair with pink highlights. 'It gans with yer hair an' all.'

At that moment the doorbell sounded: a loud peal of Big Ben chimes reverberating sonorously through the whole house. 'That'll be the caterers,' said Audrey.

'Ee,' said Cheryl, 'have I come too early?'

'Divven't talk daft, man Cheryl. Ye can come here any time.'

Cheryl smiled. 'I pulled a sickie at work. I really want to enjoy this party. I feel as though I haven't seen yus for weeks.'

'And the rest of the lasses know that the minibus is picking them up at the Red Quadrant doors straight after their shift?'

Cheryl nodded. 'I've told them.'

Audrey smiled. 'I'll be glad to see them again. It's time to make up. Life's too short to spend it fighting.' The Big Ben chimes sounded through the house again. 'Keep yer friggin' hair on!' Audrey yelled.

Left alone in the sumptuous room, Cheryl lowered herself carefully into the gargantuan leather sofa. As though overawed by the comfort, she remained perched delicately on the edge for a while, gazing breathlessly at the room. Then, with a little cry, she sank back on to the deep give and, eyes closed, wriggled her body into the generous upholstery. From the high perimeter shelf a whole crowd of toby jugs leered down at her drunkenly; among them was the African grey parrot, sleeping soundly; while, from the plates on a delph rack, shepherdesses averted their eyes coyly. Opening her eyes, and lifting her hands to her mouth, Cheryl moaned with pleasure at the scale of the opulence.

A television set, the size of a small cinema screen, dominated one side of the room. A huge marble-effect fireplace filled another wall. The top of the mantelpiece was crammed with ornaments, among them a pair of 'Love is' children standing on tiptoes to kiss, a flying dolphin, a statue of the Virgin Mary and a Red Indian whispering into the ear of a wolf. More ornaments peered out from a glass-fronted cabinet that stood almost as tall as the ceiling. As Cheryl studied the room, the cut glass of a massive chandelier glinted headily. It seemed to dazzle her, and for a moment, her eyes narrowed.

'We'll have the food served in here,' Audrey said as she swept into the room with the caterer.

'Brilliant,' said the caterer, seeming a little dazed. 'We'll just get sorted and then we'll come in and set up.'

'And make sure there's plenty to eat,' Audrey said. 'I want it posh, but not too posh, if y'kna what I mean. I want folk to be able to have decent portions. None of this stuffed spinach leaves.'

'Yes,' said the caterer uncertainly. 'Funny place this.'

'It's got a private road,' Audrey replied.

'We passed an old stately home or something. All in ruins. Could just see it in the trees.'

'That'll be the big hoose. Derwentside Manor.'

The caterer studied Audrey. 'Been living here long, have you?'

'Didn't you know?' Audrey demanded, winking at Cheryl. 'I'm the sixth Duchess o' Gatesheed. And this is me lady-in-waiting, Lady Chezza of Teams-Dunston.'

When the caterer had gone, Audrey grabbed Cheryl by the arm, 'look at this, man Chez.' She took her over to a pair of French windows, and opening them, led her friend outside on to a raised terrace. 'We can have tea and that on here come the spring.' Audrey's breath condensed on the damp early November air. All morning a feathery drizzle had tickled the mist which enveloped the old house.

'Aye,' nodded Cheryl. 'Or a crate o' Diamond White.'

Even Audrey's ringing decibels of laughter were smothered by the dense fog. The heavy, dripping silence which hung above everything seemed to muffle and slow the world. On the terrace, solid mahogany garden furniture was wrapped under green covers. There was a row of earthenware pots from which ferns uncurled. Stone steps led down to a rose garden. Audrey pointed into the mist across a chain of lawns to where some trees could just be made out. Beyond that lay forest and ruins, the vast pleasure gardens of the Derwentside Estate, at the heart of which was the Long Walk. 'That's a orchard,' Audrey said, pointing at the visible trees. 'Two acres all in all. We'll have some canny barbecues an' that here in the summer.'

'And what's that?' Cheryl asked, pointing at a huge pile of branches whose shape hung in the brume.

'Tonight's bonfire.'

'Isn't it a bit near the trees?'

Audrey shrugged. 'Ronny's in charge. Mind ye, with the weather we've been having, I doubt it'll burn at all.'

'Ee, remember the bonfires we used to have at the Teams?'

There was a pause as both women gazed at the pyre. 'We've always enjoyed worselves on Bonfire Night,' Audrey said. 'And it'll be just as good here. You'll see. In fact, it'll be better. We've really pushed the boat out for tonight.'

'Ye've come a long way from the Teams, pet.'

'Nowt's changed really. We're just living in a bigger hoose. For me it's the old things what still matter. Family, friends, Ronny.'

'Aye, I suppose what really matters nivver changes.' Dressed in her best pinstripe leggings and mohair jumper, Cheryl hugged herself against the dankness. The leggings were shiny about the knee. 'It's so quiet here,' she whispered.

Just then a loud engine roared into life, shredding the rustic peace. Shouting voices rose with the motor. Audrey smiled 'That's Bill and the bairns on the motorised microscooter. Ee, they've been on that thing since we moved here.'

Somewhere in the mist, the engine and voices could be heard passing by. Just as they faded to a steady drone on the damp stillness, a bass thump began from one of the windows up above. Cheryl stared up at the side of the house. It was an eighteenth-century, stone-built parsonage. 'That's Leeanne in the mini-gym,' Audrey informed her. 'She's on a fitness kick.' Audrey laughed. 'I divven't think this place has heard so much noise for centuries.' Audrey took Cheryl by the arm again. 'Ha'way. The best is yet to come.'

Audrey led her back into the house and ushered her through one of the doors that led off from the lounge. As she stepped into the new room, Cheryl fell silent. 'You were right,' she murmured, awestruck. 'It is a bairn's dream.'

It was another large room, with a low ceiling. One corner

was devoted to the needs of toddlers with an entire fitted play-kitchen, playhouse and boxes overflowing with toys. Another corner had been converted into a disco, complete with DJ's podium, dance floor and a metal scaffolding covered with lights. There was a dressing-up area with a rail of Disney costumes and glitzy dresses. A table-football game stood in the middle of the room, while a toy train track ran round the circumference. A spaghetti of PlayStation wires frothed from two huge televisions. On the walls were the pictures of Audrey's children and grandchildren that she had brought from the flat, and with them hung a new set, showing each child in a different Walt Disney costume.

'I've always wanted summink like this,' Audrey said quietly. 'A room special for the bairns.'

'They must think they've died and gone to heaven.'

Audrey nodded. 'Them bairns mean the world to me.' As they stood there gazing at the room, a double rhythm beat down from above: the bass of the music being played in the mini-gym above, and the heavy pounding of Leeanne on a rowing machine.

Back in the lounge the two women sank into the sofa. 'So what d'ye think of it all then?' Audrey asked as she took out two cigarettes. She lit one and handed it to her friend.

'It's amazing. To die for, man Aud. Mind ye, that place in the Meadowings was gorgeous an' all.'

'Aye.' A wistful look came over Audrey, but she expelled it with a large wreath of smoke. 'Ronny's always loved nature. And then he had the feeling aboot this place. Y'kna, the Derwentside Estate. He was looking at it the day we won the lottery. Then we came here that night. Fell asleep underneath the column. So mebbes it's meant. Besides, he didn't want to leave Gatesheed. Oh, he would have done if I'd asked him. But I didn't want to. Next summer we'll get gazebos and mebbes a swimming pool in the garden.'

'It's a bit oot in the sticks, mind, isn't it?'

'Ye wouldn't believe how dark it gets.' Audrey chuckled. 'Last neet I got up to gan and nearly ended up pissing in the attic.'

'Is it not lonely for ye? I mean, ye cannet just gan oot the door and on to the walkway for a chat nee more.'

'Why no,' said Audrey. 'It's not lonely. The family are here all the time. Terri and Toni have got their own bedrooms. And hopefully me mates'll come roond all the time. This isn't gonnae be wor last party, is it? Then there's six other private hooses on the estate as well.'

'So what they like then, yer new neighbours?'

'I divven't kna.'

'But yus've been here for a few days already.'

'Well, that's what we're having this hoose-warming party for. So everyone can get to know each other.'

'And are they all coming? All the posh ones?'

Audrey nodded. 'Ronny posted them all a invite.'

Cheryl fell into thought. 'It'll be areet, won't it? I mean, having the two sets in at the same time.'

'Two sets?'

'Why aye, the lasses from the work and yer new neighbours. I mean, they'll get on areet, won't they?'

'Why shouldn't they?' Audrey asked.

'Nee reason, nee reason.'

'After all, people are just people.' Audrey chuckled. 'I've really been looking forward to it. The hoose-warming. I haven't had a decent get-together for weeks. And this is the perfect excuse for getting legless. That burglary in the old flat was a pure sickener. Left wor with a nasty taste in the mooth. I haven't felt like it since then; not gannin' to the Catholic Club nor nothing.'

'And that's not like ye.'

'Exactly.' Audrey seemed to come to a decision. 'We're back to normal noo, mind. A good knees-up. That's what we need.' Audrey pointed at the door to the children's room. 'I'm letting the bairns dee a disco for the other bairns what come. And by the way, did I tell ye? Yus're having a make-over.'

'A make-over, what d'ye mean?'

'Hair, nails, face. The beautician's coming at four. We're all having one. I booked ye in an' all.'

'Straight up?' Cheryl bit her lip. She was profoundly moved, and smiled strangely. 'I've always wanted a make-over. To be pampered. To be special. Even for just a little bit.' She seized Audrey's hand fervently. 'Thank you.'

Audrey smiled. 'Well, we cannet have these posh bitches thinking they're better than us from the Teams. It's just as well ye've not got changed yet. We divven't want any make-up or owt on yer glad rags.'

Cheryl's smoothed down her mohair jumper, and smiled sadly. 'These is me glad rags, Aud.'

Audrey tried to disperse her embarrassment with laughter. 'We'll sort ye oot with summink, man. I've a fitted wardrobe full upstairs.'

'Ta, Aud,' said Cheryl, but for a second, resentment dulled her eyes. And then it was gone. 'Give wor summink supersexy, then. I've invited me new fella.'

'Yer new fella?'

'It's early days yet, mind. We've just started dating.'

'It's the first I've heard of it,' said Audrey in a slightly aggrieved tone.

Cheryl's voice was a little sharp. 'Ye've been busy, haven't ye?'

'I thought ye fancied Father Dan?'

'I dee. But he's not interested. Anyway, I hardly see him now that you've gone. I've got to face facts. Ye've got to get them to pick up the knife before they can butter your muffins.' There was a pause and then suddenly the room was filled with laughter that blew away the momentary estrangement.

'Who is he?'

'Aye, ye might kna him. It's Phil Heel.'

'Phil Heel?'

'Him what lives in the Square Flats.'

'Oh, him.' Audrey's face clouded again. 'D'ye kna what yus're deein', man? From what I remember of Phil Heel he's a bit of a nasty piece of work. A lady's man an' all, isn't he?'

'Ha'way, man, Audrey,' Cheryl chafed her in reply, 'he cannet be that bad, ye nivver shagged him.'

There was only the briefest of pauses before Audrey joined in laughing with Cheryl. 'What aboot big Al then, man Chez? He'll have his nose put reet oot o' joint tonight. He's been in the tanning tube waiting for ye all morning.' Their hilarity screeched out. 'Father Dan's in there at the moment.'

'An all-awer tan, is it?'

'Aye, tongue included.'

For a few moments their laughter was such that it drowned out the noise from the mini–gym above them. 'Ee,' smiled Audrey. 'It's good to have a laugh again.'

They smoked contentedly together in a companionable silence. Cheryl continued to look about the room, every now and again making little gasping noises of amazement and snorts of appreciation. Then, getting up, she went over to the French windows. 'It's a bit of a funny place this, mind, isn't it, Aud? I mean, when I was coming here with Ronny, there was like ruins an' that. They looked a bit spooky really. Ye could see them poking oot o' the mist like broken teeth. Everything's so old. I mean, this hoose itself must be canny auld.'

'Aye. Hundreds of years, I suppose.'

'Are yus not . . .' Cheryl broke off uncertainly. 'It's just that with ye having the second sight an' that. Can ye not tell if it's haunted?'

Audrey glanced around. 'I'm not sure whether I sense owt or not here.'

Cheryl gazed out over the terrace, rose garden, and lawns to where the bonfire squatted under the boughs of the orchard.

226

'There's bound to have been some lives lived here, mind. All sorts of doings.'

Audrey came over and stood beside Cheryl. There was a long silence as they peered together at the orchard. 'There is summink I've been thinking aboot actually,' Audrey said quietly. Cheryl turned to look at her. 'Aboot the, y'kna, spirit world.' Audrey seemed to think for a long time before continuing. 'Can I talk to yus aboot it? Only I divven't want to frighten ye.'

'Ye cannet frighten me. I went to see *The Exorcist* three times.'

'No, man Cheryl, this is proper real.'

'What ye on aboot?'

'Do you think it's only places that can come to be haunted?'

'What d'yus mean?'

Audrey closed her eyes. 'I've been trying to work summink oot, man Cheryl. Is it just places what can get haunted or . . .'

She broke off. Nothing was said for a long time. Cheryl gazed anxiously at her friend. 'What the hell are ye gannin' on aboot, Audrey man?' she demanded at last.

'I divven't kna really. It's just that . . . I've been wondering. Can people get haunted as well as places?'

Cheryl stepped back. She half smiled. 'Now you really are frightening me, man Aud.'

'Not half as much as I'm frightening meself.' Audrey shuddered suddenly. Opening her eyes, her voice filled the room. 'Is he haunting me?' she demanded desperately.

'Who?'

Audrey shook her head. 'He's been on me mind that much. And he never was before. It's as though he's trying to make contact with wor or summink. Or worse.' She sighed. 'To be honest with ye, these past few weeks the family have been at each other's throats. And me? Half the time I cannet dee owt aboot it. All I can think aboot is the one that's on me mind. The one what's knocking at the door.'

'Knocking at the door?'

'Wanting to come in.'

'What is it then?' asked Cheryl in a whisper.

'A face. From the past.'

'Whose face?'

Audrey flinched so violently with sudden fear that Cheryl looked about for an intruder. But they were still alone.

'Who is it that's haunting ye, man Audrey?'

Audrey lowered her head, and for a while seemed to be about to speak a name, but the word died on her lip. 'Someone I thought I'd forgotten,' she murmured, her head still lowered. 'Someone that's been dead for years. Mebbes decades. But someone that, all of a sudden, I've started thinking aboot all the time.'

'And you think this person's haunting ye?'

'Cheryl man, I'd forgotten all aboot him until we won the lottery, and then, all of a sudden, he keeps on jumping into me mind. He hangs on us like a bloody monkey. I can forget aboot him for a few hours. Mebbes even a couple of days. But then suddenly he comes back with a vengeance. Sticks his claws in me skull. And the stupid thing is, I divven't even kna him.'

'I'm gonnae shit mesel' in a bloody minute.' Cheryl shook her head. 'Me mam always said that the McPhee women had the second sight. So why do you think he's haunting you?'

'The thing is, he's likely to be . . . restless.'

'What d'ye mean, restless?'

Audrey looked at Cheryl solemnly. 'He wasn't a good man, Cheryl. In fact, he was a fuckin' bastard.'

'Look, will ye just tell me who the hell yus are on aboot?'

Audrey seemed to choke over the words before managing to spit them out. 'Me dad.'

'Yer dad?' Cheryl was amazed. 'But ye hardly even knew him.'

'I kna. That's what I'm saying. I hardly knew him, so why

do I keep thinking aboot him?' She shook her head, mystified. 'I've really been looking forward to the house-warming. Thought we could get everything sorted oot for it. Get the family an' that back together. Have a laugh. Drink to the future. But then, just now, as I was looking ootside I . . .' Audrey shook her head in bewilderment. 'I started thinking about him.' She reached out abruptly and took Cheryl by the arm. 'Ye didn't see him oot there, did ye?'

'Where?'

'Oot there, in the mist.'

'Eh?'

'Under the trees, looking over.'

'Audrey, for frigg's sake. Get a grip.'

'I thought I saw him there, and I divven't even kna what he looks like.' She tugged insistently on her friend's arm. 'I thought I saw him. That's why I'm asking, do ye think people can be haunted as well as places?'

When the door opened suddenly behind them, the women fell into each other's arms. Relieved to see the priest, Audrey and Cheryl burst into peals of laughter. 'Areet, Dan,' Audrey said. 'Been in the tanning tube?'

The priest's face was glowing with the ultraviolet light as he looked at them wryly. 'I need a drink after that horrendous experience. Do people actually go in one of those tubes for fun?'

Cheryl winked at Audrey. 'I like to gan topless mesel'. In fact, I'm gannin' up there in five minutes.'

They had only just turned from the French windows when something moved in the view outside: a figure materialising in the mist.

The figure stood in front of the bonfire for a while as though inspecting it. Then it bent down to pick up an object. The object was some kind of container. There was the sound of a liquid being poured as the figure held the container over the bonfire. Higher and higher the figure tried to slosh the bonfire so even the top branches were covered. 'What ye deein', man Al?' a voice called from the fog.

'Just putting some paraffin on it,' Al returned.

'But I've already put one lot on,' the voice said, alarmed.

'Well, we divven't want to disappoint the bairns with a bloody damp squib. It is Bonfire Neet, after all. Ye cannet deprive them of that just because yus've moved to bloody sleepy hollow.'

'Aye, but I divven't want nee accidents.' Ronny emerged from the mist, a woollen hat on his head, his ponytail beaded with droplets, his face anxious. 'For a start I think we've built it too near the trees. And then ye've splashed paraffin all over yer jacket. Yus'll have to get changed, we divven't want yus gannin' up like a Roman candle.'

'Since when did ye become such a wimp? Them bairns want a proper Guy Fawkes, and I'm going to give them one.'

'Aye, give them one, not *be* one.'

They looked over through the fog to where the stones of the house could just be made out. The steady drone of the motorised microscooter and children's voices suddenly built to a climax as the improvised vehicle roared by. 'Just a drop more,' said Al as he emptied the jerrycan over the pyre.

The bonfire was a great pile of branches and boughs, wooden palettes, cardboard boxes and, in the heart, a dark unidentifiable kernel. 'They're not tyres, are they?' Ronny asked suspiciously.

In a wheelbarrow at the foot of the pyre slumped the guy. Wrapped in a Sunderland football top, its grinning head was a joke-shop mask. 'Gan and get the ladder,' said Al. 'It's time for wor Mackem mate here to climb up top to the hot spot.' Ronny had taken a few paces when Al called him back. 'By the way, there's some more paperwork in the vanette.'

'Paperwork?'

'Ye kna. Them begging letters. The stream o' piss is thinning but the ones that do come are getting weirder and weirder. Oh aye . . .' he broke off to dig into his pocket, bringing out a dirty white envelope. 'And another ye-kna-what. We hadn't had a nasty for yonks. I thought whoever it was had given up.'

Glumly, Ronny took the envelope and plodded through the wet orchard. Behind him, he could hear Al opening another jerrycan and pouring yet more paraffin on the bonfire. As he continued on his way something soft rubbed against his cheek. He stopped, then took another step and again he felt the moist softness. Countless strands of spider silk hung between branches and from trunk to trunk of different trees, their gossamer pendulous with droplets. It was as though he was in the middle of an immense spider's web. He was gazing at the silken strands when all of a sudden, above him, he heard the honking of geese. It was distant at first, the toot of the gaggle's melancholy clarinet muffled by the fog. But then it passed directly overhead. The geese were not much higher than the top branches of the orchard, and Ronny could hear not only the individual birds' cries but also the whispering of their wings. A surprisingly delicate, haunting music.

When the gaggle had gone, Ronny carried on, every few yards feeling the explosion of softness on his cheek. The sickly smell of late autumn filled his nostrils. The mist was sharp with the mulch of the old season's windfalls: leaves and the unhusbanded fruit of apples and pears.

Crossing the cobbles of the old stable yard, Ronny went into the double garage, an outbuilding where a coach and gig had once been kept by the parson. Slowly, he approached the red Ferrari parked in the shadows. Staring at it for a long time, he reached out the tip of his forefinger as though to touch it, then turned from it decisively, and walked across to where the old vanette stood. Ronny had just taken the ladders down when he stopped abruptly. With a sudden stealth, he crept over to the doors of the garage and pulled them to. The garage fell into total darkness. Going back over to the vanette, he opened the door gently and got in. He closed the door as quietly as he could, and then put on the vanette's little light.

For a long time he sat motionless in the passenger seat where he had so often sat, gazing at the envelope Al had given him. At last he drew out the poison pen letter. Having read the threats spelt out in the tabloid lettering, he tossed it into the back. Then, impulsively he reached back into the hold of the vanette and dragged the bag on wheels towards himself. Dipping a hand in, he brought out a clutch of letters. He had read a few and was opening more when a great weariness seemed to come over him. The clutch of letters slid on to his lap and then on to the floor. Slowly, he reached into a breast pocket and brought out a photograph. It was creased and dog-eared with handling. Ronny stared at the picture of Chloe with a helpless air.

He never heard the garage door opening, and did not notice the man enter the garage until he was standing at the door of the vanette looking in at him.

'Hello, Ronny,' smiled Dan. 'I've come to find the booze.'

'Hello, Father.' Ronny fumbled the photograph back into his pocket. He got out the vanette hurriedly.

'Are you all right, Ronny?'

'Why aye,' Ronny replied with a forced brightness. 'Are ye areet, yersel', man Dan? Ye look a bit . . . yellow aboot the chops.'

'I've been in the tanning tube for ten minutes. I only did it for peace. Audrey kept rabbiting on.'

'Aye, she can be very persuasive. She's had me in there. Like summink from *Star Trek*, isn't it?'

Together they gravitated towards the Ferrari. 'Some machine that, Ronny.'

'To be honest, Father, I divven't kna why I bought it. I've nivver been interested in cars. I suppose I just thought I should. Because I could.'

Dan narrowed his eyes. 'I have a brother with a car like this.

A real Celtic tiger. He works for some investment bank in London. The Third World gets screwed, he gets the Ferrari, and I get the Teams bus.'

'I bet he gets the women an' all.'

'He does. Divorced. Twice. Yes, he gets the women. And then he loses them.'

They gazed at the car for a bit longer and then looked up at each other. 'Must be canny hard,' Ronny said softly. 'Not being allowed to, y'kna, get close to nee one.'

'It was a bloody nightmare when I was young.' Dan shook his head candidly. They lapsed into an easy silence. 'Have you got something on your mind, Ronny?' Without a word, Ronny took out the photograph of Chloe and handed it over. The priest studied Ronny closely for a few instants. 'Who is she?'

'I cannet stop thinking aboot her.' Ronny shook his head, then something deep within him seemed to burst, and he spoke rapidly. 'I divven't kna her from Eve, but I'm the only person who can save her. I mean, mebbes she's gonnae die if I divven't help her. Ye see, she needs an operation but her family cannet afford it. I can afford it. And if I divven't send her the money then she'll die. A horrible, lingering death. But then mebbes it's all a con trick. Mebbes there is nee illness. Mebbes there is nee Chloe at all . . . '

The priest studied the photograph. 'The begging letters are still coming then?' Ronny nodded. 'Let's have a drink.' The priest looked about the garage.

'Al's in charge of the booze,' Ronny said. 'He has a mate in the off-licence trade. Or something like that. He'll have stashed it in here somewhere.'

The priest handed him the photograph back. 'It doesn't really matter, you know.'

Ronny was taken aback. 'What, it doesn't really matter about Chloe?'

'Not really, no. Whether she's genuine or not. Doesn't

really matter. What I mean is that all over the world there are literally millions of Chloes.'

'What do you mean, Father?'

Dan looked at Ronny. 'Can I be blunt?'

'Why aye.'

'Well, you've got spare money. There are people with nothing. You could feed them or get them medical care. If you don't, they die. And every one of them, man, woman or child, a Chloe. Do I need to say anything more?'

Ronny exhaled softly. 'It wasn't supposed to be like this. Winning the lottery. It wasn't supposed to be aboot any Chloe. But I just cannet put her from me mind. I cannet stand to think o' bairns suffering.'

'Can I be blunt again, Ronny?' Dan pointed at the Ferrari. 'It's what I tell my brother. He's still talking to me. Just.' Suddenly the priest brought his hand smacking down on to the bonnet of the Ferrari. 'There's a couple hundred Chloes in there. They'll come with you every time you go for a spin. The dead ones will be in the boot.'

Ronny put the photograph back in his breast pocket. 'What am I gonnae dee, man?'

Dan shrugged. 'That's up to you.'

There was a long pause in which they gazed at the new car. Ronny's eyes blinked, and when he spoke his voice cracked a little. 'Why are there rich people and poor people in the world? Why do bairns have to get ill and die?'

The priest looked gently at Ronny as he put his hand on his shoulder. 'Some people have everything they want, and more. Others don't have enough. Why? I don't know. Maybe a drink will help us forget the question for a while.'

'Aye. The booze must be in here somewhere. Al'll have hoyed it in the garage to keep Bill from getting too pissed before the posh guests arrive.'

They began searching for the alcohol among the boxes, containers and black plastic bin liners Ronny had brought from the Teams. 'I haven't got roond to sorting this lot yet,' he explained. 'Not much for a lifetime's possessions when ye come to look at it.' He patted a mound of bulging bin liners. 'Before we won the lottery, this was it. The entire store o' me worldly goods. Just bits and pieces. Say if I'd been a ship that went doon, this is what would have washed up on the beach.'

'Is it all yours?'

Ronny stretched to the top of the mound, and brought down a shoebox bound with elastic bands. He looked at it for a moment, rattled it and then handed it to the priest. 'I divven't kna what's in it, but it's the only thing Audrey brought with her. Except for the photographs of the bairns and the auld dressing table.'

'Are you not curious?'

'Eh?'

The priest rattled the box himself. 'To see what's in it?'

'I am, I suppose.'

'If it was me, I'd want to know.'

'Know what?'

'What it is that's so important to her.'

Ronny shrugged. 'She'll show me it if she thinks I should see it.' Handling the box with a new thoughtfulness, he replaced it at the top of the mound. 'The funny thing aboot winning the lottery is that it doesn't change things how ye thought it would. I mean, it does in some ways. Like, it lifts ye free from loan sharks an' that . . .'

Dan winced. 'For God's sake, you hadn't borrowed again, had you, Ronny?'

'I'm afraid so. For wor anniversary. A couple of presents for Audrey and a special night for her. A night o' luxury. I borrowed it just before we won.'

'It's lucky for you that you did win then. Especially with my friend and yours taking over the Teams.'

'Don't I kna it, man Dan.' Ronny whistled with relief. 'I mean, if we hadn't won the money then I'd probably be a

235

paraplegic noo. But it's not so much that. What I mean is that winning the lottery, well, it hits you in ways ye didn't expect. For a start ye dee more thinking. And the thing is, it leaves ye with more questions than answers.'

'What do you mean?' asked Dan, searching behind the bin liners.

'Ye divven't have to gan up nee more ladders, or clean any more malls. But that's what yus'd expect. It's the different questions it brings that get me. Mebbes before, I was just too busy trying to put meat on the table to ask them.'

'Ask what?'

'What it's all aboot. Y'kna, life, the universe and everything. Your sort o' territory really.' Getting on to his knees, Ronny began burrowing through the mound of bin liners. 'Before, I suppose I just thought it was all like the roll of a giant dice. Y'kna, life was just chance. Like the lottery. Aye, that's what I thought it was all aboot. Life was just a giant lottery. Ask a lot of folks and mebbes they'll come up with summink like that. But now, now I cannet see it that way no more.' Ronny disappeared from view. 'There has to be some sense to it all. I mean, we're people, not bits o' driftwood cast up on the beach. See now? I cannet believe I could live me life like I did, thinking I was just a bloody number on a friggin' lottery ticket.' He fixed the priest with a steady eye. 'Y'kna the way bairns are always asking why? And nee matter what answer ye give them then they'll always just ask why? I've noticed it with Audrey's grandbairns. As they get older, they stop asking, because neebody can ever answer it. They get a sickener on it. But for me, deep doon, when all's said and done, that's what it's all aboot. This why. I mean, how can ye live withoot asking why? Ye cannet. Ye purely cannet.' The bags rustled, and Ronny came free at the other side of the mound. He climbed to his feet, using the bonnet of the Ferrari for leverage, and tried to smile. But he could not quite manage it.

A profound solemnity played over his features. 'And then there's the biggy.'

'The biggy?'

'Well, we're none o' wor gonnae be here for ever, are we?' Ronny cleared his throat. 'We're all of us going to have to face that last few minutes. We're all of us going to have to climb up the last ladder, so to speak. Get up on to the roof from which there isn't nee coming back doon.'

'What is it that's bothering you, Ronny?'

Ronny shook his head. 'I'm beginning to think there's more to it than the money. This winning the lottery caper. I mean, what does it point to?'

Father Dan stared levelly at Ronny. 'You're an incredible person, Ronny.'

'Am I?'

'There's not many people who win a fortune, and grow more thoughtful.'

A strange look came over Ronny's face. He seemed to be trying to bite something back for a few moments, but in the end was unable to stop himself talking. 'Audrey's got summink on her mind an' all.'

'What?'

'I divven't kna. She won't say. Mebbes it's someone from the past. Y'kna. An auld flame. Some gadgie she couldn't get awer from the past. Mebbes it's summink else.' Ronny grinned mirthlessly and suddenly clapped his hands together. He reached into a corner where a crate of bottles stood. 'Bingo!' He lifted a bottle and held it up to the light which came through the open doors of the garage. It was a crate of pale ale. 'Looks a bit oot o' date to me,' Ronny said. 'Still, Bill doesn't bother looking at the label.' As he bent down and picked up the crate, a genuine lightness buoyed Ronny's tone. 'Are ye all ready for the talent competition again this year, Father?'

'Yes. Same time as usual. Just after Christmas.'

'Well, put my name down. I'm gonnae enter this year.'

237

'You enter it every year, Ronny.'

'Aye, but this year I'm gonnae win. I've got a guitar.' Ronny tugged excitedly at his ponytail. 'Put wor Terri-Leigh's name doon an' all. She's learning the keyboard. She's brilliant already.' Ronny laughed self-deprecatingly. 'I was set on being a comedian. But now I want to be more soulful. Like Vin Garbutt. I divven't suppose ye've heard of him but –'

'Vin Garbutt? Course I've heard of him.'

Ronny beamed widely. 'Well, you're the first one that has. He's so funny. But sad an' all. There's one song aboot this Thai lass what has to become a prostitute to feed her family. Gets Aids and –'

'Aye, a proper bundle o' laughs –' Just then something clattered to the concrete floor, a broom. Dan and Ronny swung round to see Big Al standing in the shadows.

'How long have you been there?' the priest asked.

'All right,' Al answered. 'I've got one for you then.' A look of cunning glinted in his jackdaw features. 'What would yus dee if a piece of hot totty came into yer confessional, took off all her clothes and begged ye to shag her?'

Dan stared at Al unblinkingly. 'How long did it take you to come up with that?'

'Say this totty was someone like, I divven't kna, Cheryl? I mean, you're not telling me that you wouldn't at least cop a quick feel.'

'You know what, Al, I thought there was more to you than that.'

Al's opaque eye glinted. 'There's nee need to get upset, just 'cos I divven't believe in God.'

'And do you think that God believes in you?'

Half smiling, half frowning, Al wagged a finger at the priest. 'Clever, clever.'

'Is this all the booze there is?' Ronny called, rattling the bottles. 'We're wanting to droon wor sorrows.'

'Sorrows!' laughed Al loudly. 'He's won awer three million knickers and he's talking aboot drooning sorrows.'

'Audrey'll gan radge if there's not enough booze for tonight, y'kna. Ye were supposed to get Diamond White, lagers and some champagne.'

'Just a minute, marra,' Al replied as he beckoned the priest to the garage doors. His voice dropped to a whisper. 'What the hell are ye deein' confusing the poor lad? I've heard ye. He's been a bloody loser all his life, and now that summink good's happened to him you're putting a pure downer on him. Chloe? Look at the poor prick. He deserves to be happy if anyone does.'

'I agree,' the priest replied.

Suspicion sharpened Al's face. 'What's your game?'

Al stared darkly at Father Dan as the priest walked off over the cobbles of the old stable. Ronny came up behind him. 'Ye want to be careful of him, Ronny,' said Al, gesturing at the figure slipping into the mist. 'He's a bloody snake in the grass. Watch oot. Or he'll bite yer toe.' Al turned abruptly. 'I'll just gan and get the rest of the booze then.'

'Ye were supposed to have got it already.'

'Keep yer hair on, man. God, ye're turning into a reet bloody moaning minny. I just have to gan and pick it up.'

'Where is this off-licence of yer mate's?'

'North Shields.'

'That's miles away.'

'Aye, so I'd better gan in the Ferrari.'

With a quickness of movement belying his substantial frame, Al took out a pair of keys from his pocket and, bouncing over to the Ferrari, ensconced himself within. The window purred down. 'And for the last time, Ronny man, forget aboot Chloe. She doesn't exist. She's been invented to get your money.' The engine roared into life. Al revved it, a look of ecstasy on his face. 'Now this really does exist. Aye, we made the right choice here, bonny lad.'

When the Ferrari had pulled out of the garage a stack of boxes was revealed standing against the back wall. 'We said nee fireworks,' Ronny cried after the Ferrari. 'Al man, we agreed . . .'

The car stopped. Al looked out peevishly. 'What is it now?'

'We said nee fireworks. There's always accidents and –'

'I see, turn yer back on all the auld customs now that yus've moved to Gentryville. For frigg's sake, man, we've been making things gan bang on the fifth of November since we could walk. Ye might as well send Terri and Toni to elocution lessons and have done with it.'

And with that, Al powered out of the garage, whispered over the cobbles of the old stable yard and zoomed down the drive. From where Ronny stood he could hear the wheels sift through the gravel of the drive. Tentatively, he pulled at his ponytail.

Back in the garage, Ronny closed the doors, got back into the vanette and, once again, took the photograph out.

It was as he was staring at the eyes of the dying child that he grew breathless. The struggle for oxygen quickly became desperate. His mouth gaped with terror as his hands grappled with the dashboard. The model navvy came off in his wild grip and leered at him for a few moments before slipping from suddenly limp fingers. It continued to mock him from where it lay on his lap as, with his left shoulder lifted, Ronny clawed at his heart.

At last it had passed, and from the relief that followed, a look of resolution slowly grew in Ronny's eye. He sat immobilised there for a long time, flexing his arm, and all the while the resolution solidified. Finally, as though having come to a momentous decision, he took out a mobile phone.

His fingers shook as he consulted a scrap of paper in the little light of the vanette. A number of times he made mistakes, and had to begin dialling again. 'Hello,' he said when a voice answered at last. His own voice quavered. 'Is that the NHS

Direct helpline?' Ronny breathed in deeply and steadied the mobile phone with a second hand. 'No, I haven't used this service before,' he said in answer to a question. Looking at the garage doors anxiously, he began to give his address. And then the name of his doctor. He was growing increasingly nervous and frustrated, casting frequent glances at the garage doors. 'It's probably nowt,' he began after the preliminaries were over, 'but sometimes I . . . it comes awer us sometimes . . . I'm not worried or owt but I seem to get oot o' breath for nee reason . . . aye, there is pain sometimes . . . aye, doon me left-hand side . . . I mean, it's nowt really . . . but it's just comes awer me . . . it's come awer us noo so I thought I should get it put to rights . . .'

The short November day waned quickly to dusk, its fog dissolving the orchard, the lawns, the rose garden, the old parsonage and the whole Derwentside Estate beyond. The sounds of microscooter and children fell silent. Taxis appeared up the drive and then disappeared back down it, depositing the family and friends of the lottery winners. By six o'clock everyone had arrived. The excitement was growing as the caterers put the finishing touches to the buffet. 'Ee, look at them spicy potato wedges, I've nivver seen owt like that, me,' said Leeanne.

'The caterers dee all of the dos for Gatesheed Cooncil,' explained Mrs Armstrong appreciatively, leaning heavily on her metal hospital stick as she edged over to the trestle tables.

'And them boys know a pork pie when they see one,' agreed Bill.

'Aye,' nodded Leeanne. 'What a spread.'

There were baskets of Cajun-flavoured chicken wings, spiced potato wedges and vol-au-vents. Rounds of ham, turkey and beef. Brimming bowls of coleslaw, salads, pasta and rice. Trays of fresh bread rolls, pork pies and miniature sausage rolls. Pineapples, mangoes and kiwi fruit in tubs. And towers of gateaux, barrels of trifle and a dizzying Babel stack of fresh cream cakes. 'There's just everything,' said Mrs Armstrong simply.

'Where's the booze, like?' Bill demanded, stumbling and almost falling on the sherry trifle.

Just then, deafening music blasted out from the children's room. 'And a disco as well,' sighed Mrs Armstrong. 'Them new neighbours won't be able to believe their eyes. I mean, what more could ye want?'

Outside, an owl stirred from its favourite roosting place in the cleft of an oak tree. Probing the grass for the movement of small creatures, the night hunter flew silently down the long walk. Perching on one of its hunting boughs on an ancient apple tree in the orchard of the old parsonage, its eyes penetrated the fog to gaze at the lights from within the house as its ancestors had done since 1767. Entranced by the magic lantern show of silhouetted bodies on the curtain of the terrace window, it listened to the clatter of music and voices, only taking flight when something louder than everything else suddenly burst out. It was applause for Audrey's entrance.

She wore a ball gown of Regency proportions. On a rather incongruous, chunky belt was written the word ARMANI. Attached to her wrist was a bag with GUCCI lettered in silver links. Her huge gold crucifix nestled in the deep valley of her cleavage; her hair, newly dyed blonde and highlighted with pink, had been sculpted into a towering Marie Antoinette edifice. 'She looks like Elton John at his birthday party,' Al whispered to Ginga. 'Except for the baps.'

A bright glare of thickly made-up faces lit the lounge. Sparks of deep red nail polish glinted everywhere, while an overpowering scent of perfume and aftershave mixed with the dense clouds of heavy cigarette smoke. An array of flesh had been teased into titivating exposures, or wrenched there by heavy-duty but straining fabrics. And in the midst of it, Toni-Lee's camcorder lens peeked out like the nose of a curious rodent.

'What time are they coming?' someone asked Audrey. 'Yer new neighbours?'

'Seven thirty,' Audrey replied. 'We're having the bonfire at nine.'

'What are they like, Aud, yer new neighbours?' somebody else enquired.

The conversation became general. 'She doesn't know, she hasn't met them yet.'

'Hasn't met them? What yus on aboot? She's been here for days.'

'Aye, well, put it this way, once they see that spread they'll be glad they did get to know her.'

'And the disco.'

'Aye, it's like a night at the Bigg Market.'

'For free.'

'I've nivver seen owt like that spread.'

'Aye, it's a feast.'

A roomful of eyes turned to the buffet, catching the hand which had been hovering over the Cajun-style chicken wings basket. 'Nee starting yet, Al Greener,' Leeanne boomed.

Everyone stared over at Al and burst into laughter. He smiled cringingly, but a corvine resentment simmered in his eyes.

'Are they really posh, like?' someone else began. 'The new neighbours.'

'Put it this way,' somebody else answered, it was Joe O'Brien, 'the Queen Mother's family used to live here.'

There was a chorus of voices. 'The Queen Mother?'

'Eh?'

'Used to live roond here?'

'Straight up?'

'Bloody hell. It really is posh.'

'What yus on aboot, man Joe?' Leeanne demanded.

The old man shrugged. 'I've been deein' a bit research aboot the place.'

There was awe in the voice that asked: 'So she used to live here, the Queen Mother?'

'No,' replied Joe impatiently, 'but as far as I can make oot this is where her family came from.'

'What, this hoose?'

'No, man. This estate. The hoose is only the parsonage. Her place is a stately home. Or used to be. It's just ruins now.'

'Ee, I cannet believe it,' said Mrs Armstrong, deeply moved. She shuffled her unhealthy bulk a little into the deep plush of the sofa. 'So I'm sitting where the Queen Mother mebbes sat.'

'Are ye listening or what?' Joe barked. 'Her family had the big house. Anyway, what's the big deal aboot the bloody Queen Mother? Her family here, the Bowes-Lyon or whatever they call themselves, they were just coal owners.' He shook his head. 'Like a pack o' sheep. That's what yous are.' He mimicked them. 'Oo, the Queen Mother. How wonderful. How fantastic.' He snorted bitterly. 'See the Queen's mother. See all of her wealth? Killed the likes of us to build their fancy pleasure gardens, didn't they? We dug the coal so they could have a view.'

A wave of displeasure rippled through the gathering. 'Ee, ye cannet be saying things like that, man Joe,' Leeanne said.

'Why not?' the old man demanded.

'Well, some of the people at the party might be related to her. They'll still be in mourning.'

'For the love of God,' he moaned. 'Are ye really that ignorant?'

'Isn't it time to pull doon the red flag?' Paul asked. 'Nee one wants to hear them old songs any more.'

'Fads change,' pronounced Joe. 'Not the truth. Am I supposed to lie just because nee one wants to hear the truth?' His passion grew. 'And the truth is, the Queen Mother's family prospered on wor backs. They might as well have lined that bloody long walk of theirs with the broken bones o' the bairns what worked doon their pit. And I'll tell ye another

244

thing, they'd dee the same thing again if they could. Ye mark my words. They'd dee it again quick as spitting.'

A silence fell over the lounge. For a while nothing was said. All faces looked to Audrey, but they could not find her. The curtains drawn across the French windows twitched slightly and Leeanne walked over and opened them. Audrey was standing there, holding her Down's syndrome granddaughter Bernadette, gazing out into the night. 'What ye deein', Mam?'

'What?' Audrey returned, confused.

Leeanne looked at her mother strangely. 'Is everything areet, Mam?'

'I was just . . . watching . . .'

'It's just that Joe's carrying on. You'll have to make sure he behaves himself. He's cracking on aboot the Queen Mother being a murderer.'

For a few more moments Audrey seemed bewildered, then she relaxed. 'Joe O'Brien,' she called, 'there'll be nee bloody red flags here. Unless it's me deein' the flying.'

'What time's the minibus bringing the lasses from the Metro Centre?' Leeanne asked.

Audrey smiled. 'Soon as their shift's awer.'

'Is it the first time you've seen them since ye fell oot?'

'Aye, but nee one's holding a grudge.'

By seven o'clock the tension was mounting. Nobody else had arrived. 'For the last time, get off that bloody buffet, five-bellies,' Leeanne cracked.

'I'm starving, man,' Al protested. 'Building a bonfire's hungry work.' He rubbed his hands together. 'Wait until ye see the blaze, but. It'll be belter. I still think we should have got in a sack of potatoes, mind. To stick in the glowing embers. Just like we always did. And a whole bloody pig of sausages in silver foil. That's the way we always used to dee it on the fifth of November.'

There were grunts of agreement. 'Aye, we did.'

'Ee, we had some good times.'

'D'ye remember that time we built the bonfire by the river?'

'Aye, people lined the Newcastle bank just to see.'

'And when we built one on Windmill Hill.'

'They could see it from Sunderland.'

'There's always been a bonfire at the Teams. Even when it's pissing doon.'

It was at this moment that Cheryl came downstairs. She had been the last to finish her make-over. She wore one of Audrey's outfits, a sixties-style leather dress. 'Bloody hell,' Al moaned. 'They've turned her into a Page Three stunner.' Just behind her came Phil Heel. He wore a burgundy velour jacket and sunglasses, and walked with a self-confident bounce. 'What the hell's he deein' here?' Al gasped, stepping back from the buffet.

'Cheryl's new fella,' someone explained.

At half past seven none of the guests from either the estate or the Metro Centre had turned up. Gradually, those waiting fell quiet, staring with keen anticipation at the door which led through to the hall and the front door. Linzi came into the room of adults. 'Can we start the disco now?'

'Not just yet, pet,' Leeanne replied. 'They'll be here soon, and then yus can begin.'

Ten more minutes passed. 'Where is everyone?' somebody asked at last.

'It's only just getting on for quarter to eight,' came an answer.

'Aye, they're just being fashionably late. That's what rich people dee.'

'Aye, but what aboot thems from the Metro Centre? They should be here by now.'

'Ha'way, cannet we make a start on the spread?'

'I mean, there's the bonfire to light as well.'

At eight o'clock, Leeanne nodded when Linzi came up to her again. 'Gan on then, pet. Yus might as well start the disco.' She called Linzi back. 'Is yer nana not through there with ye?'

'No.'

An instant later Corky's voice burst into amplified life. 'This is DJ Corky playing the hottest, the hardest, the deepest . . .'

'They really will think they've come to the Bigg Market,' somebody chuckled.

'If they come at all,' Phil Heel commented witheringly. 'Now, ha'way, let's make a start shifting some o' that grub.'

'What d'ye mean by that, like?' Leeanne demanded.

Phil Heel was inscrutable behind his glasses. 'I mean these posh folks probably aren't coming.'

'Why not?'

'Why would they want to spend a night with the peasants?'

Leeanne was incensed. 'What d'ye mean, peasants. Mam's won the lottery.'

Phil Heel shrugged. 'As far as they're concerned, ye're still bloody scum.'

'Mam?' Leeanne called out. 'Divven't let him speak like that aboot wor.' She looked for her mother, but could not see her. She found her in the kitchen, all alone with Bernadette, standing at the sink and staring out abstractedly through the window on to the fog-bound courtyard. 'What's the matter with ye, Mam?'

As though shocked, Audrey jumped a little. With a quick breath, she recovered. 'Are they here yet?'

'No. And that Phil Heel's started on the buffet.'

At quarter past eight, people were growing restless. Everyone was staring at the buffet, poised on the edge of their seats, ready to pounce at the food as soon as they heard the word. 'They're probably all looking for somewhere to park in the fog,' Audrey suddenly decided. 'I'll just gan and see.' Carrying Bernadette, she strode out through the hall, and, opening the security locks, stepped out of the front door. On the doorstep she breathed in deeply, leaning against the door behind her. 'That's better,' she said to the girl, kissing her on the forehead. She stood there for a long time, peering into the mist, her eyes narrowed to a squint as though she was trying to pick out a single, furtive figure peeping from the night fog. 'I was your age,' she whispered suddenly to her granddaughter. 'When I last saw him. I was just your age. One morning he was there. Sitting down to breakfast. The next he was gone. I wonder if he's coming tonight. Not as I knew him. But I wonder if he's . . . here somewhere.' The owl hooted from close by, its cry reverberating against the stone of the house. Audrey bent down and nestled her face in Bernadette's hair. Even after only a few seconds, moisture had formed on the child's hair. 'It's a filthy night. And black dark. Ye'll catch yer death. Ha'way and in with you.' She threw one more piercing gaze into the brume, and paused for just an instant before turning back within doors.

Once inside, she breathed in deeply and then walked purposefully back into the lounge. 'Reet,' she announced. 'There's nee reason we shouldn't enjoy worselves. Let's start on the nosh.'

There was an audible laugh of relief as everyone surged to the buffet. Within ten minutes a din of munching jaws filled the lounge. Nothing was said for another ten minutes. At last the ravenous silence was broken by a resounding belch from Al. Just a second later a louder belch rang out. 'I divven't kna aboot this booze, mind,' Phil Heel said, wiping away the belch from his lips and holding up a bottle of pale ale to the light. 'It looks oot o' date.'

'Rubbish,' hissed Al. 'It's only just come from the brewery.' And as though to prove the point he let out a belch so resounding that the chandelier tinkled. He smiled with grim triumph.

At half past eight, at last, the doorbell rang. But under the din of the disco and the dancing, nobody heard the Big Ben chimes. Joe O'Brien just happened to be going to the toilet when the first guests arrived. Having struggled irritably with the system of security locks, the old man opened the door a few inches and peered suspiciously through the gap. 'Hello,' a man in an evening suit greeted him. Joe nodded tersely. There was an awkward pause. 'I've come for the . . .' The man fiddled with his bow tie. '. . . soirée.'

'You what?'

There was another pause. 'Is this the Slater residence?'

'Mebbes.'

'The thing is . . . They've invited me to a party.'

Joe opened the door wider, staring at the man as he stepped uncertainly over the threshold. Joe gestured towards the lounge with a terse finger and then disappeared into the toilet.

Abandoned, the guest stood there uneasily for a while then wandered to the lounge. He hovered in the doorway, flinching under the deafening boom of the music coming from the disco in the children's room. The lounge was deserted, scraps of food and empty plates everywhere. The children's room, in contrast, was heaving with dancing bodies. Just then there was a flurry of feathers and a parrot swooped at him, pecking his head as it passed. With a little scream of shock, the man ducked, then straightened up and looked about the room for his assailant. It was as he was searching for the parrot that he became aware of someone watching him. With his one eye blue and the other opaque, Al was peering at him from behind the trestle table of the buffet. 'Hello,' the guest said, embarrassed.

Al nodded, his mouthful of food making his words unintelligible. Still shovelling food into his mouth, Al closed the door to the children's room, and approached the guest. 'I met that Jeremy Clarkson once,' he said impressively, his cheeks puffed with chicken and his chin pebble-dashed with coleslaw. 'I telt him straight oot that the new Mercedes 100 was shite. And he accepted it. Have ye got change for a twenty-pound note? A tenner and two fives'll dee.' Embarrassed, the guest clutched for his wallet and opened it. In a quick swoop Al had seized the notes. 'I won't be a minute,' he

249

said, taking his plate with him and disappearing through the French windows, leaving the guest unattended again.

Bernadette was the first one to notice him standing at the doorway. He had opened the door to the children's room and was standing helplessly on the threshold. The child pointed at him, and nudged her grandmother. Audrey looked over. Then the rest followed. Almost instantly, the music stopped. 'Hello, pet,' said Audrey.

The guest blinked uneasily under the intense scrutiny of the roomful of people. 'Hello,' he managed to reply.

'Take yer coat off, love,' Audrey said, sweeping towards him.

The guest stepped back as a camcorder prodded him curiously. 'I can't stay.'

'Why not?'

He reversed further into the lounge, throwing out a staccato of excuses. 'I'm afraid we've got a prior engagement. A long-standing arrangement. We couldn't break it. I've just come to give apologies –'

'We've a buffet on,' Audrey interrupted him. 'It's lovely.'

The others followed Audrey, all eagerly gazing at the new arrival with a consuming fascination. 'Yes,' said the guest, 'it does look lovely. But unfortunately I've a prior engagement.'

'Well, at least let me make you up a doggy bag then. There's some lovely spiced potato wedges.' For a few moments the guest seemed overwhelmed by Audrey's huge hair, Armani belt and ball gown. 'And yus'd love these Cajun-style chicken wings.'

'Really, I can't . . . you see, I'm collecting my wife from *Uncle Vanya*.'

'Bring him an' all,' insisted Audrey. 'If he's an auld fella, he might enjoy the chance of getting oot.'

'No . . .' stammered the guest, retreating to the door leading to the hall. He tried to think of a convincing excuse, but couldn't. 'I've got to go ... you see, Uncle Vanya's housebound. He gets depressed.'

'Well, the more reason for ye to bring him here. Ye kna, get him out of himself.'

Suddenly the parrot swooped from nowhere. It hit him on the head. 'Who the hell let slim Jim oot?' Audrey demanded.

The guest turned on his heels, and was gone.

'He was a friendly chap,' someone said sarcastically. It was Phil Heel. 'And where's the rest of them poshos? Nee one's come from the Metro Centre neither.' He smiled at Audrey. 'Doesn't look like you're very popular these days, eh.' But Audrey wasn't there. She had left the room with Bernadette. 'Well, what are yous lot standing aroond like a box o' sad lettuces for?' Phil Heel demanded. 'How often have yus had a party at a millionaire's hoose before? Let's party!'

By nine o'clock no one else had come. 'Bob the Builder' began to throb out from the disco. 'Hey, that's our song,' Al said to Ronny.

'Have ye seen Audrey anywhere, man?' Ronny replied.

'Ha'way, ye've got to dance to this.' Al dragged Ronny on to the dance floor. A few seconds later the whole house seemed to shake. 'Bob the Builder!' they yelled.

'Can he fix it?' the rest of the gathering demanded.

'Bob the Builder!' the duet responded. 'Can he frigg!'

'I cannet stand this,' said Joe to Ginga.

With a smile, Ginga pointed at the hearing aid which he had switched off.

With difficulty, Joe managed to get up from the sofa. Gesturing for Ginga to follow him, they went into the kitchen which led off from the lounge. Joe said something which Ginga could not hear. 'I said turn on your hearing aid,' Joe barked a second time. 'Yer hearing aid, man!' In the kitchen the sound of music and dancing was still loud. 'It's nee good,' moaned Joe. 'I still cannet stand it.' With a gesture of despair, he passed through a utility room and out into the night.

The night was dark, and unrelievedly dreary. Either no moon had risen or the fog hid it utterly. The two old men crossed the cobbles of the yard slowly. Joe stopped and studied the house and the outbuildings. 'It'll want another lottery win just for the upkeep.' He paused, waiting for Ginga to speak, but his friend seemed to be in a deep abstraction. 'There'll be damp everywhere,' Joe continued. 'And dry rot. They didn't even wait for the survey. Just paid cash.' Again he waited for Ginga, but he was lost in his own thoughts. 'Well, what do ye make of it then, Ginga man?' Joe demanded at last.

Ginga nodded. 'Y'kna when we were looking aboot upstairs? Well, I heard a dog rat in the rafters. And where there's one rat there's usually one or two more of them boys.'

'Aye. It's just trouble with a capital T, this place. What on earth possessed him to buy it? He's always been a dreamer, like. But a hoose like this? It's just madness.' They stood there for a little longer, peering at the lights, then Joe shuddered. 'I cannet stand being inside there. And I'm surprised Ronny can. I kna it's only a parsonage, but it was all part o' the coal owner's empire. Queen Mother or nee Queen Mother, it's Lord Firedamp's estate.' Joe gazed up at the fog. 'It's a filthy night, ha'way, there's a Calor gas fire in the garage.'

The garage door clanked as it closed behind them. The two old friends pulled out a pair of ancient folding chairs, and set them around the Calor gas heater. 'Ye'll have to switch it on,' Joe said. 'Me hands are purely knackt.'

The heat quickly permeated the area around the fire, and the old men relaxed in their chairs. Joe flourished his stick over the bonnet of the Ferrari. 'As far as I can see, Greener five-bellies is the only person what drives it.' He narrowed his eyes in thought. A smile twinkled in his eyes. 'He hasn't really changed, mind, has he? Ronny, I mean. Same auld Ronny. At first I was worried it was gonnae gan to his heed. Y'kna, like ye hear happening. When he first telt wor at the allotments, I thought it might turn him into a monster.' He gestured contemptuously at the Ferrari. 'This monstrosity here is the only thing he's bought. Audrey, mind ye. She's done nowt but gan to the Metro Centre. Must have spent thousands. I mean, did ye see her tonight? All dressed up like a dog's dinner.' Joe broke off and mused. 'Mind ye, she's been quiet tonight. Not her usual self. As though she's got summink on her mind. Did ye not notice it? And the way she keeps on looking through the French window. As though she was waiting for someone.' Joe looked at his companion who was gazing fixedly at the little cone of blue at the heart of the Calor gas heating panels. 'And talking aboot Audrey not being herself, what is it with ye tonight, man Ginga? Ye haven't said two words.'

Ginga raised his glance from the gas and looked straight into Joe's eyes. 'I saw someone today.'

'What d'ye mean by that, like?'

There was a pause. Ginga's forehead furrowed so that his russet eyebrows formed a thick, impenetrable tangle. 'I saw her dad.'

'Whose dad?'

'Her dad. Audrey's dad. I saw him today. This morning.'

'What the hell are ye on aboot, marra?'

'What I say. I saw Audrey's dad this morning.'

'Divven't talk daft, nee one's seen hide nor hair of him for awer fifty years. He'll be lang deed, him.' Just then something landed on the roof and both old men looked up instinctively. A few moments later there was the hooting of an owl. 'I divven't trust that five-bellies, but,' Joe began again after they had listened to the owl for a while. 'He'll be scheming and skiving. D'yus kna he even gets Ronny's post delivered from the Teams address to his houseboat?' He spat. 'And as for that Phil Heel. Well, he can be after no good. He always was a spiv.'

'Joe man,' Ginga's voice was firm. 'I kna for a fact it was him.'

'Divven't talk cock and bull.'

'We used to call him the ferret. Remember? He had that quick way with him. And the little round ears. Then there's that scar.'

'Scar?'

'On his cheek. Got it doon the pit. Didn't have it seen to proper. It festered. And the funny thing is, it was in the shape of a little pick. D'ye remember?'

Joe's voice was gravelly. 'I remember.'

'Joe man, it was him.' Ginga stroked his eyebrows. 'Not much of the ferret aboot him these days. Just the ears. Like the handles of little cups. Life looks as though it's finished him. The scar was still there, but. White as snow. That's how I knew it was him.' Their long silence was filled only by the forlorn hooting of the owl above them. 'Well now,' Ginga began again. 'I wonder what he can want after all these years.'

'D'ye need to ask?' Joe's face was sour. 'If it is him, and it's a big if, then it's obvious what he's come back for. He'll have heard aboot the lottery, won't he? From what I can remember aboot that one, he'll be on the sniff for money.'

'How d'ye kna?'

'Well, why else would he hunt her oot after a lifetime?'

'I divven't kna. Mebbes he wants to make peace.'

Joe hooted with scorn. 'I doubt it somehow.'

'Ye nivver kna,' returned Ginga. 'When a man comes to the end of his days. There's nee saying what he'll want.'

Joe grew deeply thoughtful. 'That's true. Ye'll dee owt for peace. I kna it was like that with me own grandbairn. Ye change.' Joe continued to muse for a while before abruptly swatting his hand as though at a fly. 'I divven't kna why we're even talking aboot it. I think ye must be getting blind as well as deaf. There's just not nee way that that could have been him.'

'What was he called?' Ginga asked.

There was a pause between them. The Calor gas hissed fitfully. Joe shook his head. 'I cannet remember. I cannet hardly remember him. Nee one can. He's just a piece of bloody coal dust blown away lang since on the wind.'

Ginga's voice sounded far away. 'Audrey'll be able to remember him. Bairns always dee. I mean, yer dad. It's not as if he was just someone ye've passed in the street a couple of times.' Ginga rubbed his beard contemplatively. 'We all think of wor mam and dad. Orphans probably more than any. Like them what have lost a limb still feel the ache of it.'

The old men lapsed into deep thought. The Calor gas fire continued to whistle softly and a mouse could be heard scurrying under the Ferrari. 'Better not tell her owt,' said Joe at last. 'I mean, ye were probably wrang anyway. Likely he's been deed and gone these twenty years. Better not to tell her.'

Just then there was the sound of talons on the tiles above as the owl took flight. It ghosted back up the long walk, and headed expertly through a tangle of trees to another of its hunting perches: a young larch tree growing beside the walk-in opening of a long-since disused mine. Here it was that men hewed the coal that raised the column of liberty, bricked the walled garden and built the beautiful chapel. And the mouth of that disused pit was the darkest place of the night.

'Aye,' finished Joe. 'Better not tell her.'

2

The stair creaked underfoot. Breathing in instinctively, Al pressed himself against the wall. From the lounge below, the disco pumped. He was on the narrow, rickety flight of stairs that rose steeply from the first-floor landing to the attic room. At the top, a light could be seen shining underneath an old-fashioned, latched wooden door. Behind this door, voices of a man and woman could be heard in a quiet conversation. Al narrowed his eyes. Then the light went out, and the voices ceased talking.

He managed the rest of the stairs quickly and without making a sound, and on reaching the door, knelt down to squint through the keyhole. Moaning could now be heard.

The voice that suddenly called up to him from the landing below reverberated loudly. It belonged to Ronny. 'What ye deein' up there, man Al?'

Al gestured wildly at Ronny to be quiet. But it was too late. The light came back on, and a few seconds later, the door to the attic room was yanked open. Al only just had time to straighten up from his kneeling position before Phil Heel appeared. He gave Al a triumphant grin, and smoothed the slightly wrinkled shoulders of his jacket. 'Just sampling the goods, five-bellies,' he laughed, and then held his hand out to Cheryl who came to him from inside, still buttoning up her leather dress.

'What the frigg are ye prowling about for?' she demanded haughtily as she passed Al.

Like a rhino in pain, Al plunged into the room.

Ronny found him sitting in the darkness on the edge of the bed. 'Are ye areet?' he asked.

'It's her bloody loss.' Al's white eye glinted in the darkness. Ronny went to turn on the light, but Al stopped him. 'It's best not to bring it to light.' His hand strayed over the groove where the bodies had been. 'Still warm,' he whispered. 'Just think, a few moment ago her cheeks were nestling nicely against these sheets.'

Ronny stared at the bed, just discernible as a slightly lighter shade of darkness. 'Unless she was on top, which ye said she seemed to like. And then it'll have been his cheeks.'

Cursing, Al sprang up. He flicked his hand wildly as though to remove some contamination from it. Subsiding with a sigh, he went over to the single window in the attic room: a small aperture with rotting frame. Ronny came over. For a while they stood side by side, gazing at the foggy night. 'I'm sorry, marra,' he whispered. 'I suppose ye must really like her.'

Al nodded tersely. 'She's areet.' Nothing was said for a long time. When Al spoke again his voice was so changed it seemed to belong to a different person. 'I think I'm beginning to understand what ye see in Audrey.'

'What d'ye mean?'

'You're the one for questions,' Al said. 'Well, answer wor this. When does lust turn to love?'

'Come on,' Ronny said at last. 'Let's gan and light the bonfire. It's past time for that.'

But Al did not move. 'I'm not used to this, y'kna. This caring. I'm not used to any of it. Ronny man, I just divven't think I'm up to seeing that Phil Heel all awer her.' He swallowed. 'I lie in that hooseboat at night thinking of her face.'

They stole from the attic and then down the stairs, creeping through the front door. 'It's like a bloody rabbit's warren, this hoose,' whispered Al. The fog was thickening as they felt their way round the house to the back lawns. 'Christ!' Al yelped as he put his hand in a rose bush. 'Summink bit wor.'

After a fraught five minutes wandering blindly, at last they stumbled across the bonfire. They stood there looking at it, a vague, jagged shape in the darkness. 'I still think it's too near to the trees,' said Ronny. 'We shouldn't have built it in the orchard –'

'Rubbish. Ye want some o' the dead wood cleared anyway.'

'And did ye change that jacket?'

The rasp of a match silenced Ronny. The heady whiff of sulphur drifted into his nostrils. 'Let's see what we're deein',' said Al as he tossed the match into the bonfire. It seemed that the fragile flame was going to be extinguished without spreading when a corner of the newspapers stuffed at the bottom of the pyre began to curl. The flame grew, and the heavily paraffined lower branches started to crackle. 'That's better,' said Al. He looked at the flames tickling the mist. 'Nee wonder it's a tradition. I mean, there's nowt better than a bit of a burn when the spirits are doon.' In the flickering light of the early flames, the guy seemed to leer down at them with a human face. 'I only wish I could hoy Phil Heel on top of there an' all.'

Gradually, the boom of the music from the disco was drowned out by the roar of the flames.

'I'd better gan and get the bairns,' said Ronny. 'They'll want to see this.'

'Hold on a moment,' Al replied. 'Wait until it's proper going.' Light from the fire now lit Al's face, showing a staring, almost crazed look on his features. 'Anyway, I need to talk to ye.'

'Talk to me?' Ronny asked, puzzled.

Al nodded significantly, still peering into the heart of the fire. 'Put it this way: is Audrey opening up a boutique in the Metro Centre, or just receiving stolen goods?'

'What d'ye mean?'

'I was looking aroond upstairs before, and I've nivver seen so much stuff.'

'She likes shopping,' Ronny shrugged.

'All the wardrobes in your bedroom are crammed to bursting with her stuff. That attic room is an' all, where that bastard Heel was. And I'll tell ye another thing aboot him, he'll have filled his pockets if ye divven't keep an eye on him.'

'What yus on aboot, Al?'

'Then there's everything doonstairs. All them fancy drapes and frilly knick-knacks. The place is filled, and yus've only been here a few days. Add that to the price of the hoose. And the Florida trip. I mean, that alone must have come in at a tidy whack.'

'It did.' Ronny's voice sounded small against the growing noise of fire. 'Al, what are yus on aboot?'

'Ye're gonnae have to get a grip, lad. On the money. If ye divven't then yus'll end up back on a ladder. I mean, money doesn't last for ever. And once it's gone, there's nowt left.'

Ronny stared miserably at the bonfire, tugging at his ponytail. Nothing was said for a while and then Al sighed theatrically. 'So, all in all I think we're gonnae have to postpone it.'

'Postpone what?'

'Well, we were gonnae take the vanette to Terry's scrapyard at Swalwell. Remember?'

'Aye.'

'We were gonnae ask him if we could operate the levers and that. And get Toni-Lee to film it. Y'kna, the ceremonious destruction of wor beast o' burden.'

'I remember.'

'But now I think we're gonnae have to keep it.'

'What ye on aboot, Al?'

Suddenly the heat from the flames forced Ronny back a step. Al did not move. His words shot out quickly. 'How many did ye take to Florida? How much was this gaff? Does Audrey gan to the Metro Centre every day? How much did she make ye give away to her family? How much do ye think this place is gonnae cost to keep going?' Al gave a strange high-pitched giggle. 'Bloody hell, do I have to spell it oot? If things gan on like this we'll be back in that vanette within the year. Back in the vanette, back up them ladders, and back licking arses in Whickham just to make ends meet. Or not make them meet as the case may be.'

Ronny closed his eyes and fretted at his ponytail. 'I thought the worry would be awer. When we won. But ye just end up swapping one set of worries for another.'

There was a crack from the dark heart of the pyre, and foul-smelling fumes began to stir on the air. Al's giggle stopped abruptly. 'I'm sorry, Ronny. It's that Phil Heel. He's getting to us.' His voice grew more gentle. 'I'm only saying that three million-odd isn't gonnae last for ever at the rate Audrey's gannin' through it.'

The fire was roaring now, the flames leaping higher and higher, Ronny staggered back, his hands protecting his face. As he spoke, his voice was tiny, like that of a frightened little boy. 'When you win the lottery . . . you think that that's the end . . . nee more worries . . . but, see, for me? It's just leading to more. And now this. Jesus, I cannet gan back up a ladder. I'd fall off, I kna I would. I'd fall off a roof and break me back. Or . . . or . . . I'd have a heart attack and . . .' He yanked at his ponytail so powerfully that it knocked him off his balance, and he stumbled. With a scream he veered away from a sudden shoot of flames. When he looked back over he saw that Al was planting a firework in the bonfire just inches from the flames. '*Al!*' he shouted.

'Gan and get the bairns then,' said Al, his face now wearing the calm of the totally possessed. 'They'll be just in time for the big bangs.'

Ronny was sniffing the air. 'And what the hell's that smell?'

'What smell?'

'That evil ming. Like burning bloody rubber or plastic or sulphur summink . . .'

Al beamed. 'That'll be the surprise. When that hits, man, they'll be able to see wor awer in the Teams.'

'For frigg's sake,' Ronny cried as Al went on putting rockets in the parts of the pyre that the flames had not yet reached.'

'Just gan and get the bairns. This is gonnae be as good as any we've ever done.' Ronny had gone about ten yards when Al called him back. 'By the way, bonny lad, you haven't been giving money to Jimmy, have ye?' Ronny did not answer. 'It's just that he came to me hooseboat last night. Dead o' the bloody neet, and I feel someone shaking us awake. Like one of the dark friggers from *Lord of the Rings*. It was Jimmy. He was lying oot of his arse of course but he said you gave him ten grand, and that he wants more. On a regular basis.' Still Ronny did not reply. 'Ye have, haven't ye?' Al said gently. 'Yus've been giving Jimmy money.'

'I'd better gan and get them bairns,' Ronny said miserably.

Al sighed. 'The thing aboot blackmailers, Ronny lad, is that they divven't stop. Not until there's nee more blood for them to suck.'

'What we gonnae dee, man Al?' There was terror in Ronny's words.

'He doesn't kna ye live here, does he?'

'I didn't gan roond to his for a cup o' tea and give him me change of address if that's what ye mean.'

'Ye'll have to give wor a bit time to work it oot, bonny lad. This is a tough one. Ye'll have to give wor time. And for now, I just want to burn summink.'

Having crossed the cobbles, Ronny stole back into the house through the back door. His eyebrows knitted together at the silence that greeted him. The disco was not playing. He found Phil Heel in the kitchen, rifling through a drawer. 'What the hell are ye deein'?' Ronny demanded.

Phil Heel looked at him and calmly continued to search the drawer. Then he looked up at Ronny. 'I've been meaning to have a chat with ye,' he said, rubbing a greasy hand on his velour jacket and taking off his sunglasses. Underneath the glasses his eyes were small and piercing. 'What d'yus kna aboot a fire?'

Ronny's words were a whisper. 'What d'ye mean?'

'Oh, I think ye kna what I mean, lad. The question is, does Macca?'

Ronny put a hand on the kitchen table to steady himself. A porcelain salt cellar fell over. It rolled to the table edge, and then smashed to pieces on the terracotta floor. An instant later, shouts exploded from the lounge and children's room. Phil Heel closed the drawer and leered. 'We'll have a little chat in a day or two. Ye and me. Now, there's a cat fight gannin' on through there, or my name's not Phil Heel.'

Ronny stopped dead as he entered the lounge. People were screaming violently in each other's faces. A number of fights had broken out. Karen, Bill's recent fiancée, was locked in mortal combat with Michelle, one of Bill's ex-wives. Each had a handful of the other's hair and was shrieking at the top of her voice. Bill and Paddy, not succeeding in their efforts to restrain the women, were beginning to turn on one another. Meanwhile, over at the other side of the lounge, Leeanne and Cheryl were in the middle of throwing baskets of spiced potato wedges and Cajun-style chicken wings over each other's heads.

'At least I'm her daughter,' Leeanne was shouting. 'So I'm entitled to summink. I'm not just someone sponging.'

'And I'm her best mate,' Cheryl countered. 'Not just someone looking for a friggin' babysitter.'

Paul, Leeanne's husband, was buttonholing old Uncle Dick. 'I work every hour that God sends, and all we get is the same as a jailbird and some selfish hippie.'

'Divven't shout at me, pal,' Uncle Dick replied.

'And that bloody tart even gets five grand. And ye dee. No disrespect to you, but your life's over . . .'

'I can still bloody well lift me own body weight, and yours . . .'

In the children's room the table football had been knocked down, and Brosnan and Elliot were grappling over it. Skye was fighting with Brosnan on the DJ's podium, while Theresa was haranguing Corky. 'I saw ye looking at her,' she screamed.

'Looking at who?' Corky replied in disbelief.

'Michelle!' Theresa wound herself up to scream with a loudness of which her mother would have been proud. 'That Michelle cow! I'll bloody knock her into next week.'

Ronny stared, rooted to the spot. Just then Audrey came in from the hall, in one arm she was carrying Bernadette, in another was a bottle of Diamond White. 'What's gannin' on?' Ronny asked.

Drinking off the bottle of Diamond White, she shrugged, a sad bemusement on her face. Her tower of hair had collapsed and hung in ruins about her. Ronny was standing there staring when Phil Heel grabbed him by the arm. 'I'm just gonnae borrow the Ferrari, areet, Ronny?' Ronny did not reply.

The priest watched Audrey come over to him. She shook her head as she contemplated the fury all around her. 'It's all gone wrang, man Dan,' she whispered.

'You've been quiet tonight, Audrey,' the priest replied.

'I kna,' Audrey replied. With a twist of her jaws she opened another bottle of Diamond White, drinking half of it down in one draught. Suddenly she laughed without joy. 'Do ye believe in ghosts?'

'Why do you ask that?'

'Shall I tell ye why? D'yus want to kna why?' She sighed wearily. 'I've been waiting for a ghost tonight. I cannet stop mesel', man Father. Part o' wor knas it's stupid, but the other part . . .' She smiled at Bernadette. 'I mean, Ghosts an' that, why, that sort o' thing went oot with burning witches. But it's just on me mind all the time.'

'I don't know what you're talking about,' said the priest 'But talking of burning witches . . .'

The priest pointed through the French windows. The flames of the bonfire were so bright now that they lit up the intervening lawns, rose garden and terrace. 'Bloody hell,' gasped Audrey, 'that's a proper Teams flare that.' She stared at the spectacle for a while, lifting Bernadette up high so that she could see the conflagration.

'I think that fire's out of control,' Dan mused.

The flames were growing bigger, and Al was dwarfed by them: a tiny figure, irradiated with firelight. Just then the first fireworks began to go off. There was a whine as a rocket climbed higher and higher, finishing off with a spectacular bang that seemed to make the whole house shake. Instantly, people stopped arguing and fighting and gathered behind Audrey to stare through the window. They gathered there just in time to see something spinning wildly, sending out a shower of sparks that fizzed into the trees. 'Ooo!' everyone gasped.

Another rocket screamed up and then detonated. 'Ooo!' they all gasped again.

For a long time now the fire had been licking at the trees closest to the pyre, and now one of them burst into flame. There was a scream from those gathered at the French windows. 'The stupid prat's gonnae burn the hoose doon in a minute,' said Phil Heel as a second tree began to burn.

But as though entranced by the flames and the fireworks, another one of which at that moment exploded into a fantail of multicoloured sparks, the gathering seemed incapable of moving. And in the light of the fire and the fireworks, every so often disappearing in a shroud of gunpowder smoke, Al gambolled like a giant jackdaw. The children, mouths open, gazed in bliss at the blaze. 'Wow, it's better than anything in the Teams,' gasped Brosnan.

'It's brilliant,' said one of the other children.

'It's purely belter.'

The flames continued to grow and each firework was greeted with an equivalent scream from within. Audrey turned to the priest. 'They'd have had to burn me, wouldn't they?' she said softly after a while. 'If I'd been alive then. When they burnt witches.'

'Yes, they probably would have,' Dan nodded. 'They had their eye on any independent, resourceful woman.'

'I divven't kna aboot resourceful. The family's falling to pieces and I'm waiting for a dead man. I mean, what the frigg's gonnae happen next?'

Just then the French windows opened. The smell of woodsmoke, rubber, fog and gunpowder swirled in on the damp fog. A stranger entered from the terrace. He was of Mediterranean aspect. With him was a woman and a little girl of about two years of age. The woman came in last, and as she entered she looked about the lounge with a proprietorial air. She was thin and wiry, but in the strength of her body, and the gap between her teeth, she was clearly a McPhee. No one else noticed the new arrivals, so intent were they on the flames and fireworks. Only Audrey seemed to see them. 'Hello, Mam,' the woman said to Audrey.

'Donna,' Audrey whispered in amazement.

'What's gannin' on oot there then? Five-bellies practising for another insurance dodge or what?'

Chapter Five

I

The mist continued to cling to the north-east of England so that the GNER train pulling in at Newcastle-upon-Tyne Central Station some days after bonfire night could be heard from the platform a long time before it could be seen. Then, in a flurry of electric sparks, its squealing wheels lumbered into view. 'Coach G, coach G,' Ronny repeated, a piece of luggage in each hand and ponytail swinging as he scampered alongside the moving train. 'Coach G, coach G.'

'Relax, man, it's booked,' said Audrey, ambling up the platform behind him with Terri-Leigh.

Even before the train stopped, Ronny pushed his way on board. By the time Audrey and Terri had caught up with him, he had disembarked again. 'Let's have another look at them tickets, pet. We must have made a mistake. Coach G's first class.'

'I kna,' replied Audrey.

The train trundled out of the station and crossed the high-level bridge, the fog-bound River Tyne invisible below. By the time they had reached Durham, Ronny still hadn't spoken. 'What's the matter with ye, man?' Audrey demanded.

There were only two other passengers in the carriage, both about the same age as Ronny and Audrey. One was a man who spoke constantly into a mobile phone in velvet tones, the other a woman who read a small green book called *The Dark Flower*. Terri-Leigh was buried in her own book, while her grandmother flipped through a colour brochure. Ronny stared glumly at the fog. 'Will ye cheer up, for heaven's sake,' Audrey said.

Ronny sighed like a horse. 'First-class train, five-star hotel . . .'

'So? I really wanted to fly. Club class.'

'All I'm saying is could we not have done it a bit cheaper?'

'What is it with ye these past few days, have ye turned into bloody Scrooge or summink? Everything's become money. Yus're forever turning the bloody radiators doon, and if ye switch the bairns' TVs and videos off at the wall again, I swear doon –'

'Audrey love, ye can save yersel' twenty quid in a year if ye switch just one of them off at night instead of leaving it on.'

Audrey snorted. 'Twenty quid.'

At Darlington the train shuddered violently to a stop, then continued the journey at about the speed of Stephenson's Rocket.

'Anyway,' said Ronny, 'I divven't really want to gan to London. I mean, it's not all it's cracked up to be, is it?'

'How d'ye kna? Ye've nivver been.'

'Well, how d'ye kna it is? Ye've nivver been yersel'.'

The other woman in the carriage peered at the bickering Geordies over the top of her book. It was a romance concerning a sculptor and his passion for three women written in the years before the Great War.

Audrey lifted up the mini-break brochure. 'It'll be brilliant, man Ronny. Look at all o' these things. The Tower o' London, the National Portrait Gallery, Madame Two-swords . . .' Audrey smiled in rapture. 'And Oxford Street.'

'Bloody hell's teeth,' hissed Ronny. 'Ye're not gannin' shopping as well, are ye?'

'Why aye. There's the bairns' Christmases to sort.'

Ronny swallowed despairingly. 'But you've already got them.'

'Ye cannet get hardly any decent stuff from the Metro Centre. I mean, there's Hamleys and that doon here.'

'It's just what ye get from Argos, marked up aboot ten times.'

'How do ye kna?'

'Well, how do ye kna it isn't?'

'If ye say that again, Ronny, I'll bloody well −' Audrey broke off. The other passengers were looking at her. The man had paused for a moment in his phone conversation clinching a deal concerning timber rights in some Asian country. The woman peered over *The Dark Flower*. 'What d'yous want, like?' Audrey demanded. Instantly they went back to their pursuits. Audrey turned to her husband. 'Divven't ye think it's aboot time that ye expanded yer horizons? Strike oot. See yer capital city.'

'No. I've some double digging to dee doon the allotment. And the damage to repair in the orchard. Some of them trees'll have to come doon. And that fire engine knocked hell out o' the lawns.'

'Ye're hopeless.' Glancing at Terri–Leigh, a look of sadness came over Audrey. 'Are you looking forward to it, pet?'

Terri put down her book for a moment. 'I wish Toni was coming.'

Audrey reached out to her, and stroked her head. 'So do we, love. But she cannet. She's settling in with her mam, isn't she? Making a new start. Ye'll see her every day at school. And anyway . . .' Audrey paused for a moment. 'Your mam's not gonnae be inside for ever. And then ye'll be living right near Toni on Woodside Gardens.'

'I miss her, Nana.'

'And I'll miss ye an' all, pet. When yer mam comes oot o' jail, and ye move into Woodside Gardens with her. But I'll still be here for ye. Me and Granda Ronny'll always be here for you.'

Just before York, the train stopped. It stood motionless for an hour and a half as leaves were cleared from the line. Ronny began rooting about in a carrier bag. Triumphantly, he placed a Tupperware bowl on the table. 'What's that?' Audrey demanded.

'I've put some bait up.' He peeled off the lid, revealing a few battered sandwiches, party pork pies, pork scratchings and an apple.

Audrey looked at the food. 'Ye can sit here all on yer tod eating yer sarnies, but me and the bairn is gonnae gan to the silver service restaurant car.'

'And how much will that cost?' Ronny asked despairingly.

'What ye want is a healthy meal. I saw the catering box of pork scratchings getting low again. Ever since you stopped work, yus've really piled the beef on.'

Ronny stared after Audrey and Terri as they disappeared to the restaurant car. Then he popped a party pork pie in his mouth.

At an unsteady fifty miles an hour the train eventually pulled clear of the belt of east-coast fog, and began to cross England's midland plain. Fields seemed to stretch for ever on both sides. Ronny gazed at them for a while, then, twitching, suddenly grabbed the Gucci bag that Audrey had left on the table. Glancing nervously over at the door through which his wife and step-granddaughter had gone, he feverishly opened the bag. It was stuffed with cash and credit cards. After a single moment's hesitation, he took out half of the notes and the credit cards, and plunged them into his own pockets.

When the others came back, Ronny smiled at them. 'Glad to see you've cheered up,' Audrey quipped. 'I was beginning to think me husband had been changed into a basset hound.'

With a great groan of effort, the train pierced the Watford Gap. 'Look at that,' moaned Ronny. 'Hoose after hoose. Does yer heed in.'

While they were still some way away, Ronny began to assemble the luggage. 'Relax, man,' said Audrey.

'That's the last thing ye should dee.'

'What d'yus mean?'

'London? They're watching ye all the time, man. Seeing ye get off the train from the north. Waiting to strike.'

'What the hell are ye on aboot?'

'Pickpockets, man.'

The 09.12 from Newcastle shuddered into London King's Cross at 14.22. Ronny leant out of the window as it slowed. Already people were jumping on to the platform from further down the train. 'A shoal o' sardines,' he mused. 'All the plebs. Just cattle.'

'I hope ye have a nice time in London,' Audrey smiled at their fellow passengers who were waiting behind them as Ronny struggled out with the luggage.

'Listen up,' Ronny announced, producing a bumbag and tying it round his waist. 'I'll carry all wor money and credit cards an' that in here.' He tapped the bumbag. 'It's the safest way.'

'Ye look ridiculous, man,' Audrey replied.

Keeping tight hold of the suitcases, Ronny leapt on to the platform. 'Hold hands, yous two. They're like wolves. They'll try and split wor up, and then prey on the weakest.'

'I'd like to see them try,' grinned Audrey.

The trio of travellers emerged on the filthy, decrepit, cramped concourse of King's Cross Station. A phalanx of fellow travellers stood gazing up at the list of cancellations on the travel board, their faces ashen. ''Scuse me,' Ronny said loudly as he passed through them. Turning to the other two, he urged: 'Keep together, keep together.'

Caught up in a flow of bodies, Ronny found himself being carried inexorably out on the street. The stench and din of endless traffic swirled all around them as they stood there, bobbing like buoys in the current of bodies. 'Where are the taxis?' Audrey asked.

Ronny almost choked. 'A taxi? They're the worst thing,

man. It'll only be aboot a mile away and they charge ye the earth. That's if they divven't rob ye.'

'Divven't be ridiculous . . .'

But Ronny was not listening. 'Where's the tube?' he demanded, panicking in the turbulence of humanity passing on all sides. 'Where's the bloody tube?' Casting about desperately, Ronny caught sight of a newspaper kiosk. 'Ye stay here. Divven't move an inch. I'm just gonnae ask this gadgie where the tube is.'

Ronny had just turned when a filthy, emaciated figure with a beard and gentle eyes materialised from nowhere. 'Got any spare change?' he asked Audrey.

'Ee, are ye all right, pet?'

'Why aye,' the vagrant nodded. 'I was just looking for the price of a cup of tea.'

'Ye're not a Geordie are you, love?' Audrey asked. The vagrant nodded again. 'Ye're joking!' Audrey jogged Terri-Leigh who was standing there reading. 'I cannet believe it. Fancy seeing another Geordie doon here. Small world, isn't it, but? We're from Gateshead. The Teams.' Smiling, Audrey opened her Gucci bag and took out a bundle of notes. She looked at the reduced wad suspiciously.

Ronny arrived back just in time to see his wife handing a ten-pound note over to a vagrant. 'Get out of it!' he yelled. The vagrant slunk away, disappearing as instantly as he had appeared. 'Christ on a bike!' Desperately, Ronny motioned the other two to follow him. 'That was a close call.'

'He was a Geordie,' explained Audrey.

'Aye, aboot as Geordie as a cockney can get.'

'What d'ye mean?'

'They've all got a story, man Audrey. And a strategy.' Ronny stopped abruptly as they entered the concourse again. 'Y'kna, a way o' building yer trust up.'

'Divven't talk so daft, man Ronny,' replied Audrey, and lifting her head back, she filled the place with her laughter.

They descended the stairs down to the tube. Ronny was heaving like a steam train. 'Can ye manage with them bags?' Audrey asked. Sweating profusely, Ronny pushed his way to one of the ticket machines. 'We want Knightsbridge, divven't we?' Audrey said.

Ronny boomed out a raucous, false laugh. 'Knightsbridge,' he chuckled loudly. 'Good gag that.' He turned to the milling crowd in general. 'Ye mean Old Kent Road, divven't ye?' Lowering his voice, he hissed at Audrey. 'They hang aboot waiting to see who's gannin' to the posh places.'

'I'm gonnae get sick of this very quickly, Ronny man.'

Ronny stared bewilderedly at the machine. 'What kind o' ticket do we want?' he asked himself. He frowned. 'The cheapest of course.'

Audrey reached through him and pressed the buttons. 'We want three o' them One Day Travel Cards.' A crowd was gathering behind them as Ronny struggled to get the money out of his bumbag. At last the machine whirred and the cards came out. Frantically, Ronny pressed more buttons. The crowd behind grew disgruntled. 'It owes wor change,' Ronny explained to the unsmiling faces.

'Ronny,' Audrey snapped.

'But it owes wor twenty pence.'

'For frigg's sake, man. Anyone would think we were paupers. We've won the bloody lottery.'

Again Ronny's false laugh boomed out. 'Aye, a whole tenner,' he said woodenly. He was still trying to eject the small coin owing to him when Audrey jerked him away. 'I'd better keep these safe an' all,' he said, looking about suspiciously as he put the cards into the bumbag. 'They cost an arm and a leg.'

Once again, a crowd built up behind them as Ronny fiddled with the bumbag at the ticket barrier. He shrieked as he felt the belt being unfastened from his waist. 'I think I'll look after this,' Audrey said. 'Before ye give yerself a heart attack.' Ripping out the valuables, she tossed the bumbag to one side, and stuffed what was inside between her breasts. 'I'd like to see the one who tries to get their hands on that lot.'

An escalator took them underground, the strains of a busker's guitar echoing wistfully from some deeper chamber. It was a sad love song from the sixties, and glancing at each other, Audrey and Ronny smiled. The tips of their fingers touched for a moment. People of every single nation on the earth seemed to be passing them on the upward escalator. Fascinated, the Geordies listened to the fleeting snatches of the different languages, entranced as though by the fluting of migrating birds spread out on the telephone wire at the summer's end.

The platform was already crowded beyond capacity. 'Keep yer backs against the wall,' Ronny hissed to the other two as he pushed through the crush. A train came, its arrival a tornado of scalding, eye-stinging, dust-laden air. Ronny rammed a way through, but by the time they reached the doors, there was no more room left. Ronny gazed forlornly at the mass of human bodies packed together on the other side of the window. Two arms and a leg were caught in the reclosing doors. 'Ye wouldn't move animals like that,' he mused.

When they finally managed to squeeze on board a train, Ronny stood four square for the whole journey with the luggage gripped tightly between his legs and his eye fixed on the tube map on the wall. As they began to slow to their stop, he stooped down to whisper to Audrey and Terri-Leigh who sat below him. 'When I say gan, gan.' The train stopped. 'Gan!' he cried, shunting people aside in a desperate bid to get to the doors.

At last they emerged back at street level. 'Bloody hell,' said Audrey.

Ronny whistled softly. 'Millionaires' Row.'

'Knightsbridge,' said Terri.

They walked slowly down the street, wide-eyed and staring, all of a sudden shoulder to shoulder with men in dark suits and women in furs and pearls. The displays in the shop windows glittered like tiaras, there were no prices, their simplicity the sign of true wealth. Young women, laden like packhorses with intricately designed shopping bags, plodded from one shop to another. 'There's a Rolls-Royce,' Ronny said in amazement every twenty yards or so. 'There's another Rolls-Royce.'

Coming to their hotel, they stopped. Without speaking, the three of them stood on the pavement outside, gazing up. A red carpet extended on to the pavement like a tongue. A man in a top hat and livery fussed over the expensively attired guests arriving in taxis. These other guests sauntered up the red carpet and disappeared in the spinning glass of the revolving doors, their luggage carried by men in pinstripe trousers, with white gloves and epaulettes on their dress tunics. The man in the top hat raised it to each arrival and departure.

Audrey inhaled deeply. 'Ha'way, let's gan in.'

Ronny caught her by the arm. 'This isn't us,' he whispered. 'What d'ye mean?'

'I mean, we divven't belong in a hotel like this.'

Audrey shook her head. 'Ye can stay ootside here all day, pet, with yer nose pressed up against the window, but me and Terri are gannin' in.'

If one of the characters from the book being read by their fellow passenger on the train had walked in with the lottery winners, he might not have felt himself in a different time. The opulence was restrained but as substantial as the mahogany panelling of the lobby and the check-in desk. Large armchairs of burgundy leather stood grouped round coffee tables. Ironed copies of *The Times* waited to be read. The staff talked in discreetly hushed tones, moving silently. A young man carried their suitcases into a lift. The lift rose, its smooth mechanism whispering softly. 'This reminds wor of the pit lift at Watergate,' mused Ronny, puzzled by his own connection.

When Audrey came back from settling Terri-Leigh in her room, she found Ronny standing at an open window with his back to her. 'I've left her with a mug of hot chocolate. Poor bairn, she's missing her cousin.' Audrey looked about the room. 'Bloody hell,' she gasped. 'What d'yus think of the rooms?' Ronny grunted in reply. Audrey touched the head of one of the hothouse flowers which stood in a huge vase on a polished hardwood dresser. A light coating of pollen dropped on to the lid of the box of Belgian chocolates underneath. The box was tied with a green ribbon. 'There's luxury and there's luxury,' Audrey whispered as she lifted a bottle of champagne from the bucket. She took a swig. 'And this is luxury.' She replaced the bottle, and picked up the pair of flutes which had been filled by the youth who showed them to their room. She came over to Ronny at the window. 'Here, pet, have a glass o' bubbly.' Tersely, Ronny shook his head. Still he did not turn, indeed he now seemed to sag over the window sill. 'Ye might as well, Ronny, it's all part of the deal. A champagne reception.' She picked up the huge welcome card from the dresser and read it. 'Aye. Says here. All part of the Gold Star Mini-Break. A new concept in luxury. A champagne reception.' Ronny seemed to shudder. Gulping down the champagne, Audrey slowly rotated round the room. 'It's like summink from a fairy tale.' With a shrieking laugh she ran through to the bathroom. 'Bloody hell, come and look in here. It's just unbelievable. I swear doon them taps are solid gold. We'll have to get these in ours. There's a jacuzzi, and everything. Ee, Ronny, we'll have to get a jacuzzi put in. And I bet these bath lotions are worth a fortune alone. I could just spend the whole mini-break in here. D'ye fancy popping into the tub with us?'

Ronny gazed out of the window. Behind him he could hear water gushing into the bath. Down below, an endless flow of wealthy humanity and car traffic swept by. In comparison with the bright raiment of the people, the line of late autumn plane trees seemed emaciated, forlorn still points in the mania of movement.

Ronny was still gazing out of the window when Audrey emerged from the bathroom. She was naked. 'Ronny,' she whispered. But he did not seem to hear. The faded tattoo on her buttock swelled in and out of sight as she approached the window. 'Ronny,' she repeated. Ronny was staring fixedly through the window at a man standing beneath one of the plane trees, a *Big Issue* seller. He jolted when he felt Audrey's hands joining round him from behind. 'What's the matter, pet?' she breathed.

'I'm lost,' he whispered.

'Lost?'

'I mean, what's a bloke like me deein' in a place like this?'

'What's on yer mind, man?'

Ronny tugged miserably at his ponytail. 'I'm all at sea.' Suddenly words tore from him. 'When the money's gone what will happen then? Then there'll be nee way of helping bairns like Chloe. Then ye'll have to gan back doon the mall, and I'll have to gan back up a ladder. Then there's this thing what's been bothering ye –'

'When the money's gone? What are yus on aboot?'

'When we've spent it all. When there's none left –'

'Is that what's been on your mind these past few days? Us running oot of money?' Ronny nodded. Audrey kissed his ear tenderly. 'Do ye think I'm that stupid? D'yus really think I'd spend everything and leave wor back at square one? I knew ye weren't listening when I showed ye them documents this morning.'

'I couldn't take it in. Anything to dee with money just gets us reet doon.'

'So that's why ye won't come to the meetings with the bank?'

'I just haven't wanted to think aboot it, and then when Al said . . .' Ronny shivered as Audrey nibbled his other ear. 'That's nice,' he whispered miserably.

'Look, Ronny, I've just been through it with wor financial

adviser. As lang as we divven't dip into wor capital then we've got six grand a month to live off. For life.'

His voice cracked. 'What aboot the hoose? I mean, the upkeep must be –'

'We've got six thousand a month, man.'

For an instant Ronny seemed close to tears. 'Ye're not joking?'

'Why should I joke?'

'And I thought we were gonnae be stony-broke.'

'I've brought up two generations in the Teams, but I divven't kna how to look after three million poond? Is that what yus're saying?' Audrey laughed. 'Think aboot it. Have I ever not been able to cope with anything?'

'No,' said Ronny. 'Ye always cope.'

'And I'm coping now.' There was a long pause. 'There's still summink the matter, isn't there?'

Ronny nodded. 'One doon, one to gan.'

'What is it?'

'Audrey pet, what's this thing that's been upsetting you?'

Taking him by the hand, Audrey turned him round. He took her in his arms. It was then that he noticed that she was naked. 'Bloody hell,' he gasped.

'That's enough talking for now,' she murmured, leading him to the bed.

2

'She's asleep, God love her,' said Audrey as she came back into the hotel lobby.

'It's all the excitement,' replied Ronny, pulling himself upright in the deep burgundy leather sofa. 'It was great at Madame Two-swords.' He laughed. 'Just wait until them back hyem see a photo of wor standing with Tony Blair. Terri was quiet, but.'

'She's missing Toni more than she lets on an' all.'

'Bound to. They're the cwins. More like sisters than cousins.' Ronny pointed at the tray on the coffee table. 'The tea's come.'

Audrey sat down beside her husband. A piano could be heard playing Chopin in the restaurant, its music mixing with the polite hum of voices. Dotted about the large foyer other couples drank their after-dinner coffee, while the hotel staff moved between them on silent feet. On the tray, beside the intricately carved silver teapot, was an orchid. 'Who would have thought it?' Audrey mused. 'Us two in a place like this?'

'Aye.' Ronny tugged thoughtfully at his ponytail, and smiled complacently. 'I wonder how many folks born in the likes o' Keir Hardie Avenue have ever been in here?' He looked about. 'For some, mind ye, this is just second nature.' He gestured at two elderly men guzzling coffee. 'Take them, for example. Same age as Joe and Ginga. But look at the difference in lives. To the manor born, eh? And all on the freak of yer birth.'

'They divven't look very happy, mind,' observed Audrey, pointing at a man and woman who were just checking in. The thick carpets and rich wall tapestries smothered the sound, but the couple were bickering over something.

Ronny pulled his ponytail again. 'Now I wonder what's on his mind?' Grinning, he pointed at a portly, jowly old man in a woollen suit and waistcoat. With his carefully tended moustache, he looked like some General Pinochet of the Sussex heartlands. With him was a much younger woman who was wearing dark glasses.

'And I wonder what's on hers,' Audrey added. A waiter came and poured out their tea.

Ronny took a sip, and his face twisted. 'Bloody hell,' he gasped. 'It tastes like pot-pourri.'

With the air of a connoisseur, Audrey drank from her own

278

cup. 'It's Earl Grey, man. They have it in the Bainbridge privilege lounge.'

'Why, it's nee good, I want a proper cup of tea.' No sooner had Ronny spoken, the waiter materialised again. 'I cannet drink this, bonny lad,' Ronny smiled.

'What would you like, sir?' The waiter had a sorrowful face and spoke with a Latin-American accent.

'Just a normal cup o' tea, man.'

'Darjeeling, lapsang souchong –'

'Co-op 99,' Ronny interrupted him. 'Or Yorkshire Gold if ye're pushing the boat out.'

The waiter blinked a single time. 'That is not a problem.'

They lapsed back into silence, during which Ronny chomped his way through the mints. About ten minutes later, the waiter rushed through the foyer to the revolving doors where the man in the top hat handed over a box. The waiter brought it right over to Ronny and displayed the box. It was Yorkshire Gold tea.

'Blimme,' laughed Ronny. 'This really is summink else.'

They sat drinking their tea. 'I'm so glad ye're back, pet,' said Audrey. 'I mean the auld happy-go-lucky Ronny. Ye've been a different person these past few days. A proper Scrooge. It's not like ye to be like that.'

'Aye, that's all sorted noo, mind.' Ronny beamed, but for a moment a troubled look hovered about him. 'Ye've been a bit different an' all, pet.'

'Have I?'

Ronny nodded. 'Mebbes we're just getting used to it all. A delayed reaction. The winners' adviser said it might happen a few months after the event.'

'How have I been different?'

'A bit distant. Not all the time. Just occasionally. Like at the hoose-warming. I thought ye'd have just sorted everyone out when they began to fall oot. And then there was that time at Hartlepool and in the flat –'

'They can please themselves,' Audrey interrupted sharply. 'Them new neighbours and the lasses from the Metro Centre. I divven't give a toss. If they want to fall oot, then let them.'

Ronny glanced at his wife. 'A bit withdrawn. That's the word I've been looking for. A bit withdrawn. It's –'

Again Audrey interrupted him. 'As for the family, they'll make up. It's only Leeanne's who's not talking to Bill. And Donna. They didn't like wor giving her the hoose. Or Terri-Leigh's mam.'

'What was it?'

'What d'ye mean?' Audrey shot back.

'That upset ye so much on the last day in the flat? Is it –'

Audrey silenced Ronny by laying a finger on his lips. 'Aye, the adviser's right. We're just getting used to it. That's all.'

'Aye, that's right. That's what it'll be.' Ronny nodded to himself as he looked around the hotel foyer. But when he glanced back at his wife, all colour had drained from her face. 'Ee, pet, what's the matter?'

There was a loud clank as Audrey slammed her cup down on the saucer. 'So,' she said in a forced tone, 'what we deein' tomorrow? The London Dungeon or Westminster Cathedral or –' She broke off helplessly. There was terror on her face.

Ronny gazed at his wife in bewilderment. 'What's the matter, pet?'

'Ronny man, somebody's just walked awer me grave.' She stared at her husband in horror, then, reaching out to him, took his hand and impulsively pulled him to his feet. 'I've got to show ye summink. I thought I didn't have to. I thought I could get awer it. But I cannet. I'm just gonnae have to show ye.'

'What the hell are ye on aboot?'

'I divven't kna mesel'.'

She slipped from him and ran across the foyer. He stared dumbly after her. Then followed at a sprint as she disappeared in the revolving doors.

The taxi pulled up immediately at Audrey's piercing whistle. Clambering blindly in behind her, Ronny did not hear the destination his wife gave in a low voice. The red lights of the meter blurred into indistinctness as he stared at them, while outside, the West End of London, cipher of the world's wealth, passed by. When the taxi stopped, Audrey thrust money at the driver and sprang out. Ronny followed, emerging numbly into the London night. The taxi drove away, and Ronny watched it disappear. His wife was standing on a bridge. She began to cross the bridge. Ronny followed. Below them flowed the River Thames, a huge, sinewy black bladder wrack.

'Why didn't ye marry me in 1962?' Audrey asked softly, when they reached the other side. She looked back over the river where, a little distance downstream, was the Houses of Parliament.

She began to walk along the raised bank above the river, slowly at first, then quicker and quicker until she was running under the string of yellow lamps. 'I wanted to,' shouted Ronny, panting as he tried to keep up with her. 'I would have done.'

At last he caught up with her. She was standing motionless against a parapet, the Thames sliding by below her. Ronny stopped when he was still ten yards or so distant. Now the Houses of Parliament were directly opposite them. Other tourists were close-by, their Japanese and American voices rising under the stark plane trees. At that moment Big Ben chimed, its boom a vast resonance. 'I love ye,' said Ronny simply over the sound of chimes.

The chimes continued to ring out mightily. It was ten o'clock. A pleasure barge droned by on the water below, interposing loud voices and music between the lottery winners and the seat of power. 'It hasn't changed at all,' said Audrey suddenly.

'Eh?'

'This place, it's the same as it was then.'

Ronny staggered forward a few more confused yards. 'But I thought ye'd nivver been here, man Audrey.'

She exhaled grimly. 'I had to come back.' In a flurry of shocking violence her fists suddenly pounded against the top of the parapet. Chest heaving, she stopped. When she began to speak again, she appeared calm. 'I suppose I've nivver had the chance to come back before. Even if I'd wanted to. Not that I gave it a second's thought. You see, before we won the lottery, it nivver entered me mind. I nivver thought I'd ever be standing here again.'

Ronny yanked so hard on his ponytail that he lost his balance. 'I divven't have a clue what ye're on aboot, Audrey.' He stepped a little closer to his wife. 'All I kna is that I love ye. And that I cannet bear to see ye suffer like this.' Ronny watched his wife take out a cigarette. She lit it, and the smoke drifted over the parapet and lost itself above the water. 'Tell us what's hurting ye, Audrey hinny.'

'Keep back!' Audrey flared. Dazed, Ronny stepped back. But the rage continued to gush from her. Again she pummelled the parapet. Ronny watched with horror. And then the anger was over. 'Sorry, pet,' she said. She seemed deeply bemused as she looked at her grazed, raw knuckles. Another pleasure barge sailed by below: the voices a riot of carousing. 'All I knew was that he was in Woking,' Audrey began in a different, detached voice. 'So I came doon to London. Thought I'd be able to find him. I suppose I couldn't think of anywhere else to start looking.' She turned to look directly at Ronny who now stood beside her at the parapet. 'It was when I left me husband. He slapped wor aboot, ye see. Made me life a misery. Y'kna that tattoo on me arse?' Ronny nodded. 'He did that himself. Burnt it on. His initials. It was agony. Life with him was no good, so one night I took off. With Paddy and Leeanne. They were just bit bairns. We hitched a ride with a wagon taking fish doon to the south.' She nodded to herself in recollection. 'The driver was from

Alnwick. Up the Northumbrian coast. He spoke with that lovely way they have up there. He didn't ask nee questions. The bairns slept all the way. I got this far.' Audrey laid her hands on the parapet. 'The Hooses o' Parliament.' Now that Ronny got a good look at them, he could see how mauled her fists had been by the wildness of her violence. The skin hung off in strips, the cuts were red. Audrey continued gently. 'The wagon dropped us here. Just aboot this same spot. The bairns were still sleeping, heads flopping against me shoulders, like a pair o' rag dolls. I got oot the wagon with one in each arm.' Audrey looked out over the wide water below. 'It was then that I knew I'd nivver find him. With the Hooses o' Parliament just there, and the water flowing past, I knew that I'd nivver find him.' Audrey turned to look at Ronny. 'And that was that. After that I just got on with it. Went back to Gatesheed, set up me own home, brought up me bairns. And he nivver entered me thoughts again. Until . . .'

Ronny's voice was a tortured whine. 'Who?'

'I'm sorry, pet, but I cannet help mesel'. I just keep on thinking that if he's alive, he'll turn up. That he'll have seen wor in the paper. And that he'll come for me.' She looked imploringly at Ronny, and her voice, in spite of the haggard look on her face, sounded like that of a little girl. 'I mean, he would, wouldn't he? He would want to say sorry. He would want to see what I'd become. He would want to see me before he died. Any father would. I mean, how could a father not want to see what happened to their own daughter?'

'Hold on, hold on, pet. Who are ye talking aboot?'

'Him.'

'Yer dad?' cried Ronny. 'Are ye talking aboot yer dad?'

Audrey nodded. 'Me dad.'

Ronny clutched giddily at his ponytail like a drowning man being dragged to safety by the piece of driftwood he has clung to. 'This other fella, what's been on yer mind, it's yer dad?'

A sudden hunger seemed to consume Audrey. 'I mean,

Donna got to hear aboot it in Ibiza, so there must be a good chance that he'd get to hear aboot it in London.'

'But I thought he'd been dead for years. Ye've always said he was deed.'

Audrey glared distractedly at Ronny. 'What ye on aboot?'

'Ye've always said he was deed. Yer dad.'

'Aye, but only because I've wanted him to be.'

'So it's yer dad yus've been meaning? There's no one else? I mean, no other lover?'

Audrey shook her head. 'You and that. How many times do I have to tell you there's neebody else?'

Ronny sighed with massive relief. 'So everything's areet then.'

'What?' Audrey demanded, aghast.

Ronny capered and whooped loudly, causing the foreign tourists to look at him. 'Audrey hinny, yus've been giving me the proper Roy Orbisons with all this. I thought ye were gonnae leave me for someone else. I thought it was mebbes him from Shenanigans . . . I thought . . . I thought. But it doesn't matter. Thank God everything's all right.'

Audrey's scream rang out so piercingly that it reverberated against the building on the other bank with the power of an explosion. 'Ye fuckin' cunt!' she screamed. 'Ye fuckin', fuckin' cunt!' She grabbed him and pulled her arm back as though to punch him. 'Areet? Ye think things is areet? Ye think every fuckin' thing's areet? Have ye been listening to me?'

'I'm sorry, pet. I didn't mean nowt. I . . .'

The look of hatred which flashed across Audrey's features like lightning silenced Ronny. She let go of him, and he watched in bewildered torment as she boosted herself up on to the parapet. 'Aye,' she said with a strange calm as she stood above him on the wall, staring down at the slick slow of the water. 'It's areet. Me dad's probably deed anyway. And so should I be.'

Audrey tottered. An instant before she fell, Ronny could see

284

that she had already lost her balance and, letting out a little whimper, he dashed forward with his arms out. But he caught only air. He closed his eyes, paralysed by terror, waiting for the sound of the body hitting the water. But he had hardly begun to scream when he realised that somehow she was in his arms.

She crushed him to her while whispering fervently in his ear. 'I'm so sorry, Ronny. I'm so sorry. I wasn't gonnae come here. I thought we'd just have a mini-break. I mean, I didn't plan it this way. It was the last thing I wanted. But I've had to come. And I'm so sorry, but now ye're gonnae have to know it all. I'm so sorry. I'm gonnae have to tell ye the whole sorry secret.' She took his face in her hands, and brought her own face close. They did not move for a long time, their noses touching, each one's breathing indistinguishable from the other's. 'Will ye still love me when you know?'

After the earlier violence the stillness that had come over Audrey was eerie. She led Ronny through a group of tourists to a bench. They sat down there together. When she began to speak it was without tone. 'I set the bairns doon on a bench. It could have been this one. They were fast asleep. I sat with them for, I divven't kna, mebbes five or ten minutes, and then I got up to go and take me own life. I left the bairns sleeping there to go and –' Ronny jolted, but taking his hand Audrey stilled him. 'Divven't say anything, my love, 'cos I won't have it in me to try and tell this again.' She fell into silence for a while, gazing at the parapet. Then she nodded as though finding her bearings once more. 'Aye, hard to believe, isn't it? The life and the soul of the party trying to destroy herself. Well, it happened. It happened here. I stood up on that parapet, and got meself ready to jump. Said all me goodbyes to everybody. And then to the world. It was as I was aboot to close me eyes that I saw summink. Nowt really. Just a little flower growing oot o' the parapet. But I wanted to take a good look at it, since it was the last thing I'd see. So I stared at it. It was like the whole world was that flower. And that scrap of flower was a miracle. And the whole world was a miracle. Y'kna the way ye talk aboot delights? The ordinary things that can blow yer heed off if ye let them? Well, it was that flower, it just seemed to catch me.' She stared at the parapet. A slender weed could be seen peeping out. A small groundsel. She nodded. 'Aye, summink just like that. A delight. One of your little delights. Still. In the end, even that couldn't keep us. And I was just aboot to jump when . . . when . . .' An animal-like grunt tore from her. She just managed to control herself. 'When a policeman happened to come by. He shouted. I got down. Meaning to climb back up as soon as he'd gone. But he stopped. I suppose ye would. Especially in them days. A young lass with a couple o' bairns. I wasn't even twenty. He wouldn't leave us alone. Must have known I was gonnae destroy mesel'.'

Another pleasure barge shunted by below. Audrey lit a cigarette from the end of the other, and scooped her trembling hand to her mouth like a famished person feeding. Each knuckle was a pulpy red. 'But ye didn't dee it,' Ronny whispered at last. 'At the end of the day, ye didn't dee it.'

Audrey silenced him tenderly with a finger on his lips. 'Listen to what I'm saying. I was gonnae kill mesel'. And it was only because the police lad come that I didn't. Two minutes either side, and I wouldn't be here now. That river would have had me. And them bairns . . .' She stifled another animal grunt which shook her body. 'And them bairns would have woken up orphans. With nee one of their blood to ever know them. I even heard them wake. I knew they were watching me. And I was still gonnae dee it. I was that far gone. Them little faces, but I was still gonnae dee it. It was just chance that I didn't.'

'But –'

'I haven't finished yet. I haven't finished telling ye.' For five minutes, Audrey breathed deeply, staring at the groundsel, while Ronny held her hand. Meanwhile, movement continued all around them as the tourists strolled past, the barges chugged by below and above jets breasted the night sky bound for a hundred destinations. At last she was ready to begin again. 'Divven't get wor wrang, I've enjoyed me life. I love me family. Love ye. And just like I've nivver given two thoughts to me dad, I'd put the suicide oot me mind an' all. Convinced mesel' that I hadn't been serious. That I hadn't really wanted to destroy mesel'. The only thing is, since we've won the lottery, me mind's gone back to that time more and more. And I've admitted it to mesel'. The truth, I've admitted that I wanted to end it all. But there's more. For the love of God there's more. Because sometimes when I've been standing somewhere, at the sink or anywhere, I imagine I'm on that parapet again. Standing there above the river. And this time as I stand there, I jump.' She closed her eyes tightly. 'And I see the water . . . Aye. I see the water . . . closing over me like a lid . . . And in that darkness . . . in that darkness . . .' She opened her eyes and her face grew strangely twisted like something melted by a great heat. 'I want the darkness, Ronny, 'cos me daddy's waiting for us there. He's waiting for us in the darkness. Me daddy's waiting.'

'Christ,' whispered Ronny. 'Christ.'

Audrey took his hand, which she held, limp, in her own. 'See? I told ye that yus wouldn't love me nee more.' She stared at her cigarette, its blue smoke twisting and turning sinuously like a living thing. 'Sometimes I think I'm gannin' mental.' She turned to face her husband candidly. 'Am I losing my mind? I said before that I could cope with it all. But, pet, I'm not so sure aboot this. It comes over us. And then . . . and then I'm not so sure I can cope with it. Sometimes I think he's a ghost. A ghost standing in the orchard, looking over. And then I think that it's me. It's me what's the ghost.' She held up her knuckles and looked at them in surprise as though bemused by the damage she had done to herself. Then, curling into a ball, she fell to the ground, and began to butt her head convulsively while screaming as silently and desperately as a foetus being aborted.

Chapter Six

I

The fog cleared and winter came in mild over the Metropolitan Borough of Gateshead. As the days of December grew towards Christmas, the clement weather continued. Like an ants' nest disturbed by a poking stick, the Metro Centre became more and more agitated. Shoppers thronged the malls; the overflow car parks seethed with vehicles.

One morning, a taxi pulled in at the bus station and Audrey got out. Her eyes were hidden behind dark sunglasses, her dyed black hair had been combed back savagely on her scalp. She was wearing a black ankle-length coat, and carried a leather shoulder bag. Walking slowly through the Metro Centre, she went from shop to shop, yawning with boredom occasionally as she half-heartedly browsed through the clothes and the children's toys. She made a few purchases, instructing the sales assistant to send on the goods.

Audrey's meandering took her at last to Pam's Pantry. After a moment's pause, she went over to the counter. 'Is Pam not in today, pet?' she asked the teenaged assistant.

'Pam?'

'Aye, Pam. I'm Audrey.'

An older woman turned from the kitchen. 'Pam's gone, pet.'

'Gone?'

'Aye,' added the older woman, 'there's been a buy-oot.'

The teenage girl nodded. 'See this place? It's gonnae be a Costa Coffee café.' Audrey looked about the busy coffee shop.

'So what can I get ye then?' the girl asked, but Audrey seemed deep in thought. 'What d'ye want?' the assistant reiterated.

Audrey turned. 'A coffee, and a slice o' cake.' There was only one table left, the one closest to the open mall.

Audrey sat down listening numbly to the clatter of voices in the café and the pounding of the feet passing by on the mall. Every two minutes or so an announcement was made advertising a product or a lost child. The sound of cash tills could be heard ringing out like frogs in a swamp.

Her coffee and cake had just arrived when her mobile phone began to ring. 'Leeanne man,' she began wearily without waiting for the caller to speak. 'I divven't care. Leave me oot o' yer squabblings.' Leeanne spoke, and Audrey shook her head. 'I divven't care if Bill is selling the house on Woodside Gardens . . .' She took off her glasses and yawned. The voice at the other end continued to speak, but Audrey turned the phone off. Her eyes were bloodshot. Getting up, she went back over to the assistant at the counter. 'Do the lasses still come in here, pet?'

'The lasses?'

'The cleaners. Y'kna, after their morning shift.'

'Aye, they dee,' said the woman through in the kitchen. 'They'll not be long coming.'

Audrey went back to her seat, and lighting a cigarette, smoked hungrily. She opened her shoulder bag. Inside was a single object. With a cautious glance in all directions, she took out the object, and placed it on the table in front of her. It was the old shoebox. After staring at it for a long time she took off the elastic bands and then lifted the lid.

One by one she drew out the items resting in the box. The first was a scrap of paper, frail and yellow like a leaf from an old October. The pencil writing on this scrap was faded to illegibility. Secondly, she brought out half of a black-and-white photograph. A woman was the only clear thing on the picture. Closer inspection showed that she held a baby. The baby, however, like a judgement of Solomon, had been ripped in two by the tearing of the photograph. The arm of a man was just identifiable, showing that, when whole, the picture had depicted a man and woman holding a baby between them. The final thing Audrey lifted from the box was a pair of metal-rimmed spectacles.

When Cheryl arrived Audrey was still staring at the objects. Her untouched coffee had long since gone cold. 'Hello, Aud, what are ye deein' here?'

Jumping with shock, Audrey quickly replaced the objects in the shoebox. She fumbled the elastic bands on and then put it in her shoulder bag. 'I've come to sort things, man Cheryl. With the lasses.'

Just then the voices of the other cleaners could be heard arriving. They fell silent when they saw Audrey. 'Areet,' she greeted them.

One or two replied with a nod, but the others ignored her. Placing their orders at the counter, they squashed themselves in at two adjacent tables just vacated a few moments previously. Cheryl came over and sat with Audrey. 'What's the matter with that lot?' Audrey demanded loudly.

Cheryl smiled anxiously. 'Gannin' shopping?' she asked.

'What's going on?' Audrey asked, pointing at the cleaners. 'Why are they blanking wor?'

One of the cleaners snorted derisively. 'Ye can talk.'

'And what's that supposed to mean?'

'What it says.'

'And what does it say?'

'If the cap fits. Ye think ye're too bloody high and mighty to talk to us now, divven't ye?'

Audrey shook her head. 'I divven't kna what the hell ye are on aboot. It's yous what are blanking me. Some bloody friends ye lot turned oot to be.'

'Us? What aboot ye?' the same cleaner retorted.

'Eh?'

Rage rose in the heart of the cleaner. 'Audrey McPhee, what a cheek ye've got coming oot with that, after what ye've done to us.' There was a murmur of approval from the group.

Audrey rose. 'What have I done, like?'

'Ye've only gone and done the bloody dirty on yer mates.'

After the silence that followed these words, Audrey's voice was a threatening growl. 'Done the dirty?'

'Leave it alone, man,' one of the other cleaners said. 'We cannet prove nowt.'

'Prove what?'

Cheryl sat there in agony, watching the passing of the conversation as though it were a tennis match. 'Prove it or not, she's gonnae hear it,' the first cleaner said.

'Gan on then, I'm waiting,' returned Audrey, folding her arms.

But the other cleaners had got to their feet. 'Ha'way,' a third one said. 'Let's gan where there isn't such a stink aboot the place.'

A fourth woman sniffed ostentatiously. 'Aye, I think someone must have trod in some dogshite.'

The whole group began to file out of the café. 'Hey, ye!' Audrey shouted. 'Tell us what ye're gannin' on aboot noo.' But the group was moving off. Audrey strode after them. 'There must be someone here big enough to tell wor to me face what it is yus've obviously been talking aboot behind me back.'

'I will then,' shouted the cleaner who had spoken first of all. 'Ye were the syndicate manager, weren't ye?'

'Aye.'

'In charge of buying the tickets.'

'Aye.'

'Do I need to say owt more?'

'Aye, ye fuckin' dee.'

'Funny that, wasn't it?'

'What was?'

'Ye winning the lottery the night ye didn't come and watch the draw with the syndicate.'

Audrey sneered with contempt. 'Go on, say what you have to.'

'It just so happens that ye win that night. The first night ye miss with wor . . .'

Audrey roared with laughter. 'So I won with the syndicate ticket and kept the money for meself, did I?' She ran at the group of women, scattering them. 'Ye must be thick as well as ugly. For your information I gave the tickets to Cheryl before the draw so I couldn't have –' She broke off. 'What do I need to explain mesel' to yous for? If that's yer attitude then ye can just frigg off.' She turned to Cheryl. 'What aboot ye, Chez?'

There was the briefest of pauses. 'Divven't worry,' Cheryl whispered. 'I'll talk to them. I'll bring them roond –'

'Divven't friggin' bother!' Audrey shouted, but Cheryl had already gone.

The taxi took Audrey through Gateshead. She sat on the back seat as though in a daze, her sunglasses hiding the exhaustion in her eyes. The taxi had just passed under the shadow of the Dunston Rocket when Audrey tapped the glass window, and the vehicle stopped. Wrapping her coat around herself, and shrouding her head and face in its hood, she set off on foot.

The waste ground of the old rope works was desolate with December. The River Team gushed ashenly under the concrete platform, a single, hidden moorhen croaking as Audrey crossed. The wild rose avenue behind the Spartan Redheugh engineering works was also winter-bitten. Although it was mild for the time of year, there was a look of starvation about the dead grass and the skeletal briars of the dog rose bushes. Without stopping, Audrey entered the Teams. The rubble had been cleared from Keir Hardie Avenue and the earth, put to grass seed, was as freshly turned as a new grave. Two more streets had just been demolished, and another boarded with the green metal hoardings. The words GAS OFF followed Audrey as she walked up the eerily silent street.

There were few people about to see her, this strange-looking figure, dressed entirely in black like an angel of death, entering her old neighbourhood.

The parade of shops was finished now, the Londis the last to go. It was as though an epidemic had descended on the once thriving community. Audrey's heels echoed in the concrete burrow as she passed down it. She walked by the spot where she had been attacked, the dampness trickling audibly down the wall. Only when she reached the courtyard of the Square Flats did she stop. The ailing willow seemed spindlier than ever as she sat on the bench below it.

She sat there for a long time, hidden in the folds of her clothes, before finally lifting her eyes to look at her old home. Here and there the old windows and doors still peeped on to the walkways, but most were now covered with green metal hoardings. Audrey took off her shades to gaze at Flat 12A. She looked at it for perhaps half a minute, then, as though the glare from her old home dazzled her, she quickly replaced the glasses and, stumbling slightly, strode back across the courtyard.

St Mary Magdalene Church was locked, but Audrey lifted out a loose brick and retrieved the key. The greyness of the year's end did little to illuminate the interior of the church. She sat underneath the picture of *The Angelus* by Jean François Millet, and looking up at it, seemed to lose herself in it. The dark browns and greys of the painting, those thousand shades of a Northern European dusk, merged with the dimmity of the church so that the approaching night of the picture appeared to be actually falling at that moment. Utter darkness seemed to be only minutes away.

When Audrey left the church she was weighed down with an almost unbearable sadness. She had almost reached the neck of the cul-de-sac when she heard her name being called. She turned. Dan was at the upper window just as he had been on the morning after the great change in Audrey's fortunes. He called again, but Audrey continued on her way. She broke into a jog, and began to run. A black figure sprinting through the shrinking Teams.

2

All morning music had filled the house. A slow, haunting melody that seemed to be coming from the very beams and stones of the old parsonage: a folk ballad poignant in its simplicity and inevitability.

As Ronny placed yet another Christmas decoration on the wall of the children's room, he stopped for a moment to listen to the music. It was Terri-Leigh on her keyboard. Ronny smile broadly and nodded, and then stepped back to admire his work. A good half of the room was taken up by a grotto in which mannequin elves moved as they made Christmas presents. Shoulders shuddering with laughter, Ronny suddenly plunged into the grotto. When he came out a few minutes later he was dressed as Santa Claus, complete with white beard.

Still laughing, he hurried through the lounge, which was also packed with Christmas decorations and a towering tree. He ran through the hall, and yanked open the front door. The gravel of the drive crunched under his feet as he ran across it for a view of the roof. A massive sleigh, pulled by reindeer, ran across the tiles. The nose of the leading reindeer flashed. Beside the sleigh, a double life-sized Santa Claus dressed in black and white stood bent over one of the chimneys. He had a huge bag over his shoulder and on it flashed the words: SANTA IS A GEORDIE.

Ronny was still smiling when a delivery van pulled up. The smile died instantly at the sight of the delivery man stumbling towards him under the weight of his parcels. 'Just five this time,' the delivery man greeted him.

'They can't all be for us.' Ronny grabbed one of the parcels and slit it open. 'We don't need this,' he said, rattling the contents. 'We've already got two of these.'

'I cannet take it back,' reasoned the delivery man, dumping the parcels on the doorstep. 'Will ye sign this please?'

Glumly, Ronny sighed the electronic book. 'Ee, me bairns'll nivver believe it,' the delivery man laughed. 'I've got Santa's autograph.' He chuckled as he got back into the van. 'Seriously, mind, anyone would think your missus is Santa the amount of shopping she gets through. And ye? Yus're more like Scrooge.'

Ronny gazed numbly after the van as it drove away. He trudged heavily back to the house, carrying the boxes upstairs and laying them beside other boxes on the four-poster bed. A metal rail full of unworn clothes stood by the window. All at once he was overwhelmed with panic. Charging over to the dressing table, he rifled through the drawers one by one until he pulled out a purse. Casting a cautious glance at the door, he opened the purse and snatched out the wad of notes.

Stealthily as a thief, he crept to the window and lifted up the small rug lying there. A floorboard and section of carpet came up in his hands. Reaching into the cavity, he lifted out a metal biscuit box. He took off the lid, revealing a huge cache of cash. His face glinted for a moment at the sight, a cold joy suffusing him. He continued to stare at the cash, the music being played by Terri flowing out from the cavity. As though wrenching himself from a trance, he began to stuff the notes from the purse into the box. It was as he was about to put the lid back on that he heard something behind him. He turned. Audrey was standing at the door. 'What are ye deein'?' she demanded quietly.

'Nowt,' replied Ronny rapidly.

'Nowt? Pull the other one. What the frigg are ye deein'?'

'You're back soon, pet. I thought ye were meeting up with the lasses from the Metro Centre.'

'Ronny man, divven't bullcrap me, just tell us what ye're deeing with that money?'

Ronny looked down at the tin he was holding. He did not answer for a few moments. His eyes darted with thought. 'I wanted it to be a surprise,' he blurted.

'Eh?'

'It's for a Christmas present,' he decided impulsively. 'I wanted it to be a secret.'

Audrey looked coldly at him. 'But we've already agreed not to buy anything for each other. I mean, we can just gan and get what we want at any time.'

Ronny tried to rise to his feet, but got tangled in the folds of his Santa costume and sprawled onto his belly. 'Cannet we just buy one thing? One special thing . . .'

An unwanted harshness came into Audrey's eyes. 'You're lying,' she said icily. 'What else have ye been lying to me about, Ronny?'

'Eh?' replied Ronny, scrambling up bewilderedly.

'I kna what men are like.'

'What d'ye mean, man Audrey?'

'Yus've lied just now, so what else have ye lied to me aboot? Men; you're all alike. I should know, I've known enough in me time.'

Ronny writhed as though under torture. 'But I'm different. Ye kna I am.'

'Do I?'

'Aye.'

'I thought you were. But now it seems I cannet trust you either.'

'Audrey man,' Ronny moaned. 'It's nee big deal.' With a look of contempt, she walked to the door. 'Areet, areet,' he said quickly. 'It's not for a present.' Audrey stopped and turned. 'But ye'll see. Yus'll see there's a good reason. Let me show you.' He reached into a breast pocket and pulled out the picture of Chloe. 'I've been sending them money,' Ronny explained gently, handing over the photograph. 'Chloe's family. And to some of the others. Not to all of them. Just the saddest. I couldn't stand thinking of bairns suffering.'

'How long has this been going on for?'

'Since we won really. This is where I keep the money I send.'

Audrey's voice was dry. 'Why didn't ye tell me?'

'I didn't want to trouble ye.'

'Ye've been sending money withoot me knowing? But ye kna how much bairns mean to me. I'd love to have helped.' Audrey stared at her husband for a while as though puzzled by him. Then she frowned. 'How much ye been sending like?'

'About a thousand a month. All in all.'

'Christ.' Audrey shook her head. 'Ye should have telt me, man.' She thrust the photo back at him. 'Most of these'll be cons, man Ronny. Ye'll have been giving a grand a month to bloody con artists.' She looked down at the cavity; a number of letters could also be seen there. In an instant she had swooped down and plucked them out. They were all written in tabloid headline lettering. They were the poison pen letters. 'What's gannin' on, Ronny man?'

'Nothing,' he replied.

'Divven't be a prick!' Her voice resounded about the room. 'What are these?'

'Nowt . . .'

But even as he spoke, Audrey was reading them. 'Summink else that yus've been keeping from wor?'

'I was just trying to sort it out . . .'

'Ye sort things oot? That'd be a first time.'

Ronny gazed at his wife miserably. 'I kna this isn't ye talking, Audrey. I kna it's because ye're upset aboot yer dad. I kna –'

In one movement of stunning power, Audrey had ripped

the thick bundle of poison pen letters into two. She ripped them again. And continued to do so until they fell like snow from her palms. 'Get changed, man Ronny,' she said, opening the door. 'Ye look simple in that costume.'

Left alone, Ronny fell to his knees and began to gather up the litter. Terri-Leigh's keyboard was playing out plaintively. 'Merry Christmas,' he mumbled miserably. 'Ho-ho-friggin'-ho.'

When he had changed back out of the Santa Claus costume, Ronny went into the garage. He got into the Ferrari, but having sat in the driver's seat for a while, got out again, and went over to the vanette. It started only after three attempts.

He drove to the Teams, parking it outside the condemned parade of shops. He got out and stood for a while outside the old Londis. Then, closing his eyes for a moment as though steeling himself, he set off walking. The Teams' Surgery stood alone in an acreage of rubble.

The waiting room was full, and Ronny stood for a long time at reception. Three receptionists were visible through the little window, gossiping to each other as they sifted though the piles of clay-coloured medical cards. Coughing reverberated through the room behind him. 'Areet, Ronny,' someone greeted him. 'What are ye deein' slumming it?'

'I've booked me spot for the TB ward,' he quipped without turning.

At last one of the receptionists noticed him, and the glass window was slid open. 'Take a seat.'

'I've got an appointment to see –'

'There are no appointments today. It's open access. Take a seat.'

Ronny squeezed a way through to the only plastic chair not occupied. On one side of him was a frail old lady with a bewildered look, on the other a young man sat with his legs splayed widely. In front of him a baby resting on the shoulder of her mother gazed at him solemnly. Ronny smiled, but the girl did not smile back. Anxiety slowly grew in Ronny's eyes as a local radio station played out ceaselessly on ancient speakers; the frequency was not tuned perfectly and from time to time buzzed with squalls of static. 'I thought ye'd have gone private, Ronny boy,' a man Ronny's age called to him from the other side of the waiting room.

'I like to see how the other half chokes,' Ronny replied, but the anxiety did not dim in his eyes.

From time to time somebody would start to cough and coughing would spread across the plastic chairs in a raucous chorus fading eventually only to flare up again a little later. The smokers fidgeted and rocked, until finally succumbing and popping outside. The waiting patients could not hear the intercom system announcing the next patient and so organised the queue among themselves. 'It's ye next, hinny,' someone would say. 'Ye came in before me.'

People continued to address him, but Ronny, sinking into his chair, did not listen. 'Aye,' he said tonelessly. 'Is that so? Get away.'

The grubby walls, from which yellow paint was flaking, were covered in health posters. Ronny stared at one. On it was depicted a cartoon heart. In one half of the poster the heart smiled as it skipped a rope among fruit and vegetables; in the other it smoked morosely while lying on a sofa in among beer cans and pizza boxes. The patients came and went through the single door leading to the consulting room. The young man beside Ronny limped in and then out. The solemn baby disappeared and then reappeared. The bewildered old lady came back out, looking even more bewildered, her dress lifting at the back where the buttons had not been fastened properly. And all the while people coughed, and all the while people talked to Ronny; and all the while Ronny stared at the poster.

After he had been sitting there a long time, a child with an arm in a sling came in, carried by a harassed young mother. Three of the injured boy's young siblings followed behind, immediately beginning to run round and round the waiting room. The mother snapped constantly and ineffectively at the running children while the injured one sat miserably on her knee weeping inconsolably.

Then, all at once, Ronny found himself being ushered through the door himself. He pushed it open with a sinking feeling. Walking down the four or five steps of the little hall he knocked at the consulting room. 'Come in.'

The doctor was writing. Ronny hovered awkwardly at the threshold until a hand waved him to a chair in front of the desk. The doctor wore a multicoloured sari, and wrote with bewildering rapidity. For the first time in his adult life Ronny found himself on the verge of tears. He gulped back the power of his emotion, and throwing up a hand to his ponytail, yanked it until the pain caused him to blink. At last the doctor stopped writing. 'And what seems to be the matter, Mr Slater?'

Ronny lost himself in the middle of his explanation, ending with his hands pressed against his chest.

'Breathlessness, I see, a bit of nausea, chest pains . . .' repeated the doctor as she began to pump up the blood pressure sling she had tied round Ronny's arm.

Ronny forced a smile. 'Just the usual, y'kna.' But his humour evaporated instantly. He could feel the tears stinging his eyes.

'Are you all right, Mr Slater?'

'Just a bit tight, y'kna,' he lied. 'The auld blood pressure thing.'

Ronny undressed, and like an ox, suffered himself to be guided to the scales. 'You said pain down the left arm?' Ronny nodded.

The doctor weighed him and then went back to the medical notes to write down the measurement. Ronny remained where he stood, staring numbly at the needle on the scales. He could not hear what the doctor was saying to him. It was as he was standing there that the need to weep finally overwhelmed him, and he gazed in silence at the fat drop of a tear landing on the glass face of the scales. 'Just tell wor straight, man doctor. Am I gonnae die?'

3

Audrey sat at the dressing table, peering into the triptych of mirrors as though gazing through windows at a world beyond. The curtains were drawn and although it was only midday, the room was dark.

There was a soft knock at the door. Like one disturbed from a dream, Audrey jumped. She squinted apprehensively at the door as it opened slowly. 'What ye deein', man?' she snapped when she saw Terri-Leigh.

'Sorry, Nana, I didn't mean to give ye a shock.'

Running a hand over her face, Audrey sighed. 'Come in, pet.' She moved over on the seat, leaving room for the child. The two of them peered into the mirrors together. 'This was me mam's dresser,' Audrey explained. 'And her mam's before that. I used to sit like this when I was a bairn.'

'Why, Nana?'

'Just watching,' Audrey replied. 'Always just watching.'

'Watching for what?'

Audrey's fingers played over the intricacy of the wood-work, caressing the dark wood. 'Me grandad made this. For when he married me nana. Then he had to pawn his tools to buy a wedding ring. Did I nivver tell ye the story?'

'No, Nana,' Terri replied. 'Ye nivver told me that one.'

'Another night. I'll tell ye it another night.' With a sudden vehemence, Audrey embraced the child. 'Divven't grow up, pet. Divven't ever grow up. Because when ye dee then ye'll find oot the truth.' Audrey held the child inches from herself. 'Ye cannet trust men, pet. D'yus understand? Ye cannet trust a single man.'

Bewildered, the child waited for Audrey's passion to pass. 'Shall I brush yer hair like I used to, Nana?' she asked at last.

Audrey lifted a hand to the hair that was harshly scraped back against her skull. 'Ye wouldn't get a brush through here, love.' In the pause that followed she seemed to lose herself in the central panel of the three mirrors.

'Shall I read to ye then, Nana?'

She shook her head. 'Just leave us alone.'

'But –'

'Just leave us alone!' No sooner had her shout stopped reverberating than she closed her eyes and reached out gently for her granddaughter. 'I'm sorry, pet. I'm so sorry. Aye, read for me. Like you used to. We haven't done that since we moved in. And I want to kna what happened to that little donkey. I want to . . .' But Terri-Leigh had slipped out of the room.

'Terri, I'm sorry,' Audrey called. The landing floorboards creaked as she strode across them. 'Terri-Leigh . . .' The haunting music of the folk ballad seemed to stop her tracks. Then slowly, sadly, she retreated back to her own room.

She had lost track of the time she had spent sitting in front of the dresser when she heard the doorbell sounding. At the same moment, she realised that the music had stopped too. 'You get that, Terri, pet,' she called. 'It'll just be another delivery.'

But Terri did not reply. A few seconds passed. Another set of Big Ben chimes pealed through the house.

The sun had just come out, and as Audrey opened the front door, she was momentarily dazzled. When her vision cleared, she could see no one there. Neither had a parcel been left. She stepped outside, and looked down the drive. There was nobody to be seen.

She trailed back up the stairs, her shoulders stooped. In the bedroom, she drew back the curtain and gazed through the window. Across the chain of lawns the orchard could be seen, a number of its trees reduced to charred gibbets by the Bonfire

Night inferno. On a folding chair in the undamaged part of the orchard, Terri-Leigh was sitting reading. No sooner had Audrey seen her granddaughter than she spotted a second person. Hidden from the child, standing behind a scorched apple tree, an old man was watching Terri-Leigh. By the looks of him, he was a vagrant. Audrey tore out of the room. She hurled herself down the stairs four at a time.

A panel in the French windows shattered as Audrey wrenched them open. 'Terri!' She sprinted through the rose garden, across the lawns and over the soft earth of the orchard. 'Terri!' But by the time, she had reached the orchard, the intruder had gone. Audrey plucked the child from her chair and lifted her in an embrace. 'Did he say anything?' she demanded. 'What was he doing here? What did he want?'

'Who, Nana?' Terri asked, perplexed.

'Did ye not see him? I mean, he was just stood there.' Audrey pointed at the burnt tree trunk. 'He was watching ye. Did ye not see him?'

'But there wasn't anyone there, man Nana.'

Audrey stared at her granddaughter uncomprehendingly. 'But I saw him.'

'Mebbes it was a ghost,' reasoned Terri-Leigh. 'I mean, mebbes this place really is haunted.'

Audrey's tone grew matter-of-fact. 'Come in now, Terri. Read inside. It's damp out here. You'll catch your death.'

'But –'

'I said bloody well get in!'

Back at the dressing table in the bedroom, Audrey sat for a long time. When she finally stood up, she went over to the window. There was nobody to see. No one behind the tree under which she had seen the old man. Only the chair where Terri had been sitting remained. She went back to the dresser, opened a drawer and brought out a packet of cards. With eyes tight shut and her breath coming out in short, sharp stabs, she began to shuffle the deck. They were old cards and well worn, the suits depicted in a strange, stark manner. She cut the pack, and then slowly drew out a single card and laid it on the dark wood in front of her.

4

Ronny stood on the little verandah of the shack and gazed at his allotment. The spade stood in the earth where he had left it. The sweat of his digging still clung to his brow. He raised the ventriloquist's dummy to his face. 'Are ye areet, Denny?' he whispered.

'Canny, canny,' Ronny growled in return, 'and how are you, Ronny?'

'Me, Denny? I'm not so good actually.'

'What's the matter with ye, like?' the dog growled again. Ronny sighed. 'She doesn't really know. The doctor.'

'Doesn't really know?' the dog demanded.

'Not until I've been to the consultant.'

'The consultant, that doesn't sound very good.'

Ronny drew the dummy even closer to him, so that he was staring right into its glassy eyes. 'The thing is, if it is . . . what it might be . . . then I could live for another twenty years or . . . or I might gan at any time.'

'Any time?'

'Any time. Any moment. That's what she said. Any moment.'

Ronny whined like a dog then barked as he growled: 'Oh shit.'

'I say, I say, I say. What do you get if you cross a fat bastard with nee exercise and a dodgy heart?' Ronny broke off, his lips mumbling for a long time until he spoke loud enough to be heard. 'A dead body.' Whimpering, Ronny shoved a fist into his mouth. With a mighty effort, he tried to control himself. 'Course, there's a lot I can dee to help meself, like. Lose weight. Take exercise. That sort o' thing.' He trailed away, and looked at the ventriloquist's dummy with a sudden desperation. 'A dead body, Denny. You get a dead body.'

He walked stiffly over the vegetable plot, pulled the spade from the ground and began to dig again.

When Joe O'Brien came in later, he found Ronny still digging: he was standing in the hole he had made, up to his thighs. 'What ye deein', Ronny man?' he demanded.

'Areet, Joe,' Ronny greeted him, a strange brightness in his tone. 'Am I glad to see ye. Me and Denny the mutt have said everything we've got to say to each other and there's not nee one else to talk to.'

'I said what the hell are ye deein'?' the old man repeated.

'Digging.' Bending down Ronny continued to dig. He lifted the earth now with groans of strain. He had reached the clay subsoil.

'Ye've dug over yer Brussels,' the old man pointed.

'Have I?'

'And ye're as white as a sheet.' Joe came over to the hole. He jabbed his stick at Ronny. 'What are ye deein', Ronny?'

'Getting fit,' Ronny shrugged.

'Getting fit? Ye look as though yus're digging yer own grave.'

Ronny stopped digging. He wiped the sweat from his eyes as he looked at the excavation. 'Ha'way,' he said quietly as he climbed out of the hole. 'I'll make the tea.'

They sat inside the shack in silence, cradling their enamel mugs. 'What's the matter?' Joe asked at last. Ronny looked at him as though stupefied. 'With Audrey, man,' the old man added. 'What's the matter with Audrey? We've all noticed it. There might be more decorations up in that parsonage than Santa's grotto but there's summink not right.'

'What d'ye mean?'

Joe sipped his tea loudly. 'Come on, man, ye're not telling me everything in the garden's rosy?'

Misery had come over Ronny's features. 'I divven't kna what the matter with her is,' he confessed. 'Sometimes she's areet but at others ... Look, Joe, if I tell you, ye've got to swear to secrecy. Ye've got to –' He broke off. 'I've got that many things going on in me heed I feel as though I'll explode if I divven't talk aboot them. But how can I?'

For a long time Joe did not speak, and throughout the silence he peered at Ronny. 'This takes us back forty-odd year.' Ronny looked at him questioningly. 'When ye used to come doon here to see me and Ginga. Y'kna, when them lads were bullying ye.'

Ronny's voice cracked a little. 'You helped me then.'

'Aye, we did.'

'Will you help me noo? You see, I divven't kna what to dee.'

A gentleness came over the old man's face. 'There's nowt that cannet be sorted, if ye've a mind to it.'

'She says it's her dad.'

'Eh?'

'This thing what's getting to Audrey. She says it's her dad.'

'Her dad? But he's been deed for years.'

'I kna, I kna.' Ronny filled his cheeks with air. 'There's nee rhyme nor reason to it. She just says ... that since we won the lottery ... he's been on her mind.'

'How d'ye mean?'

'I divven't kna, but I'm sick of it. I wish we nivver won the lottery.'

The old man grunted. 'What's happened, cannet unhappen.'

'She's falling to pieces, man Joe. Fallen off her trolley. She's started snapping at the bairns. Especially Terri, and I kna for a fact how much she loves them all. But ye wouldn't think it if ye saw the way she's been cracking on at her. And as for the way she gets at me. Can I be honest with ye, Joe man?' The old man nodded tersely. 'I think it's summink else. Not her

307

dad. It must be another fella. She denies it of course, but what else could it be?'

Joe shifted uncomfortably under Ronny's scrutiny. 'It might be her dad after all.'

'No. It's another fella.' Ronny smiled ruefully. 'Think aboot it, Joe. Look at her. Everyone fancies her. And before me, let's face it, she wasn't exactly the Virgin Mary. Look at her, and look at me. I'm a walking bloody joke. I've got aboot as much bloody panache as a dog turd.' He flipped his ponytail. 'Baldy-lang hair, that's what they call me, and that's what I am.'

Joe stared at Ronny thoughtfully. 'Have it out with her then.'

'No. If there is anyone else, I divven't want to kna who he is. I'd rather live in ignorance.'

There was a long pause during which they continued to drink from their mugs. 'Ronny lad,' began the old man gruffly. 'Ye kna that's not the way to dee things. Remember when ye came here as a bairn, crying yer eyes out because some rogues had been taunting ye and hitting ye? Well, we didn't tell ye to run away from yer problem then. And I won't say the same now. Ye have to confront it. It's the only way. It won't go away otherwise. Ye're gonnae have to have it out with her. But before ye dee that, ye've got to look at yersel'.' Joe scrutinised Ronny. 'I mean, is there anything that ye've been deein' that's set her against ye?'

'Nowt. Not really.'

'Not really?'

Ronny wrung his hands. He paused for a moment before answering: 'I've been hiding money.'

'Hiding money?'

'I was frightened I wouldn't have enough.'

'Not have enough, what ye on aboot? Ye've won the lottery.'

'I kna, I kna, and we've got six grand a month but . . .' Ronny stood suddenly, and turning his back, leant against one

308

of the dark shelves. 'I've been giving away a grand a month to deserving causes an' that, and then there's . . . And then there's Jimmy.'

'Jimmy? What d'ye mean, Jimmy?' Joe screwed his face. 'D'yus mean that worthless specimen that used to cause all the trouble up Lobley Hill?'

'I'm having to give him a grand a month an' all.'

'Give him? What the hell are you talking aboot?'

Ronny's voice rose wretchedly. 'He's blackmailing wor. He's bloody blackmailing wor.'

There was no answer for a while. From where he stood with his head on the shelf, Ronny heard the old man sigh behind him. 'Does Audrey know?'

'She knows about the deserving causes.'

'What aboot Jimmy? Does she kna aboot him?'

'No. And I don't want her to.'

A cockerel began to crow from one of the other allotments. Joe's voice was quiet. 'How the hell did ye get into this state, Ronny son?'

'I don't know, Joe.'

'Well, ye'll have to sort him. Ye cannet be giving money to him. If ye won't gan to the pollis –'

'The pollis,' Ronny moaned. 'I cannet gan to the pollis.'

'Well then,' Joe pronounced with finality. 'You'll have to settle him yourself. In the old way. With your fists. Wait for him somewhere quiet. That Jimmy lad. I've had a few run-ins with him in me time. It wouldn't be that hard to settle his hash. Ye're about twice his size for a start –'

'D'ye still not understand?' As Ronny turned the whole shack shook. His face was creased with pain. 'I'm not that type of person. I'm not a hard man. I'm not a fighter. And I nivver have been.'

'You settled that lad what used to bully you,' replied Joe, puzzled.

'No I didn't. I kept on giving him me pocket money until I was fourteen years old.'

'But ye said –'

'I'm not like ye, Joe. I cannet meet someone somewhere quiet and settle them with me fists. I'm a loser. Pure and simple. A victim. I'm soft as shite. I've nivver been able to sort me own problems oot. Not then. Not now.'

As Ronny sat back down with a defeated smile, Joe looked at him steadily. 'So what? So ye're not a fighter. What does that matter? You're a dreamer. That's the type ye are. And that's why Audrey loves ye.' Joe nodded. 'Fighters are ten a penny roond here. But someone with a dream? Thems is a rarity.' The old man's gnarled hands played over the crook of his walking stick. 'Tell Audrey about it. She's a fighter. She'd finish the little pipsqueak off quick enough.'

Ronny's voice was a whisper. 'For once in me life, I want to be able to sort something. I want to be able to work things out.' He got up again, and reaching on to a shelf, brought down an old golden syrup tin. He popped open the lid and took out the contents. It was a wad of notes.

The old man's voice grew hushed. 'There's awer a thousand pound there.'

Wildly Ronny gestured the dark interior of the hut. 'There's little stashes everywhere in here. I cannet even remember where they are. There must be twenty grand aboot the shop!'

'For pity's –'

'And I want you to have it. You might as well. It was supposed to be for Jimmy. But I've come to a decision. I'm not giving him another penny.' Ronny held out the notes to Joe. 'Here, take them.'

'Ronny man, pull yersel' together!' Joe's shout echoed round the shack. In the silence that followed the cockerel could be heard.

'I divven't understand anything any more, man Joe,' Ronny

310

began. 'The lottery's changed it all. Even the way I think. They say it's all just one big lottery, divven't they? Life an' everything. We started as some sort of big bang, and things have just continued the same. But when ye think aboot it proper, then it cannet be. It just cannet be! 'Cos in the real lottery, ye had to buy a ticket. D'ye see what I mean? Ye had to buy a ticket.' Ronny's voice grew hoarse, and a look of wonder came into his eyes as though a great insight was imminent. 'It didn't just happen. Ye had to buy a ticket. Ye had to buy a ticket. It didn't just happen.' Ronny continued to strain after his thoughts, then suddenly started laughing. 'A loser through and through. The love of me life's pulling doon her knickers for some other fella, and I'm thinking aboot the mysteries of the universe.'

'Shut up!' Joe hauled himself to his feet. 'Yus're making a fool of yerself.' Ronny sobered instantly. 'Now listen to me, Ronny. There's nowt ye need to dee but talk to Audrey. Talk. Tell her what yus're worried aboot. Tell her aboot Jimmy.'

Ronny rose too and followed his friend out on to the verandah. 'Can I ask ye summink, Joe?'

'As lang as it's not summink daft.'

'It is daft. It's the daftest thing in the world. But that doesn't matter.'

'I haven't got time for this. I've got to milk Ginga's goat and then —'

'D'ye ever think about dying?' Ronny gazed at the old man. 'That's what I want to kna. D'yus ever think aboot dying?'

Joe continued on his way down the steps. He was halfway across the plot when he turned. 'What sort of stupid question is that to ask an auld man?'

'I'm sorry, Joe,' Ronny called. 'I'm so sorry.'

After Joe had gone, Ronny returned to the shack. Through the slow hours of the winter day, he sat there hunched over the stove, moving only to poke the burning seacoal.

Audrey found him like that as she stared through the

window of the hut. She smiled and for a few moments seemed about to knock on the glass and greet him, but at the last moment, she pulled away instead, and ran. Hearing feet on the steps, Ronny looked up, but by the time he had reached the door, there was no one there. And he stood at his door, gazing into his allotment like a man searching for a ghost.

Chapter Seven

I

After Christmas the prevailing winds of Gateshead swung round abruptly. The warm westerlies were chased away by blasts from the east as icy winds arrived all the way from the frozen steppes of Siberia.

January Sale shoppers sprinted from their parked cars to the heated malls of the Metro Centre. And the earth of the Derwentside Estate Long Walk froze to iron. The rafters of the parsonage creaked and complained. In the orchard, a wedge of ice split the finest of the fruiting trees, and with a crack that echoed across the estate like a gunshot, the tree snapped in two.

The cold spell stretched to a second day, a third, and then, deepening, to a fourth. The forest surrounding the parsonage became a vast Winter Palace. Strange birds arrived in the borough. A wayfaring group of Lapland buntings, a disorientated Siberian robin, and most other-worldly of all, arriving at sunset on wings which whistled sadly in the ice-bound bitterness of twilight, a flock of cranes.

One morning during this time of ice, Big Al was climbing up a ladder in Whickham. His frozen features peeped wretchedly from the woollen hat he wore inside the tightly zipped hood of his snorkel jacket. His hands were chapped and chilled to red claws. The bucket and rag he carried hung on his wrist. Immersed in the misery of his ascent, he could not see the Ferrari cruising towards him. It parked up behind the dirty white vanette, and Ronny got out, dressed in his old donkey jacket, which was worn over a bulging mound of jumpers. On his head was a woollen hat identical to Al's.

Ronny walked to the foot of the ladder. 'Hey, ye're up my ladder.'

Al looked down. 'So it's you.'

'How's the new job gannin', man Al?'

A huge cloud of condensed breath rose from Al's lungs as he coughed. 'I only hope me bloody wedding tackle's not as frozen solid as me bloody bucket.'

Ronny laughed. 'Ye divven't clean windows in this weather. Ha'way doon, I'll buy ye a pint. And divven't worry, I'll take ye to the Wheatsheaf.'

When he had come down from the top of the ladder, Al smiled. 'That jacket's seen better days, bonny lad.'

Ronny rubbed his hands vigorously against the coarse material of his donkey jacket. 'It's still comfortable, but.' The two men stared at each other. 'Haven't seen ye for a while, Al man,' said Ronny, jogging on the spot to keep the circulation going in his feet. At that moment the bucket slipped from Al's wrists. Landing heavily, a solid block of ice, in which the rag was contained, popped free like a cork. 'Get into the Ferrari,' Ronny said. 'Ye can drive.'

Smiling a little ruefully, Al hoisted the ladder on to his shoulder. 'No, I'd better take the vanette.' Using the heel of his clumsy hands, he tried to slide the ladders into themselves, but the catch was frozen. He struggled with it for a while.

'Al man, leave that here. Come in the Ferrari.'

'No, man Ronny, a Ferrari's not for the likes of me.' He grinned sheepishly. 'Besides, if I leave the vanette here, it'll nivver start again.'

Ronny came over and held his hand out. 'Shake hands, brother.'

Al stared at the hand a moment, and then took it. 'I'm a rogue, and you're another.'

'Blimme,' said Ronny, flinching from the deadening touch

of his friend's hand. 'It's like a block of ice, man.' He took the ladders and secured them on top of the vanette. Ye'd better let me drive. And I tell you what. We'll gan in the vanette. For old times' sake.'

'What aboot the Ferrari?'

With a shrug Ronny opened the door of the vanette, breaking the ice that had formed over the lock, and got inside. 'Have ye ever known it so cold?' he asked as Al got in the passenger seat. Blowing on his hands, Al shook his head. 'How d'ye keep warm on a ladder?'

'Ye divven't.'

The clapped-out old vanette chugged down Dunston Bank, the half-bags of cement, sand and gravel, all frozen solid, sliding across the back. 'Did ye tie the doors?' Ronny laughed just as the shoal of shovels and tools slid against the back of their seats. They drove past the old flour mill, and the coal staithes, its wooden lattice rimed in a dazzlingly blue frost. They rattled under the shadow of the Dunston Rocket and, skirting the frost-bound wasteland, entered the Teams. Another street had been demolished, its red brick glittered with frost. 'Are they going to knock the whole place down or what?' Ronny asked quietly.

The Wheatsheaf had just opened, and only a few old men sat at the bar, nursing half-pints. 'Areet, lads,' they greeted Ronny and Al. 'I thought yous would have moved to California by now.'

'Aye, well,' replied Ronny. 'I just love the winters here so much that I cannet bring meself to leave.'

Karen served them, the engagement ring from Bill prominently displayed on her finger. 'Ee, I wish ye'd sort that Leeanne oot,' she said, 'or get Audrey to. She's a reet friggin' bitch. Just 'cos me and Bill want to sell the hoose. Well, I cannet spend the rest of me life working as a barmaid. I've got me ambitions. As for that Leeanne bitch, I'll bloody slap her face for her –'

'Karen pet,' said Ronny softly. 'Sort it oot yersel.'

There was a sharp intake of breath. 'Well, if that's yer attitude. I always thought ye were different, but I see ye're just the same –'

'Two packets o' pork scratchings an' all, pet,' added Al.

He drew Ronny away into one of the dark cubbyholes of which the Wheatsheaf abounds. They sat on rickety wooden chairs. 'Bloody hell, did yus have to put up with all o' that over Christmas?'

Ronny took a deep draught of his beer. 'Divven't ask wor aboot Christmas, man Al. It was a pure nightmare. I used to love Christmas. So did Audrey. I thought it was gonnae the best ever this year. I thought it'd pull us all back together. But . . .' He broke off, and then looked at his friend. 'What was your Christmas like?'

'Canny,' said Al opening a packet of pork scratchings and popping a handful in his mouth. 'I spent it with me sister and her bairns.'

'Yer sister? But ye haven't spoken to her for ten years.'

'Well, there comes a time.'

'I'm sorry aboot not seeing ye. I was gonnae pop in on ye in the hooseboat an' that but –'

'It doesn't matter, man Ronny. We're here now. Eat them pork scratchings then, son.'

'No,' replied Ronny.

'Eh?'

'I'm trying to cut back.' Ronny looked regretfully at the unopened packet. 'So ye had a canny Christmas then?'

'The best Christmas I've had for ages. I even shagged Cheryl.'

The mouthful of beer spumed back into Ronny's glass as he choked on it. 'Bloody hell. Congratulations. I mean, well done. I cannet believe it. Brilliant.' Ronny's face, which had been fretted with anxiety, broke into a smile. But the smile faded when he heard Al's sigh. 'What's the matter? Ye look sick as a dog. Was it nee good or summink?'

'Good? It was like losing thirty years. Or ten stone.' Al shook his head slowly, an unwonted dreaminess came into both his eyes, blue and opaque alike. 'It was the real thing, man,' he said simply. 'I nivver knew anything could be that good. It was like being able to fly. D'ye kna what I mean? It was like being able to fly. And only a fat knack knas just how good that feels.'

'So what's the matter then, marra?' For a while Al sat despondently with his elbows on the table and his chin resting on a hand. Then he reached into a pocket, and placed a letter between their pints. Ronny reached for it. 'Another nasty?' Al nodded. His lips moving, Ronny read the words fashioned from tabloid headline lettering. Then he put the letter down.

'I kna who it is,' said Al in a distant voice.

'So do I,' replied Ronny.

'Do ye?'

'Aye, I dee.' A haunted look came over Ronny. 'But I've only got to pay him a grand a month for another six months.'

'What ye on aboot, man Ronny?'

Ronny inhaled wretchedly. 'Him what's been sending the threatening letters. I've been paying him.'

'Who?'

'Jimmy. But divven't worry. I've sorted him oot. Had a little chat. Went to see him. Telt him it wasn't on. And he said I just needed to pay for another six months.'

'Bloody hell.' Al took a long pull on his beer. 'But I thought ye telt me that ye weren't paying him nothing?'

'I've told ye. I've sorted it. It's only for another six months. Then the debt's cancelled.'

'Debt? Listen to yersel'. Ye divven't have a debt.'

'Shh!' Ronny urged. The two men seemed to crouch low over their glasses so that their heads almost touched. 'Look,

I've had no choice,' Ronny murmured. 'He was threatening the bairns.'

'Did ye not tell Audrey?'

'I didn't need to. I sorted it mesel'.'

Al writhed with frustration. 'Ye daft prick. Yus've sorted nothing. Six months? It'll be six years. It'll be until he's bled ye dry. Did ye win the friggin' lottery just to give it all to Jimmy?'

This time Ronny's voice rose dangerously. 'What the frigg else can I dee? Jimmy's hand in hand with Macca.'

'Shh!' Al urged. Getting up, he peered over the wooden partition behind which they were sitting. The pub was still virtually empty. Karen was on the telephone arguing with someone. He sat back down solemnly, and then spread his hands in a gesture of defeat. 'Ronny man, for the first time in me life I divven't kna what to say.'

Ronny's voice was small. 'I haven't sorted it, have I?'

'No, you haven't sorted it. And you're wrong about the letters as well.' Al began to chuckle grimly. 'Yus're aboot as wrang as it's possible to be.'

'What is it?' Ronny demanded. 'What's the matter?'

'They weren't from Jimmy. Them poison pen letters. They weren't from him.' Al rose to whisper in his friend's ear. 'They were from Cheryl.'

'Cheryl?'

'I foond oot. That's why she slept with wor. To keep us quiet. And here's me thinking it was because she liked us.' Al smiled bitterly. 'Haven't seen her since. I just telt her to piss off. Broke me heart. But what else could I do?'

They looked at each other. 'We're in the shite, aren't we?' Ronny said.

'Aye.'

'And now Cheryl. The way Audrey's been lately, I think this might finish her off. What we gonnae dee?'

Al sighed. For a few moments he looked utterly lost, then he lifted his pint and drained it. 'We'd better get back to the

Ferrari . . .' He belched. 'Knowing our luck, it'll get twocked. Ha'way, bring them pork scratchings.' They stood up. Ronny left the pork scratchings on the table. Al looked at him closely. 'Have ye lost weight?' Ronny nodded. 'Why?'

'I divven't kna,' shrugged Ronny.

'Ye look as though ye've lost loads.'

'The doctor told me that if I didn't stop eating then I'd be dead within the year.'

Al laughed. 'Glad to see ye've still got yer sense o' humour.'

They left the pub, plunging back into the frozen air. 'Here,' said Ronny, taking out a bundle of notes and thrusting it into Al's hands. 'I feel bad aboot not taking ye on as a personal adviser properly. It's only aboot a grand.'

Al plucked the cash from his friend's hand. 'See it as an investment. In fact, you have just bought yersel' a half-share in a bucket and rag.' They walked over to the vanette. 'We'll be areet. Ye and me. We're survivors.'

'I'm a dreamer,' shrugged Ronny.

'There's a place for everyone on Skid Row,' replied Al. For a moment the old cunning flashed in his opaque eye. 'Did I tell ye, I've got another Claims Direct pending?'

'Have ye?'

'Aye, against the cooncil. Me brief reckons they'll settle oot o' court.' He rubbed his hands painfully, flinching as the blood slowly began to circulate again. They stood at the vanette looking over the ladder at each other. 'Ronny man. We'll work it oot. Somehow. Jimmy. Everything. I just want ye to kna. Ye're not on yer own.'

'Aye. And there's the talent show to look forward to.'

Al winced. 'Look forward to? It's aboot as entertaining as having teeth drawn. Ronny man, why divven't ye give it a miss this year? I mean the prize money's hardly worth it to a man o' your means.'

'I cannet,' Ronny said simply. 'I dee it every year. It's tradition.'

Just then a sorrowful whispering filled the anaemic blue of the pale winter sky in which the sun hung weak and low. Both men looked up, their mingling breath rising like a geyser. 'It's them again,' whispered Al, gazing at the flock of cranes which were sweeping through the sky above. 'What the hell are they? Funniest bloody looking geese I've ever seen.'

'They're far from home,' replied Ronny.

'What they deein' here?'

Ronny shrugged. 'They came with the cold.'

For a while the two men watched the cranes as the huge birds desolately planed the sky. 'It doesn't look like they kna what to dee,' Al mused. 'So we're not the only lost fuckers roond here.' He looked back down to earth. 'Ha'way, I'll drive ye back to yer Ferrari, man.'

'No, it's areet. I'll walk. I need the exercise.'

'Exercise?'

'Aye. New Year's resolution. Since I packed in work I've ballooned.'

'Well, if it's exercise yus're wanting then why not come on the roond. Carry the ladder.'

Ronny smiled. 'Aye, I will. I will.'

'Ha'way then.'

'I've just got summink to sort first.'

'I divven't kna aboot exercise, if ye try and walk up Dunston bank ye'll end up having a bloody heart attack.'

'Well, we all have to die of summink.'

Al studied him narrowly. 'Is there anything else yus're not telling wor?'

But Ronny was already walking.

'We'll sort it,' Al called. 'We'll sort it all, Ronny boy. This afternoon when we're up the ladder.'

Ronny did not go back up Dunston bank. After Al had driven by, he doubled back on himself. Hitting the Coatsworth Road, he went into a café and ordered a mug of tea. He sat there staring watchfully out of the window, sipping the tea sweetened by three sugars, and eating a fistful of KitKats.

He was eating the third chocolate bar when he saw the one he was watching for. It was Jimmy going into the Wheatsheaf.

He did not rise immediately, but first finished his tea and snacks. As he stepped outside, the cold hit him with the power of a physical blow. Despite the bitter chill, Ronny lurked in the Wheatsheaf car park for a while, jumping on the spot and flapping his arms round his body. Then, at last, he went into the pub. Not through the main door leading into the public bar, but through a fire door in the large extension built at the back of the premises.

It was dark inside and thick with cigarette smoke. The noise of a pool ball striking another greeted Ronny and as though suddenly overcome with fear, he stopped just inside the door. For a long time he seemed to be struggling with himself before, with the forlorn look of a man with nothing left to lose, he walked on. As his eyes grew used to the dim lighting, he saw a number of pool tables over which people listlessly played. At the far end of the room, Jimmy was sitting on a bar stool with a girl next to him. Breathing in deeply, Ronny walked over.

Jimmy did not seem to see him for a while as he talked to the girl, then he grinned. 'Areet, baldy-lang hair.'

'Areet, Jimmy,' Ronny mumbled in return.

Jimmy turned to the girl. 'Ye kna baldy-lang hair, divven't ye?' The girl laughed cruelly. 'He's a proper clown,' grinned Jimmy. 'Aren't ye a proper clown?'

'Aye, I'm a proper clown,' Ronny returned in a mechanical tone.

'Come here,' commanded Jimmy. Ronny obeyed. 'Look at this,' Jimmy said to his girlfriend as he laughingly tossed Ronny's ponytail. 'Look at this.' Screeching with laughter, the girl flicked the ponytail. Ronny stood there, his eyes riveted to the ground. Suddenly his head was forced brutally up. Jimmy had yanked his ponytail. 'Buy us a pint then, baldy-lang hair.'

The man behind the bar was already pulling a pint of lager. Without any expression on his face, Ronny reached into his pocket and brought out a huge wad of notes. When the pint was poured, Ronny put the money beside it, and Jimmy pocketed it. 'That's this month's, five to gan. Ye can frigg off noo,' Jimmy said. But Ronny did not go. 'I said ye can frigg off,' he repeated sharply.

Ronny held his ground. He swallowed. 'Jimmy man, I want this sorted oot.' The youth did not reply; a malicious leer played on his baby face. 'I said I want it sorted oot.'

'I see.' Jimmy turned to his girlfriend. 'Baldy-lang hair wants it sorted out.'

'Aye, I want it sorted oot, once and for all.'

'But I thought we did sort it oot, fat boy. Pay for another six months and then yus're in the clear. Just another –'

'No.'

There was a gale of laughter from Jimmy and the girl. The barman joined in and, looking over, brandishing their cues, the pool players hooted as well. 'Baldy-lang hair! Baldy-lang hair!' they chanted. Ronny kept his nerve for a few seconds, then turned from the bar. The laughter followed him, ringing in his ears as he walked to the door.

He did not seem to notice the cold, and had reached the old metal rope works before he even realised where he was.

The chaff stalks of the willowherb thickets, which flower so beautifully in the summer, were fluffed with ice like pampas grass, and the harebell bank was a scrawl of frost. As he passed behind the Spartan Redheugh engineering works, Ronny stopped suddenly. He stood there without moving, his breath crystallising in great clouds, his eyes tight shut. Then he began gingerly to flex his left arm. At last he moved on.

Ronny jogged across the earth where Keir Hardie Avenue had stood; it was frozen to iron. Coming to a freshly

322

demolished street, he clambered over it until he stood in the midst of its wreckage. He looked at the debris about him. In among the bricks and timbers, all glinting with ice, were scraps of the lives that until recently had been lived between the four standing walls. A baby's dummy, a walking stick, and there, just at his foot, a shattered picture frame. Behind the fractured glass could be seen the faces of a family. Ronny stooped to pick it up and stared at the people captured by camera, their smiles fragmented by the shattering. He gazed at the photograph for a long time, standing motionless in the bitter night.

Dan was in when Ronny knocked. 'Come in, come in,' the priest welcomed him warmly. 'You must be freezing.'

'Aye, it is nippy.'

He examined Ronny as he sank into one of the armchairs. 'Are you all right?' Ronny did not reply. 'I've a drop of mulled wine left. It's still warm.'

'Canny.'

They sat in the living room sipping the warm red liquid. Ronny stared at the picture of *The Angelus* which hung above the gas fire. 'So you're all ready for the talent show?' the priest asked.

'Well, I'll give people a laugh,' Ronny replied bitterly. 'I mean, I dee that without trying.'

'Will you tell me what the matter is, Ronny?'

'Everyone's always asking us what the matter is these days. Ye wouldn't think we'd won the lottery, would ye?'

They continued to drink for a while without words. Then Dan broke the silence. 'How are you all? I haven't seen you for a while. Audrey wasn't at midnight Mass.'

'Aye, first time she's missed it. She just wouldn't gan. And it wasn't just that. There was a VO. To gan and see Terri-Leigh's mam. Y'kna, a visiting order to gan and see her in jail. Christmas visit. Wouldn't take the bairn. I had to gan.' Puffing his cheeks out, Ronny squashed them with his hands.

Dan watched him closely as he nursed his mulled wine. 'That's not like Audrey.'

'That's the thing. I divven't kna what is like Audrey any more.' Ronny looked at the priest with a sudden desperation. 'Will ye talk to her, man Father? Ye could put her right. Summink's happened to her. I swear down, she isn't herself. Ye could reach her. Ye could bring her back.' He reached for his ponytail and tugged gently at it. The panic had passed. Resignation spread in his mild eyes. 'I kna, I kna. There's nee speaking to her. It's since we won the lottery. Summink's been knocked loose. It's all aboot her dad. And summink aboot a river. But it's all too terrible to gan into. And all of it rolling aboot broken inside of her.' Desperate yearning filled his eyes. 'I wish we'd nivver won it.'

'I only wish I could help you.'

'I divven't need your help. I can sort things oot mesel'!' Ronny's voice resounded through the room. He stood up decisively. 'I'll sort things oot. Just ye wait and see. I'll sort them oot.' Then, giggling foolishly, he sat back down. He smiled at the priest who was gazing intently at him. 'I just divven't kna what to dee, man Father. She's been acting so . . . nasty.'

'No one said it was going to be easy,' the priest said gently. 'Love never is.'

'See, me? As far as Audrey's concerned I couldn't stop loving her even if I wanted to. Not loving her? Ye might as well ask the Tyne to gan back up into the hills.' He seemed to lose himself in thought for a while, then he clapped his hands loudly together. 'There is summink ye can dee, man Father. I've got some money. To give away. I don't need it any more. You must know someone what deserves it. A few thousand. As I say, I don't need it any more. Not now I've sorted things.'

The priest stood up and went over to the window. 'They're knocking this place down, you know.'

Ronny nodded. 'Another street's gone since I was here last.'

'I've been to the council. Seen the plans. They're not going to stop until they've knocked every single house down.' The priest turned to Ronny, his face flushed with anger. 'I intend to be the last bloody one out!' The rage turned into laughter. 'They can't build anything else here, you know. It's unsafe. All the old mine workings and clay pits undermine foundations.' He stamped a foot with shocking vigour. 'It's a honeycomb under here.' He gazed out the window a little longer then abruptly grabbed Ronny. 'Come on then,' he said, getting his coat. 'I want to show you something. You said I would know someone who deserves your money.'

Ronny had to hurry to keep up with the priest. Under a pale blue sky, they rushed along the shuttered parade of shops, passed between the Blarney stones of the roadblock, and jogged through the destroyed children's playground. Dan waited for Ronny at the mouth of the burrow. Just before Ronny reached him, both men looked up. The cranes were passing overhead again, wheeling bemusedly over the borough, making weary shapes in the blue air. The two men stared up until the forlorn flock had gone. Then they entered the burrow.

'Careful,' Dan advised. The concrete had been smoothed to a bobsleigh run, and Ronny found himself slipping. Clinging to the wall, bellied with sheets of ice, they eased themselves down the burrow. Fingers deadened with the cold, Ronny lurched through the burrow while the stalactites of icicles suspended from the roof broke against his forehead and cheeks.

'Why ye bringing wor here, man Father Dan?'

'I think Audrey used to call them the pixies,' Dan replied as they emerged on to the courtyard. 'I can't remember the last time I saw them with a toy. Or a smile. The mother's a junkie. The thing is, she's turned over a new leaf.' Dan nodded to himself. 'She's come off the drugs. Even went for a job interview yesterday. She didn't get it but she's really making an effort to change. You don't need begging letters to find people suffering, Ronny.'

Ronny followed the priest across the square, passing beneath the canopy of the willow tree. After thirty years of failing to thrive, the freak cold snap had finally finished it off. And as he passed it, Ronny sighed for the sickly thing which had at last died.

They mounted the stairs and came on to a walkway. Across the courtyard Flat 12A could be seen boarded up. Painted on the wall beside the old front door were the words GAS OFF. 'Memory lane?' asked the priest.

Ronny shook his head. 'They'll be pulling that doon an' all soon.'

The pixies lived in the last inhabited flat. There was no reply when Dan knocked. He knocked a second and a third time, then tried the door. It pushed open easily.

It seemed to be even colder inside the flat than out. The curtains were drawn, hanging in frozen strips, and it was dark. Dan tried turning on the lights but the shadeless bulbs did not respond. An evil stench hung in the air. Cursing, Dan walked straight across the room. It was the same as the lottery winners' old flat had been: open-plan with a breakfast bar separating kitchenette from living room. The priest was heading for the main bedroom. 'Come on,' he said to Ronny sharply. 'You said you were the type of person who didn't like to see bairns suffer.'

When Ronny reached the bedroom, Dan had just yanked open the tattered curtains and was standing over a mattress. Ronny could see an uncharacteristic uncertainty in the priest's posture. The double mattress lay among a debris of beer cans and ashtrays, grease-stained pizza boxes and chip papers. On the mattress was a duvet, domed slightly at its centre, as though concealing a body. It was at this dome that the priest was staring uncertainly. He hunkered down. 'Clare,' he whispered. 'Clare.'

Both men heard it at the same time, and looked at each other: a rat-like scurrying sound under the duvet, to one side of the dome shape.

'Clare,' Dan repeated urgently. 'Clare.' He turned to Ronny. 'She'll have taken another bloody overdose.' Without pausing for another moment, he reached down and pulled back the duvet. Framed by great greasy coils of hair, the green face of a dead woman stared back up at them. Shrieking instinctively, Dan dropped the duvet and fell back. Lying among the debris, he stared up at Ronny, gulping for air as he gagged. Ronny stared back helplessly.

And then they heard the scurrying again.

Ronny squatted down, but before he had chance to summon the courage to pull aside the duvet, the duvet began to move itself. It lifted and Ronny found himself staring into two pairs of inscrutable eyes set in the barely human, elfin features of the pixie girls.

They were gazing up at him with a terrified intensity, one on either side of the green face of their dead mother.

2

The cold weather continued beyond the twelve days of Christmas and Audrey never strayed from the house. One morning she lay slumped in a stupor in front of the immense television set, Diamond White bottles littering the carpet. Every so often she seized a bottle by the neck and drank deeply and joylessly.

The room was still full of festive decorations, all looking worn and tattered now. The carpet under the browning Christmas tree was covered in needles. An arid heat belted out from the radiators, and a large streamer, having come free of its Blu-tack on the ceiling, hung down just above Audrey, fluttering in the stifling waves of warmth. Cheryl sat on the edge of her armchair, looking steadily at her old friend. 'To be honest, man Audrey, I'm worried aboot ye,' she said. 'It's not like ye to just lie aboot all day. What's on yer mind, man?' Cheryl gestured at the decorations. 'For a start you should have got this lot packed away. It's bad luck after the twelfth day.'

Without replying, Audrey raised herself slightly only to light herself a cigarette. She did not offer her friend one.

'What's the matter with ye, man Audrey?'

Audrey continued to smoke absorbedly for a few moments. Then a loud burst of laughter reverberated through the room.

'What's the matter, man?' Cheryl asked in despair. Sobering, Audrey shook her head. Cheryl studied the other woman. Then she gazed about the room. 'Ha'way, let's at least get this lot packed away. It's stupid to invite misfortune.'

'What does it matter?' Audrey suddenly demanded. 'With the Christmas we had, I divven't think wor luck could get any worse.' She took a deep inhalation of smoke.

Cheryl looked at the streamer. 'Mebbes yus're right to leave them. Come to think of it, they say that you have to leave them up all year if you . . .'

Audrey reached up and tore at the streamer. A moment later the whole length of streamer fell gently down. Cheryl calmly took out her own cigarette purse and selected the longest butt. 'Ye can trust me, Audrey. Even though yer family have deserted ye. I nivver will.'

Audrey smiled. 'Thanks. That means a lot.'

'I've got some news an' all. Ye'll nivver guess. Phil Heel's proposed to us.' For a moment Audrey turned to look at the beaming Cheryl, then she slipped back into her torpor. 'And I want ye to be me matron of honour.'

'Cheryl man,' whispered Audrey, 'I wish ye'd just fuck off oot of here.'

Cheryl's eyes shifted uneasily. She smiled defensively. 'What you talking about?'

'Ye kna.'

'Do I?'

'Divven't bother pretending.'

Cheryl stood up, and clapped her hands together. 'Ye're depressed, man. I've seen it come awer ye these past weeks. It's since ye went to London. Ye divven't kna what yus're saying –'

'Chez, man, I kna it's been ye all the time.'

'Eh?'

'Do I have to gan into it, or will ye just frigg off?'

'Ee, Aud. It's nee wonder I'm yer only friend, with the way ye gan on.'

'Ye've been clever, lass. Mixing it all up. Spreading lies aboot me claiming the syndicate ticket as me own. Giving folk the wrang day so they think I stood them up. And then making me think they stood wor up. Then there's the letters. The poison pen ones.' She nodded. 'It was Al what telt wor aboot them. Still, what does it matter?' She paused for a moment. 'Now go. I divven't want to see ye no more.'

'And who have ye got now that I'm gannin'?' Cheryl demanded.

'I divven't need anyone, me.'

'That's just as well,' Cheryl spat back, her face creased with malice. ''Cos yus've driven them all from yer door. Ronny'll be the next one to piss off. The way ye treat him. Then there's the bairns yer supposed to love so much.'

In a split-second Audrey had lifted herself up from her lying position and sat bolt upright. 'What?' she demanded quietly.

Cheryl backed away to the door. 'Well, I thought ye were supposed to love them all so much but I hear ye just treat them like shite nowadays.'

'Who told you that, like?'

'Ronny's just aboot at the end of his tether . . .'

Audrey stood. She stalked over to Cheryl like a tigress. For a moment she seemed to be about to throttle her friend, then she simply shook her head. With a sigh, she returned to the sofa, and lay back down. 'I cannet trust no one no more.'

Cheryl stood there a little longer, looking over. 'It's not my fault,' she said, almost gently. 'It was ye what went and won the bloody lottery. Just remember that. It was ye what changed it all.'

Audrey stared back at her friend, then reaching down for her bottle of Diamond White, drank bitterly.

Left alone again, Audrey did not move for a very long time, her great, powerful body immobilised like a patient waiting for an operation. And as she lay there, the timbers of the old house groaned in the frost.

She must have fallen asleep because the next thing she knew was the Big Ben chimes pealing through the house. She lay there heavily without moving. The doorbell sounded again, and still she did not move. It was only after a long time that she leapt up with abrupt energy. But she did not go to answer the front door; instead she ran upstairs.

The curtains in her bedroom were drawn and she peered through a tiny gap. At first all she could see was the flock of fieldfares which had been gathering in the orchard during the cold time on account of the food Ronny had been putting out for them. The birds were disconsolate and gazed at the house from which the food came, staring vacantly as starving children. Then she saw him. The one who had been there when Terri-Leigh sat reading. An old man standing among the starveling fieldfares, he too was gazing at the house with the same vacant desperation. Audrey dropped the curtain instantly.

She sat at the dressing table and for a long time stared into the central mirror.

When at last she came downstairs into the lounge she did not seem surprised to find the old man standing on the terrace, peering into the house through the French windows. His body was frail, worn by both age and care. His large head appeared too heavy for the thin ligament of his scrawny neck. Purple pouches of skin swelled beneath stark eye sockets. Audrey made the sign of the cross.

He backed off to the far end of the terrace when she opened the French windows, averting his eyes. When at last he looked up, Audrey saw that his gaze was full of fear. 'Who are you?' she asked. 'What d'yus want?'

The old man seemed to smile at the sound of her voice, but his smile quickly faded into a mouth gaping with baffled dotage. A single tooth stood in hardened gums. Despite the tatty, scarecrow-like image he presented, it was clear that he had dressed himself up for his visit. He wore an old suit which perhaps had once fitted him, but now hung baggily over his shrivelled frame. The stained shirt he wore had no tie. He cleared his throat. 'I've come to see you.'

'I won't have beggars on my property,' she said evenly.

'I haven't come to beg.' He stepped forward, his hands extended in supplication, revealing skeletal wrists. He wore an odd pair of leather slip-on shoes: one black, the other ox blood. Now that he was so close to her, Audrey could see that the purple-tinged skin of his face was glisteningly white where the razor had knicked that morning. The tough tufts of whiskers missed by the blade showed that it was his first shave in a long time. His hands were chafed as though by unaccustomed scrubbing, although his long fingernails remained choked with filth. 'It is you, isn't it, Audrey?'

'Go on, get lost!' Her roar came out in a great cloud of condensed breath that drifted over to engulf the other for a moment. 'People like you make me sick,' she continued, speaking more quietly. 'Coming roond begging. Snooping aboot where there's bairns. Well, I tell ye, there's nee money here. So ye can piss off.'

'Did ye not get me letters?'

'Letters?'

'I've been writing to you. But ye nivver wrote back. So I've come.'

'What the frigg are you gannin' on aboot?'

The old man's lips trembled as though trying to shape words which would not come into being. 'I'm yer dad.'

The glass in the French windows rattled as Audrey slammed them shut. Calmly, she walked back through the lounge and across the hall. It was as she was mounting the stairs that her legs gave way under her and she sank heavily. She remained sprawled on the stairs for a long time, like a blackbird stunned on the roadside after being hit by the windscreen of a car. Then the Big Ben chimes rang out. As though jolted by an electric shock, she leapt to her feet, ran down the stairs, sprinted across the hall and yanked the front door open so energetically that the dying holly wreath fell from its nail.

But on seeing him, her anger seemed to evaporate instantly. 'Go away,' she whispered. 'Just go away.' Leaning heavily against the door frame, she did not look at him. Her voice was toneless. 'Look, mister, I divven't kna how ye foond oot. That I had nee dad. It was probably in the paper or summink. But I'm not being taken in by ye.'

'It's not like that.'

'I'm not being taken in by a con trick.'

'I just wanted to see you again.'

'Look, just go before I call the pollis.'

'I'm dying, I'm dying!' the old man's voice rang out. Then his tone softened. 'I'm dying.'

Audrey stared at him with no emotion. 'What do you want?'

'Just want to make my peace.'

She turned and disappeared back into the house, but she had left the door open behind her. He found her in the lounge. She was standing with her back to him at the French windows. 'The hoose,' he said, 'it's, well, it's a dream.'

'There's no money for ye.' Audrey's sudden voice was sharp.

'I'm dying, what do I want with money?'

'You must want something.'

There was a hunger in the old man's response. 'I want to see you. Talk to you.'

The old man gazed at her, squinting. He threw up a hand as though to improve his sight, like someone standing on the beach at low tide trying to spot a distant group of bathers, or the memory of a summer long ago.

Audrey shook her head in disbelief. 'How can ye dee this? I divven't kna how anyone can be as low as ye. Coming here, pretending to be . . .' She swallowed with difficulty. 'Pretending to be . . .'

For a while, neither of them spoke. After the temperature outside, the heat within was savage, and beads of sweat crowned the old man's brow. The sweat threw into relief a mark on his face, an ancient scar, dried hard and white in the shape of a small pick. He began to struggle with something in the pocket of his threadbare overcoat, but his fingers could not manage what he wanted. Bewildered, he tugged ineffectually at the pocket. Then he closed his eyes as though in resignation.

He seemed to have drifted into his own thoughts and for a while he did not even realise that Audrey had come over to him and, reaching into the pocket, had drawn out the small object with which he had been struggling.

The object seemed to mesmerise her. Walking over to the sofa, she sat and gazed at it. It was a photograph. Just half of a ripped one. On it a young man could be seen and part of a baby that he was holding. The rest of the baby lay invisibly beyond the torn edge. Just discernible in the teeth of the tear was the elbow of a woman.

'I divven't come with any excuses,' the old man said at last.

Audrey continued to stare at the photo for a little longer, then she got up, and with a sudden explosion of energy, dashed from the room. The stairs thudded under her speed as she took them three at a time. Then thudded again as she pounded back down them. She came back into the room with

333

a shoebox, bound by elastic bands. The elastic bands played a forlorn, dying note as she took them off with trembling hands. She listened to this sound until it had completely faded. Then she held out the shoebox to her father.

His gnarled fingers were already clasped round the box when suddenly she jerked it back, hugging it closely to herself like a newborn baby in need of comfort. Still cradling the box as though it were a living thing, she sat on an armchair.

The old man stared at her. 'I won't bother you no more after this. I just had to see you. Talk to you. To make some peace.' He waited for Audrey to speak. But she was staring at the box, rocking it now slightly on her breast. 'I've not been back long. It's all changed. When the bus stopped from London, I got back on. I couldn't believe that it was Gatesheed. It was like a different place.' He cleared this throat. 'What can I say to ye, man Audrey?' The old man's gnarled features were racked with pain. 'I didn't mean it to be like this. It just happened. I didn't mean not to be yer dad. Somehow, it just happened . . .' All of a sudden his breathing rattled. He knocked his chest with a fist but when he spoke again his voice was dogged with phlegm. 'I've spent me life doon south. In exile. A brickie. All my life building walls. And the funny thing is, I've lived long enough to see all the buildings I put up come back doon again. All just been a waste of time really. But I nivver stopped thinking aboot ye. Not one day would gan by –'

'I don't want to know!' Audrey's shout echoed about the room for a few moments before being smothered by the lavish chintz of the furnishings and the drooping decorations. She did not speak for a long, long time, and when she did, her voice was just a whisper. As she spoke, she stared down at the box at her breast, held there like a feeding infant. 'I used to wait for ye, coming back from the pit. Every day I waited for ye coming off yer shift. I knew it was you by the sound of your boots on the step. And I was always so happy that ye were back. I was so happy to hear ye coming that I danced.' A smile played on Audrey's face. 'Even when ye were on the back shift and I was in bed, I waited. I waited 'cos I could tell by the sound of yer boots coming up the stairs. And then when ye were back, I could sleep. I would still recognise that sound, if I heard it now. Aye, there's some things that gan too deep for the forgetting.' The old man tried to speak, but he could not muster the words. 'I waited the night ye didn't come back,' Audrey continued. 'I waited and waited. Four years auld. And waiting, always waiting. To hear the creaking of boots on the step. Or on the stairs. I waited to hear what I nivver would hear again.' For the first time Audrey looked directly in her father's eye. 'And I kept on waiting 'cos nee one ever telt wor that ye weren't coming back.'

'Oh, God,' her father said with the soft listlessness of the broken. 'Oh, God.'

Audrey suddenly leapt up and towered over him. It seemed that she was going to knock the frail old man to the ground and murder him.

'I nivver had any other family . . .' he managed to say, not flinching from his daughter. 'Ye were me only bairn. I've got nothing. Nobody. And now I've got to die alone. In a home. I've got to die all alone in a home.'

For a few more seconds she loomed over him threateningly, then stepped back. A cold cruelty sparkled in her eyes. 'Ha'way,' she said, and gestured for him to follow her. He followed meekly as she led him to the children's room. In a sudden access of violence, she ripped down the masses of Christmas decorations that had been placed around the photographs of the children. She watched him look up at the framed pictures. There was little sap left in the old man's face; like the willowherb in November he had withered to a stalk, but there was enough remaining in the shape of his face to prove kin with a number of the children looking down. 'Your flesh and blood,' she whispered. 'All of them. Your blood.'

Her voice dropped to nothing more than a whisper. 'You could have had a family. Been one of us. Loved. Cared for. But now I'll make sure you die alone. And the day ye die, see me? I'll dance on yer friggin' grave, 'cos I kna ye'll be on yer way to hell.'

But her father was too lost in the portrait gallery to pay attention to the desolation in these words. He smiled as he stared at the unmistakable likenesses. But the smile faded, and a sigh of infinite regret escaped his lips. 'Ye're reet,' he nodded. 'Ye're reet. It's what I deserve.' He shook his head. 'I didn't mean to be a bad person. Somehow, it just happened.' He continued to gaze at the pictures. 'All these grandbairns and great-grandbairns,' he murmured. 'It was me what won the lottery. But I lost me ticket. Somehow, I just lost me ticket.'

When he came back into the lounge, Audrey was waiting there calmly with the shoebox. She handed it to him. 'It's yours,' she said simply.

In the time that he had spent in the room the old man seemed to have become more of a ghost than a man. There was a strange detachment about him. With an almost imperceptible nod he took the box and opened the lid. One by one he took out the objects. First he drew out the glasses. Putting them on, his eyes seemed to swell painfully behind the lenses like a rabbit with myxomatosis. 'I left these on the dresser,' he whispered. 'When I left. When I . . .' He broke off. For the first time, he was seeing his lost daughter in unrelieved detail. 'Ye're the spit of yer mam. She was a fine-looking woman. Aye, yus're the spit of yer mam.' With the glasses still on he took out the scrap of paper. His lips moved as he read the barely legible words to himself, turning the paper to the light. Then he nodded. 'Yes. I wrote that. Valentine's Day, 1946.' And having spoken he bowed his head. For a long time neither moved, then the movements of the old man were betrayed by a light scuffing. His hand was in the shoebox, and he was trying to pick up the other half of the torn photograph which had lain there for half a century. Time and time again the picture eluded him as he attempted to lever it up, his fingers unable to get a grip.

With an air of calm, Audrey suddenly reached over, and picking it up, handed it to him. At last the photograph, ripped asunder so long ago, was whole. 'Go now,' Audrey said in a matter-of-fact voice. 'Now that yus've ruined me life twice. Go now.'

'Audrey . . .' But her back was turned. Only the shape of her chin was visible to him: a tightly clamped set of jaws. He brought the shoebox round to his daughter, and held it out. 'Here, Audrey . . .'

'No,' she said quietly. 'It's yours. I divven't have nee need for it no longer. Do what you want with it. Hoy it in the bin if ye want. No matter.' She shook her head. 'It's funny, I've waited for this moment all me life. Waited for you to come back. Waited and waited and waited. And when it happens? It means nothing.'

The old man was holding a hand out. 'Audrey, in God's name, divven't let wor part like this.' She stared at the hand, but did not move. He held it out for a long time until it was clear that she would not take it, then at last he left. Audrey did not watch him going, although when he reached the French windows, she suddenly called out abruptly. 'There's just one thing I've got to know.'

He turned to look at his daughter, his lips trembling, life returning momentarily to his eyes. 'Anything.'

'Why?'

As the old man swallowed, his Adam's apple bobbed in a throat which was pleated with age like the neck of turkey. 'I've told ye, Audrey. There is nee why. It just seemed to happen.'

'No. I mean, why did ye come back now?'

'I saw you in the paper. By chance. I divven't read the

paper. It's funny. I just saw it by chance. There was one on a bus.' He looked at her hungrily. 'For pity's sake, will ye not make peace with me?'

Audrey shook her head. 'It's too late.'

The starveling fieldfares gathered on the terrace and, staring in at the warmth of the room within, did not even move aside as the scarecrow-like figure emerged back into the bitter chill and shuffled through them.

Without showing any emotion, Audrey watched her father from the window. He passed slowly through the frozen orchard, and for a long time she caught glimpses of him between frozen trunks. Until all at once, he had gone.

Mechanically, Audrey mounted the stairs, sat down at the dressing table and peered into the central mirror. She pulled back the locks of her unruly hair so that she might see her face fully. 'Mam,' she whispered with the smile of a little girl. 'He came back. After all the waiting. But it's too late.' The smile faded. 'Mam, I always wanted to tell ye summink. Can I tell ye now?' Audrey breathed in deeply. 'Ye didn't know this, but I was always waiting for him to come back. When ye foond wor sitting on the stairs, when ye saw wor staring through the window. I was waiting for him. I was always waiting for him. When you saw me sitting here, staring in the glass, I was always waiting for him.' She reached out as though to touch the face of the woman peering back out at her. But her finger found only the cold glass.

Chapter Eight

I

The cold snap stretched to a second and then a third week. And on the evening of the annual St Mary Magdalene's Talent Show the stars in the black night sky crackled like frost. 'So where is she then?' Joe asked.

Ronny looked up with bloodshot eyes. 'She's not well.'

'Not well?'

'Na, she's not feeling well. I left her lying in bed.'

'It seems to me that Audrey spends a lot of her time in bed these days.'

The silence of the allotments surrounded them. The animals were well foddered inside the shacks, and the only sounds were the occasional moan of wood and corrugated metal, writhing under the clench of the cold. Ronny's stove was crammed with burning sea coal. 'The whole family's there,' Ronny continued, gazing glumly through the open door of the stove at the orange glow. 'Waiting at the Catholic Club. No doubt they'll end up murdering each other before the night's out. But at least Terri-Leigh should have finished her spot by then.' Ronny tried to lift his spirits. 'Hey, Joe man, you should hear her. She sounds brilliant. She's got real talent. Who would have thought it? If she'd been born in Whickham, or somewhere with a piano, she might have been another Mozart. As for me, well –'

'Ronny man,' Joe barked, 'ye want to forget all this tomfoolery and concentrate on that wife of yours.'

'What and disappoint everyone what's come for a good

laugh?' One of Ronny's hands was clenched in a fist. He opened the fist slightly and glanced furtively at what he held there. 'We'd better be gettin' there worselves. As soon as Ginga's given the goat fresh hay, we'll get off.'

'What's the matter with her, like?' Joe demanded peremptorily.

'What d'ye mean, Joe?'

'Audrey. Why isn't she coming tonight?'

'She's gone doon with a bug.'

Joe stared sceptically at Ronny. The younger man was dressed in a burgundy cabaret suit, complete with frilly shirt and chunky bow tie. 'Ronny lad,' Joe said quietly, 'ye need to get a grip.'

'Leave us alone,' returned Ronny wretchedly.

Joe nodded grimly. 'Aye. Ye will be alone if ye divven't get it sorted out. 'Cos ye and bloody Audrey are well and truly on the rocks.'

Ronny flicked at his ponytail despondently. 'She's changed completely. Everything that meant owt to her before, now stands for nothing. And there's nothing I can dee.'

'Course there is. Have it out with her. Drop me and Ginga now. Go back, and have it out with her.'

'But –'

Joe's voice rose to a shout: 'For God's sake, man, divven't be so bloody lily-livered, go and grasp the nettle. Make her come with ye to the talent show. Ye sorted Jimmy, didn't you?'

'Course I did.'

'So why cannet ye sort Audrey oot?'

Again Ronny opened his fist and peered down at what he held.

'And what's yus've got there?' Joe demanded irritably.

Ronny held up a jewellery box. As he opened it a frail version of the Theme from *Love Story* played out in the shack.

Ronny lifted out the two pendants on a finger. 'We nivver did celebrate it.'

'What?'

'Wor anniversary.'

In silence, Ronny drove the old friends to the social club. When he had dropped them he pressed the vanette on through the wintry streets of Gateshead. It was a Saturday night and despite the cold the usual band of near-naked revellers was in evidence. They thronged the bus stops and packed the taxis, running from pub to pub in shrieking groups.

The gritters were out again, plodding their lumbering way, lights flashing forlornly. Ronny drove behind one as he entered the rural portion of the borough, the nose of the vanette straying perilously close to the large vehicle. The private road of the Derwentside Estate was treacherous and the vanette slid and skidded uncontrollably. When he was only halfway to the parsonage, Ronny bumped the vehicle up on to a patch of frozen grass and got out. He gasped at the cold, and froze motionless for a moment, before hurrying on his way.

From a distance, the house seemed to lie in total darkness, but as Ronny came through the orchard, he could see that a single light shone in his and Audrey's bedroom.

The house was silent. Ronny listened from the foot of the stairs, and then again on the landing of the first floor. There was nothing to be heard. He had not turned on any lights, and the light from the bedroom could be seen pooling under the door. For some reason, Ronny found himself knocking gently before entering. 'Audrey,' he whispered. 'It's me.'

Audrey was not in bed. She was sitting at the dressing table, applying make-up. She was dressed in a black PVC miniskirt and a black PVC jacket with a collar of fake leopardskin. Ronny stared at her in puzzlement. 'I thought ye were ill?' he said. Then a smile burst over his face. 'So you are coming after all. To the talent show. And dressed like you used to be. I knew you would, I knew . . .' he trailed off under a sharp glance from Audrey. 'You're not coming to the talent show, are you?'

'No.'

'Where are you going?'

'Just leave us alone,' Audrey replied in a small voice.

For a few moments it seemed that Ronny was going to say something, but he only gave a nod and withdrew.

Groping his way through the darkness, Ronny descended the stairs. He stood for a long time in the lounge. A blood-red moon was rising, and its lurid light flooded through the French windows, drenching his features. It was in the shine of this light that he saw the stand of videos. Walking over to the stand, he selected one and sat down to watch it.

It was Toni-Lee's film, the footage she had so painstakingly collected ever since the lottery win. The smiling faces of the winning-night party grinned at Ronny from the screen. Voices were raised in jubilation above the pounding celebration of the 'Birdy Song'. And then the lottery winners, dancing together, filled the picture. Ronny watched unmoved for a while, then suddenly picked up the remote control and hurled it at the television with all his might. It glanced off the side, and came to rest against the skirting board, with the visual fast-forward button jammed. As Ronny sat there numbly, the life of their past six months flickered rapidly before him. He watched unflinchingly as the smiling faces flashed by. Gradually, the smiling became replaced by frowns and arguments, and still he continued to watch. Then calmly he got up and switched it off. 'Sort it out,' he said to himself wistfully. 'You've got to sort it all out now.'

Standing in the red-tinged moonlight he took out the jewellery box from his pocket. The theme from *Love Story* sounded even more distorted. He held the double pendant out into the bloody moon beams and gazed at the halved discs.

Audrey was still sitting at the dressing table when Ronny came back for her. There was a strange edge to his voice as he began to speak. 'We'll have to go now. To get the first acts. At the talent show.'

'For the love of God,' she whispered. 'Leave me alone.'

'No.' Ronny's voice was quietly firm. 'You cannet miss it. Not with Terri-Leigh playing, and me . . . I kna ye really want to gan. Ha'way, pet, let's just forget aboot what's been happening. Let's just imagine we nivver won. And tonight? Tonight we're celebrating wor anniversary.'

'What the frigg are ye on aboot?'

'That's the important prize. Our love. The family. Not winning the lottery.'

Audrey looked up at Ronny with a sneer. 'I can't trust you. You lied to me.'

'I only did it to look after ye and the bairns.'

Contempt flickered over Audrey's heavily made-up face: as beautiful and dangerous as a Gateshead Cleopatra. 'You? You've nivver looked after us. I should have known you were no good when it took you forty years to get up the nerve to ask us to marry ye. Then ye bring us to this dump. I wouldn't mind, but it wasn't even ye what won the lottery.'

For a moment Ronny wavered. Then he pushed himself on. There was a click as he opened the jewellery box, then the music began to play out shakily. 'I love you,' Ronny began slowly, 'more today than yesterday. But less than tomorrow. All wor problems? I'll sort them. We'll gan to the talent show. And then we'll gan to the Poacher's Pocket. Just like we were going to before we won –'

The music stopped abruptly as Audrey snatched the box. She also yanked the pendants from her husband. In three steps she had reached the window. A sharp draught of icy air slashed the room as she opened the window. Her arm flexed powerfully a single time as she threw the objects into the night. The window crashed closed again.

Like a child Ronny rubbed his eyes with the heels of his

343

hand. 'I can't go on. Without you, Audrey, I might as well be dead.' He fell to his knees and threw his arms around her waist.

She tried to push him away but he would not let go. It was only when she punched him hard on the back, winding him, that he let her go. Looking at him with revulsion, she picked up a mobile phone from her dresser. 'Taxi for McPhee,' she said.

Ronny smiled. 'I divven't blame ye, love. I kna I'm not good enough for ye. I'm ugly, me, and ye? Ye are as beautiful as a summer's evening. The Beast only gets Beauty in Disney films. And as for baldy-lang hair . . .' He broke off to stare at his wife. Then, as though suddenly inspired, he demanded: 'What do you want me to be? I'll be anything. Just tell me what you want me to be. I can do anything. I've even sorted that Jimmy.'

'What?'

Ronny nodded vociferously. 'He was blackmailing us. But I didn't bother telling you. I didn't need to. I just sorted him out myself.'

'You sorted it yourself?' said Audrey witheringly.

'I just told him not to mess with me.'

Audrey threw her head back and brayed with laughter. Her whole body shook. And through her open mouth, her lucky gap tooth was revealed in all its glory.

The grief on Ronny's face seemed almost a leer as he shuffled, still on his knees, to the dressing table. The blade of the pair of scissors he picked up glinted in the single light. Audrey continued to laugh in helpless mockery. The scissors were very sharp, and Ronny recoiled with a gasp as he cut his finger on the blade. A single bead of blood fell on to the frill of his cabaret shirt. He stared at the drop of blood for a long time. A shadow seemed to fall over his face.

Lifting the scissors, he held them like a knife, gazing at the tip. 'If it hadn't been for the lottery everything would have been areet,' he said simply. He had turned very pale, and thick beads of sweat clung to his brow. 'Winning was the worst thing that happened.'

'I kna,' Audrey replied.

Ronny flexed his arm as he took another knee-step towards Audrey. In her hilarity she did not seem to see the scissors that he was brandishing near her. 'I'm sorting things out,' he rasped. With no further warning he stabbed the air violently. There was a single snip, and his ponytail fell to the floor. 'Look,' he said, begging up at her on his knees like a puppy. 'Look. Will ye have me back now? Will ye have me now that there's nee more baldy-lang hair?'

A loud horn sounded outside. Audrey got up. 'That'll be my taxi,' she said, and left without another word.

Ronny remained on his knees, staring down at the shank of hair. He felt the severed stump where the ponytail had been. A shrill giggle reverberated round the room. Then, hurling himself on to the bed, he began to punch himself: on the head, on the face, on the body, everywhere. He curled into a ball, but continued to rain his fists down on himself. When the first paroxysm of his rage had passed, he yanked his shirt up and grabbed handfuls of his belly fat. He pulled at it so savagely that it seemed he would tear his own flesh asunder. Then he lay without moving, bruised and bleeding.

When he got up at last, he was round-shouldered and his step was slow. He wandered like a ghost through the rooms of the parsonage, gazing numbly at their emptiness, until he finally found himself out in the courtyard. The moon had disappeared, smothered in the first heavy clouds for a long time. As he stood there, he suddenly felt something soft on his cheek. He tilted his head to the heavens, and felt the rushing brush of feathers. His lips parted and the tender spot of his tongue felt a soft, repeated melting. It was snowing. Blinking as the flakes hit his eyes, he stared up. A million flakes were descending from the sky.

He moved through the orchard silently, and emerged on the

road. The vanette was where he had left it. He got in and turned the key. As he dropped the vanette off the bank, Ronny bounced high on his seat, his head striking the roof. Automatically, he lifted a hand to his ponytail where it encountered the sharp bristles of the stump.

Heedless of the danger, his headlamps describing a whitened wilderness, he drove recklessly down the private road, and then, having skirted the silence of the snowbound trees and the Derwentheugh coke works country park, he entered the built-up portions of the borough. The snow was now a blizzard, masking traffic lights and street signs. The visibility was down to about ten yards, but Ronny did not stop driving. Even when he could see nothing through his window, he kept on driving, leaning right out into the wind, eyes squinting in the blizzard. At last, face and hands numb, he reached the car park of the Wheatsheaf.

The back bar of the Wheatsheaf was crowded and Ronny had a struggle pushing his way to the bar. A jukebox was playing but was drowned by human voices. 'Where's Jimmy?' he yelled when at last he managed to reach the bar.

The barman nodded in the direction of the pool tables, and biting his lip, Ronny began to push through the bodies in the direction indicated.

Jimmy was taking a shot when Ronny reached him. The youth continued to play, the pool balls slapping together violently. Doggedly, Ronny stood there, waiting. 'Not ye again, Ronny boy,' Jimmy said at last. 'Ye're beginning to get on me wick.'

Jimmy's opponent, a tall, acned lad of about the same age, potted a ball. Jimmy frowned. The next shot took Jimmy round to where Ronny stood. But Ronny did not move. 'There's twenty quid riding on this game,' Jimmy said quietly. 'So be a good prick, and get oot the way.'

Ronny's fists whitened as he clenched them. 'I want a word with ye,' he said deliberately.

346

'If ye divven't get oot me way, I'll fuckin' kill ye,' growled Jimmy. And then he suddenly made as though to launch himself at Ronny. 'Boo!' Flinching, Ronny stepped back, lifting his hands in protection. Laughter rang out. Ronny peered through the web of his fingers to see Jimmy and his mate mocking him. 'Boo!' said Jimmy, repeating the same movement.

'Boo!' his mate laughed.

'Ye're a bit red in the face, Ronny lad,' Jimmy derided him. 'Look like yus're gonnae have a heart attack.'

Ronny blundered his way back through the room and flung open the door. It was still blowing a blizzard and his footsteps creaked. There were four or five inches of snow already on the ground, and more swirling down all the while. The vehicles in the car park were disappearing into mounds of snow.

The vanette was snowbound. Opening the back, Ronny took out one of the old NCB shovels, and began to clear away the snow from the wheels. As he was doing this he felt a tap on his shoulder. He turned. It was Jimmy. 'What do you want?' Ronny asked.

Jimmy watched as Ronny continued to shovel more snow, the metal of the blade silent. 'I lost me twenty quid. It was your fault. I'm a bit short of cash at the minute an' all, Ronny boy.'

'The payment's not due until next month,' replied Ronny tonelessly.

Menace crept into the youth's voice. 'The payment's due when I say it is.'

'That's not fair,' said Ronny.

Laughter was the reply. 'Me fuckin' heart bleeds for ye. Anyway, divven't fuck aboot, it's the bloody Antarctic oot here. Gan to the cashpoint. Get us two hundred and fifty now, and sort it oot with the bank tomorrow for a grand.' Jimmy rubbed his hands together. 'I'll let ye into a secret. I've had a little chat with a mutual friend. I think ye kna him. Phil Heel.

347

It was very interesting.' Jimmy's voice suddenly sharpened. 'I kna it was ye and Audrey, man fat lad. Calling the pollis on Macca that time. So divven't fuck wor aboot. Canny expensive, a bit of news like that. Really I should be milking ye for the next ten years with news like this.'

Without replying, Ronny set to shovelling again. Jimmy reached out to grab him by the ponytail. 'Friggin' hell,' he wheezed with derision. 'Baldy-lang hair's only gone and cut his ponytail off.'

'Leave me alone,' Ronny whispered. 'Please, just leave me alone.' Something broke in his voice. 'Leave me alone before ye regret it.'

Coming round to the front of Ronny, Jimmy slapped his head with both hands. 'Baldy nee hair! Baldy nee hair!' the youth taunted him. 'Baldy . . .' With a little cry, Ronny had shaken Jimmy from him and strode away. Jimmy's voice was quiet. 'Ye'll regret that, baldy nee hair fat lad.'

From the snowy darkness Ronny lumbered at him like a great bear. There was a high-pitched squeal of pain as the first blow of the shovel caught the young man on the shoulder and knocked him to his knees. The shovel was raised again. Stunned, Jimmy was just able to raise his hands in protection and parry the first blow, but again and again the shovel was brought down on him until a broken finger and a dislocated thumb caused him to writhe in agony and drop, for a moment, his guard.

Unimpeded, the shovel bit deep into his neck and hurled him down into the pile of snow cleared by Ronny. Breathless with shock, Jimmy looked up to see the NCB shovel poised above him like a guillotine. 'Ye'll friggin' kill me with that thing,' he said. Then gathering his wits, he scrambled to get on to his feet. But the next blow smashed his kneecap. Like a crab now, he desperately tried to scuttle across the snow-covered car park, but implacably, Ronny strode after him. Time after time he raised the shovel and brought it down with all his strength. Jimmy screamed a final time as the cold metal struck him on the head. He seemed to rise a little, before subsiding in a silent heap on snow crimsoned with blood. And now there was silence, except for the heavy breathing of the man with the shovel.

Chest heaving, Ronny stared down at the inert body. He seemed unable to take in what he saw, and his eyes squinted in confusion. Then, with a little squeal, he flung the shovel away and began to run. The clatter of the shovel was deadened by the snow, and Ronny's footsteps were also smothered. A thin layer of flakes was already covering the lifeless body.

Ronny ran blindly, the sound of his own heart beating the only noise in the snowy silence of the Gateshead streets. On and on he ran, falling repeatedly, and repeatedly picking himself up, and without even brushing off the snow, pressing on. He was crossing the ring of wasteland which surrounds the Teams when suddenly he fell head first. The snow cushioned his fall, but he lay there, stunned. It was only when he pulled himself into a sitting position that he realised he was right on the edge of the concrete slab that bridges the River Team by the old rope works. He sat there baffled, shivering, his legs dangling above the river. He was still for a long time and then, all of a sudden, with both fists, he began to smite the left side of his chest, where his heart lay. 'Stop, ye bastard,' he whispered, between blows. 'Stop. Yus're gonnae pack in some day anyway, so pack in now. Now. Now. Now!' Ronny waited and waited, but his heart continued to thump dully in his ears. His voice was a whimper. 'Why won't you stop and make it easy for me? Why won't you let me . . .'

In one moment it had been done. Shuffling forward slightly he had eased himself over the edge of the bridge. Although the drop was only ten feet or so, to Ronny it felt as though he was falling into a darkness that would last for ever. Then there was a dull clump. The River Team was frozen solid. He hit the

349

surface feet first, following an instant later with his face. His nose broke with the tiniest of snapping sounds.

Sprawled on the frozen river with his hands and face pressed against the ice, he listened to the Team. 'Ye an' all, eh?' he whispered. 'Ye let me doon.'

Wearily, he rose, and went on his way.

He was halfway across the piece of featureless, iron-bound land where Keir Hardie Avenue used to stand when he became aware of a desolate whispering all around him. He stopped in his tracks and looked about. He had stumbled across the lost flock of cranes. They were too weary to fly away, and suffered the man to walk right among them. One or two stretched exhausted wings, but the rest could only whistle softly. In the darkness, with long necks and nose-like beaks, they looked like a group of emaciated old men, abandoned and baffled.

2

The St Mary Magdalene's Catholic Social Club was stifling with heat from the packed scrum of bodies. On the stage Kenny Rogers was doing his second karaoke version of 'Coward of the County'.

Audrey's family was scattered through the audience, no one sitting in a group of more than two or three, ignoring each other whenever they happened to meet at the bar, or going to and from the toilet.

Al was pacing at the back. The priest came over. 'I'm going to have to announce the winner now,' Dan said.

'Give him another five minutes,' replied Al.

'But he won't win anyway.'

'I kna.' Al shook his head. 'But he's entered every year.'

Dan nodded. Kenny Rogers came to the end of his song. 'Shall I dee that again?' he asked the audience. But before he could start, the priest had leapt on to the stage and seized the microphone.

For a while he said nothing, just gazed at the faces. Gradually the attention of the room turned to him. He smiled sadly. 'They're knocking our homes down,' he began at last. 'They say the Teams is finished. And who knows? Maybe this is the last gathering of its kind. The end of an era. So let's enjoy ourselves.' Applause rang out, and he waited until it was finished. The faces looking at him seemed suddenly gentle. 'I'm proud to be an honorary Teamser,' the priest announced, 'and I'll tell you this, they'll have to do more than just knock our houses down to take away our pride.' More applause broke out, taking even longer to die down. 'So let's put away all our resentments and disagreements, because now I want to call back one of our own. The best of us.'

To cheering and shouting, Terri-Leigh was drawn back on to the stage. The moment she began to play, the boisterous crowd fell silent. It was a song that had grown from the River Tyne and the people who had lived and worked there two hundred years ago. All those lives and livelihoods were long gone now, and only the river still ran.

The song was halfway through when the door to the club opened. Standing at the back, Al was the only one to notice. It was Ronny. 'Areet, bonny –' began Al, but broke off when he saw the state of his friend.

Half frozen and dishevelled, Ronny's velour cabaret suit was ripped to shreds. There was a wild staring look in his glassy eyes. Al could see blood on his frilly shirt. His nose was twisted and caked with dried blood. Watching the girl playing her keyboard on the stage, Ronny smiled. 'See? Didn't I tell ye she was the best?'

When she had finished there was no immediate applause. People seemed to breathe in before bursting into a deafening clapping. And, clapping louder than all the rest, Ronny approached the stage. 'Our final act of the evening,' Dan said at the microphone as he spotted him crossing the crowded room. 'The one, the only, Ronny the Dreamer.'

The stage lights dimmed as one of the Geordie Shamrocks played a drum roll. In the partial darkness Ronny's state remained unrevealed. With a grunt he hauled himself on to the stage and took the microphone from the priest, who patted him on the back. Holding the microphone gingerly, Ronny walked to the middle of the stage, then paused and, as though lost, looked about. A single light came on, and above him the disco globe spun. Its sparkling panels caught his eyes and he gazed up at it. It seemed to dazzle him.

The single light died, and for a while there was total darkness. 'I say, I say, I say . . .' Ronny's voice called out eerily. 'What d'ye get if ye cross a . . . if ye cross a . . . if ye cross a . . .'

There was squall of feedback as the microphone hit the floor of the stage, rolled across it and fell off the side just as a strobe light exploded into life. As though in slow motion, the strobe light caught Ronny staggering to the back of the stage, hitting the back wall and bringing down handfuls of the straggly silver paper as he grabbed at it in the attempt to hold himself up.

Mercilessly, the strobe light turned the death act into something from a silent comedy, and the audience roared with laughter as Ronny clawed desperately at his throat as though trying to clear a sudden obstruction to his breathing. To more general hilarity, his convulsive movements brought him back to the edge of the stage where, having gulped grotesquely, he collapsed and lay there on his back, not moving.

Chapter Nine

I

The tide had turned. Through the small hours of the night, black with the coal shoals lifted from the bed of the sea, it had been climbing the long slope of the north-east coast, but now, having held its line for the briefest of instants, it was on the ebb. The slate grey of a February dawn revealed a scattering of toiling figures, fanned out across the wide curlew's beak sweep of the otherwise deserted Hartlepool beach. They were harvesting the sea coal left on the beach by the tide.

Everywhere, the sea coalers worked in pairs, raking the sea coal into piles before shovelling it into the backs of a whole fleet of ancient Land-Rovers.

Closest to the sewage overspill pipe stood a vehicle different from all the rest. It was a vanette whose once white bodywork was encrusted with copper rust.

The wind was blowing off the sea and the men shovelling the sea coal into the vanette were already drenched. One wore a snorkel jacket, the other a donkey jacket. Both had pulled their woollen hats low over their features. The man in the snorkel jacket seemed to have different coloured eyes: one blue, the other white. His companion seemed drawn, a recently grown beard doing little to soften the pinched look around his mouth.

With constantly bent backs and knees working like hinges, their shovels whirred. The sea coal, fine-grained as congealing tar, sifted through itself in the air before hitting the hold of the vanette, salt water cascading back out of the vehicle through every hole and perforation in the metalwork.

When they had filled the vanette, the man in the snorkel jacket got into the driving seat. 'That's it,' he smiled. 'We'll show these Monkey Hangers what a pair o' Geordie lads can dee. I'll take this lot to Warren's depot.'

Without replying, the man in the donkey jacket began to rake up more sea coal.

The man in the vanette looked in concern at the other. 'Ha'way, man Ronny, come with me and have a rest. We divven't want ye having another bloody angina attack.'

Ronny shook his head. His voice was toneless. 'No, you're areet, Al man.'

Close to where Ronny toiled, a little group of wading birds were harvesting the tide line themselves, digging at the softness with their tiny beaks. As Ronny worked, he kept these birds in the corner of his vision. A string of gulls hung over the breakers twenty or so yards from land, holding their position in the wind like a line of kites.

When Big Al came back, they began to shovel up the sea coal Ronny had just piled. 'Beats freezing yer bollocks up a ladder this eh, Ronny lad?' Al laughed. 'I mean, if ye've got to freeze yer bollocks off then ye might as well as dee it by the seaside.' Al gazed at Ronny as he shovelled. His friend had lost weight, his shoulders had a rounded shape. He rarely talked. 'Some of the Monkey Hangers are gannin' oot for a pint doon the Pot Hoose when the tide chucks in. D'ye fancy it?'

'No,' Ronny replied, still toneless.

They filled their second load even more quickly and soon the vanette was lumbering back up the sea defences to Warren's new depot. The beach was getting larger on the ebb, a vast swathe of pristine sand. Like the wading birds, Ronny was following the tide line, piling the sea coal as it became exposed. The gulls kept their strict formation above the white waves, as though controlled by some expert kite master.

354

As the light began to improve, the container ships and bulkers could be seen strung out on the offing as they waited to enter Teesport. Ronny paused in his work to stare at the shipping, and so deeply was he lost in the sight that he did not see the small figure approaching him over the sand. The figure was carrying a large flask which he set down in the sand, ten yards behind Ronny. Sitting down himself, the man watched Ronny for a long time before reaching out to the flask and unscrewing its top. Steam rose. 'Ronny,' he called gently.

On hearing the voice, Ronny swung round, the sharp terror of the hunted on his bearded face, his feet ready to sprint, even though the sea was the only way he might fly. But the fear dissipated instantly when he recognised the dark, craggy features of the newcomer. 'Areet, Youssif,' he greeted him.

'Good coal today, Ronny,' said Youssif, whose thick accent had grown under a sun far brighter than the one now rising barely perceptible behind the slate-grey clouds. He looked appraisingly at the piles of sea coal Ronny had heaped. 'We get another load before the tide is gannin' on turn, Ronny my friend?'

'If we're lucky,' Ronny nodded. Youssif was pouring tea from the flask into a plastic cup, and the fragrant smell drifted into Ronny's nostrils. He walked over and sat beside Youssif, who handed the cup to him.

Youssif watched the other man closely. 'So what is the tea like this morning, my friend?'

'Spot on,' Ronny replied, sipping.

'Yes,' mused Youssif. 'Spot on. The real thing. A breath of home.'

Sitting on the sand together, passing the cup between themselves, their eyes blinked against the cold wind that harrowed off the sea. The huge grey hulk of a container ship materialised on the grey horizon, loomed larger and then sailed into the Tees bay. The gulls continued to bob above the waves and, across the foreshore, the wading birds darted. 'It's a big sea,' said Youssif after a while. 'Such a big sea.'

'Just gans on and on,' Ronny said. He pointed. 'Norway's awer there somewhere.'

'Angry too.'

'Angry?'

'It's always throwing itself at the land. Never rests.'

'No, I suppose it doesn't.' Ronny lifted a work-gnarled finger to prise a piece of sea coal from his eyes. 'We used to swim here when I was a bairn. It was bloody freezing.'

They fell into silence, listening to the crash of the waves and the clamour of the wind. 'How lang you live?' Youssif began after a while. 'If you just started walking?'

'What, into the sea?'

Youssif stuck his fore and middle fingers into the sand. 'Start here and just walk . . .' His hand walked as far as he could reach until he overstretched and fell forward. He sprang back nimbly.

Ronny considered the question. Subconsciously, his hand reached up to where the ponytail had once grown, but clenched quickly into a fist when he found nothing there. 'Ye'd be deed in less than ten minutes.'

They fell into deep thought, each considering the heaving sea, moving only to pass or accept the rapidly chilling cup. When Youssif unscrewed the flask again and poured out more tea, the fragrance of the southern herb mingled with the acrid tang of the North Sea. Both men breathed in deeply. 'It's the wind,' mused Ronny. 'I've been coming here since I was a bairn, and there's always been a wind. We call it the Chewer.'

As Youssif sipped his tea, his eyes narrowed appreciatively, disappearing into his gaunt features. 'Ronny, my friend, a wind also blows in the mountains where I was born.' His hands cradled the cup as he held the infusion up to his nose. 'It is drier than this one. Than your Chewer. But it also has teeth. Only in the spring is it soft.' He chuckled aridly. 'Like the

356

caress of the woman you love. Or the hair of your first-born falling against your cheek. But spring is short in the mountains.'

'Aye,' nodded Ronny, 'it is roond here an' all.'

They continued to sit there, two motionless figures peering at the perpetually shifting sea, framed by a bay lined with chimneys, furnaces and power stations. Youssif pointed at the gulls hanging on the wind. 'These we do not see in the mountains. These white ghosts.' He pointed at the waders. 'And these little ones are not there either.' A shadow passed over his features. 'Everything is so different from home.'

'They're called knot,' said Ronny after a while.

'Knot?'

'Comes from a king what ruled once. Canute, they called him. Tried to prove that he could stop the waves coming in. Or that he couldn't. One of the two.' Ronny shrugged. 'It's just an English story. Some fella walking his dog telt me it.'

Youssif nodded. 'Will you teach me more of your English? I have learnt so much from you already. Tell me some more about the rivers of your home.'

Ronny shook his head self-deprecatingly. 'Ye divven't want to be learning the lingo from me, man Youssif. I speak pure Geordie.'

'The same as the other sea coalers?'

With a smile on his face, Ronny shook his head vehemently. 'Thems isn't really Geordies. They're Monkey Hangers, man.'

'Monkey Hangers?'

'Even their mayor's called Hangus Monkey.' Ronny shot a glance at the toiling men, the nearest group of whom were fifty yards distant. 'It's another old story. And divven't ever let them hear ye tell it. A couple o' hundred years back, a ship docked from the South Seas. On board was a monkey. When they saw it, they didn't kna what to dee. They'd nivver seen a

357

monkey. They thought it was a Frenchman so they took it to prison and hanged it.'

Both men creaked with laughter as they continued to drink the tea. 'Ronny,' said Youssif abruptly. 'What are you doing here?'

Ronny shrugged. 'Me cousin owns the depot.'

'Yes, Warren is the big fish round here.'

Ronny smiled. 'Aye. He bought the depot a few months back. With his mam, Queenie. He came into some money.'

Youssif studied Ronny closely. 'But what are *you* doing here?'

'What's anyone deein' here?' Ronny peered out to sea. He did not speak for a long time. 'Here's a story for ye. In me last life I was a millionaire.'

'And here's one for ye. In my last life I was a writer of love stories.'

Both men laughed so much that they fell back helplessly in the sand. Still they laughed, and the little knot and the gulls above the waves gazed at them wonderingly. When Ronny finally pulled himself back on to his feet, he was amazed to see that Youssif had disappeared. He peered down the beach, and saw him walking swiftly back to his own pile of sea coal, carrying the flask of tea under his arm as though it were his only possession.

Big Al returned and the two of them worked harder than ever. Al tried remonstrating once more. 'Gan easy, man Ronny, with your heart . . .'

But the answer stung him into silence. Ronny stopped in his shovelling for a moment, breathed in deeply and looking at the sea said expressionlessly: 'There's worse places to die.'

By the time the third load was nearly finished, the tide was on the turn. They started shovelling even more quickly. 'D'yus kna Youssif?' Ronny said, without faltering in mechanical dig-lift-throw.

'Ye mean Arnie's side lad?' Al nodded his head down the

beach to where Youssif was digging with the driver of his Land-Rover.

'Aye, him. What's his story?'

Al shrugged. 'Same as all them others.'

'What others?'

'Refugees. Asylum seekers or whatever ye call them.'

'What d'ye mean?'

'Well, they've all been through the same sort of thing, haven't they? Come doon the Pot House for a quick pint after the tide. There's always a few in. They'll tell ye.'

'Does Youssif gan in?'

'Youssif? Nivver seen him there.' Al stood back and looked calculatingly at the tide. The tip of the pipeline was still many yards clear of the sea. 'I'll take this lot to Warren's sharpish. Then we'll get the fourth load in.'

Ronny watched Al trundle away over the beach. The February day was made of countless shades of grey: the slate of the sea, the lead of the sky, the scattered dust of the beach, and the cold, husked embers of the coastal defences; it was as though all that remained of the world were the ashes after a great fire. Lowering his gaze, Ronny set to raking the last pile.

The sweat dripped from them as they shovelled up the final load. One after another, the Land-Rovers trundled away and did not return. 'So where's he from then?' Ronny asked as Youssif, passing in the last Land-Rover to leave, waved at them.

'He's a Kurd or summink.'

'Where's that, like?'

'Bloody hell, man Ronny. Me O level was in woodwork not geography. All I kna is that it's a lang way from Hartlepool.'

'Mountains. He said he was from mountains.' Ronny flicked his head to clear the sweat from his eyes. 'He's always gannin' on aboot the mountains. When he was a bairn he used to watch the big birds of prey soaring. And once, he caught an eagle's feather. Kept it. Gave it to his first bairn as a present –'

'I divven't like the look of that tide,' Al interrupted Ronny. 'So stop yammering aboot Youssif and start shovelling.' Al spat surreptitiously, adding in a quiet voice: 'Anyway, ye divven't want to kna his story.'

'What d'ye mean?'

''Cos it's fuckin' depressing, that's why.' They worked at their hardest now, ignoring their aching backs and knees. 'Bloody hell,' grunted Al, speaking in gasping breaths, 'who'd have thought we'd ever be back working with coal? Started with it at fourteen, and now finishing with it forty-odd years later. And nee machinery nor nowt. Just bloody muscles. I saw a programme on it once. On the Discovery channel at yours. In the days when we had satellite telly. The monks what lived at Blackhall bloody rocks just up the coast there. Thems were deein' what we're deein' now. Fifteen hundred years ago.'

Ronny looked at the sea coal thoughtfully. 'Aye, but they didn't have a vanette.'

A burst of bitter laughter rang out from Al. 'Fifteen hundred years of progress and what d'yus have at the end of it? A rusty, clapped-oot auld vanette.' Ronny smiled as Al laughed louder and louder. 'I wouldn't mind so much if it was a proper van . . .' Al's sudden hilarity made him struggle to articulate. And Ronny started to laugh too. 'But it's not. It's not big enough to be a van. It's only half cocked. Half baked. A half-pint.' Al's heavy body heaved with mirth. 'We win the lottery and we still come oot of it with a vanette . . . I mean, ye think that there might have been room for a full-sized van somewhere in them millions.' He leant helplessly against his shovel, laughing hysterically now, and joined by Ronny. 'But no, no. We've still got a vanette . . . we've still got a vanette . . . we've still got the bloody vanette . . .'

For a while Ronny seemed to forget his worries as he

laughed with Al. But abruptly his joy evaporated. 'Ha'way, man Al. That tide's not hanging aboot.'

Al looked at the sea, and sobered instantly. 'Christ, we're gonnae be cutting it canny fine.'

They dug with such frenzy that the sea coal seemed to form a curtain sealing them from the rest of the world, and nothing was said until they both sat in the vanette. 'I suppose he had to flee in a hurry,' Ronny began again.

'Eh?' demanded Al, turning the key.

'Youssif. Had to get away from someone what wanted to torture him or summink. Left his family withoot time to even kiss them goodbye. And them still waiting for him back on the mountain.'

'Aye, well, that's where yus're wrang,' snapped Al. 'But divven't goad wor. I'm not telling ye the story. Not with the way ye keep on looking at the sea and talking aboot good places for dying.'

The tide had risen dangerously, and as the waves broke, the tip of the pipeline disappeared beneath its froth. Al's opaque eye seemed to glint delightedly. 'Shall we risk it?' And without waiting for an answer he began to drive into the sea.

A wave had just broken and it fizzed deafeningly as it receded, drowning the complaining screeching of the vanette as it ploughed into the water. Suddenly the gears ground and, for a moment, the wheels spun into soft sand before jolting free. On they drove towards the tip of the pipe. The water lay only at the top of the wheels, and it seemed that they were going to make it easily. Then the large wave came.

They were engulfed in an instant, sealed within a dungeon of salt water. In these moments of submersion it was not completely dark in the cab of the vehicle, but ashen and confused as the dawn which had just broken. Fear immobilised them both as they felt themselves floating under the rushing water as though the vanette were a submarine. But there was worse to come. When the wave had broken over them, the water remained at bonnet height and, as they looked out over the engulfing grey, it seemed that they were cast adrift in the middle of the sea. 'Friggin' hell,' whimpered Al. 'Friggin' hell.' The grey sea appeared to spread for ever: vast, featureless, lonesome. Al's voice was only a murmur. 'Friggin' hell.'

Both acted at the same time, forcing their doors open against the weight of the water. Al slipped out, and breasted the water to the shore. He had reached it when he realised that Ronny was not with him. 'Ronny!' he shouted at the top of his lungs. 'Ronny!' But there was no sign of his friend. Swearing softly, Al crashed back into the sea. Now the waves lifted him off his feet, causing him to dance a deadly hornpipe on the shifting softness of the sand. And the further he went out, the more desperately he was forced to dance. 'What the fuck are you doing?' he screamed when he reached the vanette.

Ronny was sitting there in his seat. He had not moved. 'I cannet get oot,' he said, his calm words further quietened by the wound-up window.

'Eh?' shrieked Al.

Remaining placid, Ronny indicated the vanette door, mouthing: 'I cannet get oot.'

'Open yer window then!' Al yelled, banging against the window, and then clinging to the roof as a wave lifted him off his feet. 'Open yer window.' But Ronny merely shrugged in reply. 'For frigg's sake, stir yersel'!'

Al punched the window wildly, but it did not break. He battered it repeatedly until suddenly he found himself punching air. Ronny had unwound the window. The two friends were able to look at each other for only an instant before the biggest wave so far crashed over them.

Gasping for air, at last Al found himself bobbing free of the fizzing water. He gagged on the salt he had swallowed as he stared about desperately, trying to find the vanette in his disorientation. Having spotted it, he ploughed his way over to it, but when he managed to reach it, Ronny was gone. 'Ronny!' Al's voice screeched at the blind sea. 'Where are ye?'

The ten seconds during which Al searched for his friend seemed to Al to stretch out as limitlessly as the sea around him. The top of the vanette was the only feature visible in the entire world. Then he caught sight of Ronny's head, bobbing like a seal. But Al's instinctive smile disappeared as quickly as it had appeared. 'Ronny man,' he screamed. 'Ye're gannin' the wrang way. Ye're swimming oot to sea. Ronny man . . .' A wave took hold of Al, and suddenly he found himself out of his depth. His legs fought desperately for the seabed, but like a cartoon character treading air on the wrong side of a cliff, he felt himself plunging.

Once he came up for air, and a second time. And somehow he managed to claw himself back up to the surface a third time. But he knew as his head dipped below that he could not climb again. A silence such as he had never known before sealed itself over him. It was then that he felt the arms around him, gently but insistently pulling him up. Puzzled at first, his face was lifted free of the water, and he saw that he was being buoyed by Ronny. A grim, precarious, desperate ten minutes followed. One moment it seemed that the beach was close by, another had the pair being taken further out.

When at last they reached safety, they lay on the beach for a long time, drenched and exhausted. The vanette had disappeared under the waves. Nothing was said until Ronny broke the silence. 'So what's his story then?'

'Eh?'

'What's Youssif's story?'

'Ronny man, we nearly drooned.' Al lay back and panted like a beached whale. 'Areet then,' he began in a matter-of-fact tone. 'This is what happened to Youssif.' He pointed across the waves to the string of container and bulker ships waiting entrance to Teesport. 'They smuggled themselves in one of them big ships. Youssif and his family. He put his wife and bairns under a tarpaulin some place. Pulled it geet tight. To keep them safe from prying eyes. Then hid himself some place else. Come the end of the voyage, he lets them out.' Al paused for a moment, and taking off his wet woollen hat, squeezed the sea water from it thoughtfully. 'They were dead. Every one of them. Wife, bairns, the lot. Asphyxiated. He'd wanted to hide them. 'Cos they hoy stowaways awer board, y'kna. But he ended up hiding them so well that he'll nivver find them again.' Al looked up at Ronny who had go to his feet. 'Ha'way, let's gan and get a pint. Mebbes a wee dram. Warm worselves up. Come low tide, Warren'll winch the vanette oot.' But Ronny was walking away. 'Where the fuck are ye gannin' noo, Ronny?'

'I'm gannin' hyem,' Ronny returned.

'Eh?'

'Just back to the caravan.'

'For God's sake. We've had a friggin' brush with the grim sea coaler. The least we deserve is a drink.'

But Ronny did not turn. Al watched him walking along the beach, growing smaller and smaller until he was just the size of a gull over the breakers at low tide. Then Al got up, and went in the opposite direction.

Ronny walked south, hugging the sea until the esplanades and jetties stopped abruptly, giving way to sand dunes. And still he walked, gazing at the blast furnace which stood like a giant's gallows across the bay, at the huge toxic car battery of the nuclear power station, and at the seals which lay on the little skerries close at hand. Turning from the sea at last, he threaded a way through some deserted sand dunes before coming to the caravan site. In February it wore a desolate air: the only sign of life was the plastic woodcutter on one of the roofs, wielding his axe with murderous abandon in the stiff wind.

Ronny walked across the empty, windswept little site. The stretch of grass beside his caravan was gouged to the sand

364

below with the deep treads of the vanette. The black grains of sea coal were scattered around like seeds. The caravan had subsided. Its wheels and axle having collapsed, it was shored up with wooden fish crates. More fish crates stood as a step.

It was dark inside. Ronny plodded down to the bottom end where two sleeping bags lay on the floor, curtained off from each other by a piece of ragged sheet. A small pile of clothes lay on either side of the sheet and a couple of carrier bags: the only signs of habitation. With a grunt he collapsed on to one of the sleeping bags. There was little else in the gloomy caravan. On a shelf stood teabags, tins of baked beans, a loaf of bread blueing with decay, and a bottle of St Ivel Five Pints. Lying flat on his back, Ronny stared up through the gloom to the ceiling, dark with damp.

Suddenly the caravan's little curtain was opened, and in the meagre light that came in, Ronny looked over to see a figure sitting at the little plastic-covered table. 'Where've you been?' Audrey asked gently.

He did not reply nor move, but lay flat on his back and closed his eyes.

Audrey spoke with the urgency and rapidity of breaking dam water. 'I've looked everywhere for you. How have ye been living, pet? We've worried worselves sick. Why did ye discharge yersel' from the hospital like that? Nee one knows where yus've been. What yus've been deein'. We didn't even kna if ye were . . .' Still lying there motionless, Ronny began to weep. Audrey came over and knelt down beside him. 'We've been so worried about you,' she whispered. 'I've been at the end of me tether. I've been in every hospital this side o' York.'

'How's the bairns?' Ronny said quietly, still weeping.

'They want ye to come back. We all just want yus to come back. The whole family. We just want you back.'

'Me?'

'All of us. Toni's back with us at the parsonage. Donna's in

365

Ibiza. Terri's missed ye. She's broke her little heart since ye've been gone.' Audrey paused for a moment. When she spoke again her voice was abject, utterly stripped bare. 'We all just want ye to come back, man Ronny.'

'I've missed them bairns. God, how I've missed them.' Ronny kept his eyes shut. Screwing them tightly as he wept.

Audrey cradled his head on her lap. 'Jimmy didn't die, man Ronny. Ye didn't kill him. It was Macca what nearly finished him off. After ye'd done him. When he found out that he'd been muscling in on his patch. It wasn't just you. He'd been deein' his own deals all awer the shop. So Macca settled him.' Lying down beside her husband now, Audrey's passion grew. 'So ye can come back now. Ye haven't done nowt. Ye can come back. Ye can come back. YE CAN COME BACK!' Audrey hid her face in the crook of his arm. 'Please come back,' she whispered, barely audible. 'I'm so sorry. Please come back.'

'I wanted to kill him, Audrey. I wanted to kill him. I'd got so that I wanted to kill a man.'

'It was my fault,' she whispered. 'Mine. Mine.' She breathed in deeply. 'I've taken me clothes off for more men than I've had hot dinners, but I've nivver felt so naked in me life before. Ronny, I need ye. I kna that I divven't deserve it, but if ye give wor a second chance ye'll nivver regret it. Please. I love ye. I always have.' Nothing was said for a long time and Audrey was so still that Ronny thought she must have fallen asleep buried into his side.

'Audrey,' Ronny said at last. 'If I had everything there was to have, everything in the world, I'd hoy the lot in the Tyne just for the chance of having you.'

And now Audrey began to weep. There was no aggression left. No anger. No energy. Just the soft flow of tears. 'A fog came awer me when we won the lottery. A fog. And all I could think of was me dad. You picked me off the ground and loved me, and I hurt you. And the bairns. What mean the world to me. I hurt them. And it was only when I was in that taxi the night of the talent show that it came to me. I was halfway to a club in the Bigg Market when it came to me. I said to meself, What the hell am I deein' gannin' to the Bigg Market on the pull when the real love of me life and me grandbairns and me family are . . .' Audrey broke off. Her voice cracked. 'Ronny. It was because of me dad. I didn't mean it. It was because of me dad.' Still weeping, she lifted a hand to her cheeks. Her fingers came back moist. She gazed at them. 'I'm blubbing like a babby.'

'I love ye,' said Ronny simply.

She looked at him in bewilderment as he held his arms out, and her weeping became a torrent of relentless sorrow. 'I only ever loved ye and the bairns. Terri. Toni. And the rest of them. And then I foond mesel . . . gannin' to the quayside . . . all dressed up in . . . me miniskirt and . . . and . . . and . . . I realised what was happening . . . but by the time I got to the Catholic Club . . . ye were lying on the stage . . . and I thought ye were dead . . . I thought ye were dead . . . the fog lifted . . . but it was too late . . . because I'd missed Terri's big night . . . and I thought ye were dead . . .' She gulped convulsively.

'I love ye,' Ronny repeated.

'Do you?' she asked in profound disbelief. He nodded. She reached out and laid a hand on his cheek. 'Ronny,' she asked, 'why do you love me?'

'Because you're Audrey.'

'My Ronny,' breathed Audrey. 'My Ronny. The strongest man I know. My rock.'

'Me?' Ronny replied softly. 'I'm a pushover.'

'No. Not deep doon. Deep doon yus're the strongest man I kna. See ye? Ye are strong enough to stay gentle when everybody else is getting the boot in. And I love ye, Ronny. I love ye.'

Both fell silent simultaneously as though suddenly realising that their arms had entwined round the other. 'Come back to us, me love,' Audrey whispered. 'We'll make it like it was before.'

'Me bonny Gatesheed lass,' replied Ronny simply.

They rolled over the sleeping bag and kissed, their bodies joining with such tender power that it seemed impossible that they would ever be prised apart.

2

In March they began to prepare the land, and the allotments rang with the happy cry of many voices. Towards the end of the month, the weather grew warm and spring-like. 'Reet,' said Ronny as he stood on the black earth. 'Come and get yer seeds, everyone.' There was a rush as the children dashed across the soil. Each in turn received a tiny seed which they held reverently in the palm of their hand. 'Divven't drop it, man Keegan,' Ronny warned the little boy.

'Have ye got yours there, Terri?' Audrey asked, coming over from the far end of the patch.

'Yes, Nana,' Terri smiled.

'Here's yours and here's mine,' said Ronny, dispensing a seed first on Audrey's palm, and then on his own. They looked at each other and grinned.

'And ye, Joe man and Ginga,' Audrey called to where the old men sat talking on the veranda. 'And ye, Bill and Leeanne. Ha'way, the lot o' yous.'

When everyone was ready, the children crouching above the black earth of the seedbed, the middle-aged folk bent at the waist, and the old ones stiffly reaching down, Ronny smiled. 'Now,' he said, and the seeds were dispensed by the many-handed drill, and then covered over with soil, poking fingers and giggles.

'What do we dee next, Granda Ronny?' Brosnan asked.

Laughing, Ronny shrugged. 'Watch it grow.'

'We could gan and get an ice cream,' Brosnan suggested.

They walked up the sunken lane, made by the generations of cartwheels, and in the hawthorn brakes above, many of the little birds of the northern summer were already singing: the chiffchaff, the willow warbler and the blackcap. And joining with this sound that causes the heart to surge each year on its renewal, was the babbling music of the children. Al and Cheryl walked up the lane too, Al's hand constantly roaming over Cheryl's buttocks and waist as he whispered endearments in her ear. Behind them all came Ronny and Audrey. Holding hands, they did not need to speak.

A skylark soaring above the spoil heap meadows of the Watergate Redevelopment greeted them as they emerged from the lane, and everyone paused for a few instants to watch and listen. Higher and higher the bird rose, until no one could see it, and only its song remained. Then the children hurried on, the shop and its ice creams beckoning them. 'We'll all cross together,' Audrey called.

But Terri-Leigh had already stepped out on to the road.

'Ha'way, everyone,' Audrey cried. 'We'll cross together. Ha'way . . .'

The car seemed to come from nowhere. Audrey saw it an instant before Terri-Leigh did, and for the rest of his life Ronny would never forget the look in her eyes when she realised what was happening and that she could do nothing to prevent it. A cry tore from the grandmother's lips as the child was hit.

Having remained at the side of the road when her cousin crossed, Toni-Lee was the closest of all of them to the tragedy, and she was able to see the surprise on Terri-Leigh's face at the sudden revelation that the speeding car was the angel of death.

The little girl was hit and briefly soared as though she herself was a bird, before landing, smashed broken on the road. And only the distant skylark's song remained in the air, the same sound on either side of the small life just taken.

369

Chapter Ten

I

The day of the funeral was both harsh and beautiful. A fresh wind harried clouds across the ultramarine sky so that one moment the sun shone warmly, the next the air was cut with the blade of midwinter. In the cemetery the municipal gravediggers could not decide whether to wear their coats.

There were two gravediggers working together: a man and a woman. The man was small, and the woman tall, at least a foot higher than her male companion. For now their fluorescent municipal jackets hung on a nearby gravestone. They were digging quickly. The mechanical digger had just stopped working, and they had not yet cleared the earth into a single pile so that the mourners might approach the graveside. In among the sea of gravestones that lined the hillside cemetery, the heads of the gravediggers could be seen bobbing in and out of view as they dug, the blades of their spades glinting.

No expense had been spared on the funeral cortège that was winding its way through the streets of the Metropolitan Borough of Gateshead. The rest of the traffic stopped, and people stared from open doorways and windows.

Four huge horses pulled the hearse. These death horses were draped in black. And black plumes spumed from their black, masked headdresses. The sallow-faced driver, himself wearing a black cape and black top hat, flicked the horses' withers with a sharp whip. Up the hills and down the banks of the borough, the cortège wound itself between the tower blocks and the endless rows of Tyneside flats, the crunch of its carriage wheels and the clatter of its shod hooves resounding in the otherwise hushed streets. And those within their homes heard this strange music as it cut through the spell of radio and television, and came to their doors and windows to see who was passing.

The hearse was glass-panelled and gigantic. The coffin resting in the nest of flowers was so small that it caused the onlookers to shiver. 'We Will Always Miss You, Terri-Leigh' read the simple words of the floral tribute.

Four funeral directors attired in top hats and tails flanked the clattering carriage. And behind the hearse came the long line of mourners.

They were nearing the cemetery now. Audrey had walked the whole journey with her eyes glued on the little coffin box, while beside her Ronny had not looked up from the ground as though counting each little stone and pebble of Gateshead. Their arms were wound round each other like two pilgrims nearing the end of a journey, keeping each other on their feet through the fear that should one fall then the other would too. The rest of the family followed, all enmity cast away, supporting each other. Toni-Lee held her mother's hand. The bereaved mother, out of prison for the funeral, was chained to her warders. From time to time Bill sobbed. As did Corky, walking hand in hand with Theresa. Leeanne was carrying one of her children, and the rest bunched in a silent group. Cheryl was pushing Cara in a pushchair, while Al and Father Dan walked to one side of her.

A police helicopter buzzed overhead, hanging above the cortège, bothering the horses like a monstrous blowfly. All in all, the mourners formed a tail that was half a mile long, and even when the hearse had reached the grave, the rest took a long time to gather. It seemed that the Teams had gathered for one last time to mark the passing of one of their own. The gravediggers, having just finished in time, gazed in amazement.

'Who is it?' the woman asked one of the mourners from the edge of the congregation.

'That bairn what was knocked doon by the hit-and-run,' the mourner replied. 'Little Terri-Leigh McPhee. Her nana was the one what won the lottery. Much good it'll dee her now.'

The gravediggers withdrew. There were so many people that nothing could be seen of the graveside. 'It's a long time since we had this many,' the man remarked.

'We nivver have had,' his female colleague returned.

The coffin was raised on to the four pallbearers: Ronny, Dan, Paddy and Audrey. And resting on those broad shoulders it appeared to be even smaller.

'I remember it now,' the woman gravedigger whispered. 'It was in the papers. The driver was speeding on Whickham Highway.'

'And them winning the lottery an' all.'

The woman sighed. 'All the money in the world cannet give them what they want now.'

When the crowd had settled, Dan began. 'It's not a day for words,' he said. 'They'll come later.' A sharp wind raked the mourners. 'We're too sad to speak. We loved this little girl, and she's been taken from us. We're angry and lonely. We can't see the reason behind it. Why did we have to lose her so young?' He broke off, then, closing his eyes for a moment, continued doggedly. 'She was the light of our hearts. A ray of sunshine. A treasure. And all we can say is thank you for what we had of Terri-Leigh. And without her the world is darker. But it's because of her brightness that we feel so hopeless now.' The priest bowed his head. 'People might want to know where God is in all of this. She's with us here. Breaking her heart.'

As the coffin was lowered into the earth, the cold wind blew again and people shivered. The silence of the thousand people was edged by a bitter chill. A silence disturbed only by the occasional cough, bitterly strangled sob, and by the soft sigh of the grains of earth hitting the lid of the coffin as the chief mourners began to drop the soil.

It was just then that the music began. Toni-Lee was holding a tape recorder. She had recorded her cousin playing one of her folk ballads. It was her favourite tune, the one she had most often returned to; everyone recognised the melancholy air but nobody knew the words. A full verse and chorus had been played when suddenly a voice began to sing. People looked about for the singer whose voice was a thin wisp, worn by the years, but nevertheless owned an aching sweetness.

> The cow's come hyem but I see not me hinny.
> The cow's come hyem but I see not me bairn.
> I'd rather lose all me cows than lose me hinny.
> I'd rather lose everything than lose me bairn . . .

It was old Mrs Armstrong who sang, and everyone listened; even the municipal gravediggers, sitting on a bench at a far remove, paused as they ate their sandwiches. 'Ee, what a bonny song,' the woman said.

'Aye,' replied the man simply.

And as the ballad continued, the sun flickered free of the clouds and the air grew warm so that the song telling the story of a lost child and the bitterest of pain known to parents, took on an unbearable tenderness.

> Fair-faced is me hinny, her blue eyes are bonny,
> Her blonde hair in ringlets, hung sweet to the sight;
> Oh, off ye gan, Daddy, seek wor lost lassie,
> Please bring back to her mammy, her only delight . . .

Those at the edges drifted away first, in ones and twos. In time only friends and family remained. And they too left, leaving but two mourners at the graveside. These two, a man and a woman of advanced middle age, did not move but stood there bent slightly over the grave like a willow with two trunks.

The municipal gravediggers were standing at a discreet distance from another funeral. This was as different a burial as could be imagined. There were no crowds to mark the passing of this person. A vicar was turning his pages as quickly as he could, and just one woman stood there, whose dress made the merest reference to mourning in the black leather gloves she wore. 'Funny that, isn't it?' whispered the male municipal worker. 'The whole o' Gatesheed turns up for the bairn; hardly a single bugger shows his face here.'

'Well, ye kna the story,' replied the woman, taking out a tin of rolling tobacco and beginning expertly to roll a cigarette.

'Do I?'

'Why aye.' The woman nodded at the single mourner who was checking his watch. 'That's her from that retirement home. Well, today they're burying the auld gadgie neebody knas.'

'Oh aye,' said the man vaguely. 'It was in the paper.'

The woman nodded. 'Poor auld bastard. He didn't have nee family, and the home didn't want to foot the bill. Canny expensive things funerals.' Having rolled her cigarette, the woman paused to lick the paper. Drawing her colleague behind a tall mausoleum, she lit the cigarette. 'So who was gonnae pay for it? The council refused, but the home said that the body was industrial waste. A council disposal job then. That's why they pay their rates.'

'So who is paying?'

'I divven't kna,' the woman shrugged. 'But they thought they'd better get rid of the body before the national press got hold of it. I mean, can ye imagine the headlines about the council and the home?'

'Christ, aye. Doesn't look good. Arguing the toss over a human body. When all's said and done, mebbes neebody

374

wanted him but he was still a human body.' The man watched the smoke from his colleague's cigarette drift over the mausoleum, melting into the locked door of the sepulchre like a ghost. 'Was there not *nee* family at all?'

'Not that they could trace.' She pursed her lips. 'Makes ye think, mind. A whole life, and at the end of it, what are yus?'

'Industrial waste.'

At Terri-Leigh's grave, Audrey and Ronny had still not moved.

The cemetery was built on a hill, gravestones terracing the slopes, and Terri-Leigh had been buried at the summit. Now that the crowds had gone, the panoramic view over Gateshead was revealed in full. All the landmarks were visible. To the south were the wide, empty arms of the Angel of the North. To the west, the rolling farmland beyond Lobley Hill and the giant beanstalk of the Dunston Rocket. To the east, the new gleaming buildings of the Baltic Art Gallery and Concert Hall. And to the north, straight ahead of them if they looked up for a moment, the Teams bounded by its two rivers.

From here the destruction could be truly seen. Emptiness, vacant plots and piles of bricks where life had been. Only the Square Flats seemed to be left.

Ronny and Audrey had still not left the graveside when the gravediggers walked by. Their shift was finishing and they carried their spades over their shoulders as their forebears had carried scythes. 'I tell ye what,' the woman was saying. 'I'm feeling lucky tonight. I think I might gan and get mesel' another lottery ticket.'

'Me too,' mused the man. 'Why, ye've got to live in hope.'

Heads bowed and hands clasped low, Audrey and Ronny continued their vigil over the grave. Just then a distant rumble could be heard from the north, like thunder in a gathering storm. A little while later they heard another rumble, this time so loud that they looked up. A huge, impenetrable fog hung over the Teams.

Mutely, they watched the monstrous sight and as they did so, they realised that this was no fog but smoke: great billowing pillars of dark grey smoke. Very slowly the smoke began to clear, drifting across the Metropolitan Borough of Gateshead, and when it had cleared sufficiently, they saw that the Square Flats no longer stood in the Teams. They had gone in a mighty blast of dynamite.

And suddenly a grey darkness fell over the graveside as though evening had fallen all at once. The pillars of smoke, carried on the cold wind from the Teams, had reached the cemetery, eclipsing the sun. The lottery winners stared up blankly at the billowing darkness.